'Beware of the Mon... mured. 'He's a sod for getting his hands into girls knickers. Especially horny little blondes in red miniskirts. Right, you've only got an hour as the pub opens at six.'

'But it's only four o'clock.'

'I close at five. That gives me time to change and get ready for an evening of heavy drinking in the local. You're . . . you're not married, are you?'

'No, why?'

'You're a bit of all right. Nice figure, firm thighs, well-rounded titties—'

'Excuse me,' Samantha cut in angrily. 'I'd rather you didn't . . .'

'Sorry, it's just that I'm looking for a wife. You'd do quite nicely.'

'Are you asking me to marry you?'

'No, no, no . . . Yes. You see, most of my female customers are old and wrinkled. Tits like empty leather bags, if you get my meaning. It's not often I get a tasty young bit of . . . a lovely young lady visit my haunted mansion.'

RAY GORDON

Dark Desires

NEW ENGLISH LIBRARY
Hodder & Stoughton

First published in Great Britain in 2003 by Hodder and Stoughton
A division of Hodder Headline

A New English Library paperback

3

A CIP catalogue record for this title
is available from the British Library

ISBN 978 0 340 82163 3

Typeset in Plantin by Hewer Text Ltd, Edinburgh
Printed and bound in Great Britain by
Mackays of Chatham plc, Chatham, Kent

Hodder and Stoughton
A division of Hodder Headline
338 Euston Road
London NW1 3BH

Dark Desires

I

Samantha stood in front of her dressing-table mirror and gazed at the reflection of her young body. Wearing a white blouse and short pleated skirt, she looked smart in her school uniform. But it was what lay beneath her clothes that fascinated her. Lifting her skirt and focusing on the material of her tight panties faithfully following the contours of her sex lips, she grinned. This was what men wanted, she mused, pulling her panties to one side and exposing the fleshy swell of her hairless vaginal lips. Gazing at her tightly closed vaginal crack, the pinken wings of her inner lips protruding invitingly from her valley of desire, she knew that men watched her in the street and thought their male thoughts of illicit sex.

'If I knew then what I know now,' she breathed, concealing her virginal sex crack with her panties and lowering her skirt. But she did know. With the mind of an experienced adult in the body of a young and naive girl, Samantha knew only too well. But this must have been a dream, she thought, looking around her bedroom. She was twenty-two years old now. Her schooldays were far behind, drifting in the memories of her mind. She couldn't really have travelled back in time, could she? No, this had to be a dream.

Samantha eyed her balding editor despairingly as he sat behind his desk, grinning at her. He knew that she didn't

want the assignment. She'd said that an undercover operation to expose a man who purported to harbour ghosts in his mansion was ridiculous. What was the point? she wondered, twisting her long blonde hair around her slender fingers. Gerry Andrews was charging people to visit his so-called haunted mansion. He was a charlatan. What of it? The punters loved the prospect of coming face to face with a ghost as they roamed the mansion, and Gerry Andrews was raking in the cash. Where was the problem?

'Sam, Sam,' Dave sighed, leaning forward across his desk, his hands clenched. 'This could be a big one. It's a blatant rip-off, baby.'

'Don't call me *baby*,' Samantha snapped. 'I'm twenty-two years old, for Christ's sake.'

'OK, OK. Right, this is the highly devious plan. Andrews—'

'Gerry Andrews is an eccentric, Dave,' Samantha broke in. 'The punters know full well that there are no bloody ghosts in his ramshackle mansion. He's just trying to bring some money in to run the place. The electricity bill alone must be—'

'Listen to me, Sammy baby. Andrews is ripping off the public. Fifty-odd punters a day at twenty quid each? The crook's raking it in. That's a grand a day, for fuck's sake. The *Daily Moon* is a pillar of the community. We're here to give the public the truth. We're here to—'

'Sell newspapers?'

'Yes, of course. But . . . *you* are here to do a job, Sammy.'

'Can't you put John onto this one?' she sighed.

'John's a prat, you know that as well as I do.'

'John's all right. He . . .'

'He fancies you.'

'Of course he doesn't,' she laughed.

'He fancies you rotten, any fool can see that. Anyway, a beautiful young blonde such as you will be able to get in with Andrews. Show him a bit of thigh and—'

'I'll show you a bit of fist, in a minute.'

'Into fisting, are you?'

'Pardon?'

'Look, there's no such fucking thing as fucking ghosts, Sam. This bloke is a fucking charlatan and he's taking money under false pretences.'

'OK, OK – I'll do it,' Samantha finally conceded, raising her blue eyes to the ceiling.

'I knew you wouldn't let me down, babe. Right, get your arse to the mansion and take a look round. Hidden speakers, tape recorders, lighting . . . Look for anything . . .'

'I know what to look for, Dave.'

'Excellent. Give us a ring on your mobile when you've sussed the joint, OK?'

'OK,' she agreed, holding her hand out.

'What is it?'

'Money, Dave. I'll need some money.'

'Shit,' he cursed, opening his desk drawer. 'There's twenty.'

'Is that all?'

'That's what Andrews charges.'

'I don't even get a cup of tea?'

'Fucking hell, you'll be the ruin of me,' he sighed, thrusting a second twenty-pound note into her hand. 'I want a result on this one, Sam.'

'Yeah, yeah, I know.'

'Try to show a little enthusiasm, babe.'

'If you keep calling me *babe*, I'll show you—'

'A little bit of tit?' he chuckled.

'A little bit of blackmail.'

'Blackmail?'

'I might just have to have a chat with your wife.'

'Oh, that.'

'Yes, that. How you can carry on with your secretary is—'

'Cool?'

'*Un*cool, Dave. She's half your age, for fuck's sake.'

'Don't I just know it,' he sniggered. 'Actually, she's younger than my daughter.'

'You're despicable.'

'That's not what she says. Do you know, last night she got me on the bed and—'

'I'll call you later,' Samantha cut in, walking on her long legs to the office door. 'You'd better take one of your pills before you get too excited and keel over.'

Reaching Andrews's mansion, Samantha parked her VW Golf and walked towards the stone steps that led up to the huge oak doors. At least the sun was shining, she mused, dreading the thought of traipsing around a dilapidated eighteenth-century building. Looking down at her red miniskirt, she wished she'd worn jeans. She should have gone home and changed before embarking on a ridiculous mission to search an old mansion and expose an eccentric as a charlatan. But this wouldn't take long, she decided. A quick look round, make a few mental notes, and then home to an evening meal and on to the pub to meet her boyfriend.

Climbing the steps, she was greeted by a middle-aged man wearing a peaked cap, a checked shirt and brown corduroy trousers. Looking him up and down, she couldn't

help but laugh at his brown brogues. This was Mr Andrews she knew as he grinned at her and licked his narrow lips. Gerry Andrews, locally infamous for his eccentricity, he could often be spotted riding an old boneshaker bicycle through the local village. He was harmless enough, Samantha thought, focusing on the long black hair sprouting from beneath his cap and cascading over his suntanned face. Completely mad, but harmless enough.

'Afternoon,' he greeted her, raising his cap in a most gentleman-like manner. 'The ghosts are rampant today.'

'I'm sure they are,' Samantha murmured, unable to show the slightest inkling of enthusiasm.

'Kept me up all night, they did,' he complained. 'Moaning and groaning, banging and humping around . . .' His words tailing off, he looked down at her naked thighs. 'I wouldn't mind keeping *you* up all night, banging and humping,' he sniggered.

'Where do I buy a ticket?' Samantha asked dismissively, not so sure now that Andrews *was* harmless.

'There are no tickets. Just bung me the cash and you're in.'

'There you are,' she said, passing him a twenty-pound note.

'And there's your change,' he returned, passing her a one-pound note.

'Change? But . . . I thought that the entrance fee was twenty pounds.'

'Yes, that's right. That's your change.'

'One-pound notes went out years ago.'

'Don't you want your change? If not . . .'

'No, no, I'll keep it. Is there a guide or do I just wander around aimlessly until I'm confronted by the ghost of a headless woman?'

'Just wander around.' Looking over his shoulder as if making sure that they were alone, he leaned forward. 'The ghosts will find you, if they want to,' he whispered mysteriously.

'That *is* reassuring.'

'Beware of the Monk of all Perversions,' he murmured. 'He's a sod for getting his hands into girls' knickers. Especially horny little blondes in red miniskirts. Right, you've only got an hour as the pub opens at six.'

'But it's only four o'clock.'

'I close at five. That gives me time to change and get ready for an evening of heavy drinking in the local. You're . . . you're not married, are you?'

'No, why?'

'You're a bit of all right. Nice figure, firm thighs, well-rounded titties—'

'Excuse me,' Samantha cut in angrily. 'I'd rather you didn't . . .'

'Sorry, it's just that I'm looking for a wife. You'd do quite nicely.'

'Are you asking me to marry you?'

'No, no, no . . . Yes. You see, most of my female customers are old and wrinkled. Tits like empty leather bags, if you get my meaning. It's not often I get a tasty young bit of . . . a lovely young lady visit my haunted mansion.'

'Sorry to disappoint you, but I'm a lesbian,' Samantha announced unashamedly, hopefully putting an end to the subject.

'A lesbian?' he echoed, flashing her a lecherous grin. 'That's even better.'

'You do know what a lesbian is?'

'Too right, I do. Er . . . I don't suppose you do shows? I could hire out my banqueting hall and we could—'

'Shows?' Samantha breathed incredulously. 'Certainly not. And to answer your next inevitable barrage of questions. Yes, I am wearing panties. They're red. And, yes, I masturbate, using a vibrator. Happy now?'

'Good grief, you must be psychic.'

'No, just worldly wise.'

Leaving the man examining the twenty-pound note, Samantha entered the building and looked around the huge entrance hall. Antique furniture covered in layers of dust, cobwebs hanging from the high ceiling . . . Gerry Andrews didn't need a wife. He needed an army of cleaning ladies. There again, she supposed that the cobwebs and dust were in keeping with the notion of an old haunted mansion. Years of dust and cobwebs were consistent with the presence of ghosts, she reflected. As were thunder and lightning and blood-curdling screams echoing in the dark of the night. But it was the afternoon and the sky was blue, so there'd be no thunderstorms. Unless they were pre-recorded on tape. Wondering where to start, she picked up a leaflet from a table.

'Female masturbation lessons every Friday at six,' she read, her blue eyes frowning. 'Candles supplied.' There was far more to Mr Gerry Andrews than fake ghosts, she mused, tossing the leaflet onto the table. But he was a likeable character, in a most peculiar way. Doubting that he'd ever find a wife, she felt cold and shivered as she again wondered where to start. The scent of musk filling her nostrils, she walked across the threadbare carpet and climbed the huge staircase. There were no other visitors, which she thought odd. But this was hardly the sort of place for a family outing. *Candles supplied?*

A distant, blood-curdling scream echoing around the building as she wandered into a large room, Samantha shook her head and sighed. The eerie sounds were obviously coming from hidden speakers, and she half expected to see someone covered with a white sheet leap out of the shadows and shout *boo*. 'This is crazy,' she murmured, sitting on a tatty chaise longue by the window. The eerie sounds growing louder, she gazed around the room. They were coming from a large wooden cabinet standing by the far wall. If there was a speaker in the room, the cabinet would be an excellent place to hide it. From her low position, she could see a wire running along the skirting board and up to the base of the cabinet.

Sure that she'd found what she was looking for, she left her seat and tried the cabinet door. As she'd expected, it was locked. But it didn't take much effort to yank the door open, breaking the ageing lock. 'Well, well, well,' she whispered, discovering a small loudspeaker at the back of the cabinet. Closing the door, she followed the wire along the skirting board to a hole in the floor. *Shit*, she thought, wondering how to get to the room below as eerie sounds continued to emanate from the wooden cabinet. She also wondered why she was stuck in a dingy old mansion when the sun was shining and her stomach was calling for food.

Leaving the room and smiling at a young couple as she made her way along the landing, Samantha descended the stairs and slipped through an oak door. The wire ran down the wall and, again, through a hole in the floor. Pleased to think that there were at least two other visitors in the building, she crossed the empty room to a small door. Unless the visitors were ghosts? Trying the door's handle, she was determined to discover why it was

locked. Things locked normally harboured secrets, she mused, pushing with her shoulder against the door. Grinning as another ancient lock broke and the door swung open, she found herself at the top of a narrow staircase. Finding a switch, she turned the light on and closed the door before creeping down the stairs to what appeared to be the basement.

The eerie sound of dripping water echoing around the basement wasn't fake she knew as she looked up at the low ceiling. Hoping that the water dripping from long strands of green slime didn't come from a toilet, she took her mobile phone from her belt and punched in Dave's number. 'Fuck it,' she murmured, realizing that there was no signal in the basement. Looking around and noticing a pile of magazines stacked on a shelf, she grabbed one and opened it. 'God,' she breathed, gazing at a photograph of a huge purple knob about to enter a gaping pussy hole. Gerry Andrews didn't want a wife, he wanted a whore-slut. Checking her watch as thoughts of diving into bed with her boyfriend filled her mind, she tossed the magazine onto the shelf.

Gazing at the piles of old furniture and cardboard boxes strewn around the basement, Samantha could see no sign of the wire and reckoned that she was wasting her time. Again wondering what point there was in exposing Andrews, she decided to call it a day and go home. It wasn't as if Gerry Andrews was a criminal, she mused. The crazy man was only trying to make a few pounds. Dave would have a go at her for letting him down, she knew. But there'd be nothing he could complain about if she told him that she'd not found anything suspicious. If he really was hell-bent on exposing Andrews, then he'd have to go to the mansion and check it out for himself.

A pinpoint of red light glowing in a dimly lit corner of the basement caught her eye and she noticed a computer and video equipment on a desk. This was proof enough she knew as she switched the monitor on and found herself looking at the entrance hall. The computer appeared to be controlling a tape recorder, probably sending eerie sounds to various rooms as visitors entered. Gerry Andrews was a charlatan, all right. But what of it? Should she expose him? She pondered, watching the young couple walking through the hall and leaving the building. His ghost scam was harmless enough, after all.

Walking up the narrow steps to the basement door, Samantha was horrified to find that, despite the broken lock, it was somehow firmly secured once more. Turning and yanking the handle, she began to panic as she thought that she might be trapped. Yanking again on the handle, she hammered on the door in the hope that someone would hear her. There again, hammering sounds emanating from the basement would be deemed to be the antics of ghosts. No one was going to investigate, she was sure. Checking her watch, she reckoned that Gerry Andrews would be closing up before long and would come down to switch the computer off. She'd have a little explaining to do, she reflected, descending the steps and making herself comfortable in an old armchair. But if she said that she'd lost her way and had somehow ended up in the basement, the eccentric would believe her.

After an hour, Samantha was becoming fearful. Her mobile phone didn't work in the basement and there'd been no sign of Andrews. Imagining being locked in the bowels of the mansion all night, she again thought about her boyfriend. She'd arranged to meet Zak in a local wine

bar at seven and then go on to see a film. The time approaching seven, she reckoned that Zak would contact Dave and . . . and what? Dave wouldn't know where she was. He'd probably mention that she'd gone to the mansion, but he'd not assume that she was still there.

'Who's there?' she breathed, sure that she heard someone murmuring in the shadows. Leaving her chair and gazing into the shadowy corners of the room, she felt that she wasn't alone in the dingy basement. Reckoning that it was nothing more than the eccentric's electronic ghosts – and her imagination running wild – she flopped into the armchair and closed her eyes. Resigning herself to the fact that she would probably have to remain in the basement all night, she decided to stay calm. There was no need to panic, she thought, trying to reassure herself as a dull thud resounded throughout the ancient building. As Dave had said, there were no such fucking things as fucking ghosts.

'There you are,' Zak said, smiling as Samantha stood next to him at the bar.

'I . . . I must be dreaming,' she breathed, looking about her. 'I was locked in the basement and—'

'Basement?' Zak murmured. 'What are you talking about?'

'I was in a chair and . . . I must have fallen asleep.'

'Sam, I have no idea what you're talking about. Now that you're here, would you like a drink?'

'Er . . . vodka, please.'

Waking with a start, Samantha leaped out of the chair and looked around the basement. It was a dream, she was sure. But it had been so real. Zak, laughter drifting

around the bar, the chink of glasses . . . She'd never had a dream where she'd known that she was dreaming. Finally retaking her seat, she thought that she must be tired. The anxiety of being trapped, fear gripping her, weariness and the heat of the day overwhelming her . . . Recalling the time she'd been locked in a cupboard at school, her thoughts turned to those heady days. Her best friend, Angela, had come to her rescue after one of the boys had thought it fun to lock her in the cupboard. In the dark of the cupboard, Samantha had panicked, believing that everyone would go home and she'd be stuck there all night.

'Sam,' Angela called from the classroom doorway. 'Aren't you going to join us?'

'Er . . . yes, yes,' Samantha breathed, looking about the classroom. This was another strange dream, she was sure as she walked up to her friend. 'Where are we going?'

'To the party, of course,' the girl replied, frowning. 'Are you feeling all right?'

'Yes, I . . . I'll be with you in a minute.'

'We're going to be late as it is. By the time we've got home and changed . . .'

'I'll only be a minute, Angela.'

Half opening her eyes, Samantha stared at the computer standing on the desk. She was in the basement, there was no doubt about that. But her dreams had been so real, she thought, closing her eyes again. Wondering whether she could choose what she wanted to dream about, she recalled her bedroom at her parents' house. The bay window opened out onto the beautiful garden where the

lawn seemed to stretch for miles down to the huge rockery and pond. She'd always loved the garden, and her bedroom, and had been sad to have to leave home to get a job on the outskirts of London.

'This is it,' Samantha breathed, finding herself lying on her bed in her room. Lifting her head off the pillow, she looked down at her naked body. Her fingers toying between the firm hillocks of her warm love-lips, she immediately knew what she was doing. Very often, when her parents were out, she'd strip off and lie on her bed with her slender thighs parted. Masturbation had played a major role in her younger years. Having discovered the delights of her clitoris at a very early age, she'd masturbated regularly, sometimes twice a day. And now, in her strange dream, she was young and carefree and masturbating again.

Her fingertip rubbing the solid nubble of her erect clitoris, she breathed deeply as her young womb contracted and her juices of passion flowed from the virginal hole of her pussy. Massaging her pleasure spot faster, the smooth plateau of her stomach rising and falling, the petite mounds of her barely developed breasts heaving, she finally reached the apex of her self-loving. Her naked body shuddering uncontrollably, she gasped and whimpered as her orgasm rocked her very soul. The brown teats of her sensitive nipples painfully hard, she squeezed and pinched her milk teats and tossed her head back as her orgasm peaked.

Reaching beneath her thigh and slipping a finger into the tight sheath of her sex-wet vagina, Samantha massaged the creamy walls of her pussy, adding to her incredible pleasure. She remembered this well, the illicit

massaging, the heavenly sensations, the immense relief her orgasms had brought her. Her early discovery of masturbation had taken her a step further along the path to womanhood. She had left behind her dolls and toys: her clitoris had taken over, demanding appeasement at every opportunity. She'd watched her young breasts grow and develop, and she'd massaged her nipples whenever she lay in her bed, delighting in the new and wondrous sensations of sex. And now, in her peculiar dream, she was there once again.

Her orgasm finally receding, she lay quivering on her bed, recalling again her younger days and her illicit sessions of self-loving as she ran her hands over the mounds and curves of her naked body. She'd toyed with a candle one evening as she'd lain in her bed. Slipping the waxen shaft deep into the sheath of her virgin pussy, she'd gasped and squirmed as the sensations had permeated her young womb. Her candle had become her friend, her lover. Wondering where the wax dildo was, she looked around her.

'This is my bedroom,' she breathed, slipping her cunny-wet finger out of her hot vagina. Looking around the room at her school uniform hanging over the back of the pink armchair, her books piled on the windowsill, she propped herself up on her elbows and caught her reflection in the dressing-table mirror. She was about fourteen, her hair in those silly plaits her mother used to insist on. Was this a dream? She mused on the possibility, running her hands over the small mounds of her rock-hard breasts, her inquisitive fingers examining the sensitive teats of her nipples. She could feel her body, hear the birds singing in the garden . . . This couldn't be a dream. This was real.

At fourteen, she hadn't known that she'd eventually live in a London flat with the boy across the road. Zak was a silly teenager in those days, shouting out daft comments about sex as he passed Samantha in the street. Her fingertip again massaging the solid nub of her young clitoris, Samantha breathed deeply. As she'd grown and got to know Zak, she'd allowed him to touch her, to massage the solid protrusion of her ripening clitoris and—

'We're home, Samantha,' her mother called. Leaping off the bed, Samantha smiled. Her mother's voice was comforting, and she wanted to go downstairs and meet the young woman . . .

But her thoughts turned to the mansion, the basement. Suddenly finding herself sitting in the armchair and gazing across the dimly lit basement, she looked down at her red miniskirt. Confused as she tried again to convince herself that she'd been dreaming, she jumped as a creaking sound echoed through the room. It was just gone eight o'clock, and the prospect of spending the night in the basement wasn't at all appealing. Whether or not the sinister sounds were electronically produced, she wasn't going to stay in the dungeon all night.

'Fucking hell,' she breathed, futilely trying her mobile phone again. Dave must have wondered where she'd got to, she mused. He'd probably tried to call her mobile and thought that she'd switched it off. Wishing she'd not ventured down to the basement, she wondered where Gerry Andrews was. He lived in the mansion, she knew that much. But it was such a huge place that he wouldn't hear her if she shouted. This was Dave's fault, she thought angrily. The idea of exposing Andrews as a

charlatan was a waste of time. Everyone locally knew that the place wasn't haunted. Why tell them what they already knew? Picturing Dave sitting behind his desk, she wished she'd told him that she wasn't going to . . .

'Dave,' she breathed, wondering what the hell was going on as she found herself standing in front of his desk.

'Ah, Sammy baby,' he said, looking up and grinning at her. 'How did you get on?'

'The mansion . . .'

'What mansion?'

'Gerry Andrews. I went to his mansion and . . .'

'That eccentric nutter? What the hell did you go there for?'

'You sent me there this afternoon.'

'What *are* you talking about? You've been to the meeting at the town hall, right?'

'Meeting?'

'The bypass discussion. You were supposed to be—'

'That was years ago, Dave.'

'Years ago? Sam, the meeting was this afternoon. You were supposed to be covering it, if you remember.'

'I . . . I don't know what's happening. The meeting was in nineteen ninety-eight.'

'It *is* nineteen ninety-eight, for fuck's sake. Look, I know you've only been here for a few months, but . . .'

'I've been here for four years, Dave. This is two thousand and two.'

'Two thousand and . . . Have you been drinking?'

'No, of course not.'

'I think you'd better go home and have a rest.'

'Yes, yes I'll do that,' she breathed, eyeing the calendar on the filing cabinet. *July, nineteen ninety-eight*.

'I take it that you didn't go to the meeting?'

'I . . . No, I suppose I didn't.'

'You suppose? What is it, Sam? What's wrong with you?'

'The mansion . . . I'm locked in the basement.'

'*What?* Fucking hell, I haven't got time to play games. Go home, for Christ's sake. Perhaps you'll make more sense in the morning.'

'Dave, I need help.'

'You're telling me you do. Perhaps it's the heat. Go home and we'll talk about this tomorrow.'

Back in the basement, Samantha gazed at her trembling hands. These weren't dreams, she knew. But it wasn't possible to go back in time and . . . No, of course it wasn't. Time travel was the stuff of movies. Shaking her head, she recalled starting at the newspaper back in ninety-eight. She *had* been to a meeting at the town hall about the controversial bypass plans. 'That was four years ago,' she breathed shakily, wondering whether it was the basement that was a dream. 'Perhaps I'm dead,' she murmured, trying the door again. Looking round for something to smash the door with, she noticed a hefty wooden pole leaning against a cardboard box.

'Fuck it,' she cursed, realizing that the oak door wasn't going to splinter even as she repeatedly hit it with the wooden pole. This was a crazy situation, she mused. Andrews must have been upstairs somewhere. Surely he'd come down to check the computer equipment at some stage. But perhaps not until the following day, she thought fearfully. Deciding to try to dream about the man, she wondered whether it would be possible to tell him that she was trapped in the basement. Sitting in the

chair, she closed her eyes and concentrated. But her thoughts turned to Zak.

Finding herself in the bar, standing several feet behind Zak, Samantha stared in disbelief at him. His arm around Angela's waist, he whispered in the giggling girl's ear, kissing her neck and moving his hand down over the pert cheeks of her bottom. Samantha couldn't believe that her best friend would behave like this, let alone her boy-friend. Moving closer, she stood behind the couple. They'd both had too much to drink, that was obvious. But that was no excuse for their underhand behaviour.

'With any luck, she won't be back for ages,' Zak said.

'Where did she go?' Angela asked.

'God knows. She was here one minute, and then . . . Let's not talk about her. Did you enjoy the other night?'

'You know I did,' Angela giggled.

'You like it up your bum, don't you?'

'Yes, but keep your voice down. I don't want the world to know about us.'

'If Sam doesn't come back, how about—'

'Why don't you dump her, Zak? You know how good we are together. We could fuck every night if you dumped Sam.'

'We *do* fuck every night,' he laughed. '*Almost* every night, anyway. She doesn't seem to mind me going out. As long as she thinks I'm meeting the lads, there's no problem.'

'Yes, but . . .'

'Her dad's got money, Ange.'

'Are you really going to marry her?'

'Yes, but that won't affect us. Once I've married the daft bitch and got my hands on her old man's cash, we'll

take off to some Greek island or other and fuck all day and all night.'

Slipping into a shadowy corner of the bar, Samantha knew that this had to be a dream as she watched Zak kissing Angela's full mouth. Returning to her classroom, her bedroom, the office, the wine bar . . . These were all dreams. There was no way that Zak and Angela were fucking behind her back – was there? Her shoulders slumping, Samantha let out a sigh. She wanted to confront Zak, but if this was a dream . . . There was one way to discover whether these were strange dreams or . . . or something sinister.

Thinking of the basement, Samantha again found herself sitting in the armchair. Perhaps the whole thing was a dream, she thought, looking around the dimly lit dungeon. Perhaps, after visiting the mansion, she'd gone home and was now in bed dreaming. She'd been tired, and might have fallen asleep on the sofa. Dreams, or reality? She had to discover what was going on. Concentrating her thoughts on an event that had taken place during her schooldays, she wondered whether she could change the future by changing history. If she was travelling back in time, then surely by changing events . . .

'You're a pretty little thing,' the vicar said, his deep voice echoing around the church as he grinned at Samantha. 'I asked you to stay behind because I wanted to talk to you. You enjoy Sunday school, don't you?'

'Yes,' Samantha replied, sitting on a pew and swinging her legs.

'You're growing up, Samantha. You're in your teens now, growing to be a fine young lady. As you know, I

take photographs for the church magazine. I'm looking for a model, Samantha. Not for the magazine, but for my own private collection of photographs.'

'A model?' she echoed, cocking her head to one side.

'How would you like to be my model?'

'Yes, all right,' she replied eagerly in her naivety.

'Let's have a look at your legs. Lift your dress up and show me your legs.'

Slipping off the pew, Samantha pulled her skirt up over her stomach, revealing not only her legs but the tight material of her panties hugging the swell of her hairless sex lips. This was no dream she knew as the vicar knelt in front of her and ran his fingers up and down the firm flesh of her inner thighs. She'd gone back in time and had returned to the church where she'd stayed on after the others had gone home that fateful Sunday afternoon. At the time, she'd not known what it was that the cleric had wanted. Taking photographs had seemed innocent enough to an innocent mind. But now she knew the truth. *If only I knew then what I know now*, she thought, watching the vicar's glazed eyes as he focused on her tight panties. But it *was* then, and she *did* know.

'You'd like me to take some photographs, wouldn't you?' the vicar asked, his fingertip dangerously close to the triangular patch of her white panties.

'Of my legs?' she queried, feigning puzzlement.

'Yes, and your . . . My camera is in the office, Samantha. Would you like me to take a couple of photographs now?'

'All right,' she replied, following the man.

This was exactly how it had happened, she recalled, watching the priest close the office door behind her. He'd coaxed her gently, telling her that she was going to be a

famous model and he was going to help her. He'd taken several shots of her legs, asked her to sit on his desk and part her thighs so that he could take *real modelling* photographs. But things were different now, she mused, watching him fiddling with his camera. By changing what had happened, could she change history? She pondered the question.

'Why don't you sit on the desk?' the vicar asked, just as he'd asked all those years ago. 'That's it,' he said, kneeling on the floor. 'Now lift your skirt up and I'll take a couple of photos of your legs.' Holding her skirt up, Samantha listened to the click of the camera as she had on that fateful afternoon after Sunday school. The vicar moved in, ordering her to part her thighs and focusing on her tight panties as she obediently complied. Samantha remembered clearly what had happened next, but she was going to try to change that. Could she change the course of events?

'Why don't you lie on the desk with your dress pulled up?' the vicar asked, rising to his feet. 'That way, I'll be able to take some good photographs of your legs.'

'All right,' Samantha murmured, slipping off the desk. Discreetly pulling her panties to one side, she climbed onto the desk and lay with her dress pulled high over her stomach. 'Like this?' she asked, wondering at his reaction.

'Er . . . yes, yes,' he replied shakily, eyeing the smooth lips of her young vulva. 'That's absolutely . . . That's perfect, Samantha.'

Samantha was enjoying playing her wicked games as the vicar repeatedly clicked the camera shutter, but she was determined to discover whether she was dreaming or not, and whether she could change history. If she returned to the day Zak had asked her out and she'd declined his offer,

would she have still shared a flat with him? This was nonsense, she mused. The concept of travelling back in time was ridiculous. She had to be dreaming. The basement, the school classroom, the vicar . . . She must have gone home to bed after leaving the mansion and . . .

'What I'd really like is to take some photographs of you without your dress,' the priest said, his hands visibly trembling as he licked his lips.

'What? You want me to take all my clothes off?' Samantha asked, surprised.

'That's what real models do. Would you like to be a real model?'

'That would please my dad,' Samantha said, clambering off the desk and unbuttoning her dress. 'He'll be pleased when I tell him that—'

'Yes, but . . . Samantha, it's . . . it's best not to mention this to anyone,' the vicar stammered. 'You see . . .'

'There we are,' she trilled, allowing her dress to slip down her young body to her ankles.

'You, er . . . you don't wear a bra?' he asked, gazing longingly at the small mounds of her fresh breasts.

'No, my mother won't let me,' she replied dolefully.

'Right, well . . . I'll just go and lock the main doors, Samantha,' he said, again licking his lips as he left the office. 'I won't be a minute.'

This was what had happened before, she recalled. He'd gone to lock the doors just as someone had walked into the church. He'd got talking to them and had said goodbye to Samantha as she'd walked past him and left the church. He'd not got a glimpse of the smooth lips of her young vagina on that occasion but, apart from that, this was exactly what had happened. Hearing voices, she pulled her dress up and buttoned the garment before

leaving the office. It was happening as before. Talking to an elderly lady, the vicar smiled at Samantha and said goodbye as she left the building. He'd cornered her again the following Sunday, she recalled. Many times he'd lured her into his office after Sunday school and the day had inevitably come when he'd—

'This is crazy,' Samantha breathed, finding herself sitting in the armchair, her wide eyes looking around the basement. Experimenting with her dreams or whatever they were was getting her nowhere, she knew. Feeling hungry, she knew that she was going to have to do something to escape the basement before long. 'That's it,' she murmured, having an idea. Closing her eyes and thinking back to when she'd arrived at the mansion, she imagined herself walking up the stone steps to be greeted by Gerry Andrews. Miraculously finding herself standing on the steps, she gazed at Andrews as he raised his cap and greeted her.

'The ghosts are rampant today,' he said. 'Kept me up all night, they did. Moaning and groaning, banging and humping around—'

'You must listen to me,' Samantha interrupted him. 'I was here earlier and . . .'

'I'll do you a discount if it's a repeat visit,' he offered, eyeing her naked thighs.

'No, no – you don't understand. In your basement, there's a computer and video equipment.'

'Who told you that?'

'I've been down there. I mean, I *am* down there. The door's locked and I can't get out. Please, go to the basement and . . .'

'You're down there?' he chuckled. 'Are there two of you? You're not a clone, are you?'

'Listen, this is serious. Go down to the basement and unlock the door.'

'That door is to be kept locked at all times.'

'I'm . . . There's someone locked in the basement. You must let them out.'

'All right, as you wish,' he sighed. 'You stay here and man my post.'

'What post?'

'The punters – you stay here and take their money.'

'Oh, yes. Please, go and unlock the door. And leave it unlocked.'

Sitting on the low wall as the man wandered into the building, Samantha tried not to think about Zak canoodling in the bar with Angela or about anything else that might whisk her away to another time and place. There'd be an opportunity to confront Zak and her so-called best friend once she'd escaped from the basement. And time enough to try to work out exactly what had been going on. Dreams? She thought about the matter for the umpteenth time. This was no dream she knew as she turned and saw Andrews approaching.

'I've unlocked the door,' he said, smiling at her. 'But there's no one down there.'

'Did you leave the door open?'

'Yes, I did. The basement is out of bounds to visitors, young lady. I don't understand why you—'

'Thanks,' she broke in, moving towards the door. 'I'll explain everything later.'

'Hey, you can't go in without paying.'

'I'm not going in yet. I . . . I have to get something from my car.'

Trotting down the steps and walking to her car, Samantha thought again about the basement and once

more miraculously found herself sitting in the armchair. There were so many unanswered questions, she mused. What would happen if she went on one of her trips and never returned to the basement? Had her body remained in the armchair when she'd visited her parents' house? She'd been about fourteen when she'd been in her bedroom . . . Was she dead?

Deciding to make her escape before it was too late, she bounded up the steps and tried the door. 'Shit,' she breathed, finding it locked. Andrews had opened it before she'd originally ventured into the basement. Realizing that she had to get him to open the door at a later time, after she'd gone down to the basement, she returned to the armchair and sat down.

Closing her eyes, she did her best to concentrate on Gerry Andrews. Not knowing where he was, what he was doing, she couldn't picture his surroundings. *Come on, come on*, she urged mentally, trying to imagine him in the local pub. What did the pub look like? What was Andrews wearing? She couldn't go to him in her dream unless she knew where he was. For some reason, her thoughts turned to the vicar. She'd tried to blot out the memory of the evil man and his church as she'd grown. Keeping away from him, she'd told no one of her Sunday afternoons in his office.

She recalled one particular afternoon when she'd been to Sunday school as usual. The others had left, the vicar had hovered . . . And Samantha had hovered. She'd not known why she'd stayed behind. Perhaps she was intrigued by the man of God, his peculiar interest in her young body. Was it his attention she'd craved all those years ago? Her parents were usually too busy to spend time with her, take an interest in what she was doing.

The vicar had always given her his undivided attention, taken a great interest in her. And now she knew why . . .

Samantha remembered the incident well. She'd followed the vicar to his office to look at the photographs he'd taken of her. Gazing at pictures of her legs, her thighs, her exposed panties, she'd asked him why her face wasn't in any of the shots. He'd stammered some reply or other, mumbled his excuses. And had then suggested that she pose naked for him. Growing up in the country village with fairly strict parents and no brothers or sisters, Samantha was gullible, far more naive than most girls of her age. And the vicar was a man of God, a man to be trusted. Wasn't he?

'Slip your clothes off and I'll get the camera ready,' he said as Samantha found herself going back in time and standing in his office.

'*All* my clothes?' she asked. Now she knew then what she knew now. 'Even my panties?'

'Well, er . . . yes, yes – of course. You do want to be a model, don't you?'

'Yes, I do,' she replied, unbuttoning her dress and allowing the garment to tumble down her slender body to her feet.

'Very good,' he praised her, his dark-eyed gaze glued to the ripening teats of her small breasts. 'And now your . . . your panties.'

'No one's ever seen me naked,' she breathed, slipping her thumbs between the tight elastic of her panties and her slender hips.

'Samantha, I think it would be best if you didn't tell anyone about our modelling work,' he said, obviously desperate to gaze at the fleshy swell of her love lips.

'You don't think I should tell my parents that I'm going to be a model?'

'No, no. For goodness' sake . . . Er . . . take your panties off and we'll get started.'

Deliberately hesitating, Samantha teased the pervert. She was old enough back then, she mused, tugging her panties down an inch or so. Old enough, but still too young. Things were different now, she reflected. She was an adult in a young girl's body. An adult who understood men, what they wanted. His pathetic lies about modelling had worked back then, but now? Now he came across as a sad pervert. Was this the time for her long-awaited retribution? Finally tugging her panties down, she stepped out of her clothes and stood naked in front of the trembling man.

'Yes,' he breathed, kneeling on the floor and gazing longingly at the sparse blonde fleece of her vulva. 'You'll make a fine model.'

'You like my pussy?' she asked, concealing a grin.

'Is that what you call it?'

'I don't like the word *cunt*. That's what my friends call it.'

'I see,' he murmured, adjusting his solid cock through his cassock. 'Do you and your friends talk about your pussies?'

'Yes, all the time.'

'Do you touch yourself there?'

'Well, I . . . I'd better not say anything.'

'You can tell *me*, Samantha.'

'Well . . . yes, I do touch myself. I rub myself there in bed at night. It feels nice.'

'Has anyone else ever rubbed you there?'

'No, no, they haven't.'

She remembered this Sunday afternoon well. The forbidden event indelibly etched in her memory, she knew that she'd never forget the vicar's intimate attention. But she was about to change history. The vicar wasn't going to touch her, massage her budding clitoris to orgasm, as he'd done all those years previously. Grabbing her clothes, she told him that she'd just remembered that her father was due to meet her at the church. The cleric panicked, holding his hand to his lined forehead and urging her to dress quickly.

'Why didn't you say so earlier?' he asked. 'If your father—'

'I've only just remembered,' she broke in. 'You can still look at my cunt, if you want to.'

'Yes, I . . . no, Samantha. Dress and get out of here.'

'You can look at my cunt next Sunday,' she said, smiling at him.

Leaving the man with his rampant erection, Samantha skipped up the aisle to the main doors. He was watching her, she knew, as she left the cold building and emerged into the bright sunshine. He'd not had his wicked way with her that time. Maybe the next time she dreamed of visiting him, she'd allow him to rub her clitoris, perhaps let him run his wet tongue up and down the virginal valley of her pussy. Thinking about wanking his cock, bringing out his spunk, she opened her eyes and gazed around the basement. The dreams, or whatever they were, were fun. But Samantha had to grasp the stark reality of her imprisonment and escape the basement. Feeling hungry, she wondered whether she'd ever see the light of day. Was this death? she mused. Had she slipped and fallen down the basement steps? Perhaps this was heaven. Or hell.

2

Waking with a start, Samantha looked at her watch. Eight-thirty. The morning had come, she thought, hauling her aching body out of the armchair. Gerry Andrews would be around soon she was sure as she climbed the steps and tried the basement door. He'd come down and check the computer and video equipment before opening for business – he *had* to. Her stomach rumbling, her head spinning, she knew that she should eat something before long.

'This is turning into a fucking nightmare,' she breathed, checking the monitor and gazing at the entrance hall. There was no sign of Andrews, and she began to imagine that he'd gone away for a week or more. She'd die in the basement, she thought fearfully, flopping back into the armchair. Unless she was already dead. Shaking her head, she realized that she had to be sensible. She was only in the basement, she reflected. There were daily visitors to the mansion, and Gerry Andrews would have to check the equipment at some stage. It was just a matter of time she knew as her stomach rumbled and she thought about the small café in the shopping precinct that did all-day breakfasts . . .

'Yes, miss?' a waitress asked, walking up to Samantha's table.

'Oh, er . . . a full English, please,' Samantha replied, the smell of food making her mouth water as she looked around the café.

'Tea or coffee?'

'Coffee, please.'

Looking around the café again, Samantha wondered whether her body was still in the basement, sleeping in the armchair. She couldn't be in two places at once, she mused, pressing her fingertips into the smooth flesh of her naked thigh to make sure that she was real. Had she somehow transported her body to the café? she pondered. This was all too confusing she decided as the waitress placed a cup of coffee on the table. No matter how much she thought about it, she knew that she'd never discover exactly how she was flitting from one place to another – from one *time* to another.

Sipping her coffee, she looked at an old man sitting in the far corner. She scrutinized him, deflecting her thoughts from the vicar for fear of finding herself in his office once again. After she'd eaten, she could go where she liked, she mused. She had to eat before doing anything. She was pleased when her breakfast arrived. Eating would take her mind off everything else she knew as she thanked the waitress. Wondering whether she'd still feel hungry once she was back in the basement, she thought again about being in two places at the same time. If she really was travelling through time, then it *would* be possible to be in two places at once, she decided.

After her breakfast, Samantha left the café and slipped into an alleyway between the shops. When returning to the basement, she didn't want anyone to see her vanish into thin air. She thought about it. Anyone looking at her would . . . She had no idea what they'd think when she

suddenly disappeared. Concentrating on the basement, she found herself sitting in the chair. Her hunger gone, she hoped that Andrews would check the computer and video equipment before long. He must have noticed that her car was still outside, she mused. After a day or two, he'd call the police.

All Samantha could do was wait. But she'd spend some time experimenting, she decided. Rather than sit around doing nothing while she waited for Andrews, she thought that she might as well try a few dreams, visit places in the past and . . . A fresh thought struck her. Could she travel *forward* in time? Before attempting to move into the future, she thought it best to practise travelling back in time, to discover more about her new-found gift.

Closing her eyes, she thought about the vicar and his office. He was an evil man, she reflected. It was too late now to tell people about his wickedness and expose him as a sad pervert. He'd deny everything, claiming to be a man of God and . . . Unless she could change history, she mused again. If she arranged for someone to visit the church and discover the young Samantha naked in the vicar's office . . . It was worth trying, she decided.

'Oh, hello, Samantha,' the vicar said, smiling as he walked up the aisle towards her. 'I haven't seen you in a long time.'

'No, I . . .' Samantha began, realizing that she was still in her twenties. Something had gone wrong with her timing. 'I was just passing and thought I'd pop in.'

'I'm pleased you did.'

'I wanted to ask you about Sunday school,' she said, deciding to worry him.

'Sunday school?'

'*After* Sunday school, to be precise. The times you took me into your office.'

'Oh, er . . .' he stammered, rubbing his chin. 'I don't remember . . .'

'*I* remember everything. Do you still have the photographs?'

'Samantha, that was a long time ago. I'm not into photography any more.'

'No, but you're still into young girls.'

'No, I . . .'

'I know everything, vicar.'

'You . . . you work for the local paper, don't you?'

'Indeed, I do.'

'That all finished years ago, Samantha. There was no harm done, was there? All I did was take a few photographs.'

'No harm done?'

'Nothing happened, did it?'

'You tell me.'

'All I did was—'

'I know what you did, vicar. Do you remember when I lay on your desk with my knickers pulled to one side?'

'No, no, I don't.'

'Where are the photographs?'

'Gone – thrown away years ago. Don't forget that *I* know something about *you*, Samantha.'

'Me?' she breathed, frowning at the man. 'What do you mean?'

'I'm not going to say anything but . . . I would suggest that you forget about my taking photographs of you. The words *altar* and *sixteen years old* might jog your memory.'

Sitting on a pew as the priest went into his office to

answer the phone, Samantha knew what he was talking about but pushed all thoughts of the event to the back of her mind. That was a long time ago and . . . The vicar knew nothing about it – he couldn't have known. She was innocent, she mused, and decided to test her theory about changing history. If she went back in time and changed one particular event, she could then move to the present and ask the vicar about it. The event would have to be memorable, she thought, a plan coming to mind. An event so shocking, so wicked, that the vicar would remember it for the rest of his days . . .

'Ah, there you are,' he said as Samantha slipped back in time and wandered into his office in her Sunday dress. 'I've got the camera ready.'

'What is it you really want to do?' she asked, her long blonde hair framing her angelic face.

'Er . . . what do you mean?'

'You take photographs of my legs, and my panties . . .'

'Your panties?' he echoed, frowning at her.

'My panties are in the pictures, aren't they?' she asked, wondering at what stage of the abuse she was. Was this the first time he'd taken photographs?

'It's your legs, Samantha. You have the legs of a model. Perhaps your panties were in some of the pictures, but . . .'

'You'd like to take photographs of me with nothing on, wouldn't you?' she asked, knowing that, one Sunday afternoon in the near future, he'd suggest that she should slip out of her dress. 'That's what you'd really like, isn't it?'

'Well, I . . .'

'That's what you're working towards, isn't it?'

'Samantha, you're a lovely girl. You're very pretty and
. . . If you want to get into modelling, then I can help
you. I have a friend in the business. He's seen some of the
photographs I've taken and he's very interested in you.'

'So, you want me to take all my clothes off?'

'Yes, yes, I do. If you're serious about modelling,
then . . .'

'All right,' she breathed, unbuttoning her dress. 'You
do know how old I am?'

'I, er . . . yes, I know how old you are. But there's
nothing wrong with taking photographs, Samantha.'

He was right, there was nothing wrong with taking
photographs, she thought, tugging her dress down and
stepping out of the garment. But the vicar wanted to do far
more than that, she knew. Wondering whether he'd lured
other young girls into his office, she looked down at the
firm mounds of her petite breasts, her elongated nipples.
He was going to have to remember this, she mused,
recalling her thoughts. *An event so shocking, so wicked,
that the vicar would remember it for the rest of his days.*

'Do I look like a model?' she asked, slipping her
panties down and revealing the fleshy swell of her vulval
lips to his wide eyes. 'Do you think I've got what it
takes?'

'God, yes,' he breathed, staring at her feminine in-
timacy.

'Do you think I'm all right, down there?'

'Down there?' he murmured, gazing at her ripening
nipples.

'My pussy. I've often wondered whether it looks
right.'

'Let me see,' he said shakily, dropping to his knees.
'You look . . . It's perfect, Samantha.'

'No, I mean inside my crack,' she coaxed him, sure that he'd not be able to control his base male desires. 'I'm not sure that it's right.'

'Stand with your feet apart and I'll take a look,' the priest instructed her, his face flushing, his hands trembling.

Allowing him to part the soft pads of her outer labia, exposing the intricate inner folds of her sex crack, Samantha knew that she was leading him on. This had happened, she reflected. But it had taken many, many visits to his office before he'd gained her confidence, before he'd dared to touch her there. The incidents in the vicar's office hadn't left her psychologically scarred or disturbed her in any way. He'd not raped her or forced her to do anything. His interest had been in the beauty of her young body. He'd touched her, even slipped his finger into the hugging sheath of her wet vagina. He had eventually taken things further, masturbating her, bringing her intense orgasms and even lifting his cassock and getting her to—

'Is that nice?' he asked, his fingertip massaging the pink funnel of flesh surrounding her virginal sex duct.

'Yes, yes, it is,' she replied. 'Although I usually rub myself higher up. That's where it feels really nice.'

'Do you mean there?' he asked, his trembling finger massaging the swelling protuberance of her sensitive clitoris.

'Oh, yes,' she gasped. '*That*'s where I rub myself.'

In her tender years, her vulval flesh was more sensitive, her clitoris more responsive. As she'd grown, her orgasms had stayed incredible, but were never as intense as they had been. Her sex hormones had run wild during her early teens, she reflected as the vicar took great

delight in massaging her solid clitoris. She'd masturbated regularly, toyed with her inner lips, stroked her stiffening nipples, fingered the tight sheath of her vagina whenever the opportunity had arisen. At twenty-two, she was still incredibly sensual, craving sex as much as the next girl. But her early teens had been her prime years.

'Shall I lie on the desk?' she asked, her breathing fast and shallow. 'My legs are wobbly. I can't stand properly.'

'Yes, yes,' the cleric replied eagerly, standing and moving some papers off the desk.

'That's far more comfortable,' she said, sitting on the edge of the desk and reclining. 'You'll be more comfortable if you pull a chair up,' she enticed him, her naked buttocks over the edge of the desk, her thighs parted wide.

'Now that is a good idea,' he replied, dragging a chair across the room. 'Now I'll be able to check you properly.'

Samantha knew that he wouldn't be able to resist the temptation to kiss the fleece-covered flesh of her mons, lick the creamy wet valley of her young pussy. His fingertip massaging her solid clitoris, he parted the fleshy cushions of her outer quim lips with his free hand. He was gazing at the inner folds of her young pussy she knew as her clitoris responded to his illicit massaging by transmitting ripples of pure sexual bliss throughout her trembling body. Her climax nearing, she gripped the sides of the desk, arching her back as the birth of her orgasm stirred deep within her rhythmically contracting womb.

'It's coming,' she gasped, her head tossing from side to side, her legs twitching, as the vicar quickened his masturbating rhythm. His finger sliding deep into the

tight canal of her vagina, massaging her inner flesh, he finally leaned forward and swept his wet tongue over the sensitive tip of her painfully hard clitoris. Sucking and mouthing on her pleasure spot, he drove a second finger deep into the drenched sheath of her convulsing pussy, pistoning her sex duct and sustaining her massive orgasm.

Listening to the sound of her squelching juices of sex, Samantha whimpered in her incredible coming. Letting out a scream of delight as her climax peaked, gripping her naked body, she spread her young thighs further. Again and again, tremors of sex rocked her very soul, taking her to heights of ecstasy she'd never known before. Her teenage juices of desire streaming down between her pert buttocks, trickling over the brown ring of her anus, she gripped the sides of the desk harder as the vicar worked between her young thighs. Her nostrils flaring, her stomach rising and falling jerkily, she felt the ripe nipples of her young breasts harden as her pleasure rolled through her quivering body.

Her orgasm finally beginning to recede, her clitoris retreating beneath its pinken bonnet, she lay gasping for breath as the vicar sucked the last ripples of pleasure out of her cumbud. Quivering uncontrollably on the desk, her naked body glowing in the aftermath of her forbidden climax, Samantha knew that the time was right for the unforgettable event. Lifting her head and gazing at the grinning vicar as he slipped his cunny-wet fingers out of her sex duct, she licked her lips provocatively.

'Why don't you rub your thing up and down my crack?' she asked huskily. 'Don't put it in me, just rub me with it.'

'Yes, yes,' the vicar breathed excitedly, leaping to his

feet and lifting his cassock. 'Have you ever seen a penis?' he asked, proudly displaying his solid cock to her staring blue eyes.

'No, never,' she replied, grinning as he retracted his foreskin fully and exposed the purple head of his penis.

'Rub the knob up and down my crack and make me have that feeling again.'

Wasting no time, the vicar slipped his purple glans between the swollen pads of her girl-wet vaginal lips, breathing heavily as his knob glided up and down her creamy valley of desire. The silky-smooth head of his cock repeatedly sliding over the swelling nub of her ripening clitoris, Samantha knew that he'd pump out his spunk, the white liquid filling her gaping sex valley and running down between the firm cheeks of her buttocks. She'd hold back if she could, time her climax with his and heighten their forbidden pleasure.

Would he be able to restrain himself? She asked herself the question as his gasps of male pleasure resounded around the office. Would he be happy enough to spunk her sex crack? Or would he drive his knob deep into the virgin sheath of her young cunt and fuck her naked body? He knew her age, he knew that she was a virgin. He hadn't hesitated to lick her clitoris, to finger the tight sheath of her chaste vagina. His male desires would surely get the better of him and he'd pump her young cunt full of his creamy spunk, she was sure. He was about to come she knew as he let out long low moans of pleasure. Her clitoris swelling, pulsating in the beginnings of her climax, Samantha lifted her head and watched the man of God fucking her drenched sex crack.

'Yes,' he gasped, his sperm jetting from his knob-slit, filling the valley of her vulva and running down between

the firm cheeks of her rounded buttocks. Her clitoris exploding in orgasm beneath his sweeping glans, she wondered why he'd not succumbed to his male needs and slipped his knob into the velvety sheath of her spasming cunt. Was he afraid? Her naked body shook violently as her orgasm gripped her very soul. Perhaps even a perverted vicar had some morals, some decency about him.

'Put it in me,' she cried, knowing that this would be a forbidden act that the man would never forget. 'Put your cock in me.' His throbbing glans suddenly driving deep into the virginal sheath of her cunt, tearing down her curtain of virginity, the priest grabbed her hips and fucked her naked body with a vengeance. Samantha could feel his spunk gushing into her, bathing her cervix and lubricating the illicit union. Her orgasmic juices mingling with his semen, squelching as he repeatedly thrust his throbbing glans deep into her convulsing body, she felt the outer lips of her pussy rolling back and forth along the sex-slimed shaft of his huge cock.

The vicar had done it now, she mused, her clitoris massaged by his thrusting cock-shaft. He'd committed the forbidden act, used his position of trust as a so-called man of God to fuck a young girl to orgasm and flood her tight cunt with his spunk. As he slowed his pistoning rhythm, his cock beginning to deflate, Samantha lay on the desk gasping for breath as her own orgasm subsided. Trembling uncontrollably, she wondered whether he'd recall the forbidden act. If he did, then she could change history. If he had no recollection of fucking her senseless, then . . . then she wouldn't know what to think. Taking the notion to the extreme, she wondered what would happen if she became pregnant by the vicar. Her entire future would change, but that wasn't possible, was it?

'I have to go,' Samantha sobbed, feigning tears as the cleric finally slipped his spent penis out of her abused vaginal sheath.

'Are you all right?' he asked concernedly.

'You shouldn't have done that,' she wailed. 'You . . . you fucked me and—'

'You asked me to, Samantha. For God's sake, I hope you're not going to go telling people that I forced you to have sex?'

'I . . . I have to go,' she stammered again, grabbing her clothes and fleeing from the office.

Hiding behind a pew, Samantha concentrated her thoughts on the basement as sperm oozed between the inflamed lips of her pussy. Suddenly finding herself back in the armchair, dressed in her blouse and miniskirt, she let out a wicked chuckle. The vicar *had* to recall the forbidden fucking, she mused, wasting no time and thinking about visiting the man in the church. In her mind, she pictured herself at twenty-two years old, meeting the vicar after all those years. She wondered if he would make out that he remembered nothing of the event. If he lied, then . . .

'Ah, vicar,' Samantha said, walking down the aisle towards the man.

'Samantha,' he greeted her. 'It's lovely to see you. How are you?'

'I'm fine. I was just passing and thought I'd call in. Do you remember when you had me on your desk?' she asked directly.

'Had you on my desk?' he echoed.

'Stripped me of my virginity.'

'What *are* you talking about, Samantha?'

'You fucked me in your office.'

'I . . . I never did anything of the sort.'

'You took filthy photographs of me, didn't you?'

'Filthy? Yes, I took photographs of you. But they were never—'

'You don't remember having sex with me?'

'Good grief, girl,' he gasped. 'I never did anything of the—'

'Are you sure?'

'Of course I'm sure. For goodness' sake, I hope you're not going to tell . . .'

'It's all right, I'm not going to say anything to anyone. What you did to me all those years ago was *very* wrong, and I can't say that I like you for the way you treated me, but . . .'

'All I can do is apologize, Samantha,' he murmured, hanging his head. 'You were such a beautiful . . . you *are* such a beautiful girl. I . . . I just couldn't help myself. There was no harm done.'

'And who are you abusing now? You might as well own up because I know what's going on.'

'She told you?' he gasped disbelievingly.

'Yes, she did.'

'Caroline is . . . She's—'

'Too young, vicar. I'll be back to discuss this with you.'

'Samantha, I . . .'

'We'll talk about it later, vicar. I need to chat with Caroline first.'

'Samantha, please . . .'

Leaving the church, Samantha realized that she had to do something to put an end to the evil man's abuse of young girls. She also realized that she couldn't change

history. That put paid to her idea of resitting her exams to get better grades. *If I knew then*, she mused, deciding to return to the mansion and make an effort to escape from the basement. Finding herself in the armchair once again, she leaped to her feet as she heard someone trying the door handle.

'Thank God,' she breathed as Gerry Andrews opened the door and trotted down the steps.

'What are you doing here?' he asked her.

'Waiting for you,' she replied, smiling as she climbed the steps.

'But . . . how did you . . .'

'I'll be back,' she said, reaching the open door. 'I'll explain everything later.'

Fleeing the mansion, Samantha climbed into her car and drove to her flat. Sitting in the lounge with a cup of coffee, Samantha pondered on the recent events. Her visit to the mansion, the school, vicar's office, the café and wine bar . . . The whole episode now seemed like a strange dream. *Travelling in time?* She giggled inwardly. If that really was possible, the benefits would be amazing, she concluded. Recalling Zak and Angela kissing in the bar, she decided to try another trip in time. This wasn't going to work she was sure as she lay back on the sofa and closed her eyes. Time travel was only possible in the movies . . .

'She didn't come home last night and there's been no word from her today,' Zak said, his voice coming from behind a door as Samantha found herself standing in Angela's hall. 'God only knows where the daft bitch has got to.'

'Forget about her, Zak,' Angela giggled as Samantha

crept up to the bedroom door and spied through the crack. 'I'm hungry again, and I want to eat your cock.'

Staring in disbelief at her best friend lying on her bed, gobbling on Zak's erect penis, Samantha knew that this wasn't a dream. Whatever power or force she'd tapped into, she was able to transport herself anywhere she wanted to go. Watching Angela licking the bulbous knob of Zak's cock, she felt her stomach churning, her hands trembling. If this was how her boyfriend behaved behind her back . . . Closing her eyes, she returned to her own lounge and grabbed the phone.

'Angela, it's Sam,' she said as the girl answered the phone.

'Oh, hi,' Angela trilled. 'Where have you been? Zak . . . He called earlier and said that you'd not been home all night.'

'I had to sort something out to do with work. Is Zak there?'

'Here? Er . . . why would he be here?'

'On your bed with you, naked.'

'*What?* Sam, I hope you're not suggesting that Zak and I are having—'

'Oral sex? Yes, I am. My phone call interrupted you, didn't it? You were sucking his cock, Angela.'

'I . . . But . . . where on earth did you get that idea?'

'I was only joking, you daft bitch. As if you'd do that, for God's sake.'

'Yes, er . . . that's right,' the girl said, forcing a laugh. 'I'll call you later, OK?'

'Yes, yes, that's fine. You and your jokes, Sam. For a minute, I thought that you were serious.'

'Of course I wasn't. It would be funny if it was true, wouldn't it? OK, we'll talk later.'

Replacing the receiver, Samantha wasn't sure whether she was actually transporting herself through time and space or whether she'd gone mad. Had something in the mansion influenced her? *There's no such fucking thing as fucking ghosts*, she mused, recalling Dave's words. Something had happened she knew as she slipped out of her clothes and stepped into the shower. Nothing happened without reason, she thought, shampooing her long blonde hair. There was a cause and a reason for everything. Although, for the life of her, she didn't know what reason there could possibly be for her to be able to travel through time.

After her shower, she dressed in a short skirt and T-shirt. Ringing the office to tell Dave that she wasn't feeling well and was taking the day off, she breathed a sigh of relief to discover that he'd gone to London. Now that she had the day ahead to experiment with her new-found talent, she decided to return to her schooldays. There'd been one particular teacher whom she'd never forgotten. Mr Graham, the geography master, was a middle-aged man who took an interest in his young female pupils. He might have been innocent, his intentions honourable, but he had the habit of putting his arm around the girls, his hand dangerously close to their pert breasts.

Samantha had enjoyed geography and had always sat at the front of the class opposite Mr Graham's desk. One afternoon, she'd noticed that her geography teacher was gazing beneath her desk, his dark eyes wide, his gaze obviously fixed on something. Looking down, she'd realized that her short skirt had ridden up her naked thighs. Mr Graham was a respected member of the community. On the board of school governors, he was

in line for the post of headmaster. But, respectable as he was, he seemed to have a fascination with Samantha's school knickers . . .

'And that is the peninsula,' the geography master said, gazing at his fresh-faced pupils. Looking down at her base thighs beneath the desk, Samantha pulled her short skirt even further up and parted her legs. She remembered well how the man's gaze had repeatedly returned to her exposed flesh. But, this time, Samantha knew exactly why he was gazing beneath her desk with a strange glint in his eyes. She'd already established that she couldn't change history, but she could have some fun with her new talent.

Gazing at the triangular patch of Samantha's bulging panties as he sat at his desk, his wide eyes staring hard, the teacher mumbled something about the class leaving the room quietly. As he gazed at her blatantly displayed panties, Samantha fiddled with her books until her fellow pupils had left the room. Feeling wicked, she waited until the teacher looked away momentarily before slipping her hand between her young thighs and pulling the crotch of her panties to one side. Gazing beneath her desk again, his eyes bulging, the man obviously couldn't believe what he was seeing.

'What do you think you're playing at?' he asked her, walking towards her desk.

'Playing at?' she echoed, not expecting this sort of response as she cocked her head to one side. Frowning, Samantha played the innocent, her blue eyes reflecting naivety. 'I don't know what you mean, sir. I'm just putting my books away.'

'Your knickers, girl,' he said sternly. 'You deliberately—'

'My knickers?' she breathed. 'What about—'

'You know very well, Samantha,' he interrupted. 'Girls who behave like that are obviously asking for just one thing.'

Deciding to see how far the man would go, Samantha knew that he wouldn't recall the episode. She'd be safe enough playing her wicked games. This *was* only a game, she thought, realizing the power of her young body as the man gazed at the mounds of her small breasts billowing her blouse. But she wondered why she was playing sexual games. Was it because she found the thought of an adult mind in a teenage girl's body exciting? *I know now what I didn't know then.*

'Unless you want me to report your despicable behaviour to the headmaster, I suggest that you lift your skirt up and take a look for yourself,' Mr Graham said.

'Oh,' she gasped, standing and raising her short skirt. 'I'm sorry, sir. I had no idea that my knickers—'

'Pull the front of your knickers down,' he ordered her sternly.

'Pull them *down*?' she breathed incredulously, realizing that he was taking the bait. 'But, sir . . .'

'Unless you want to find yourself in a great deal of trouble, you'll pull your knickers down.'

Complying with the teacher's perverted request, Samantha feigned shock, gasping as he knelt in front of her. Lifting her skirt up over her stomach, she pulled her panties down her shapely thighs to her knees as Mr Graham gazed longingly at the tightly closed crack of her vulval flesh. His dark eyes bulging as he focused on the creamy-white stain in the crotch of her school knickers, he obviously couldn't control his base male instincts. But how far would he go, she wondered again, delighting in

the illicit game. Would he touch her? Would he slip his finger between the pinken wings of her inner lips and explore the inner sheath of her young pussy?

'You've been misbehaving of late, Samantha,' he growled.

'May I go now, sir?' she asked, jutting her hips forward a little.

'Not until you admit to deliberately pulling your panties to one side.'

'I had no idea, sir,' she breathed, her long blonde hair veiling her angelic face as she hung her head. 'I was just sitting at my desk . . .'

'You *wanted* to show me, didn't you?'

'Show you, sir?'

'Your crack, Samantha. You wanted to show me your crack. Go to the back of the classroom and bend over the computer desk.'

Again warning her that she'd be in serious trouble unless she did exactly as he said, he followed her to the back of the room. This might not have been what had happened all those years ago, Samantha reflected, tugging her panties up as she walked. But it was exactly what the man would have *liked* to have happened. Leaning over the desk in the corner of the room, Samantha knew that they couldn't be seen behind the bookshelves. As Mr Graham lifted her skirt high up over her back and pulled her panties back down around her knees, she wondered what he was going to do. The fleshy swell of her vaginal lips was protruding between her slender thighs she knew as he hovered behind her. Would he touch her there?

'I will not tolerate bad behaviour,' he said sternly, running his fingertips over the rounded cheeks of her naked bottom. 'You behaved like a common tart, Sa-

mantha. Exposing yourself like that . . . You did it deliberately, didn't you?'

'Sir, I was only sitting at my desk and—'

'Don't make the situation worse by lying, girl. Admit it. You exposed your crack deliberately.'

'Yes, sir.'

'Why?'

'Because . . . because I felt sexy, sir. I often feel sexy.'

'So you thought you'd pull your knickers to one side and show me your crack?'

'Yes, sir.'

'And what did you expect me to do?'

'I . . . I don't know.'

'I don't know, either. But I'll tell you what I'm going to do now, Samantha. By way of a punishment, I'm going to spank you.'

'Please, sir, I . . .'

'You only have yourself to blame, Samantha. Perhaps you'll think twice about behaving in such a despicable manner in future.'

His palm meeting her tensed buttocks with a loud slap, the teacher held Samantha down over the desk with his free hand as she squirmed and struggled. She'd never been spanked before, and found the degrading experience quite exhilarating. Her naked buttocks beginning to sting as loud slaps echoed around the classroom, she felt the nub of her sensitive clitoris swelling. This was a real turn-on, she thought, her knuckles whitening as she gripped the sides of the desk. Her young body trembling, her small breasts pressing hard against the desk, she gasped as the geography master spanked her burning bum cheeks unrelentingly.

'Have you pulled your knickers aside and shown your crack to anyone before?' he asked her, halting the spanking.

'No, never,' she replied, sobbing to add credence to her act.

'Are you sure? Tell me the truth, Samantha.'

'Yes, I have done it before,' she confessed. 'When I'm waiting for the bus, I sit on the seat in the shelter and do it.'

'And men see your crack?'

'Yes, yes – they do.'

'Why do you behave like that?'

'Because it excites me, sir. It makes me feel very sexy and—'

'And you go home and masturbate?'

'Yes, I do,' she admitted softly, her pretty face grinning beneath the gold curtain of her long hair. 'Most days when I get home from school, I go to my bedroom and masturbate.'

As he resumed the spanking, telling her that she was a naughty little schoolgirl, Samantha wondered whether all men harboured debased thoughts about schoolgirls. Mr Graham was obviously deriving immense sexual pleasure by administering the spanking, but what were his innermost thoughts? Given the opportunity, would he sink his purple knob deep into the tight sheath of her virgin cunt and fuck her as she was pinned down over the desk? Wondering what he was up to as he again halted the spanking, she let out a rush of breath as she felt the tip of his finger pressing softly against the brown ring of her anus.

'What are you doing, sir?' she asked.

'Have you ever touched your bottom-hole?' he

breathed shakily, massaging the sensitive brown tissue surrounding her anal inlet.

'Never, sir,' she replied, telling the truth for once.

'Has anyone else ever touched you there?'

'No,' she replied, truthfully again. 'Sir, it's not right to—'

'It's not *right* to expose yourself the way you did, Samantha. In fact, it's wicked. For the way you've behaved, I should, by rights, spank you until you scream. However, I'm not a hard man. Let's turn this dreadful situation round to our mutual advantage.'

'What do you mean, sir?'

'You're obviously at the age where your teenage sex hormones are running wild. You expose yourself because it excites you. You sit in the bus shelter displaying your crack to strangers and then go home and masturbate. You're obviously very keen to learn, hungry for experience. That's where I can help you.'

'Help me, sir?' she echoed, jutting her crimsoned buttocks out as he continued to massage the sensitive tissue of her tightly closed anus. 'What do you mean, sir?'

'Seeing as it's the end of the day and everyone's gone home, we have the time and the opportunity to . . . I was thinking that I might help you to gain a little experience. Do you like me massaging you there?'

'Well, I . . . yes, I suppose I do.'

'Good, good. You see, young teenage girls need to be led gently along the path to sexual experience. Fumbling teenage boys have no idea . . . Let's just say that I know what I'm doing, Samantha. Now, I want you to relax and enjoy the sensations.'

Closing her eyes as Mr Graham's finger slipped past her tightening anal sphincter muscles and drove deep

into the dank sheath of her hot rectum, Samantha felt a quiver run through her contracting womb. No one had ever fingered her most secret hole, explored the hot depths of her tight rectum. Zak had never ventured into the gully dividing the pert globes of her buttocks, let alone suggested anal intercourse. Is that what he'd done with Angela? Samantha shivered at the thought, quivering as the geography master massaged the walls of her spasming rectum.

'I wonder what my father would say,' Samantha breathed, deciding to worry her teacher.

'Your father?' he echoed, his finger stilling within the tight duct of her bottom. 'You're not thinking of telling him about this, surely?'

'Well, I . . .'

'Samantha, you don't seem to understand the gravity of the situation. You have behaved atrociously. By rights, I should not only report your behaviour to the headmaster, but tell your parents about your dreadful . . . I thought you liked what I'm doing?'

'Yes, I do. But . . . it's wrong, isn't it?'

'We're alone, so no one's going to know about us. I'm teaching, you, Samantha. You *do* want to be taught, don't you?'

'Yes, if that's *all* you're going to do. I mean, I don't mind what you're doing to me, but I don't want you to do anything else.'

'You mean this?' he asked, slipping a finger into the burning sheath of her vagina. 'Are you going to tell me that you don't like that?'

'No, I . . . I don't mind that.'

Fingering her two sex holes, his penis obviously fully erect, the man was going to have to do something to

appease his swollen knob. But what? Samantha wondered, her juices of lust streaming from the virginal canal of her young pussy. Would he pull his cock out once she'd gone and wank himself to orgasm? Would he fuck her? Pondering on sucking the sperm out of his purple knob, she grinned as he slipped his fingers out of her tight sex sheaths and planted a kiss on the stinging cheek of one naked buttock. The feel of his wet tongue running up her anal valley sending incredible sensations of crude sex rippling throughout her young body, she hoped that he was going to tongue-fuck the sensitive inlet of her once-private hole . . .

'Sam,' Zak called from the hallway as Samantha opened her eyes and found herself sitting in the lounge. 'Oh, there you are,' he said, walking into the room. 'Where the hell did you get to last night?'

'Er . . . I . . .' she stammered, somewhat disorientated as she wondered why she'd returned to her own place. 'I had to work.'

'Are you all right?' Zak asked, brushing his long black hair back with his fingers.

'Sorry, I must have fallen asleep.'

'Angela called me and said that you rang her,' he mentioned nonchalantly. 'She reckoned that you thought I was at her place.'

'I was joking,' Samantha chuckled.

'What happened to you in the wine bar? You arrived late and then—'

'You remember that?' she asked.

'Of course I remember. Angela turned up just after you'd left. Why didn't you say that you had to go? You were there one minute, and the next . . .'

'I . . . I'm sorry, Zak,' she sighed. 'I've not been feeling too good for a couple of days. That's why I've not gone into work.'

'Oh, right. Look, I can't stay. I have to meet a couple of the lads. It's just a little business I have to see to. I'll only be an hour or so.'

'Yes, yes, that's fine,' Samantha said, knowing only too well where the two-timing bastard was going.

'I'll see you later.'

As he left, Samantha not only wondered where her relationship was going, but where her life was heading. Wishing, as she gazed around the room, that she'd never visited the mansion, she pondered again on her ability to travel through time. This was amazing, she knew. But it might also prove to be very dangerous. If she ventured back to her schooldays and, for some reason, was unable to return . . . Was it wise to go back and relive events? And did she really want to know what Zak got up to with her best friend?

Still not sure whether she'd been dreaming, she thought that she might have been having premonitions while sleeping. In her sleep, she might have seen Angela sucking Zak's cock. *A sixth sense?* she mused. No. Zak had remembered her visiting the wine bar. And she'd been locked in the mansion basement at the time. Again wondering why she'd left the classroom and returned to the lounge, she thought that perhaps Zak calling her from the hall might have been the reason for her un-timely return. Was it some kind of fail-safe thing? In times of trouble or danger, she'd automatically return to the present and—

The phone rang. 'Hello,' she said, answering it.

'Hi, Sam, it's Angela.'

'Oh, hi. How are you?'

'I'm OK. I was thinking about what you said earlier.'

'Oh?'

'What made you say that I was sucking Zak off?'

'I told you, it was a joke.'

'Yes, but . . . what made you think of even joking about such a thing?'

'When we were in the wine bar and Zak was saying how much you liked it up your bum . . .'

'*What?*' the girl breathed surprisedly, obviously shocked. 'But you weren't there.'

'Angela, I was standing next to you. Zak was talking to you, saying how much you liked it up your bum. And you said that you didn't want the world to know. Don't you remember?'

'No, I . . . I don't. Zak wouldn't say anything like that.'

'I think you must be losing your memory, Angela.'

'Er, yes . . . I think I must be. Oh, there's someone at the door. I'll . . . I'll talk to you later.'

Grinning as she replaced the receiver, Samantha knew that she'd confused the other girl. Although it was sad to think that Zak was screwing her best friend, the discovery of her boyfriend's infidelity had made Samantha realize that she wasn't bothered about her relationship. She'd known Zak since they were at school and they had progressed from being friends to becoming lovers. Having never played the field, Samantha had become stuck with Zak. There were more important things in life than Zak, she concluded. Were there more important things than sex?

Again pondering on her increasing fascination with sex, she thought about her geography master. It was a

shame that she'd been whisked away just when things were becoming interesting. Her visit back in time to the vicar's office had been interesting, she mused. Eager to time travel again, she thought about money. If she visited a bank . . . Horrified as she realized that she was thinking about stealing money, she knew that she was going to have to control herself, her new-found power. Having sex was one thing, but to steal money?

Pushing such thoughts out of her mind, she realized how many times and places she could return to. School-days, parties, friends . . . There were dozens of incidents she'd like to relive, not least the school camping holiday. She'd shared a tent with Jane, a young girl who was not only extremely attractive but incredibly sexual for her tender years. Samantha tried not to recall how old she'd been when the girl had run her hands over her half-naked body. Two schoolgirls in the privacy of a tent, their young bodies . . . Samantha had feigned sleep, halting what could have been a most rewarding experience. She'd been too young, she reflected. Too young to want to learn – but now? Wondering whether to return to that fateful night, she knew that she could change the course of events and enjoy the most intimate sexual relationship with Jane. Did she want to tongue another girl's vagina?

3

'Sammy, baby,' Dave said as Samantha answered the phone. 'How are you?'

'Feeling a little better,' she replied. 'Sorry I couldn't come in today.'

'No probs. So, what happened at the haunted mansion?'

'Well, I . . . I couldn't find any hidden speakers or anything. But I . . . I did see a ghost.'

'A ghost?' he laughed. 'It wasn't a naked young girl with firm titties and—'

'Dave, I'm serious. Gerry Andrews might be an eccentric, but his mansion is haunted. Look, I'll tell you about it in the morning. I should be all right by tomorrow.'

'OK, babe. You rest today and get here nice and early tomorrow and tell me a ghost story.'

'I will. And thanks, Dave.'

Wondering why Dave hadn't flown off the handle over her failure at the mansion, Samantha hoped that he'd forget about exposing Gerry Andrews as a charlatan. Turning her thoughts to her new talent, she wondered about moving forward in time. To take a peek into the future would be fascinating, she mused, sitting on the sofa and closing her eyes. Knowing what was going to happen, she could be the first on the scene as news stories

broke. With her knowledge of the future, she might even get a job on a national paper. Trying to picture herself about ten years older, she realized that she might discover something that she'd be better off not knowing.

Her thoughts again turning to the time she'd been on a school camping trip and had had the opportunity to experience lesbian sex, she wondered whether to return to that fateful night. Her friend, Jane, had been a little older than Samantha, and vastly more experienced. Recalling the girl's fingers stroking the unripe teats of her sensitive nipples, she remembered the wondrous quivers of pleasure coursing through her young body. When the girl had tried to slide her hand into her panties, Samantha had thought how wrong it was and had crossed her legs. She'd often wondered what it would have been like to feel another girl's hand stroking her vaginal lips and masturbating her clitoris to orgasm. It wasn't so much that she'd longed to indulge in lesbian games, but she still wished she'd taken the opportunity to experience mutual masturbation with another girl . . .

Lying on her back, Samantha looked up at the moonlight shining on the green canvas tent as Jane's hand slipped beneath her T-shirt and worked its way up to the petite mounds of her young breasts. She remembered this well – the arousing sensations, the girl's fingers nearing the sensitive teats of her barely developed breasts. But she also remembered the guilt, her incredible embarrassment and shyness. In her tender years, she hadn't thought of her friend's caresses as experimenting with sex, learning, discovering. She'd been riddled with thoughts of wrong-doing, naughtiness. But things were different now.

Breathing heavily, Samantha lay still and pretended to

be sleeping as Jane's fingers reached her painfully erect nipples. Her stomach rising and falling, she felt her juices of arousal seeping between the swelling lips of her vagina and wetting her panties as her friend squeezed and pulled on her young milk teats. Jane's hand exploring the rock-hard mounds of her petite mammary spheres sent wondrous sensations through her young pelvis and Samantha waited expectantly for her friend to explore the virgin crack of her sex-wet pussy. To feel the girl's fingers there, massaging, teasing, would be an amazing experience, she knew.

As Jane's hand left her breasts and ran down over the smooth plateau of her stomach, Samantha recalled turning over and crossing her legs at that point, halting the lesbian proceedings. But, this time, feigning sleep, she lay on her back and parted her thighs to allow her lover access to her virgin flesh. Jane's fingertips moved over her lower stomach slowly, teasing her firm flesh, tantalizing her before tentatively slipping beneath the elastic of her panties to the sparse blonde pubes sprouting from the mound of her mons. Samantha waited in anticipation as the girl's finger slipped into the top of her moist sex valley, locating the solid nub of her sensitive clitoris.

Samantha's new talent was amazing, she reflected. To be able to go back in time and experience the delights of those early days of sexual discovery was like a dream come true. She mused on the paradox of an adult mind in a young virgin body, her clitoris responding beneath Jane's inquisitive fingertip. The possibilities were endless, the fun she could have was limitless. The vicar, her geography teacher . . . But there was one time in her past, one horrendous experience she'd never want to relive. Trying to push thoughts of the horrifying event

out of her mind, she breathed deeply as her lesbian friend attended her solid pleasure bud.

Travelling further down the wet divide of her swollen vaginal lips, Jane's inquisitive finger rounded the firm curve of Samantha's pubic bone and ventured into the hot sheath of her virgin pussy. This was the first time that her young body had been invaded in this way, the first time she'd felt the nerve endings of her inner vaginal flesh stirring. The other girl's finger slipping further into the hot sheath of her pussy, Samantha could feel the petals of her inner lips opening, gripping her friend's intruding finger. Her clitoris sending beautiful sensations of lesbian sex through her contracting womb, Samantha trembled uncontrollably as she continued to feign sleep.

With no embarrassment or inhibitions, she felt that she could let herself go. Nothing mattered, she mused, relaxing completely. Jane wouldn't recall the lesbian fingering. There was nothing to worry about. Parting her thighs further as her love juices flowed and her clitoris pulsated, she breathed in the scent of Jane's long black hair as the girl leaned over and kissed her cheek. Slipping a second finger into Samantha's tightening vagina, Jane expertly massaged her inner flesh, inducing her girl-milk to flow in torrents from the tight sheath of her young vulval duct.

'Is that nice?' Jane asked, her fingers stirring the hot juices bubbling within Samantha's sex sheath.

'Yes,' Samantha murmured, the girl's hot breath playing on her stomach as she kissed and licked the indent of her navel.

'Do you want me to lick your cunt?' Jane asked huskily.

'I . . . I think so,' Samantha breathed, never having heard the word used before at her tender age.

'I want to tongue your cunt, Sam. You'd like that, wouldn't you?'

'Yes,' Samantha replied shakily, her young body becoming rigid.

Tugging Samantha's panties down, Jane snaked her wet tongue around the top of her camping companion's sex crack, sending incredible tremors of pleasure coursing through Samantha's quivering body. Her fingers leaving Samantha's vagina, her tongue licking the drenched entrance to the younger girl's tightening pussy, Jane mouthed and gobbled on the intricate inner folds of Samantha's once-sacrosanct vulval slit. Her tongue entering Samantha's vaginal duct, she licked deep inside her virgin pussy, waking the sleeping nerve endings and sending ripples of pure sexual bliss throughout her young friend's body.

'You taste nice,' Jane breathed, her tongue snaking up Samantha's sex valley to the solid nubble of her expectant clitoris. 'It's been very hot today, making your pussy wet and very tasty. You haven't had a shower, have you?'

'No, I haven't.'

'That's good. I like my girls hot and tasty.'

'Have you done this to other girls?' Samantha asked, feigning naivety.

'Oh, yes,' Jane giggled. 'I thought you knew that I have quite a reputation at school. Girls come to me when they reach the age where they start thinking about their cunts. I teach them to masturbate. I teach them licking, fingering, clit sucking . . . I think you're old enough to learn, Sam.'

'Yes, yes, I am,' Sam replied.

Feeling the girl's wet tongue snaking around the erect

nubble of her protruding clitoris, Samantha arched her back and breathed deeply in her illicit act of lesbian sex. Jane certainly knew what she was doing, she reflected, her clitoris responding beneath her friend's sweeping tongue. Her teenage hormones driving her wild, her girlfriend taking her arousal to almost frightening heights, Samantha parted her slender legs as wide as she could. Offering the open sexual centre of her young body to Jane's snaking tongue, she let out whimpers of pleasure as her womb contracted and her juices of lesbian desire flowed from her inner nectaries.

Grabbing the torch, Jane examined her friend's vaginal crack, opening her sex hole and peering inside the cream-drenched sheath. 'You're a virgin,' she breathed, eyeing Samantha's hymen. 'I like little virgin girls. Oh, and you have a few pubic curls sprouting just above your crack. You've shaved, haven't you? Or is it that . . .' Saying nothing, Samantha quivered as her lesbian friend continued the close examination of her most private place by torchlight. The fleshy cushions of her outer lips stretched further apart, her bared sex hole gaping wide open, Samantha hoped that she wouldn't be whisked back to her own time before she'd experienced a lesbian-induced orgasm.

'Come,' Jane whispered, discarding the torch and licking the solid protrusion of Samantha's pulsating clitoris. 'I want you to make lots of sex juice. Come now and pump out your girlie juice and I'll drink it.' The girl's words heightening Samantha's arousal, she tossed her head back and grimaced as she teetered on the brink of her clitoral eruption. As Jane stretched the fleshy pads of her vulval lips further apart, fully exposing her inner folds, her sex-wet vaginal entrance, Samantha clutched

the older girl's head and ground her bared cuntal flesh hard against her hot mouth.

'Yes,' she cried, her young body shaking violently as her clitoris exploded in a massive orgasm. She could feel her sex juices pumping from her rhythmically contracting vagina as Jane sustained her amazing pleasure with her sweeping tongue. Her clitoris pulsating intensely, her stomach rising and falling, she let out a cry of lesbian pleasure as her orgasm peaked and her lust juices gushed from the burning sheath of her virgin cunt. Again and again, electrifying tremors of sex coursed through her young body, her muscles convulsing fiercely as she rode the crest of her climax.

'No more,' she finally gasped. Ignoring her lesbian lover, Jane thrust at least three fingers into the juice-flooded canal of Samantha's hot pussy, taking her to yet another peak of ecstasy as she mouthed and sucked on her orgasming clitoris. Her pleasure finally beginning to recede, Samantha closed her legs, trapping Jane's pistoning fingers and halting the illicit massaging of her inner flesh. The older girl's fingers slipping out of her juice-flooded sex sheath, Samantha lay quivering uncontrollably in the aftermath of her lesbian-induced coming. Jane wanted her to reciprocate she knew as the girl pulled her T-shirt over her head and slipped her tight panties off. Was this what Samantha wanted? Did she want to lick and suck another girl's vagina?

'Please,' Jane breathed, grabbing the torch and lighting up the firm mounds of her young breasts. 'Suck my nipples and lick my wet cunt.'

'Jane, I . . .' Samantha began, confusion welling in her racked mind as she deliberated on Jane's crude request.

'You know you want to,' Jane coaxed her. 'Come on, Sam. I made you come, so now . . .'

'All right,' Samantha finally conceded. 'Lie on your back and open your legs.'

Samantha knew that this was an opportunity not to be missed as she picked up the torch and shone the beam on Jane's vulval flesh. Her eyes wide as she realized that the girl had no pubic hair, she gazed at her tightly closed sex crack, the pinken petals of her inner labia protruding alluringly from her valley of desire. Focusing on the hairless lips of her vulva, the perfectly formed hillocks rising either side of her creamy-wet crack, she felt her stomach somersault. Jane looked so young without her pubic fleece, she thought, running her fingertip over the smooth surface of her outer labia. Very young – but far from innocent.

Leaning over her friend's naked body, Samantha pushed her pink tongue out and tentatively licked the protruding wings of Jane's inner lips. The salty taste waking her taste buds, she sucked the fleshy folds into her hot mouth and savoured the flavour of the other girl's genital flesh. Breathing in the perfume of her vulval crack, the heady scent driving her into a sexual frenzy, Samantha yanked the girl's vaginal pads wide apart and sank her tongue into the hot depths of her vagina. She'd never tasted her own vaginal cream, let alone sucked out the juices of arousal from another girl's pussy. Slurping and sucking, she drank the lubricious milk from Jane's vaginal canal. The more she drank, the more the juices flowed. Her fresh face wet with the girl's sex fluid, Samantha moved up Jane's hot valley of desire, sucked the solid protuberance of her clitoris into her mouth and swept her tongue over the sensitive tip.

Writhing and squirming, Jane let out rushes of breath as Samantha worked between her thighs, nibbling her engorged inner labia, sucking her swollen clitoris into her wet mouth. The girl was nearing her climax Samantha knew as her clitoris swelled to an incredible size. The gasping sounds of lesbian sex reverberating through the night air, Jane finally cried out as her pulsating clitoris erupted in orgasm within Samantha's hot mouth. Gripping Samantha's head, forcing her orgasming clitoris into her hot mouth, Jane shook violently in her intense coming.

'Finger my cunt,' she gasped. 'Finger-fuck my cunt.' Complying, Samantha drove three fingers into the tight wet sheath of her friend's vagina, stirring her sex cream as she repeatedly thrust her fingers into her spasming sex sheath. The squelching sound of the girl's bubbling juices filling her ears as she managed to piston Jane's contracting vagina with four fingers, Samantha felt her own clitoris swell in anticipation of another girl-induced orgasm. Desperate for the feel of Jane's tongue between the engorged outer lips of her vulva, she crawled over her friend's body and placed her knees either side of her head.

'You're learning fast,' Jane said, grabbing Samantha's hips and pulling her gaping vaginal crack down over her open mouth. Samantha fervently tongued Jane's cuntal sheath as the girl's wet tongue slipped into her own pussy and licked the creamy walls of her hot cunt. The double tongue-fucking sending shuddering waves of ecstasy throughout Samantha's young body, she sucked out her friend's juices of desire, drinking from her steaming cunt as the girl reciprocated and drank from Samantha's virgin quim.

Their vaginal juices flooding each other's faces, the two girls squirmed and writhed in their lesbian entwining as their mutual pleasure heightened until they both shuddered in the explosions of their orgasms. Their girl juices gushing from their open vaginal holes, their clitorises pulsating in each other's gobbling mouths, they cried out through mouthfuls of vaginal flesh as they shook violently in their lesbian coming. Fingering each other's spasming cuntal sheaths, squelching their cream-bubbling cunts, they continued to suck and mouth on their pulsating clitorises until their immense pleasure began to subside.

'God,' Samantha breathed, her young body collapsing over Jane's naked body. 'I've never known anything like it.'

'There's nothing better than two girls together,' Jane giggled, lapping up Samantha's flowing juices of lust.

'Don't you think you'll ever marry?' Samantha asked, knowing now that the girl ended up getting married.

'If I do, I'll still have lesbian relationships. My plan is to have a training school.'

'A training school for what?'

'Young girls. I believe that young girls, such as you, shouldn't automatically conform to society. They're expected to go out with boys and eventually get married. They should have a choice. And I'm going to give them experience, sexual experience, so that they can then decide.'

'You seem to have got it all worked out,' Samantha said.

'Oh, yes. My training school will give young girls the opportunity to explore each other's bodies, have sex with each other.'

'It sounds interesting. I'll ask you about that when we're older,' Samantha giggled . . .

Finding herself sitting on the sofa back in her lounge, Samantha looked around her. The phone wasn't ringing and there was no sign of Zak, so why had she returned? It would have been nice to have stayed for a while longer and enjoyed a little more lesbian sex, she reflected as she went into her bedroom and grabbed her address book. Sitting on the sofa, she found Jane's number and called her. Would she really have lesbian relationships even though she was married? And as for a training school for young girls . . .

Deciding to slip a bit less further back in time and meet the older Jane, Samantha closed her eyes and pictured the girl's house. She'd last visited her about four years previously, and had a pretty good idea of how it looked. Picturing Jane standing in her lounge, Samantha concentrated, imagining herself standing in the lounge with her. With the ability to travel back in time, Samantha knew that she could discover everything about anyone. Everyone had skeletons in their cupboards, she mused, pondering again on Jane's idea of a training school for young girls . . .

Finding herself standing on a landing, Samantha listened to Jane yelling at someone. Thinking that she must be arguing with her husband, Samantha moved to the door and spied through the crack. Gazing in horror at a young girl's naked body bound to a wooden frame with rope, Samantha immediately realized that Jane had gone ahead with her idea of a training school. A rubber ball-gag in the girl's mouth, her breasts bound tightly with thin

rope, her nipples painfully ballooning . . . Lowering her eyes, Samantha focused on her hairless vaginal lips stretched tautly around a huge candle. This wasn't training, she mused, staring at the young girl's arms stretched high above her head, her wrists bound to a rope hanging from the ceiling. This was sexual torture.

Jane was dressed in a black leather catsuit. Her long black hair framing her pale face, her full lips glossed with black lipstick, her nails painted black, she appeared witchlike as she wielded a leather whip. Looking at the girl again, Samantha wondered how old she was. She was young, that was for sure. Too young for this, she mused, focusing on the ropes bound around her ankles holding her feet wide apart. Her long blonde hair matted with perspiration, her angelic face reflecting fear, she gazed at her mistress as the woman raised the whip above her head.

'How did you get in?' Jane asked, flinging the door open wide as Samantha coughed.

'Oh, I . . . I came to see . . .' Samantha stammered, looking around what could only be described as a torture chamber. 'I came to join you, to help you with the training.'

'In that case, you'd better come in,' Jane said. 'This is Caroline.' She introduced the young girl. 'She . . . let's just say that she won't experience lesbian sex. She insists that she prefers boys when she hasn't even tried sex with another girl.'

'So, you're whipping her?' Samantha asked, gazing at the thin weals fanning out across the girl's small breasts.

'Of course,' Jane replied in a matter-of-fact tone. 'It's part of the training, Sam.'

'So, you wanted her to have sex with you?'

'The girls have sex with me to give them experience. How on earth can they choose between male and female when they've never experienced sex with a female? Caroline refuses to lick me and—'

'Do the girls come to you through choice?' Samantha asked, knowing only too well what the answer was.

'Not exactly,' Jane giggled. 'They're brought to me by the procurer.'

'The procurer?'

'She's a friend. She's a schoolteacher and, in her position, she gets to know which girls are suitable candidates. She brings them to me to be punished. The training isn't only about experiencing lesbian sex, Sam. It helps young girls to shape up. Caroline, for example, is a real troublemaker at school. She disrupts the class, plays the fruit machines in the arcade rather than going to school . . . After spending a day with me, she'll be a model student.'

'What about the girl's parents?' Samantha asked, frowning as she gazed at a shelf lined with huge vibrators. 'I mean, don't they—'

'The girls understand that they'd be in real trouble if their parents discovered my training school. I've only had one girl go running to her parents. After I convinced her father that the girl was lying, he dealt with her in a most severe manner. A few days later, the procurer brought her to me and I dealt with her. We've talked enough, Sam. Now that you're here, you can start by pulling the candle out of Caroline's cunt. You'll find some metal clips and chains on the shelf over there. Fix the clips to her cunt lips and then hang those weights on the chains.'

Kneeling in front of the girl, Samantha gazed at her hairless outer lips stretched tautly around the huge

waxen phallus. The solid shaft of her clitoris forced out from beneath its pink hood, Caroline must have been in some pain, Samantha reflected as she eased the candle out of the girl's tight sex duct with a loud sucking sound. Looking up at the fear mirrored in the girl's wide eyes, Samantha knew that Jane had gone too far. Obviously, her torture chamber had been designed purely to bring her sexual gratification. The idea of a training school was nothing more than a front for her debased abuse of young girls. Samantha couldn't allow this to continue she knew as she noticed several pairs of handcuffs hanging from hooks on the wall. Seeing, too, several bamboo canes propped in the corner of the room and a small table cluttered with speculums and hideous-looking instruments, she knew that Jane had to be stopped.

'What does your husband say about all this?' Samantha asked as Jane passed her the metal clips.

'Geoff is all for it. We're a team, Sam. I offer the girls lesbian sex and he—'

'*Offer?*' Samantha echoed. 'Don't you mean *force*?'

'Whatever,' she quipped. 'Geoff teaches them the heterosexual stuff and I teach them about lesbian sex. Don't you see that we're giving the girls valuable experience? When they leave here, they're ready to face the world. If one of our girls finds herself in a position where her boyfriend is demanding oral sex, she'll not only be prepared for it but know how to do it properly. There's nothing they'll come across during their lives that they've not experienced.'

'The heterosexual stuff . . . Basically, Geoff fucks them?'

'Yes, he does. Vaginal sex, anal, oral . . . As I said, they leave here fully prepared for the world.'

Fixing the metal clips to Caroline's swollen outer labia, Samantha gazed at the girl juice streaming from her gaping sex hole and coursing down her inner thighs. If Dave wanted a sensational story for the newspaper, then this was it she thought as Jane passed her two heavy weights. Gerry Andrews and his so-called haunted mansion were nothing by comparison with Jane's illicit torture chamber. Young girls dragged to the chamber by the so-called procurer, whipped, fucked, sexually abused by Jane and her husband . . . *This* was the sort of story Dave should be chasing.

'Fix the weights to the chains and stretch the bitch's cunt lips,' Jane ordered Samantha. 'No, no. You've fixed the clips to her outer lips. Fix them to her inner lips, Sam.'

'But that'll really hurt her.'

'That's the whole idea,' Jane laughed. 'The girls won't learn if we're lenient with them. No pain, no gain. Right?'

'Right,' Samantha murmured, fixing the clips to the sensitive wings of Caroline's protruding inner labia.

'I made her drink several pints of water earlier. It shouldn't be long now before she learns about degradation by pissing herself in front of us.'

Coming to the conclusion that Jane wasn't normal, was probably verging on insane, Samantha stared at Caroline's painfully stretched inner lips as the weights swung between her parted thighs. Thinking back to the school camping trip, Samantha realized that, even then, Jane had been hooked on lesbian sex with younger girls. Relieved that she'd originally crossed her legs that night, she pondered again on her new talent of time travel. Perhaps the idea of the gift was to enable her to put a stop to the activities of people like Jane. Was it a gift? She

turned the question over in her mind, hearing Jane moving about behind her.

'Geoff should be back soon,' Jane said, passing Samantha a thin bamboo cane. 'Give the insolent little bitch a good whipping while we wait for him. Whip her tits hard.'

'Jane, I . . .' Samantha began, standing up.

'What's the matter? Give her tits a good caning and then Geoff will show her the delights of a good arse-fucking.'

'She's probably a virgin, Jane,' Samantha murmured, gazing into the girl's wide eyes.

'Of course she's a bloody virgin,' the woman laughed. 'There'd be no point in Geoff fucking a girl who wasn't a virgin. The whole idea is to give the girls experience. Once he's fucked her little pussy and spunked in her sweet mouth, he'll do her tight arse. By the time young Caroline leaves us, she'll be prepared for anything the world throws at her.'

Tentatively tapping the firm mounds of Caroline's petite breasts with the cane, Samantha frowned as the girl winked at her. Was this some kind of game? Why would the girl wink at her if she was genuinely fearful? Feeling a little easier, Samantha caned her small breasts harder, watching the brown teats of her nipples rise and stand proud from her chocolate-brown areolae as the bamboo repeatedly struck them. The girl's eyes closing, Samantha reckoned that she was enjoying the abuse of her young breasts. This *was* only a game she knew as Jane's giggles resounded around the room.

Caning Caroline's young breasts, watching her areolae darken, her milk teats rise, Samantha felt her own juices of arousal seeping between the swollen lips of her vulva.

She had to admit that this was a turn-on as she repeatedly lashed the girl's rock-hard breasts. Looking down at her victim's painfully distended inner lips, the heavy weights swinging between her slender thighs, she realized that she was as bad as Jane as she felt her clitoris swell in anticipation of lesbian sex.

'Ah, that will be Geoff,' Jane said as the front door closed. 'Now we'll have some real fun.'

'Samantha?' Geoff breathed, bounding into the room. 'What are you doing here?'

'I've come to help with the training,' she replied, gazing at his black hair cascading over his rugged face.

'Caroline's ready for you, Geoff,' Jane said, unbuttoning his shirt and releasing his belt. 'Show Sam how you fuck our little girlies.'

'Oh, I will,' he chuckled, kicking his shoes off and stepping out of his trousers.

'Geoff has the biggest cock you've ever seen,' Jane laughed as he tugged his shorts down and revealed his erect organ. 'There. Now tell me that you've seen a bigger cock.'

'No, no, I haven't,' Samantha replied, gazing in awe at the huge weapon.

'*You* can have some of this,' Geoff laughed, running his hand up and down the solid shaft of his massive penis. 'A nice length of my cock sliding right up your wet cunt—'

'That's a good idea,' Jane broke in. 'Slip your clothes off, and Geoff will teach you . . .'

'No, I don't think . . .' Samantha began.

'Are you saying that you don't want Geoff's magnificent cock?' Jane breathed, running the leather tails of the whip through her fingers.

'No, it's just that—'

'Good. In that case, strip off and bend over that table.'

Slipping her skirt and top off, Samantha knew that she'd be better off going along with the perverted pair rather than trying to oppose them. Geoff wasn't a small man in any respect, and Jane wouldn't hesitate to use the whip. Standing naked in front of Jane, Samantha wondered whether she should concentrate on her lounge and try to return to her own time. Gazing at Geoff's massive cock, his huge balls, she felt her juices of lust oozing between her engorged inner lips as her clitoris swelled and pulsated. She couldn't resist the temptation, the lure of such a magnificent penis, she knew as she watched the man fully retract his fleshy foreskin, exposing his ballooning purple knob. Walking across the room, she leaned over the table and projected the rounded cheeks of her firm buttocks. Her arms stretched out across the table, she closed her eyes as Geoff stood behind her.

'This is to ensure that you don't escape,' Jane said, clamping handcuffs around Samantha's small wrists.

'Jane, no,' Samantha cried, pulling on the cuffs fixed around the table legs. 'I don't want—'

'What you do or don't want doesn't concern us,' Jane snapped. 'It's what *we* want that matters.'

'That's right,' Geoff rejoined, slipping his swollen knob between Samantha's puffy outer lips. 'I doubt that young Caroline wants my fucking great cock shoved up her tight little cunt, but she's going to get it.'

'And *you*'re going to get it shoved up *your* pretty little cunt,' Jane laughed, slapping Samantha's rounded buttocks with the palm of her hand.

'Jane, take the cuffs off me,' Samantha said firmly. 'It's one thing having Geoff—'

'You don't seem to understand,' the woman cut in. 'This is our training school, our institute of correction. Not only do we train and correct young girls, but anyone of any age who needs educating in the fine art of disciplined sexual pleasures.'

'Jane, what you're doing is illegal. You can't bring girls here and—'

'Illegal?' Jane laughed as Geoff slipped the swollen plum of his massive cock deep into Samantha's tightening vagina. 'There's nothing illegal about our activities here.'

'Nothing illegal?' Samantha gasped as Geoff's penis partially withdrew and then thrust back deep into the hugging sheath of her pussy. 'How old is Caroline? Tell me that.'

'Her age is of no consequence,' Jane retorted angrily. 'She has been brought here because she needs to be trained, corrected. And, by the way you're arguing, you're in need of some serious correction yourself. We do not tolerate insolence, Sam. The very point of this training school is to deal with people like you. All right, Geoff. Give it to her, really hard.'

Her naked body rocking back and forth as the man grabbed her hips and repeatedly drove his solid cockshaft deep into her tight vagina, Samantha knew that she was in line for the whip. But she could leave the torture chamber and return to her lounge at any time she knew as her vaginal muscles spasmed, gripping the pistoning penis like a velvet-jawed vice. She'd enjoy the crude fucking, take his spunk deep into her vaginal throat, and then go home to her lounge before Jane whipped her naked buttocks.

'I always fancied you,' Jane said huskily as her hus-

band's penis squelched Samantha's copious vaginal juices. 'I used to look at you at school and imagine your little pink pussy.'

'I remember you in the tent that night,' Samantha gasped, her vaginal muscles gripping the solid shaft of Geoff's thrusting cock.

'Oh, yes. I remember that well. You were sleeping and I . . . I really wanted to stick my tongue between your hairless little love lips and taste your cunt. Still, I have you now. When Geoff's finished fucking you, I'll tongue-fuck your little pussy and suck out his spunk.'

The woman really was a nymphomaniac, Samantha reflected, hearing the deafening crack of the leather belt lash Caroline's naked body. The girl moaning through her nose as the leather tails cracked again, Samantha decided to return to her own time and then visit Jane. She had to stop the woman she knew as Geoff grunted and pumped his sperm deep into her contracting vagina. Closing her eyes, she thought about her lounge, concentrating on sitting on the sofa. Again, she thought about the sofa, sitting there and looking around the lounge. The feel of Geoff's huge cock inflating her vaginal canal, the sound of her squelching sex juices resounding around the room, she knew that something was blocking her, preventing her from returning to her own time.

'Did you enjoy that?' Jane asked her husband as he stilled his spent cock deep within the inflamed sheath of Samantha's sperm-flooded vagina.

'God, yes,' he breathed. 'She's pretty slack in comparison with the little virgins, but she's not a bad fuck.'

'And I'll bet she tastes nice,' Jane giggled. 'Hold still, Sam. I'm going to suck Geoff's spunk out of your little pussy.'

Again trying to return to her own time, Samantha closed her eyes and concentrated as Jane's warm tongue snaked into her sperm-drenched vaginal sheath. Jane's lips pressing hard against the pinken funnel of flesh surrounding Samantha's burning sex hole, the older girl sucked hard, drinking the heady blend of Samantha's girl-juice and her husband's sperm. Fearing the leather whip as Jane sucked her sex canal dry, Samantha couldn't understand why she was unable to return to her lounge. If she was going to lose control over her time travelling like this, then she was going to be at risk, she knew. Again imagining being stuck back in her school-days, she let out a yelp as Jane spanked her naked buttock with the palm of her hand.

'A good whipping is in order, I think,' Jane said huskily, rising to her feet and grabbing the cat-of-nine-tails. 'You have a perfectly rounded bottom, Sam,' she giggled. 'Perfect for the whip.'

'No,' Samantha cried as the leather tails swished through the air and landed with a loud crack across the tensed globes of her naked bottom.

'You've been asking too many questions for my liking,' Jane hissed. 'I don't like being questioned about my training school by someone who knows nothing about the fine art of discipline and sexual gratification. When we were in that tent, I wanted you. I wanted you really bad. Ever since that school trip, I've thought about you, Sam. I've thought about your sweet little cunt, your tight arse . . . And now I have you.'

The whip landing squarely across her quivering buttocks again, Samantha bit her lip and grimaced as the stinging pain permeated the taut flesh of her naked bottom. A rush of hot liquid streaming down her inner

thighs as her bladder drained, she knew that her degrading act would only heighten Jane's pleasure, drive her on to abuse her naked body in the extreme. Listening to the golden liquid splashing on the floor between her feet, the swish of the whip repeatedly flying through the air, the deafening crack of the tails biting into her burning buttocks, Samantha let out a scream.

'Please,' she cried, her anal orbs glowing a fire-red. 'Please, no more.'

'No more?' Geoff chuckled. 'Jane's only just begun. And there's plenty for you to look forward to. My cock in your mouth, my cock up your arse, your tongue up Jane's arse . . . Relax and enjoy your visit to our den of correction.'

'Den of corruption,' Samantha spat back.

'She really *is* in need of correction,' Jane hissed. 'And I'm the one to correct her.'

They were both insane perverts, Samantha thought as the whip swished through the air again and struck the fiery cheeks of her rounded bottom. And they were going to have to be stopped. Once she returned to her own time – if she was able to return – she'd phone Jane, she decided. She'd call at her house for a coffee and a chat, gain the woman's confidence and trust, and then expose her and her evil husband. Wondering who the procurer was as the leather tails repeatedly bit into the stinging flesh of her naked bottom, she knew that she couldn't take much more of the gruelling punishment . . .

'Thank God,' Samantha gasped, sitting on the sofa in her lounge and looking around the room. Her buttocks stinging like hell, she wondered why she was feeling the pain now that she'd returned to her own time. There

again, her hunger pains had gone when she'd returned to
the basement after eating breakfast. There was so much
that she didn't understand about her time travelling, she
mused, grabbing her address book and dialling Jane's
number. Praying for the woman to be at home, she
grinned as she answered.

'Jane, it's Sam,' she said, wondering whether she'd
interrupted a session of sexual abuse.

'Oh, hi, Sam. How are you?'

'Fine, fine. I just happened to be reminiscing about my
schooldays and remembered that camping holiday we
had.'

'God, I remember it well. I've not seen you for at least
a couple of years. What news have you got?'

'Not much. I'm still with the newspaper, still with Zak
. . . well, just about.'

'Why don't you come over for a chat? I'm not doing
anything in particular, so come over now.'

'OK, I'll do that. Give me fifteen minutes and I'll be
with you.'

'Great. I'll put the kettle on.'

Replacing the receiver, Samantha rubbed her stinging
buttocks as she grabbed her handbag and left the flat.
This was going to be extremely interesting, she mused,
the sun warming her as she walked down the street.
Wondering whether she should confront Jane, she
decided to make out that she'd heard rumours of an
illegal sex den in the area. Perhaps throw in a couple of
frighteners, such as *Word has it that a schoolteacher is
involved and young girls are—*

'Sam,' Zak called, crossing the street. 'Where are you
off to?'

'I want you out of my flat,' Samantha stated firmly.

'*Your* flat?'

'It's in my name, Zak. It's my flat, OK?'

'But—'

'You can move in with that slut you're screwing.'

'What slut? I don't know what you're talking about.'

'Angela – the tart who loves it up her arse and likes you fucking her filthy mouth.'

'Sam, this is crazy.'

'Yes, I agree. To think that I'm chatting to Angela on the phone while you're naked in bed with her is crazy.'

'Hey, hey. You've got it all wrong, Sam. Let's talk about this, OK?'

'I don't want to talk about you fucking her arse, Zak. Move out, OK? I want you out by the time I get back.'

Leaving the man dumbfounded, Samantha walked on with a spring in her step. She couldn't afford to pay the rent on her own, but she'd worry about that later. She didn't need Zak and his cheating ways. And Angela . . . Angela was going to pay dearly for her betrayal. Approaching Jane's house, Sam tried to forget about the cheating pair and took a deep breath. This was going to be interesting, but it might also prove to be dangerous, she thought as she walked up the front path and rang the bell.

'Sam,' Jane said warmly, beaming and opening the door. 'It's great to see you.'

'And you,' Samantha said, smiling as she stepped into the hall.

'Come into the kitchen and we'll have a coffee. So, how are things?'

'Fine,' Samantha replied, eyeing the other woman's miniskirt, her long legs. 'How's Geoff?'

'He works away most of the time now that he's been promoted. He's in Zürich at the moment.'

'You must get bored all alone here?'

'No, not really. I have a few friends to keep me company. So, what have you been up to? How's the newspaper business?'

'I'm looking into some rumours at the moment. Apparently, there's a schoolteacher in this area who lures young girls to some sort of illegal sex den. I think she—'

'A schoolteacher?' Jane echoed, anxiety mirrored in her dark eyes.

'I shouldn't really say anything, but . . . She's known as the procurer. There's a house somewhere around here where she takes young girls and—'

'The procurer?' Jane murmured, her face turning pale. 'What else have you discovered? Who knows about this, apart from you?'

'No one. I've not even told my editor yet. I think I'm on to something big.'

'Go on,' Jane said, her trembling hand spooning coffee into two cups.

'The schoolteacher takes young girls to a house where a woman and her husband sexually abuse them. I've spoken to one of the girls. She's not told me a great deal but—'

'What's her name?' Jane asked, spilling the milk as she poured it into the cups.

'She wouldn't tell me her name.'

'What does she look like?'

'Oh, I don't know. Dark hair, young . . . It doesn't matter what she looks like. The point is—'

'I need to know what she looks like, Sam.'

'Why?'

'Because . . . because I think I might know who's involved.'

'Really?'

'I too have heard one or two rumours. The other day, I overheard someone saying something about a married couple who seem to have a lot of young girls visit their house. I thought nothing of it at the time, but now . . .'

'Who was this person?'

'Just someone in a shop. I don't know them. But I did think it odd that they were talking about schoolgirls going to a house and something about a schoolteacher . . . Yes, that was it. They said that a schoolteacher was in on the game. As I said, I didn't think anything of it at the time. Tell me what you know and I might be able to help in some way. You never know, I might even bump into this woman again.'

'All I know is what this young girl told me. She said that there's a special room with a wooden frame, whips, handcuffs . . . Apparently, the woman wears a catsuit.'

'Didn't she say where the house was?'

'She was rather vague about that. I intend to get more out of her.'

'Yes, yes – I'm sure you will.'

Sipping her coffee, Samantha wondered what to say next as Jane changed the subject by talking about her husband's work. She'd said enough for the time being, she decided. To drop any more hints would only lay her open to suspicion. It was best to leave it at that. She'd eventually try to discover the identity of the so-called procurer. The schoolteacher would lead her to the young girls, and then she'd be in a position to do something about Jane and her perverted husband.

'I'd better be going,' she said, finishing her coffee.

'Already?' Jane asked, frowning at Samantha.

'I've got a story to write up this evening. To be honest, I didn't realize how late it was.'

'Well, it's been nice seeing you. Do keep me posted about this sex den or whatever it is.'

'Yes, yes, I will.'

'When are you seeing the young girl again?'

'She's . . . she's coming to see me tomorrow morning,' Samantha lied, an idea coming into her mind. 'About eleven o'clock.'

'OK, I'll give you a ring and we'll chat again when you have more time.'

'Yes, I'd like that.'

Leaving the house, Samantha reckoned that Jane would be lurking somewhere in the street around eleven o'clock the following morning, hoping to get a glimpse of the non-existent girl. With Jane's husband in Zürich, this would be an ideal opportunity to go to the sex den and . . . and what? Thinking that she might take a few photographs as evidence of the debauchery, she finally reached her flat to find Zak moping around in the lounge. He wanted to talk, he announced as she dumped her bag on the coffee table and flopped onto the sofa.

'Talk about what?' she sighed.

'Us, Sam. What's all this crap about Angela and me?'

'You tell me. All I know is that you were naked on her bed with her. And don't deny it because you were seen.'

'*Seen?* If I *was* there, no one could have possibly seen me.'

'She wants you to dump me so that you can fuck her every night. As you told her, you fuck her most nights as it is.'

'I . . . Who have you been talking to?'

'Just get out, Zak. I don't want you or your cock

anywhere near me. Particularly as you stick it up her arse and fuck her there.'

'All right, all right. If you want me to go, then I will. But you're making a big mistake, Sam.'

'*You* made the mistake, Zak. The only mistake I made was trusting you. Oh, and I mistakenly thought that my so-called best friend really *was* my best friend.'

'I don't know who's been telling you these lies, Sam. But I intend to find out.'

'Never in a million years will you understand this, Zak. You told me, and Angela told me.'

'*I* told you? What the hell do you mean? Are you saying that I lied by telling you that I was screwing Angela?'

'No, you didn't lie. You told the truth, as she did.'

'I think you've lost it, Sam. I don't know what's happened to you, but you've lost the plot.'

'All I've lost is a cheating man and a bitch of a friend. And I have to say that both losses are very much to my liking. Now I can get on with my life. And *you* can get on with fucking that slag's arse.'

'You'll be sorry, Sam. I really love you and—'

'And wanted to get your hands on my father's money?'

'Your father's . . .' he stammered, obviously stunned. 'I've never given a thought to his money.'

'His money is the very reason you didn't want to leave me. You told Angela that, so don't deny it.'

'That bitch has been talking to you, hasn't she?'

'She proved to be a bitch to me, Zak. And now she's proving to be a bitch to you. She's told me everything, you fool. Girls stick together, Zak. Guilt got the better of her and she told me everything.'

Grinning as he stormed out of the flat, Samantha felt good inside. Her new talent was inexplicable, but the

benefits it was bringing her were incredible. As much sex as she wanted, discovering people's dark secrets . . . There was no limit to what she could do she knew as she decided to have an early night. She'd go into work the following day, she decided, climbing beneath the quilt. There were one or two people in the office she wouldn't mind learning a little more about. There was Sally, John . . . Christine was a dark horse. It might be worth taking a look around her flat, delving into her private life. Tomorrow was going to prove most interesting.

4

'So, what happened at the mansion?' Dave asked, perching on the edge of his desk.

'It's not a hoax,' Samantha replied. 'I saw a ghost, Dave. I know that you're going to laugh at me, but—'

'So there's no fucking story?'

'No, there's not. However, I'm onto something that will . . . Let's just say that this could be the biggest story this crummy little paper has ever had.'

'Crummy little paper? Fuck me. I like that.'

'Young girls lured to a den of sex by a female schoolteacher. A married couple whipping the girls, fucking them, sexually abusing them . . .'

'This is more like it. Go on.'

'It's a training school, a correction centre. In truth, it's a den of iniquity. Handcuffs, vibrators, whips, speculums, instruments of sexual torture . . .'

'Fuck me, this is brilliant. OK, names, addresses . . .'

'No, not yet.'

'Sammy baby, this isn't one of your whims, is it?'

'I've been there, to the torture chamber. You're not getting anything until I've got more, OK?'

'Shit, you always do this to me. OK, OK, I agree. But keep me posted, for fuck's sake.'

'I will, don't worry.'

'How the hell did you stumble across this?'

'I know the woman who runs the torture chamber.'

'Fucking hell.'

'I was at school with her.'

'Double fucking hell. OK, so what's your next move?'

'I've set something up to get her out of her house this morning. Her husband is away on business, so the place will be empty.'

'Be careful, Sam.'

'I will, don't worry. I'll need a camera.'

'Grab one from Derek on your way out. And for fuck's sake, keep me posted.'

'Don't I always?'

'Like fuck, you do.'

Leaving the building, Samantha drove to Jane's house and parked a few doors away. Sure that the woman would take the bait, she checked her watch. Ten-thirty. Within minutes, Jane left her house and drove off. Clutching the camera, Samantha walked up the front path and slipped around the back of the house. This was nothing new to her, she reflected, trying the back door. Her various exploits, even as a journalist on a crummy local paper, had taken her on many interesting and dangerous missions. Noticing the dining-room window ajar, she opened it and clambered into the house.

So far, so good, she thought, slipping into the hall and creeping up the stairs. Apart from photographs of the torture chamber, she was hoping to find names and addresses of the young victims. Doubting that Jane would leave such information lying around, she slipped through a door and found herself standing in the sex chamber. This wasn't evidence, she mused, taking several photographs. There was nothing illegal about a married couple setting up a sex den in their house.

Looking around the room, she discovered a small diary. 'Yes,' she breathed, opening the diary and flicking through the pages. 'P,' she read, hoping that stood for procurer. Deciding to steal the diary, she took several more photographs of the room before leaving the house. Jane would obviously discover that the diary had gone, but she'd have no idea who the thief was. With any luck, she might have become complacent and think that she'd mislaid it. Sitting in her car, Samantha read through the diary. There was nothing about the young girls, no names or addresses. But at least Samantha now reckoned that she had the phone number of the schoolteacher involved. Grabbing her mobile phone, she dialled the number.

'Oh, hi,' Samantha said as a woman answered. 'Geoff put me onto you.'

'Geoff?' she queried.

'You are the procurer?'

'Er . . . who is this?'

'My name's Sally. I've known Geoff and Jane for years. After a tour of their house, if you get my meaning, Geoff suggested that I give you a call.'

'What about?'

'I have a similar room at my place and . . . I need a supplier. Look, can we meet to discuss this?'

'Well, I . . . I'll give Geoff a ring and then get back to you.'

'He's away in Zürich at the moment. Give Jane a ring. She'll tell you about me.'

'OK, I'll do that now.'

'You can get my number by using dial-back.'

'All right, give me a few minutes.'

As the woman hung up, Samantha dashed back to

Jane's house and clambered through the dining-room window again. This was risky, she knew as she waited by the telephone. The woman might realize that it wasn't Jane, she mused. And they might even have some sort of code to authenticate their identities. If she could only discover who the woman was and where she lived . . . Lifting the receiver as the phone rang, she prayed that Jane wouldn't return just yet. She put on a muffled voice.

'Hello,' Samantha said softly.

'Jane, it's P.'

'Oh, hi.'

'A woman just rang me and said that Geoff had put her onto me. Her name's Sally.'

'Oh, yes. She's . . . she's interested in our set-up and wants to start a similar thing.'

'She's OK, then?'

'God, yes. I've known her for a long time.'

'Are you all right? Only, you sound different.'

'I think I have a cold coming on. I'll be all right.'

'Right, I'll ring this woman back. OK if we meet at your place?'

'Er . . . I'd rather you didn't. I have some people coming round and Geoff's away.'

'I suppose it'll be all right to meet her in a pub.'

'She's genuine, believe me.'

'OK, talk soon.'

Replacing the receiver, her hands trembling, Samantha slipped out of the house and went back to her car. This was bloody risky she knew as she waited for the woman to ring. Once she discovered where the woman lived, she could slip back in time a day or two and take a look around her house for evidence of her part in the debauchery. It might have been an idea to visit the school

where she taught, Samantha thought, tapping the steering wheel as she waited impatiently. Calling Dave, she asked him to get the address from the woman's number. He complained but finally agreed to call his contact at the phone company. The phone rang the moment she'd finished talking to Dave and she pressed the button, grinning as the woman asked for Sally.

'That's me,' Samantha said. 'Did you talk to Jane?'

'Yes, I did. I think we'd better meet in a pub, if that's all right with you?'

'Of course. When and where?'

'There's a wine bar in the High Street. I think it's called the Grapevine.'

'Yes, I know it.'

'I'll head there now.'

'All right. I'm wearing a red miniskirt and white blouse. I have blonde hair and—'

'I'll find you, don't worry.'

'OK, I'll see you soon.'

Starting the engine, Samantha drove to the High Street and parked in the supermarket car park opposite the wine bar. She knew that the teacher would eventually talk to Jane and realize that she'd been set up. And when she described 'Sally', it wouldn't take long to work out that it was really Samantha. What with that and the missing diary . . . Noticing a young woman entering the wine bar, Samantha climbed out of her car and locked the door. She wouldn't have a problem flannelling the woman with stories of sexually abusing young girls, but she knew that it wasn't going to be easy discovering where she lived.

Walking into the bar, Samantha ordered an orange juice as she watched the woman out of the corner of her

eye. She was in her late twenties with shoulder-length auburn hair. Her full lips furling into a smile as she looked at Samantha and walked towards her, she wasn't at all unattractive. Wearing a short blue skirt and matching blouse, she looked nothing like a schoolteacher, Samantha thought, wondering what to say as the woman looked her up and down as if she was for sale. Wondering whether she was a lesbian, Samantha introduced herself as Sally.

'Please to meet you,' the woman said, her brown eyes staring at Samantha's elongated nipples pressing through her blouse. 'You can call me Lucinda. So, you're interested in setting up a room?'

'Yes, I am,' Samantha replied eagerly.

'How do you think I can help?'

'Girls – young girls.'

'That's your preference?'

'Oh, definitely.'

'I see. What has Jane told you about me?'

'Not a great deal. She said that you're the procurer, that you're a schoolteacher . . . You supply Jane with young girls. That's what I want you to do for me.'

'And what do I get in return?'

'What does Jane give you?'

'You don't know?'

'Jane was pretty secretive, Lucinda.'

'She gave you my mobile number. I don't call that secretive.'

'Telling me your phone number was hardly giving anything away. I've known her for many years, known about her room. When I said that I'd like to start up, she suggested that I call you. Actually, it was Geoff's idea. So, can you help me or not?'

'I might be able to. I'll have to make one or two checks before I—'

'So will I,' Samantha cut in, deciding to take a firmer stance. 'I'll need to know which school . . .'

'No, no. You've come to me, Sally. I'll do the checking and I'll ask the questions.'

'In that case, I think we'll leave it at that.'

'As you wish. Although I must say that you don't seem very keen.'

'I'm extremely keen and I have money. But I don't deal with evasive people. I need to know exactly who and what I'm dealing with, for obvious reasons.'

'So do I, Sally.'

'Of course. The truth is that I've been in this business for several years now. My original supplier . . . He went out of business. I'm now looking for someone I can trust, depend on and—'

'I would have thought that Jane would have been a good enough reference?'

'The way I look at it . . . I don't trust anyone, Lucinda. And you'd be wise to do the same.'

'I think we can sort something out between us. As for the financial side of things—'

'I don't want to talk about it here,' Samantha interrupted her. 'If you're interested in supplying me, then I'll come to your place this evening.'

'My place?' The schoolteacher laughed. 'Oh, no, no . . .'

'I don't think this is going to work out.'

'Be reasonable, Sally. I've never met you before, and you're asking for my address?'

'Excuse me for a moment,' Samantha said, answering her mobile.

'Sammy baby, it's me. Can you talk?'

'No, but you can.'

'I've got it. Twenty-five Ivy Road. Her name's Jones, Kitty Jones.'

'OK, thanks. So,' Samantha said, smiling at the woman as she switched her phone off, 'it looks as if we're at logger-heads.'

'Even Jane doesn't know where I live. In a business such as this—'

'I'll be straight with you,' Samantha broke in. 'I've already checked you out. Does Ivy Road mean anything to you? It should, seeing as you live there.'

'You know?' the woman gasped. 'But how on earth . . .'

'I've been in this game for quite some time. There's no way I'd meet you in a bar without doing a little homework first, Kitty.'

'You know my name? Well, I must say that you're pretty shrewd.'

'Shrewdness has nothing to do with it. OK, your place this evening?'

'Why not? About seven?'

'OK, I'll be there.'

Leaving the wine bar, Samantha grinned as she walked to her car. This was going to be easy, she mused. Slip back in time a day or two, check out the woman's house . . . Exposing her old schoolfriend wasn't something Samantha relished, but she knew that it had to be done. Driving to Ivy Road, Samantha wondered how many perverts were involved in the group. Perhaps it was just Geoff and Jane, she reflected. Parking a few yards from the teacher's house, she closed her eyes and concentrated . . .

'So you understand?' Kitty asked as Samantha found herself standing in the hall.

'Yes,' a girl replied. 'Don't worry, I won't blow it.'

'There's a lot of money at stake, Caroline. Have you shaved?'

'Of course I have. Look, nothing will go wrong. You worry too much.'

'I always worry when there's money at stake. If they discover that this is a set-up, that you're seventeen years old . . . You *do* know what to expect, don't you?'

'Yes,' the girl sighed as Samantha spied through the crack in the door. 'The whip, handcuffs . . . God, I'm not stupid.'

Frowning, Samantha realized what was going on as she gazed at Caroline. This was the very young and innocent victim she'd met in the torture chamber, she reflected. *Not so young and not so innocent*, she mused. So that was the schoolteacher's game, she thought. Supplying teenage girls to Jane and her husband and making out that they were not only very young but unwilling. Wondering how much money Kitty was raking in, Samantha knew that her story was dead. Dave wasn't going to be at all happy, she thought, gazing through the crack in the door.

'I have to be careful,' Kitty breathed. 'The last girl almost ruined everything.'

'What happened?' Caroline asked.

'She made it blatantly obvious that she wasn't young and naive and then she mentioned working in an office. Luckily, she realized her mistake and added that it was a Saturday job. Anyway, don't worry about her. You're a virgin, you're naive, gullible, frightened . . .'

'Kitty, we've been through all this.'

'I know, I know. The woman, Jane, asked me whether I really was a schoolteacher after the last girl almost

fucked things up. If they ask which school you go to, it's a private school called Lodge Mead, OK?'

'OK. So, when are we going there?'

'This evening. Get here at five and you'll have time to change into your school uniform. I'll take you to the house at six and, when Jane opens the door, I'll bundle you into the hall. You'll cry and say that you won't be bad at school again and I'll hand you over to Jane for your punishment. You've had half the cash and you'll get the other half when I pick you up at ten o'clock.'

'This is easy money for four hours of sex,' Caroline giggled.

'With any luck, they'll want you again. I have a few girls who are regulars now.'

'Do they get the same money each time?'

'No. The first time is the best because they're supposed to be virgins. After their first visit, the money halves.'

This was clever, Samantha reflected as she crept up the stairs. Jane and Geoff were the gullible and naive ones, not the girls. Again wondering how much money was involved, Samantha slipped into a room housing a desk and a computer. There was no time to take a good look round, but she'd come back again when Kitty was out and search the house thoroughly. Hoping that the computer contained some interesting information, she hovered on the landing as the front door closed. Listening to Kitty making a phone call, Samantha grinned when she realized that the woman was talking to Jane.

'Her name's Caroline,' she said as Samantha crept down the stairs. 'Stealing. I caught her stealing cash from the bursar's office. Her father is something big in the City and if it comes to light . . . Oh, yes, she's young,

all right. She's terrified that her father will be told of her thieving. Not only would she be expelled, but her father . . . Let's just say that she'll be putty in your hands. Jane, the last girl *was* a virgin. Just because her hymen wasn't intact . . . Of course I'm sure. Yes, I know that Geoff likes them untouched and I can assure you that they've never had sex. As I said to you before, girls experiment. They masturbate from a very early age and often stick things up their pussies. God, I know I did. Yes, that's fine. I'll bring her round at six. OK, see you later.'

Shaking her head, Samantha thought again how clever the scam was. But where did Kitty find the girls? And how did she get together with Jane and Geoff? Reckoning that Kitty might have been supplying others with young girls, Samantha closed her eyes and concentrated on returning to her own time. Finding herself sitting in her car, she started the engine and drove off. Reaching her flat, she had an idea and rang the schoolteacher.

'I'd like to see a sample,' she said as the woman answered.

'A sample? You mean, you want to see a girl?'

'Yes, that's right.'

'I'm afraid that's not possible.'

'A photograph?' Samantha persisted.

'I do have a portfolio of my girls, but—'

'Ah, that's good. I'd like a girl straight away.'

'I can't get a girl for this evening. These things have to be arranged.'

'Then arrange something for seven o'clock.'

Hanging up, Samantha reckoned that she might get a story out of this after all. The girls were in their mid to late teens, but this was prostitution at the very least. Not quite as scandalous and sensational as Samantha had

initially thought, but a story worth going after. Spending several hours packing Zak's things and dumping them by the front door, she didn't answer the persistent phone caller. It would have been Dave after an update she knew as she took a shower and checked her watch. Deciding to walk the short distance to Kitty's house, she grabbed her bag and left the flat. Doing her best to plan what she was going to say as she rang the doorbell, she took a deep breath and composed herself.

'Come in,' Kitty said, looking up and down the street as Samantha entered the house. 'In the lounge.'

'Nice place,' Samantha remarked, following her into the lounge and sitting on the sofa. 'You must earn a lot as a schoolteacher.'

'It's not bad,' Kitty replied.

'Seeing as you're not a teacher and there is no Lodge Mead . . .'

'How the hell do you know so much?' the woman asked, shaking her head and frowning.

'This is a dangerous business. As you'll appreciate, I can't be too careful. You know what I want, Kitty. I want a young girl. May I see the photographs?'

'I can do better than photographs. There's a girl upstairs. One hour, that's all you can have with her. Two hundred, up front.'

'I've not brought any money with me.'

'In that case—'

'I'll take a look at her,' Samantha cut in. 'If I like what I see, then . . .'

'You'll have to get the cash first.'

'You don't trust me, Kitty? Look, I'll have an hour with her and then go and get the cash. If you don't want it that way, then we'll have to forget it. You did say that

these things have to be arranged. I wasn't expecting you to come up with the goods. That's why I didn't bring any money. Bear in mind that I intend to become a valued customer, Kitty.'

'All right,' the woman finally conceded. 'She's tied up in the spare room. No more than an hour because I'll have to get her cleaned up and take her home. In fact, it might be an idea to make it fifteen minutes.'

'Is that all?'

'Seeing as you have no money with you . . . Look at this as a taster.'

'All right, fifteen minutes. Where do you get the girls from?' Samantha asked.

'I can't tell you that. Suffice to say that they're very young and I . . . I have a friend who works with young girls. It's not been easy arranging this at such short notice.'

'I appreciate it,' Samantha said. 'As I said, if I like the girl, then I'll become a good customer.'

'I'll take you to her.'

'Right,' Samantha said, following the woman to the door. 'I'm in real need of fresh meat right now.'

Walking into the spare room, Samantha gazed at a young girl's naked body lying on the bed. Her limbs spread, her wrists and ankles bound with rope, she looked extremely young, with a boyish figure and no pubic hair. This was an excellent scam, Samantha mused, eyeing the girl's petite breasts, her elongated nipples, as Kitty checked her gag. The woman had obviously chosen her girls well.

'I'll leave you to enjoy yourself,' Kitty said, moving to the door.

'I'm certainly going to do that,' Samantha replied,

running her fingertips over the girl's naked vaginal lips.

'Her name's Julie, by the way. I'll be back in fifteen minutes.'

Sitting on the edge of the bed as the woman left the room and closed the door, Samantha smiled at her young victim. Parting the fleshy swell of the girl's vulval lips, she peered at the intricate folds nestling within her wet valley of desire. Slipping her finger into the girl's snug sex sheath, Samantha breathed deeply, her stomach somersaulting as her arousal heightened. She wasn't a lesbian, she mused. But she was beginning to enjoy the feel of another girl's hot vagina.

'You're not a virgin,' she murmured. 'You're not innocent and you've not been brought here against your will. In fact, you're only too willing to have your cunt abused. You're not so young, either. I'd say that you're at least seventeen or eighteen.' The girl's blue eyes frowning, she stared hard at Samantha. 'OK, this is the deal. You're going to tell me who you are, where you live and how Kitty met you and got you into this.'

Slipping her finger out of the girl's hot vaginal duct and removing the gag, Samantha hoped that she wouldn't scream out. The girl was obviously too stunned to say anything as she looked at Samantha. And probably too frightened. After all, Samantha could have easily been an undercover cop. Slipping two fingers back into the tight sheath of Julie's young vagina, she pressed hard against her pubic bone and grinned at the girl.

'OK, we'll start by you telling me how old you are.'

'Seventeen,' the girl confessed softly.

'How did you get into this scam?'

'I can't tell you.'

'I think you can,' Samantha returned, digging her

fingernails into the girl's inner vaginal flesh. 'Talk, or I'll . . .'

'All right,' Julie gasped, her pretty face grimacing. 'I met Kitty through a friend. I was working from home and—'

'As a prostitute?'

'Yes. I met Kitty and she told me about her business.'

'How many clients does she have?'

'God knows. Dozens, I reckon.'

'I see. OK, you're working for me from now on.'

'Working for *you*?'

'If you want to stay out of trouble, you'll report back to me. I want names and addresses of all the clients. I want to know how many girls are working for Kitty and their names and addresses.'

'But there's no way I . . .'

'It's up to you, Julie. Either you work for me, or . . . . I really don't think that you want to know what the alternative is.'

'All right,' the girl sighed.

'What's your phone number?' Samantha asked, pulling her fingers out of the girl's vagina and taking her mobile phone from her bag. 'I intend to make sure that you're telling the truth before we go any further.'

Punching the buttons as Julie revealed her number, Samantha listened to the ringing tone. She had no idea where this was going to lead, she mused as an answer machine took the call. 'Hi, this is Julie. I'm not here right now but—' Switching her phone off, Samantha wondered what to do. It crossed her mind to make some serious money out of the scam, but she reminded herself that she was supposed to be getting a story for the paper.

'OK, so you've been truthful so far,' she said, slipping

a finger back into the girl's vaginal duct again. 'How many clients do you see each week?'

'A dozen or so.'

'How much?'

'I get half. Usually around a hundred.'

'One hundred for each client you entertain? Miss Kitty *is* doing well, isn't she?'

'We all do well. And there's nothing illegal about it.'

'Isn't there?'

'It's prostitution, that's all. The punters believe that we're young but, if there was ever any trouble, we could all prove our ages. So who are you? A cop?'

'I intend to take over the operation,' Samantha announced, her finger sliding in and out of the girl's drenched vagina. 'Is there anyone else running this besides Kitty?'

'No, it's just her.'

'Good, good. Right, I have your phone number so I'll be in touch.'

'Kitty has been running this for years. Why don't you set up your own business?'

'That's exactly what I intend to do. Using her girls and her clients. Talking of which, give me a few names of your clients.'

'I don't know,' Julie sighed. 'Fred, John, Ian . . .'

'Geoff?'

'Yes, Geoff and his wife Jane. You know them?'

'Yes, I do. Anyone else locally?'

'I shouldn't think that they give their real names. There's one man who calls himself Dray. Another goes by the name of Clayton.'

'Clayton?' Samantha echoed. 'That wouldn't be Clayton Hargreaves, would it?'

'Yes, that's right. Do you know him?'

'I've heard of him,' Samantha said, imagining Zak's best friend fingering young girls' hairless pussies. 'Do you go to his place?'

'No, no.'

'Where, then?'

'There's . . . Here, sometimes.'

'There's what? What were you about to say?'

'Kitty has a place. We work from there.'

'Where is it?'

'Look, I . . .'

'Where is it?'

'OK, OK,' Julie gasped as Samantha again dug her fingernails into the creamy walls of her vagina. 'It's a flat above the chemist in the High Street.'

'There are no flats there.'

'It's a dancing school. I should say, it *looks* like a dancing school. The punters look at the girls through a two-way mirror and make their choice. Dressed in a leotard, Kitty takes a girl into a back room where the punter is and—'

'The girl feigns shock and fear?'

'Something like that. The punters think that it's genuine. They believe that they really are choosing from a group of innocent young girls. That's why they pay . . . They pay a lot.'

'How much for a dancer?'

'Three hundred upwards.'

'Very clever,' Samantha breathed. 'Kitty's quite a business woman, isn't she?'

'She's bloody clever,' Julie said. 'You imagine a man in his fifties or sixties able to choose from a group of young girls in leotards. The one he picks is brought to him in

the back room and he can spend an hour with her. The older guys love it. They pay up without question.'

'I'm sure they do. Right, I'm going now. I'll be in touch.'

'I like you,' Julie said, smiling at Samantha. 'I reckon that you're all right.'

'Thank you. And I reckon that you're all right, too.'

'Don't you want . . . you know?'

'What?'

'Don't you want to lick me?'

Her stomach somersaulting, Samantha realized that she very much wanted to lick and taste the young girl's hairless vulval crack. Sighing, she checked her watch. She had about five minutes before Kitty hammered on the door. Time enough to . . . But, she wondered, was this really what she wanted? Confusion flooded her racked mind. Gazing at Julie's pert breasts, her ripening nipples, she knew that she was heading down a road to a life of lesbian relationships with anyone and everyone. But Julie looked so young, so fresh and . . . innocent?

Setting between the girl's splayed legs, Samantha ran her wet tongue up Julie's sex groove. Lapping up her flowing juices of arousal, her tongue snaking into her vaginal entrance, she felt her own love juices oozing from her hungry pussy as she sucked and mouthed between the girl's naked thighs. Quivering, Julie lifted her rounded buttocks clear of the bed, forcing her naked vaginal flesh hard against Samantha's mouth as her juices of lust gushed from her spasming vaginal sheath.

'You're good,' Julie gasped as Samantha sucked her solid clitoris into her hot mouth and swept her tongue over the sensitive tip. 'God, I'm going to come already.' Fervently mouthing and sucking on the girl's ballooning

clitoris, Samantha drove three fingers into the tight sheath of her teenage cunt and massaged her creamy inner flesh. Crying out as her orgasm erupted within her pulsating clitoris, Julie shook violently in her lesbian-induced coming. Her naked stomach rising and falling, her nostrils flaring, she pumped out the creamy product of her orgasm, splattering Samantha's flushed face with her sex juices as she screamed out again.

The sound of the girl's squelching juices sending Samantha's libido rocketing, she finger-fucked Julie's young cunt and sucked hard on her palpitating clitoris to sustain her incredible pleasure. It was amazing how her life had changed in a matter of days, she reflected, her full lips pressed hard against the pinken flesh surrounding the girl's orgasming clitoris. From a comparatively dull life with Zak to enjoying sex both with men and young girls . . . But why had she been blessed with the gift of time travel?

'Your time's up,' Kitty called, banging on the door.

'All right,' Samantha replied, her mouth leaving Julie's clitoris as the girl floated down from her sexual heaven. 'I'll phone you,' she whispered, slipping her girl-wet fingers out of the burning sheath of Julie's cunt. 'I'll ring you later this evening.'

Replacing the gag, Samantha kissed Julie's flushed cheek before composing herself. She'd have liked to have spent an hour or more with the teenage beauty, but she'd have the opportunity to pleasure the girl's body again. Particularly now that Zak was moving out of the flat, she mused, walking across the room and opening the door. With her cheating boyfriend out of the way, she was free to do what she liked when she liked. Descending the stairs, she found Kitty standing in the lounge doorway

with her arms folded. The woman didn't appear to be too happy, and Samantha hoped that she'd not overheard her conversation with Julie.

'When do I get the money?' Kitty asked.

'I'll drop fifty round tomorrow.'

'Fifty? But—'

'That's not bad for fifteen minutes, Kitty.'

'All right. Before you go, tell me how you know so much about me.'

'I've told you. I've done my homework.'

'Yes, but no one knows about Lodge Mead School.'

'I've been looking for a supplier for some time now. When Geoff put me onto you, I checked you out by watching you, following you. It's not difficult to check up on someone. Once I found out where you lived, I got your name. I'll see you tomorrow.'

Leaving the house, Samantha went home to discover that Zak had taken his things from the hall. Relieved, Samantha flopped down onto the sofa, her thoughts turning to the dancing school as she wondered how to pay the rent without Zak's money. Kitty was raking in the cash, more cash than any small-time newspaper journalist could ever hope to earn. The idea was brilliant, Samantha thought, picturing a group of leotard-clad young girls practising their ballet routines. Cashing in on men's thirst for young girls was . . .

Finding herself standing outside the dance room, looking through the open door at half a dozen young girls, Samantha slipped behind the door before she was noticed. The girls looked so young in their leotards. Their breasts obviously flattened by tight bras, their hair tied in ribbons, they were practising the splits. Looking up and

down the passageway, she noticed a door at the far end. Sure that the potential customers were behind that door, looking through a two-way mirror, she stole along the passage and listened. She could hear the deep voice of a man remarking on a petite blonde as she pressed her ear to the door. She was desperate to learn more, but there was no way she could walk into the room and show herself.

'Oh, er . . .' she murmured as Kitty walked towards the door. Frowning, Samantha wondered why the woman ignored her as she opened the door and said something to the customers. 'Kitty?' Samantha said as she closed the door and walked back to the dance room. This was amazing, she mused. The woman couldn't see or hear her. Walking into the small room, Samantha gazed at three men as they looked through the two-way mirror.

'I'll bet that cute little blonde's got a tight cunt,' one man said, obviously unaware of Samantha as he sat on a sofa. 'Hairless, tight, wet, hot . . .'

'I'm going for that skinny dark girl,' another said. 'Just look at the way she opens her legs.'

Leaving the room, Samantha joined the young girls. Wondering why no one could see or hear her, she realized the great potential of her gift. She could go anywhere at any time and spy on anyone, she reflected. Watching Kitty walk up to the dark girl and whisper something in her ear, Samantha knew that she was going to be taken to the customer. Following as they left the room, Samantha eyed the girl's slim figure. The tight material of her leotard clinging to her pert buttocks, she certainly looked the part. Watching as Kitty led the girl into another room, Samantha followed and stood by a glass-topped trolley piled with speculums and other metal instruments.

'The fitness examination?' the girl asked, gazing at an examination couch.

'Yes,' Kitty said, grinning. 'He's going to examine you, check you over to make sure you're fit enough for the ballet exam next week. Do your stuff and tell him that you're worried about your fanny. Only don't put it like that.'

'I won't,' the girl laughed as Kitty opened the door. 'I'll say that my little pink cunt hurts every time I get fucked by a horse.'

'God, no. Come to the office when you're done and I'll pay you. Right, I'll send him in.'

Again wondering why she couldn't be seen or heard, Samantha watched the middle-aged man enter the room and smile at the young girl. The dancing school was a brilliant idea, and the doctor scam was sheer genius, she thought. The man even had a stethoscope around his neck and a file in his hand, Samantha observed as he asked the girl to remove her leotard. There was no way that he'd think that this was a set-up, that the girl was in on the scam. As far as he was concerned, Kitty had gone to great lengths to have the girls believe that this was a real surgery and that the visiting doctors were genuine.

'You're taking the exam next week?' he asked as the girl stood before him in her small bra and panties.

'Yes, that's right,' she replied softly.

'Hop onto the examination couch and I'll take a look at you,' he said, looking through the file. 'It says in your notes that you had an ankle strain last month. Is that giving you any trouble?'

'No, it's fine now,' the girl replied, lying on her back on the couch.

Samantha hovered in the corner of the room, watching

the so-called doctor stand by the couch and press his fingertips into the girl's lower stomach. The surgery, the fake notes . . . This really was a brilliant scam, Samantha mused. Moving his hands down to her legs, he kneaded the firm flesh of her young thighs, his fingers dangerously close to the tight crotch of her pink panties. He obviously realized that he had to come across as a genuine doctor, so how was he going to get his fingers into the girl's tight little pussy? Samantha pondered on the problem as he mumbled something about muscular development.

'Slip your panties and bra off, please,' he said, moving to the trolley. Lifting her rounded buttocks clear of the couch, the girl pulled her panties down her slender legs and unhooked her bra. Lying naked on the couch, her thighs deliberately parted, she gazed at the ceiling in her feigned innocence. Her vulval lips devoid of pubic hair, her sex crack tightly closed, she certainly looked the part, Samantha mused. Her small breasts topped with delicious milk teats, she'd obviously been chosen for her boyish figure.

Kitty was a very clever woman, Samantha thought again. Knowing exactly what men wanted, she'd set up the perfect scam. The so-called doctor probably believed that if the girl told her parents that she'd been examined, they'd think nothing of it. As far as he knew, this was a genuine dancing school and Kitty told the parents about the fitness examinations.

'Have you had any pain in your lower stomach?' he asked, pressing his fingertips again into the soft flesh just above the gentle rise of her naked mons.

'Yes, a little,' she replied softly. 'I sometimes get pains lower down.'

'There?' he murmured, his fingertips pressing into the swell of her vulval lips.

'Yes, inside.'

'I thought as much,' he murmured, parting her thighs wider. 'It's probably nothing to worry about, but I'll check down there just to be on the safe side.'

Samantha watched as the fake doctor's trembling finger slipped between the fleshy pads of the girl's outer lips and sank deep into the tight sheath of her vagina. *So far, so good*, she thought. But how was he going to explain that he was going to force his cock into her little cunt and fuck her? Kneading the small mounds of her rock-hard breasts with his free hand, he was obviously becoming desperate to have his wicked way with her. Noticing the crotch of his trousers bulging with his erection, Samantha moved closer as he slipped his finger out of the girl's pussy and smiled at her.

'Everything seems to be in order,' he said. 'Are you on any medication?'

'No,' she replied. 'Miss Kitty did give me a sedative earlier because I had a headache. But I'm not taking any pills or anything.'

'Are you feeling sleepy?' he asked.

'Yes, I am.'

'I would imagine that it's the sedative. Just close your eyes and relax while I check your ankle.'

Grinning, Samantha realized what the ploy was. Kitty would have told the impostor that she'd given the girl a sedative to knock her out. The scam got better and better, she thought, watching the girl's head loll to one side as she feigned sleep. Wasting no time, the man grabbed her feet and pulled her down the couch until the firm cheeks of her bottom were over the padded

edge. Grabbing a chair, he sat between her splayed thighs, her naked vaginal lips only inches from his face as he stared longingly at her most private place.

Moving in, he parted her swollen vulval lips with his fingers and licked the intricate folds nestling within her yawning vaginal slit. Lapping at her open love hole like a dog, he forced her outer lips further apart and exposed the full length of her erect clitoris. Standing by the couch, Samantha watched the man fervently lapping up his patient's vaginal cream, his tongue darting in and out of her tight sex hole as he stretched the hairless cushions of her outer lips apart to the extreme.

Although this was prostitution, Samantha felt a little jealous of Kitty. The woman was running an amazing business and obviously earning a fortune. Apart from supplying individuals such as Jane and Geoff with young girls and running the dancing school, Samantha wondered what other pies she had her fingers in. Recalling Kitty mentioning an office, Samantha left the room and wandered along the passageway. Spying through a partially open door, she noticed a desk and slipped into the room.

This was the office, all right, she mused, sifting through a pile of papers on the desk. Finding a phone bill and a letter concerning the rent for the dancing school, Samantha knew that Kitty wouldn't be stupid enough to leave any incriminating evidence lying around. Opening the top drawer of a filing cabinet, she discovered a file containing information about the girls. Shaking her head, she again had to admire Kitty for her cleverness as she read through the notes. Dance routines, comments on each girl's progress, fitness, diet . . . To all intents and purposes, this was a genuine dancing school.

Closing the filing cabinet, she turned as Kitty wandered into the room and sat at the desk. This might be interesting, she thought as the woman lifted the phone and punched the buttons.

'Hi, Gerry,' she said. 'How's it going?'

Gerry? Samantha mused. This wasn't Gerry Andrews, surely?

'That's great. As you know, I've only got a few days here. Yes, I'll come over this evening. Really?' she giggled. 'Er . . . no, I don't think we want a pretty little pair of sisters who are keen to become ballerinas. What did you say to her? A five-year waiting list? That's good. Some woman came here the other day, asking whether her daughter could join the school. I told her that we were full. I do like the waiting-list idea. OK, I'll be over this evening.'

Watching the woman hang up and leave the office, Samantha couldn't believe that Gerry Andrews was involved in the scam. There were lots of people with that first name, she mused, leaving the office and walking back to the surgery. Gerry Andrews had his ghost scam to be getting on with. He wouldn't involve himself in prostitution, would he? Whoever Kitty had been talking to, Samantha reckoned that she was about to move the dancing school. The haunted mansion would be an ideal place, she thought, entering the surgery. But she just couldn't imagine Gerry Andrews becoming involved in such a scam.

The 'doctor' was running the swollen globe of his erect penis up and down the young girl's vaginal valley, obviously lubricating his weapon-head in readiness to impale her on his huge shaft. Samantha moved closer, watching the man open the girl's vaginal entrance with

his fingers and slip his ballooning knob into the tight duct of her wet vagina. His shaft gliding along her sex duct, he breathed heavily as he drove his knob fully home. His huge balls pressing against the rounded cheeks of her naked bottom, her lower stomach bloated, he massaged the erect nub of her exposed clitoris. The girl played her part well, her breathing slow and deep, her young body completely limp as the man withdrew his cock-shaft partially and rammed his glans back deep into her young cunt.

'Dirty little bitch,' the man breathed, slipping his cunny-slimed cock out of the girl's vaginal sheath. Lifting her feet high in the air, exposing the tight entrance to her rectum, he pressed his glistening knob hard against the delicate tissue of her anus. Watching as his bulbous glans slipped past her defeated anal sphincter muscles, Samantha felt her own clitoris swell as her arousal soared. Focusing on the girl's sensitive anal tissue stretched tautly around the man's solid shaft, the creamy liquid oozing from her gaping vaginal entrance, Samantha found herself seriously wondering whether to set up her own illicit business.

'*Yes*,' the man breathed, the slurping sound of his squelching sperm resounding around the surgery as he repeatedly rammed his orgasming knob deep into the girl's tight rectal duct. Holding her legs high and wide, he fucked the girl's tight arse with a vengeance as Samantha watched the crude act in awe. A very good actress, the young victim didn't bat an eyelid as the man drained his swinging balls and filled her bowels with his creamy spunk, her naked body rocking with the crude fucking.

Her thoughts turning to Gerry Andrews, Samantha

closed her eyes and concentrated on his haunted mansion. Although she was sure that he wasn't involved with Kitty, she wanted to check out the mansion thoroughly. Perhaps there was a hell of a lot more to Gerry Andrews than met the eye, she reflected, recalling the leaflet about female masturbation and candles. The mansion would certainly be an ideal home for Kitty's dancing school. Her mind drifting as she listened to the impersonator grunting in his forbidden pleasure as he arse-fucked the young girl, Samantha felt herself leaving the 'surgery'.

5

'This has to be finished today,' Gerry Andrews said, waving his hand around a large room.

'It will be,' a man in paint-splattered overalls replied. 'Another three or four hours, and I'll be done.'

'I hope so. The floor's going down tomorrow. The last thing I want is to have to put off the flooring people.'

'Don't worry, Mr Andrews. Not only will I be out of here soon, but the paint will be dry by the morning.'

'All right,' Andrews sighed, leaving the room.

Following him, Samantha knew that the preparations were for the dancing school as he went into a small room. And this was to be the surgery, she thought, looking about her. An examination couch, a trolley topped with a host of hideous-looking medical instruments . . . Andrews wasn't the eccentric that people believed him to be, she reflected. Like Kitty's dancing school, his eccentricity was a front. Wondering when and where he'd met Kitty, she thought it ironic that she'd set out to expose him as a charlatan when all along he'd been in league with Madam Kitty.

Following the man along the hallway and through another door, Samantha looked around the tiled room. Two showers, wooden benches . . . Watching Andrews open a small vent, she gazed wide-eyed as he fiddled with a video camera. This was obviously a bonus for the

punters, she mused. There'd be a room somewhere where they could view the dancers through a two-way mirror and then watch the girls taking a shower on a TV monitor. This was all rather ingenious, she thought as Andrews closed the vent and left the room. And, no doubt, highly profitable.

Still following him, she walked into what appeared to be a small lounge. There was the two-way mirror, she observed, looking through a huge glass window at the man decorating the dance room. On a small table, a TV monitor showed the shower room in crystal-clear colour. Wondering what other tricks Andrews had up his sleeve as he stared at the monitor, Samantha was about to return to her own time and go home when a female voice called out.

'In here,' Andrews called.

'Hi, Gerry,' a pretty blonde in her early twenties trilled, breezing into the room. 'Two dancers have turned up.'

'What?' he breathed, his dark eyes frowning. 'They've come *here*?'

'Apparently, Kitty sent them here for your approval.'

'We're nowhere near ready yet. All right, Jenny,' he sighed. 'Where are they?'

'In the correction chamber.'

'Kitty shouldn't have sent them here without letting me know,' he complained, following the blonde. 'She only had to pick up the bloody phone.'

'I suppose she thought that you'd want to take a look at the new recruits. You might even think it prudent to try them out.'

'Now, that *is* a thought,' he chuckled. 'I think it prudent for me to become chief girlie tester.'

'Prudent or disgusting?'

'*Disgusting* is the appropriate word, Jenny. Let's take a look at the little darlings.'

Samantha frowned, wondering what horrors the correction room held as she followed Andrews and the girl along the hallway. Although, after seeing Jane's sexual torture chamber, she had a pretty good idea what the correction room was all about. Slipping through an oak door and descending a wooden staircase, she looked around the large room. Whips, chains, a rack, handcuffs . . . Noticing two young girls standing by a leather-topped table, Samantha made herself comfortable on an old chesterfield sofa as Andrews approached the new recruits.

'Gerry Andrews,' he said, introducing himself and grinning at the little beauties. 'So, you're going to work for us?'

'Yes,' the taller girl replied. 'Kitty sent us.'

'OK, so you know the set-up?'

'She told us all about it. We know Caroline, one of the dancers. That's how we got onto Kitty.'

'Well, they certainly look the part,' Andrews said, turning to Jenny.

'That's what I thought,' she murmured pensively. 'OK, girls, strip off and let's have a look at you.'

Shaking her head, Samantha realized that there was far more to the scam than she'd initially thought. Supplying girls to Jane and Geoff, the dancing school, and now this? Watching as the girls disrobed, she gazed at their boyish figures, the petite mounds of their pert breasts, the hairless flesh of their pouting vaginal lips. She had to agree with Andrews. The little beauties really did look the part. There was money in this, Samantha mused

again as the girls stood in front of Andrews and displayed the gentle curves of their naked bodies. Big money.

'Carla, isn't it?' Jenny asked, stroking the brown protrusions of the tall girl's erect milk teats.

'Yes, that's right,' the girl replied softly.

'We need to test the correction frame, Carla,' Jenny announced.

'Correction frame?' the girl echoed, cocking her pretty head to one side.

'This is the correction frame,' Gerry said enthusiastically, walking towards a wooden frame on the far side of the room. 'Some punters . . . I should say *all* the punters enjoy caning young girls' bottoms. The crossbar, here, is for . . . Come over here, Carla. I'll demonstrate.'

Watching the girl join Andrews by the wooden frame, Samantha wished that she was involved in the scam. This was more fun that journalism, she mused. And certainly more rewarding – not only from a financial point of view. As the girl leaned over the bar and touched her toes, Samantha eyed her hairless vaginal lips swelling alluringly between her slender thighs. This was a sight that men wouldn't hesitate to pay for, she reflected. And to fuck the little beauty from behind . . .

'These handcuffs slip around your ankles, like this,' Gerry said, kneeling on the floor and pulling the girl's feet wide apart. 'There we are. And then I cuff your wrists to your ankles, like so.'

'And then I take a nice, long, thin bamboo cane,' Jenny giggled wickedly. 'On second thoughts, why don't *you* punish her?' she asked the other girl. 'What was your name again?'

'Faye,' the petite girl murmured.

'There is one thing we must get right,' Gerry said. 'As far as the punters will be concerned, Carla will be here to be punished. The dancing girls will obviously be taken to the surgery to be examined by the doctor, but Carla . . . This is the scenario. Carla has been brought here by her schoolteacher to have her wickedness corrected. I think we should begin with Carla owning up to her naughtiness. Imagine that I'm a punter, Carla. What have you done wrong, girl?'

'Nothing,' Carla whimpered.

'You must have been very naughty at school to have been brought to me.'

'I . . . I haven't done anything.'

'Your teacher informed me that you swore at her.'

'No, no, I—'

'Are you denying it?'

'Please, I only said—'

'You're lying,' Gerry snapped, running his fingertips over the smooth flesh of her unblemished buttocks. 'You do realize that you're going to get the cane?'

'No, please . . .'

'Please, what?'

'Please, sir. I promise to—'

'It's too late for promises, girl. You're going to get the cane and . . .'

'But I . . .'

'Sir.'

'Sir, I . . .'

'You're not arguing, are you?'

'Sir, please don't . . .'

'Arguing, lying, insubordination, foul language . . . I'll correct your wicked ways, my girl. If it's the last thing I do, I'll—'

'All right, Gerry,' Jenny cut in. 'I'm sure the girls have the idea. Faye, take the cane and punish her.'

Grabbing the thin bamboo cane, Faye stood behind her young friend as Andrews and Jenny stepped back. Samantha watched the girl raise the cane above her head in readiness for the first gruelling strike. The cane swished through the air and landed squarely across Carla's naked buttocks, the deafening crack resounding around the room as the young girl let out a yelp. Samantha grinned. Her clitoris swelling as she noticed the girl's vaginal juices oozing between the fleshy hillocks of her vaginal lips, Samantha knew that she was really getting into this. Having spent years living with Zak and covering boring town hall meetings for the newspaper, this was a completely new world. A world that Samantha was determined to explore to the full. From setting out to expose Gerry Andrews, she'd moved on to Jane and Geoff and was now witnessing . . .

These people shouldn't be exposed, she decided. Where was the harm in pleasing dirty old men? Kitty and Gerry had obviously gone to a lot of time and expense setting up the dancing school and the correction room, not to mention the surgery. So why spoil not only their business but the pleasure they were giving the punters? *Live and let live*, she mused as the cane swished through the air and struck Carla's twitching bottom again. *Fuck and let fuck*.

'Lick her cunt,' Jenny ordered Faye, grabbing her arm and halting the caning.

'But I thought that we—' Gerry began.

'I want to see what sort of lesbian show they put on,' Jenny broke in, her pink tongue licking her succulent lips provocatively.

'We're supposed to be naughty schoolgirls,' Carla whined, looking up between her parted thighs. 'We're supposed to be punished, not—'

'Lick her cunt,' Jenny hissed, forcing Faye to her knees.

'We're not lesbians,' Faye complained.

'Suck the cum-juice out of her tight little cunt,' Jenny ordered her sternly. 'Do it, or I'll cane you. And, believe me, I know how to cane a naughty little girl.'

The woman was clearly showing her true colours, Samantha mused as Jenny pushed the girl's face hard against Carla's crimsoned buttocks. She'd obviously succumbed to her lesbian desires. Gerry didn't seem to mind the change of plan, Samantha thought, watching the man's grinning face as Faye licked her friend's creamy vaginal crack. Perhaps the girls weren't suitable candidates after all, Samantha mused. It seemed rather odd that they were keen to work for Kitty and yet they weren't into lesbian sex.

'Fist her cunt,' Jenny ordered Faye, grabbing a jar of Vaseline from a shelf and passing it to the bemused girl. 'Grease her crack and shove your fist deep into her tight little cunt.'

'Jenny,' Gerry whispered, taking the woman's arm. 'I really don't think—'

'*I* run the correction room,' Jenny stated firmly. 'That was the arrangement, wasn't it?'

'Well, yes, but . . .'

'There are no buts, Gerry. *I* run the correction room. This is *my* domain, all right?'

'Yes, yes, of course. I have several things to do so I'll leave you to it.'

Frowning, Samantha knew that Jenny wasn't to be

messed with. She was certainly an ideal person to run the correction room, she thought as Gerry left and closed the door behind him. Walking to the door, Jenny turned the key, the heavy lock clunking as she imprisoned her young victims. Watching Faye smearing Vaseline over her fingers and into Carla's vulval crack, Samantha wondered whether it was possible to sink her fist into the tight sheath of the young girl's vagina. Supposing that anything was possible, she moved closer and watched the girl forcing four fingers into her whimpering friend's sex duct.

'I hope that you two understand the situation,' Jenny said as Faye sank half her hand into Carla's tight vagina. 'You'll be working directly for me. Although Kitty and Gerry run the show, as I said earlier this is *my* domain. At the moment, you are the only girls who will be working in the correction room. I didn't mention it to Gerry but Kitty sent you here to see me. The idea being that I check you out, ensure that you're the right girls for the job. Faye, you're making a right mess of that,' she complained, grabbing the girl's long blonde hair. 'Pull your fingers out of her cunt, for shit's sake.'

'I'm sorry, but I . . .' Faye began, her fist leaving Carla's well-greased vagina.

'Stand by that wall with your hands above your head,' Jenny snapped. Samantha knew what was about to happen as she watched the girl take her position below two pairs of handcuffs hanging from chains. 'There we are,' Jenny giggled, cuffing her victim's wrists high above her head. 'Now I'll show you what cunt-fisting is all about.'

Grabbing the jar of Vaseline, Jenny greased her fingers and knelt in front of the quivering girl's naked body.

Gerry had gone, the door was locked, Carla was in no position to help her young friend . . . Both girls were at the mercy of the lewd lesbian. Settling beside Jenny, Samantha watched her yank Faye's fleshy vaginal lips wide apart, exposing the pinken funnel of creamy-wet flesh surrounding the entrance to her tight sex sheath. The girl was in for a rough time Samantha knew as she focused on her erect clitoris forced out from beneath its protective hood. As Jenny slipped two fingers into the tight duct of her well-greased vagina, the girl let out a whimper. She was in for one hell of a rough time.

'What's the matter with you?' Jenny snapped.

'I . . . I thought this was a set-up to con the punters,' Faye murmured, her long blonde hair veiling her pretty face as she hung her head. 'If I'd known that this was for real. If I'd known that I'd be tortured like this . . .'

'What are you talking about, girl? This *is* a set-up, as you so aptly put it. All I'm doing is enjoying myself. Perks of the job,' Jenny giggled, forcing four fingers into her young victim's vaginal sheath. 'I get to play with you when – how shall I put it? – when business is quiet.'

'When business is quiet, we won't be here,' the girl returned, her flushed face grimacing as Jenny's fingers drove deeper into her tight cunt. 'Kitty said that we'd get a phone call when we're needed, so—'

'Do you want the job or not?'

'Well, I . . . I thought . . .'

'Five, six, seven hundred a week? If you don't want that sort of cash, tax free, then—'

'Of course we want it,' Carla chipped in. 'What Faye means is that we thought we'd be earning money from the punters. Not by having to put up with a lesbian bitch like you . . .'

'I *beg* your pardon?' Jenny hissed, her fingers sliding out of Faye's sex duct as she stood up and walked across the room to the tethered girl. 'A lesbian bitch?'

'I meant . . .'

'You're determined to be the first to test the correction room, aren't you?' Jenny asked the naked girl, taking the thin bamboo cane from the floor and raising it above her head. 'You dare to call me a lesbian bitch?'

'I . . .'

'You've just made a grave mistake, young lady.'

Watching the cane fly through the air and land across Carla's pert buttocks, Samantha winced. Jenny *was* a sadistic bitch, she reflected as Carla's yelps reverberated around the correction room. But the girls must have expected to be sexually abused. They could hardly play the part of naughty little schoolgirls sent to the correction room to be dealt with by perverted men and hope to get off lightly. The girl should never have called Jenny a lesbian bitch, Samantha mused, focusing on the reddening flesh of Carla's naked buttocks. To call the woman names while Carla herself was bent over the wooden bar with her feet and ankles cuffed was asking for trouble.

'You have a nice little bottom,' Jenny said, lowering the cane to her side. 'I have a strap-on dildo that you might find enjoyable. Have you ever had the pleasure of an arse-fucking?'

'No, and I don't want it,' Carla riposted, struggling against the handcuffs.

'If a punter wants to shove his cock up your arse and fuck you . . . I really don't think that Kitty did a good job of vetting you. You don't want this, you don't want that . . . What you do or don't want doesn't bother me,' Jenny giggled. 'This is my domain, Carla. And you are—'

'Shall we stop this crap?' Faye cut in. 'We were supposed to be here for—'

'Not you as well?' Jenny hissed. 'I can see that I'm going to have to teach you both a lesson you'll never forget.'

Lashing Carla's naked buttocks with the cane, the woman was obviously possessed. Samantha could do nothing but watch as the young girl's shrieks resounded throughout the correction room and Faye screamed her own protests. Again halting the gruelling punishment, Jenny took two metal clips from a shelf and stood in front of Faye. Pulling at the girl's elongated nipples, she fixed the clips over the sensitive protrusions and giggled as Faye gritted her teeth and grimaced. Taking two chains, she fixed them to the clips and hung heavy weights from the dangling ends. Faye's breasts became distended into taut cones of flesh and she whimpered as her mistress let out a wicked chuckle.

'You'll pay for this,' Faye breathed, looking down at her painfully stretched and abused nipples.

'This is a test,' Jenny announced. 'If you want to work for us, and earn yourself a fortune, then you'll have to pass the test.'

'You mean that, once we've passed the test, we won't have to go through this again?' Carla asked in her naivety.

'That's right,' Jenny replied. 'The idea is that, if you can endure whatever I put you through, then you'll be able to take anything from the customers. That, Carla, is why I'm going to continue with the caning.' She grinned, grabbing the bamboo stick and standing behind the trembling girl. 'Remember that this is purely a test.'

Lashing the girl's glowing buttocks again, Jenny let

out a grunt each time she brought the cane down. This was no test, Samantha knew as she watched the crazed woman thrashing the sobbing girl. The caning was purely to satisfy her lust for sadistic pleasure. Wondering why Gerry Andrews was involved in such a thing, Samantha pondered on his haunted-mansion scam. What was the point of it? Why run the risk of having people milling around the mansion looking for ghosts when he'd obviously have to keep the dancing school undercover? Nothing made sense, Samantha reflected, listening to the thrashed girl's screams as the cane repeatedly swiped the naked globes of her burning bottom. Samantha also wondered what Julie was up to. Deciding to phone to find out whether she'd got the names and addresses of the girls and the clients, she also thought it would be a good time to visit the perverted vicar again.

Carla couldn't take much more Samantha knew as she gazed in horror at the scarlet flesh of the girl's tensed buttocks. Again and again the cane swished through the air, cracking loudly across the fiery orbs of her naked arse, jolting her young body as she let out piercing yelps. Her vaginal fluid streaming between her pouting vulval lips, coursing down the pale flesh of her inner thighs, Carla was nonetheless obviously deriving some pleasure from the gruelling beating.

'Yes,' Jenny trilled as golden liquid suddenly flowed in rivers down Carla's thighs and splashed onto the floor between her feet. '*That*'s what I like to see.' Continuing with the merciless thrashing, Jenny struck the backs of the girl's slender thighs, delighting in her act of sexual torture as thin weals fanned out across her urine-wet flesh. Thrashing the girl harder, Jenny appeared to lose

herself in the sadistic punishment. Moving back up to Carla's naked buttocks, she repeatedly lashed the scarlet globes of her young bottom with the bamboo cane until the girl screamed out. Undeterred by her victim's pleas for leniency, she continued with the unmerciful beating until the cane snapped in two.

'Let that be a lesson to you,' Jenny gasped, discarding the broken cane. 'And now for you, young lady,' she said, grinning wickedly as she walked towards Faye's tethered body.

'My arms ache,' the girl complained, raising her head and looking up at her cuffed wrists.

'Your arms ache?' Jenny said mockingly. 'Oh, you poor thing. I know what we'll do. To take your mind off your aching arms, I'll thrash the soft lips of your little cunt.'

'No, please . . .'

'Your nipples are coming on nicely. Stretching into beautifully suckable little teats. I'll leave the weights to do their job while I thrash your hairless little cunt with a leather strap.'

Dragging a high chair across the room, Jenny forced the girl to sit. Her arms high above her head, Faye could do nothing as the woman pulled two more chains down from the ceiling and fixed leather slings to the ends. Placing the girl's ankles in the slings, she moved to the wall and turned a handle. Watching her victim's feet rise, her legs opening wide, Jenny took a leather belt from a hook on the wall. Samantha gazed at Faye's full vaginal lips, the gaping valley of her vagina, as Jenny knelt on the floor in front of her victim. To slip her tongue into her lesbian valley of desire and lick her there . . . Trying to control her inner yearning, Samantha felt her panties

filling with her pre-orgasmic juices. Perhaps the time had come to return to the tent and lick the cream out of Jane's hairless pussy crack.

'Are you comfortable?' Jenny asked, breaking Samantha's reverie.

'Hardly,' Faye retorted, her buttocks just resting on the chair, her naked body virtually hanging from her cuffed wrists and ankles.

'That's what I like to see,' Jenny giggled. 'A young girl's hairless cunt gaping wide open, her cunt-milk streaming from her defenceless little hole . . . You look so young, Faye. You could easily pass for—'

'How long are we going to be chained up like this?' Carla asked.

'For as long as it takes,' Jenny returned. 'The more you complain, the longer it will take.'

Raising the leather belt, Jenny lashed Faye's naked vulval hillocks, the loud crack echoing around the correction room as the trembling girl let out an agonizing scream. The weights still hanging from her painfully stretched nipples, she grimaced and yelped as the leather belt lashed her stinging outer labia again. The pinken petals of her inner lips swelling with each swipe of the belt, she wriggled and squirmed, trying to bring her thighs together in an effort to protect the most sensitive part of her teenage body.

Powerless to halt the gruelling thrashing of the girl's genitalia, Samantha could do nothing but watch the horrendous sexual torture. As lash after lash resounded around the room, Jenny continued with the cruel vulval thrashing, chuckling wickedly as the young girl's naked pussy reddened beneath the punishing leather strap. Realizing that the lewd sight was heightening her own

arousal, Samantha felt the hot juices of her pussy seeping into the tight material of her panties. She couldn't believe that the sexual torture was exciting her, sending her libido through the roof as she watched Faye's vulval flesh turning a fire-red.

Watching the girl's cunt lips swelling to an incredible size as the genital strapping continued, Samantha wondered how much Faye could endure. Again and again, the leather belt lashed her crimsoned vaginal flesh. Her inner lips inflating, the inflamed red petals protruding from her gaping valley of lust, she screamed out as Jenny thrashed her harder. Samantha watched in awe as the girl's burning pussy lips ballooned, her juices of arousal streaming from the gaping entrance to her young cunt. The belt striking the pale flesh of her inner thighs, lashing her vulval crack, Faye again screamed out in agony as her sadistic tormentor continued the genital torture.

Finally discarding the leather strap, Jenny moved forward and ran her wet tongue up the full length of the girl's inflamed vaginal crack. Tasting her there, lapping up her flowing juices of lust, she forced the fleshy hillocks of her vulval lips wide apart and drove her tongue deep into the wet heat of her sex sheath. Gasping, her eyes closed, her naked body trembling uncontrollably, Faye was obviously enjoying the lesbian cunt-tonguing. Mouthing and slurping on her young victim's vaginal flesh, Jenny drank from the helpless girl's vagina, sucking out her cunt-milk and swallowing hard until she'd drained the girl's sex sheath . . .

Wondering what Zak was doing as she recalled his wet tongue running over the solid nub of her clitoris,

Samantha found herself standing in Angela's lounge, staring at the young couple sitting on the sofa. Zak was complaining about money, saying that there was now no chance of getting his hands on Samantha's father's cash. That was all he'd wanted, Samantha reflected, watching Angela tugging his zip down and hauling his erect penis out of his trousers. As the girl lowered her head and sucked his purple crown into her wet mouth, Zak pushed her aside and leaped to his feet.

'What the hell are we going to do?' he asked, zipping his trousers.

'I was hoping to suck out your lovely sperm,' Angela giggled.

'Ange, this is serious. I thought that I'd be marrying Sam and . . . We've invested money in this and now . . .'

'And now all you have to do is get Sam back,' Angela sighed. 'Get her back, marry her, and we'll be home and dry.'

'That's easier said than done,' Zak breathed. 'Shit, I've spent money on her, thinking that . . .'

'OK, so you've spent a couple of grand on a holiday and ring. Get her back, for Christ's sake. Get her back and—'

'I'll ring her later. I'll say that you came on strong, led me on and all that. I'll proclaim my love for her and . . .'

'And she'll take you back with open arms.'

Samantha couldn't believe what she was hearing as she stood in the corner of the room and gazed at the scheming pair. Her father had plenty of money, but there was no way Zak was going to get his hands on it – even if he *did* marry Samantha. Zak was a bastard, that was for sure. To think that he'd not only been screwing her so-called best friend, but the evil pair had been after her father's

money . . . Coming up with an idea, Samantha sat in an armchair and grinned.

'Tell her that there was nothing in it,' Angela said. 'I'll speak to her and explain that we were attracted to each other but it was nothing more than ships passing in the night. If I make out that you want nothing to do with me any more, she'll come round.'

'I hope so,' Zak sighed. 'What I want to know is how the fucking bitch found out about us. How did she know that I was on your bed and—'

'It doesn't matter how. The point is that she knows and now you've got to sort it out.'

'Yes, you're right. When I told her father about my business plans, he seemed pretty interested. I was sure that he was going to invest and . . .'

'Zak, just work on getting Sam back. Marry her as soon as you can, and then we'll talk about her father's money.'

'I'll ring her now,' Zak said enthusiastically . . .

Returning to her own time, Samantha sat in her lounge and mulled over her plan. Zak needed to be taught a lesson she knew as she gazed at the telephone. Apart from giving Zak a necessary shock and enjoying a life of crude sex, she wondered what else she could do with her talent. Thinking again about setting up a dancing school and making money from perverted men, she wondered whether to stay on at the newspaper office or give up her job. She'd need money, but—

'Hello,' she said, grabbing the ringing phone.

'Sam, it's me,' Zak murmured. 'I think we need to talk.'

'Yes, you're right,' Samantha agreed readily.

'There was nothing between Angela and me, I swear.'

'I know, Zak. I suppose I just thought that . . . I'm sorry, too.'

'Does that mean that we're back together?'

'Zak, my father has just given me some money. Quite a lot of money, actually.'

'Oh?'

'He wants me to buy a house and invest the rest so that I can live off the interest.'

'How much, exactly?'

'Several hundred thousand.'

'Christ, several hundred . . . Er, well . . . I'm very pleased for you, Sam. We've talked about marriage many times. Why not go for it? Apart from this silly misunderstanding, we're pretty good together.'

'Yes, yes, we are. But I'm not sure about marriage just yet, Zak. Maybe in a year or so we can get married and . . .'

'Whatever you say. I wasn't trying to rush you. It's just that . . . well, I have plans. The sooner we're married the better. Perhaps in six months we could . . .'

'I suppose we could at least start making plans for the wedding.'

'That's great. Look, I'll come round and—'

'I'm about to go out. Give me a call later and we'll get together, OK?'

'You bet.'

''Bye for now, Zak.'

Replacing the receiver, Samantha rubbed her hands together gleefully. This was a silly game, she mused. But a game worth playing after the way Zak and Angela had treated her. Still unable to believe that the evil pair were after her father's money, she paced the floor, thinking

about her plan. It would serve Zak right if he lost every penny he had, she mused, wondering how to get him into serious trouble. It was about time the vicar had his come-uppance, too, she reflected, wondering how to get in touch with the other girls he'd abused. Thinking about his office, her Sunday-afternoon visits, she suddenly found herself standing in the church . . .

Looking down at her Sunday dress, her black shoes and white ankle socks, Samantha wondered what stage of the abuse she'd returned to. Had the vicar approached her yet? Or was this visit well into the proceedings? Hearing movements in the office, she walked across the church and peered through the crack in the door. Watching the man sitting at his desk and scribbling in a diary, she knocked on the door.

'Come in,' the man of God called. 'Oh, Samantha,' he said, grinning as she wandered into the office. 'How are you? Did you enjoy your sixteenth birthday?'

'Er . . . yes,' she replied, recalling that her mother had made her wear white ankle socks and her hair in plaits until she was about eighteen.

'I thought that the christening went well. Why aren't you at the party with the others?'

'I . . . I wanted to see you,' she replied, recalling the christening she'd gone to when she was sixteen. 'Vicar, the things you did to me when I was young . . .'

'What things?' he asked her, frowning.

'Sex.'

'Sex?' he chuckled. 'What *are* you talking about?'

'Don't make out that nothing happened. You know very well what I'm talking about.'

'Yes, I do,' he sighed. 'And I hope that you're not

trying to make out that you don't remember the time that you were drunk in the church with three men.'

'What do you mean?' she asked, her eyes wide.

'I was watching from the office, Samantha. I've never said anything but, if you're now going to threaten me . . .'

'I . . . I wasn't drunk,' she stammered, recalling her worst nightmare.

'Weren't you? Don't give me that rubbish. You were naked on the altar. The men were . . . I can't bring myself to think about the disgusting way in which you behaved.'

That fateful evening was the horrendous nightmare that Samantha had blocked from her mind. During a friend's party, she'd drunk far too much and had gone to the church with three men to have a laugh. Things had quickly got out of hand and . . . She'd not known that the vicar had witnessed the crude acts she'd been forced to perform. The men had been in their mid-twenties. They'd stripped her, groped between her legs, squeezed the mounds of her firm breasts and plied her with vodka. She recalled swigging from the bottle as she'd danced on the altar. To think that the vicar had been there all along . . .

'So, Samantha,' he breathed triumphantly. 'Would you like me to inform your parents of your despicable behaviour?'

'They forced me,' she said softly.

'Forced you? Good grief, you were blind drunk.'

'That's what I mean. They took advantage of me. They used and abused me, the same way you did when I was young.'

'I don't like your tone, young lady,' he said sternly. 'I suppose Zak was at the party while you were here with those men? Shall I tell him what happened?'

'Zak and I are finished, so—'

'Finished? Don't give me that.'

'We're *about* to finish,' she said, realizing that her relationship with Zak wouldn't end until she was twenty-two.

Wondering why the vicar had never previously mentioned her sex session on the altar, she thought that he might have been waiting to use it if she threatened to expose him as a pervert. Confused, she didn't know what to do as he eyed the mounds of her firm breasts billowing her tight blouse. There was no way she could expose him now, she reflected. Even though Zak was no longer with her in her real-time life, the last thing she wanted was the vicar telling all and sundry about her drunken behaviour with three men.

'I'll be back,' she said, leaving the office and fleeing the church. Wandering through the woods behind the churchyard, she sighed as a tear rolled down her cheek. Her ability to travel through time was doing more damage than good, she mused. Returning to the vicar's office, recalling the three men . . . She didn't even remember who the men were. No one at the party seemed to remember them, and she'd thought that they'd gate-crashed. She'd been too drunk to remember where Zak had been, too drunk to . . . Perhaps Zak screwing Angela was some kind of revenge, she thought. Zak had always been a dark horse, she mused. Perhaps he'd been screwing Angela all along. She imagined Zak taking Angela to the woods, screwing her in the bushes . . .

Samantha gasped and held her hand to her chest as she found herself standing in what appeared to be a derelict warehouse or old barn. Her new talent was all very well,

she reflected, looking around at rusted farm machinery and bales of straw. But she had no real control. She could have been anywhere at any time, she thought, wondering why she'd travelled to the barn. There was a reason for everything. Wasn't there?

'And who might you be?' a young man asked as he approached.

'Oh, er . . . hi,' Samantha said, wondering why he was wearing a suit. He obviously wasn't a farmworker, she decided as she wondered how to explain her presence. 'I was out for a walk,' she began.

'Out for a walk?' he said, frowning. 'You're miles from anywhere.'

'Yes, I know. I . . . I got lost.'

'You'd better come with me,' he said, taking her hand. 'I'm driving into town in about ten minutes so I'll drop you off.'

'Which town is that?'

'There is only one town near here,' he said softly, leading her across the barn to a side door. 'And this is it,' he laughed, opening the door and pushing her into a small room.

Picking herself up, Samantha looked around the room and noticed a teenage girl sitting in the corner. The door closing, the sound of a heavy bolt sliding across, she knew that she'd landed herself in trouble as she looked up and noticed iron bars criss-crossing a small window. Huddling in the corner on the floor, the girl said nothing as Samantha asked her who she was and what she was doing locked in the small room.

The girl was extremely attractive with her blonde hair in a bob framing her angelic face. Dressed in a short skirt and T-shirt, she appeared to be clean, indicating that she

might not have been held captive for very long. Samantha eyed the little beauty's panties as she sat with her chin resting on her knees. The red material bulging with her puffy sex lips, concealing her undoubtedly creamy-wet sex crack, she looked exceptionally sexual. Wondering why her time travelling only seemed to lead her to debased sex as she thought longingly of breathing in the scent of the girl's moist panties, Samantha asked her how long she'd been there.

'I know your tricks,' the girl retorted angrily.

'Tricks?' Samantha echoed, somewhat puzzled. 'What do you mean?'

'I won't tell you anything about my father, so don't bother asking.'

'Your father? I wasn't going to ask you anything about . . . What are you doing here? Why has that man locked you up?'

'You know why. I just hope that my father doesn't pay up. Then you'll have to kill me and . . .'

'Kill you?' Samantha breathed. 'You've been kidnapped and he wants money from your father?'

'Don't play innocent with me. You know damn well that I've been kidnapped.'

'Look, I know nothing about this. I'm not working with that evil man. Whatever you might think, I . . . What's your name?'

'Anne.'

'OK, Anne, I'm going to help you.'

'Yeah, right.'

Rising to her feet, Samantha knew that it would be easy enough to return to her own time and get help. But she had to discover the exact location of the barn, and the time and date. She didn't recall any news of a kidnap-

ping, and began to wonder just how far back in time she'd travelled. Hearing movements outside the door, she looked at the girl, noticing the fear apparent in her expression.

'Oh, dear,' a middle-aged man murmured as he opened the door and stared hard at Samantha. 'We have an intruder.'

'I found her lurking in the barn,' the younger man said, hovering just outside the doorway.

'This rather complicates matters, I'm afraid. What's your name?'

'What's going on here?' Samantha asked.

'That's what I'd like to know. You're not bad-looking. I'll tell you what we'll do. You strip off and—'

'And you can go to hell,' Samantha said angrily.

'I'm sure I will, when my time comes,' the middle-aged man laughed. 'You have a choice, young lady. You either strip naked or—'

'Never.'

'In that case, sweet little Anne will have to oblige. Come with me, girl.'

'Leave her alone,' Samantha snapped.

'The choice is yours,' he chuckled. 'Either you strip off, or we take the girl outside and . . .'

'All right,' Samantha finally conceded, knowing that she had to play for time in order to discover the location of the barn.

'No, no,' the man said as she moved towards the door. 'I want you to strip in here.'

'What? In front of—'

'Yes, in front of Little Miss Innocent.'

Unbuttoning her blouse, Samantha slipped the garment over her shoulders as the young girl watched with

wide eyes. Still sure that she could save herself by flitting back to her own time, Samantha unhooked her bra and allowed the silk cups to fall away from the firm mounds of her young breasts. Her nipples rising in the relatively cool air of the old building, the chocolate-brown discs of her areolae darkening, she tugged her skirt down her slender legs and kicked it aside, along with her shoes. The teenager watched with bated breath as Samantha slipped her thumbs between the tight elastic of her panties and her shapely hips. Perhaps she'd never seen a naked woman before, Samantha mused, again imagining breathing in the heady girl-scent of the girl's moist panties. Was she a virgin?

Tugging her panties down her long legs, the hairless flesh of her vulval lips coming into view, Samantha watched the man's eyes widen as he focused on the creamy-wet slit of her vagina. She knew what he wanted as she felt her clitoris swell in expectation of crude sex. And he could have it as long as he left the girl alone, she decided. Standing with her feet apart, her naked body shamelessly displayed to her captor, she knew that the girl was going to be stripped and used for illicit sex.

'Not bad,' the middle-aged man murmured, his obvious arousal bulging his trousers. 'Not bad at all.'

'I'm glad you like it,' Samantha breathed, running her hands over the spheres of her young breasts. 'Why don't we go somewhere private and . . .'

'Who needs privacy?' the younger man chuckled, leaning in the doorway. 'We don't want privacy. We want the little tart on the floor there to see exactly what she's going to get.'

'Let's get the little tart to lick the big tart,' the middle-aged man chortled.

'What a good idea. Go on, little tart. Lick the big tart's cunt out.'

'No,' Samantha snapped. 'Do what you want with me, but leave the girl alone.'

'Do it,' the younger man snapped, grabbing the girl's arm and dragging her across the room. 'Do it, or *I*'ll lick *your* dirty little cunt out.'

Watching the girl kneel in front of her, Samantha closed her eyes as she felt the teenager's wet tongue running up and down her vaginal crack. Wrong though it was, she realized that she was deriving immense pleasure from the enforced lesbian act. Her juices of arousal seeping from her tight sex hole, trickling between her engorged inner lips, she let out a sigh of satisfaction as the girl's tongue swept over the swelling protrusion of her sensitive clitoris. The pouting lips of her vulva parted by the girl's fingers, she breathed deeply as she felt Anne's tongue slide into the sex-wet hole of her contracting vagina.

'A photograph,' the middle-aged man said. 'The girl's father has one of her tied up and gagged. How about a shot of his little girl licking out a tart's wet cunt?'

'Perfect,' the younger man agreed. 'I'll get the camera.'

'Perhaps a few shots of my cock fucking her pretty little mouth might persuade him to come up with the money?'

'Or both our cocks fucking her pretty little mouth?'

'Even better.'

The crude words battering Samantha's racked mind, she knew that she had to do something before the girl was crudely stripped of her virginity by the evil pair. Not wanting to simply disappear into thin air, she wondered

how to get rid of the men for a few minutes to enable her to make her escape. The younger man leaving the room to get the camera, she smiled at his accomplice and suggested that he close the door and strip off.

'We don't need your friend,' she said, licking her succulent lips provocatively. 'I'm sure you have more than enough to satisfy both of us.'

Grinning, he turned and was about to lock the door when he spun round on his heels. 'Oh, no,' he said, shaking his head. 'No tricks, young lady.'

'Tricks?' Samantha echoed surprisedly. 'I thought that you might enjoy . . . Obviously not. It's strange to think how wrong I was.'

'Wrong?'

'I thought that you were a real man. Oh well, never mind. Perhaps I should be going after your friend. I'll bet his is a lot bigger than yours.'

'I know your game. And it won't work.'

'What game's that?' the younger man asked as he entered the room, clutching a camera.

'She was trying to . . . It doesn't matter. OK, take a few shots of daddy's little girl licking out a woman's wet cunt.'

'My pleasure.'

Listening to the camera shutter clicking as Anne's tongue snaked deep inside her tightening vagina, Samantha tried to deny her soaring libido. Wondering again about her obvious leaning towards lesbianism, she wondered whether she should let go and appease her inner desires. Did it matter whether she was deriving pleasure from a male or a female tongue? She pondered the question, her clitoris painfully solid between her splayed love lips.

Hearing movements in the barn, the two men dashed out of the room to investigate. This was her chance to escape Samantha knew as she looked down at Anne, clutching the girl's head . . .

She was about to push her away when she suddenly found herself back in her lounge with the girl still at her feet. Horrified to think that she'd taken the girl back to her own time, she wondered what to say as she stepped back and watched Anne climb to her feet.

'Where are we?' the teenage beauty asked, looking around the room.

'I'll explain later,' Samantha replied.

'But . . . where are we? I don't like this. God, we must have—'

'It's all right,' Samantha soothed her. 'Anne, what date is it? When were you kidnapped?'

'The date? How did we get here?'

'I'll explain everything later. Just tell me the date.'

'It's September.'

'And the year?'

'Nineteen ninety-four.'

'Ninety-four?' Samantha gasped. 'Christ, that's eight years ago.'

'Eight years ago? What are you talking about?'

'If you're here with me, then . . . I wonder whether you're still in the barn?'

'You're going to have to tell me what's going on,' the girl sighed, flopping down onto the sofa. 'Eight years ago? Am I still in the barn? Where am I now?'

'In my flat. It's two thousand and two, Anne. Eight years after you were kidnapped.'

'You're mad,' she laughed.

'Far from it.'

'Don't tell me that you're a time traveller,' Anne giggled. 'How did you do it? What's the trick?'

'I'll tell you later.' Samantha breathed pensively. 'What's your surname?'

'Wilkinson.'

'Anne Wilkinson? Yes, I remember reading about the kidnapping in the paper. And it was on the television. Anne, you were never seen again. Everyone assumed that you . . . Everyone assumed the worst.'

'I really have no idea what you're talking about. All I know is that I was in the barn and now . . . How did we get here?'

'Shit,' Samantha sighed. 'This wasn't supposed to happen. How the hell am I going to get you back to your own time? And if I do get you back, you'll die.'

'Die?'

'Phone your parents. Tell them that—'

'OK,' the girl said eagerly, grabbing the phone and punching the buttons.

Shaking her head, Samantha slipped into her bedroom and grabbed her dressing gown. Returning to the lounge, she wondered what Anne's parents would think. Their daughter had been missing for eight years. To suddenly get a phone call from the girl would . . . Listening as Anne said hello to her mother, Samantha sat down beside her.

'It *is* me, Mum,' Anne said, frowning. 'What do you mean? Of course I'm not a crank. Is Dad there? Mum, this *is* me. It's Anne . . .'

'Perhaps that wasn't such a good idea,' Samantha breathed as the girl hung up.

'She didn't believe me. She said that I was a crank and—'

'I'm sorry. I should never have suggested calling your parents.'

'What's going on?' Anne asked, a tear rolling down her cheek.

'I only wish I knew. Look, I really don't know what to do. You'll have to give me time to think. Are you hungry?'

'Yes, I'm starving.'

'Help yourself to whatever you want in the kitchen. I'm going to take a shower and get dressed.'

'Where are we? I mean, where is the flat?'

'London.'

'I'd better go home.'

'No, Anne. You must stay here.'

'Why?'

'Because . . . because I have to work this out. You can't just walk into your parents' house after eight years and . . . Stay here with me until I've worked something out, OK?'

'If you say so. I couldn't get home, anyway. I live in Hampshire and I don't have any money.'

Wandering into the bathroom, Samantha realized that she was up against a serious problem. Taking the girl back to her own time would inevitably lead to her demise, and yet she couldn't stay in the future. Slipping her dressing gown off and stepping into the shower, Samantha wondered again why her time travelling always led her to crude sex. Someone or something was behind her ability to travel through time she knew as she shampooed her long blonde hair. Perhaps she'd been gifted with time travel in order to achieve something, she mused. Was it to save the young girl from her dreadful fate? But if it turned out that she was unable to change history, Samantha was certain that the girl would die.

6

'I know that, Dave,' Samantha sighed, pressing the phone to her ear.

'You said that you'd keep me posted. I've heard nothing from you . . . If you weren't such a little beauty, I'd sack you. So, what have you discovered about this sex den?'

'Nothing, yet.'

'Nothing? For fuck's sake, Sammy . . .'

'Dave, do you remember that kidnapping about eight years ago? Anne Wilkinson . . .'

'I remember it very well. What's that got to do with it?'

'What happened, exactly?'

'The girl was never found.'

'Were the men caught?'

'The kidnapper was never caught. Why did you say, *men*? No one knew who the kidnapper was.'

'I don't know. I just assumed, I suppose.'

'Why the interest?'

'I heard something about it the other day. I was young at the time and don't recall the details. Were there any clues as to where the girl had been held?'

'No, nothing at all. Extensive searches were carried out for several months. Countryside, towns, villages . . . Nothing came up.'

'OK, thanks, Dave. I'll be in touch.'

'You'd better be. I miss looking at your nipples pressing through your—'

''Bye, Dave.'

Hanging up, Samantha wandered into her bedroom and
gazed at Anne sleeping beneath the quilt. The girl had
washed and eaten and had then slept well all through the
night. Samantha had been tempted to slip into the bed
beside her but had managed to control her rampant lesbian
desires and sleep on the sofa. Thinking how angelic Anne
looked, Samantha pulled the quilt back, exposing her
naked body. Her breasts were small, her ripe nipples
standing proud from the dark discs of her areolae. She
was extremely attractive, Samantha thought, eyeing the
sparse blonde curls barely concealing her tightly closed sex
crack as she rolled onto her back and spread her limbs.

Pulling the quilt up, Samantha left the room and closed
the door. Trying to push thoughts of lesbian sex to the
back of her mind, she flopped down onto the sofa in the
lounge and tried to work out what she was going do with
the girl. Anne would have been in her early twenties by
now, she mused. She might have married and had children, but now . . . This was a bloody mess, she thought.
Anne was going to have to take on a new identity, Samantha decided. No one would believe that Anne was *the*
Anne Wilkinson. And no one would have believed that
Samantha had been drunk in the church with the three
men. They'd have thought her to be a common tart, if
they'd discovered what she'd done on the altar . . .

'God,' Samantha breathed, looking down at her naked
body as she stood by the altar. 'I . . . I didn't want to
come back here. I—'

'I'll bet you want to come off,' a man chuckled,

squeezing the small mounds of her teenage breasts.

'No, I . . .' The alcohol blurring her mind, she clung to the altar to steady her swaying body. 'I don't want to be here.'

'How about a mouth-fucking?' another asked, pulling her head back by her long blonde hair and kissing her full lips.

'Or a bum-fucking?' the third man suggested, cupping the smooth, firm globes of her arse in his hands and squeezing them hard.

As her naked body was lifted onto the altar, Samantha realized the shocking truth about that fateful evening. She'd tried to convince herself that she'd been too drunk to stop the crude abuse of her young body. She'd subconsciously persuaded herself to believe that she'd been forced to commit the crude sexual acts with the three men. In reality, she'd been only too willing to go to the church with the men and allow them to fuck and spunk her wet orifices. The skeletons in her cupboard were escaping she knew as several fingers drove deep into the wet heat of her teenage pussy.

'Suck it,' a man gasped, his knees either side of her head, the swollen knob of his solid penis hovering above her open mouth. Taking his glans into her wet mouth, Samantha ran her tongue over its silky-smooth surface, sucking hard as another penis slipped into the tight sheath of her teenage cunt. Pondering on her age in her alcoholic haze, she wondered why she'd ever done such a thing at sixteen years old. The drink had obviously influenced her, but to allow three men to . . .

'God, she's got a tight little cunt,' the man fucking her pussy gasped. 'This is a nice change after my wife's slack cunt.'

'Think yourself lucky,' the man pushing his cock into Samantha's mouth laughed. 'A man of your age fucking a young tart . . .'

'I'm only forty-five,' the man retorted.

Forty-five? Samantha mused. She'd not realized how old the men were. They'd obviously gatecrashed the party looking for sex. Samantha had enjoyed being chatted up, thought it would be a laugh to go to the church and . . . The men quipping about each others' ages, Samantha was shocked to learn that the man fucking her pretty mouth was in his fifties. The alcohol had blurred her vision at the party. She recalled the three men chatting to her, suggesting that they go to the church to have some fun. But she'd not realized how old they were.

Her teenage pussy flooding with sperm, her naked body rocking, she swallowed hard as her mouth filled with sperm. A finger slipping between the taut cheeks of her buttocks, she jolted as a finger drove deep into the tight sheath of her rectal duct and massaged her inner flesh. She vaguely recalled the crude abuse of her young body as she repeatedly swallowed the gushing sperm flooding her mouth. She'd been spanked, arse-fucked . . . And the vicar had witnessed the crudities from his office.

Looking up at the man as he slipped his spent cock out of her mouth, Samantha thought that she recognized him. To her horror, she realized that he was a friend of her father. Looking back, she recalled him asking her about the party, asking whether she'd had a good time. He had obviously been trying to discover whether or not she could remember him fucking her. Several times over the months after the crude fucking, he'd asked her about

the party. She hadn't recognized him as one of her abusers, but now . . .

Her naked body was rolled over as the other man yanked his deflating cock out of her sperm-flooded vagina. She lay on her stomach and gripped the sides of the altar as her legs were yanked wide apart. As one man tried to force his fist deep into her teenage pussy, another began spanking the taut flesh of her naked buttocks. The pain permeating her anal globes, she couldn't believe that one of the men was her father's friend. He'd never visited the house, but she knew him from the odd occasion when he'd picked her father up in his car to go to some business meeting or other. She couldn't even recall his name, but she knew that he had something to do with her father's work.

'Hold her down,' a man breathed, clambering onto the altar. Samantha could feel hands clutching her thighs and arms as the man's solid glans stabbed at her anal entrance. His huge knob slipping past her defeated anal sphincter muscles, gliding along the tight tube of her rectum, he let out a sigh of satisfaction as he completely impaled her on his massive penis. Feeling as if her pelvic cavity was inflating to bursting point, that her anal ring was about to split open, she stared wide-eyed at a bulbous knob hovering close to her mouth as her head was pulled up by her hair.

'A double-ended fuck,' the owner of the engorged cock laughed, driving his knob to the back of Samantha's throat. The inflamed tissue of her anus rolling back and forth along the huge penis fucking her tight arse, her mouth bloated by another massive prong, her eyes bulged as a finger slipped into her anal canal alongside the solid organ. A hand slipping beneath her naked body,

fingers forcing their way into the tight sheath of her sperm-drenched cunt, she knew that the crude sex had only just begun.

She recalled staggering home late that fateful night and swaying as she'd almost fallen through the front door before climbing the stairs to her bed. Thankfully, her parents hadn't woken. Thinking that she was sleeping over at a friend's house, they'd not been expecting her. Had they seen the state she was in, they'd have questioned her far into the night, probably grounded her for several months. She'd woken the following morning with a blinding headache, and with sperm oozing from the burning holes between her slender thighs. Zak had asked her where she'd got to, and she'd lied about feeling ill and going home early. She'd never mentioned the church to anyone. Not knowing who the men were, she'd blocked out all memories of her night of wanton whoredom.

'Coming,' the man fucking the tight sheath of her rectal canal gasped, his spunk lubricating the illicit pistoning of her burning arse and gushing deep into her bowels. As sperm sprayed from the dilated hole of her anus, she realized that she'd tried to block out all memories of that night because of her guilt. She'd done her best to erase memories of her visits to the vicar's office because she'd blamed herself for leading the man on. She wasn't the innocent young teenage girl she'd thought herself to have been, she knew.

'Swallow it,' the man shafting her pretty mouth gasped as his spunk jetted from his throbbing glans and filled her gobbling mouth. Complying with his crude request, Samantha drank from his fountainhead, sperm dribbling down her chin as spunk trickled from her pistoned arse and bathed the valley of her teenage cunt. This was sex at

its crudest she mused as fingers massaged her inner vaginal flesh. Her young body used and abused, she knew that'd she'd been only too willing to commit the vulgar acts with the three men.

She was going to have to accept that she *had* behaved like a common slut she knew as her clitoris swelled, sending wondrous ripples of illicit sex through her convulsing womb. Perhaps that night in the tent with Jane had sparked her curiosity in sex, she reflected. Perhaps the vicar's interest in her young body had excited her, had caused her to lead him on. Perhaps the time she'd cheated on Zak . . . That was another skeleton she'd not only locked in the cupboard but had denied existed.

She'd just got serious with Zak, meeting him after school and spending weekends with him, when someone else had caught her eye. Chris was in his late twenties, and had an eye for young girls. Samantha had met him at the school disco. He'd gone there to pick up his young sister and had got chatting with Samantha. Talking about her beautiful hair, admiring her curvaceous young body, he'd made her feel good. He'd arranged to meet her in the woods behind the church the following afternoon after school. She'd lied to Zak, saying that she was going to a friend's house after school.

Meeting Chris in the woods, Samantha had felt grown up when he'd taken her head in his hands and kissed her full mouth. She recalled her juices of arousal seeping into her school knickers, her clitoris swelling, as he'd squeezed the mounds of her young breasts through her white blouse. She'd played around with Zak, wanking his cock as he'd masturbated her clitoris to orgasm. But she'd not gone any further with him. When the young man pulled her down onto the soft grass and

slipped his hand up her skirt, she knew that she wanted full-blown sex.

Chris was so much older than Zak, and so much more experienced. His finger slipping between the tight elastic of Samantha's knickers and the top of her inner thigh, he'd massaged the soft swell of her pussy lips. She'd melted in his arms, desperate to feel his solid cock gliding into the tight shaft of her young vagina. Within minutes, he'd stripped her naked and was sucking her sensitive milk teats into his hot mouth, massaging her clitoris and fingering her virginal cunt.

'Please, I want you to take me,' Samantha recalled begging him as he'd slipped out of his clothes and settled between her splayed legs. His penis had glided deep into her young cunt with ease, filling her, bloating her pelvic cavity as she gasped and squirmed in her sexual ecstasy beneath his muscular body. She'd looked up at the trees high above her as she'd listened to the squelching sound of her vaginal juices. He was big, his huge cock almost splitting her pussy open as he pistoned her young body gently. Increasing his fucking rhythm, he'd rocked her young body, breathed words of love as his swinging balls had repeatedly smacked the rounded cheeks of her naked bottom. Breathing heavily, he'd pumped his spunk deep into her cunt as she'd reached her shuddering orgasm and cried out in her ecstasy beneath the swaying trees.

Samantha had thought that she'd found love as Chris had fucked her and taken her to her sexual heaven. He'd slipped his spent penis out of her inflamed vagina and licked and sucked her young clitoris to another mind-blowing climax. He'd mouthed her milk-teats, fucked her again and taken her to heights of sexual satisfaction she'd never thought existed. She'd arranged to meet him

again, but he hadn't turned up. Later, she'd heard that he was married. Devastated, she'd thrown herself at Zak, fucking him at every opportunity in an effort to forget about Chris. What other skeletons was she denying? She asked herself the question as the three men rolled her onto her back and ran their hands over her naked teenage body . . .

'Hi,' Anne breathed, wandering into the lounge with the quilt wrapped around her.

'Oh, er . . . Good morning,' Samantha said, looking around the room and wondering what had brought her back from the church. 'You slept well.'

'God, I was so tired last night. What time is it?'

'Ten-thirty. Would you like some tea or coffee?'

'Tea, please. Where are my clothes?'

'I washed them last night. I'll put them in the tumble drier in a minute. So, what are we going to do with you?'

'I don't know,' Anne sighed, sitting on the sofa next to Samantha. 'All this stuff about going back in time . . . I can't believe that—'

'I'll prove it to you,' Samantha cut in. Leaping to her feet and switching the television on, Samantha found a news channel. 'Watch the news,' she said, moving to the door. 'You'll soon see that we're in two thousand and two. I'll go and make the tea.'

Leaving the room, Samantha went into the kitchen and filled the kettle. Wondering whether to return to the barn to try to discover the identity of the men, she realized that there'd be no point. Pondering on the kidnapping, the fact that the girl had never been found, she wondered whether it was down to her intervention. Anne had vanished, the men had never been caught . . . Eight

years was a long time, she reflected, wondering whether she could somehow make Anne appear older.

Recalling the events in the church as she waited for the kettle to boil, Samantha shook her head. She'd been only too willing, she reflected. And she'd fucked Chris in the woods and lied to Zak. Pouring the tea, she realized again that she had to accept that she hadn't been the sweet young girl she'd thought she was. A common slut? Or simply a girl experimenting with sex? Where was Chris now? She turned the questions over in her mind as she carried the tea into the lounge.

'I didn't put sugar in it,' she said, placing the cup on the table.

'Thanks,' Anne murmured abstractedly. 'I've been watching the news and . . . How the hell did I move forward eight years?'

'I don't know,' Samantha replied, gazing out of the window. 'I don't know how I'm able to go back in time, let alone bring you forward. The point is, what do we do now that you're here? I can't take you back to the barn.'

'How about taking me back to just before I was kidnapped?'

'I'm not sure, but I don't think that's possible. The newspapers, the TV news . . . Everything would have to change if you hadn't been kidnapped. You can't just appear out of thin air and go home. Apart from your age . . .'

'I know,' Anne sighed. 'I've been thinking about that. All I can do is . . . I don't know what I'm going to do.'

'Don't worry about it now. You can stay here for the time being. In a few days, we'll find you a job and a flat and—'

'I'm too young to get my own flat.'

'Anne, you're going to have to lie about your age. As for your identity, you'll need a National Insurance number and . . . I really don't know what to do.'

'How about a fake passport? And a birth certificate?'

'That's a thought. I'll make some enquiries. I don't think you should leave the flat. Someone might recognize you and . . . We'll change your hair and get you some new clothes. With make-up, I'm sure we can add a few years to your looks. Do you have brothers or sisters?'

'No, I'm an only child. How about telling people that I'm your sister?'

'That's a good idea. I'd be able to vouch for you and . . . I might even be able to get you a job at the newspaper. I'm a journalist, by the way. Anne, what we did in the barn . . .'

'I liked doing that to you,' the girl confessed sheepishly.

'Did you? Have you ever done that with another girl?'

'No, I haven't.'

'No boyfriends?'

'No. There is . . . there *was* one boy at school I liked. I suppose he's eight years older now.'

'You're very attractive, Anne. But you're also very young and I don't think we should . . .'

'I'm very hot,' Anne breathed, tossing the quilt aside and revealing her curvaceous young body as she reclined on the sofa. 'It must be summertime.'

'Yes, yes, it is,' Samantha replied, gazing longingly at the younger girl's full sex lips rising either side of her creamy-pink vulval crack. 'I'd better go and dry your clothes.'

'Sam, what I did to you in the barn . . . Do you want to do it to me?'

'I . . . I don't think we should,' Samantha breathed, her clitoris swelling between her fleshy love lips.

'Why not?'

'Because . . . When I was your age, I did things that I now regret. I've only just realized that . . . It doesn't matter what I've realized. The thing is that you're young, you're learning and . . .'

'If I'm learning, then you can help by teaching me.'

'Yes, but . . . It's not that simple, Anne. When you're older, you won't thank me for . . . If we were to . . .'

'What did you do when you were my age?'

'I fucked men. In fact, I allowed three men to fuck me on a church altar.'

'Three at once?' the girl gasped.

'I'm not proud of it, Anne. The point is—'

'Please,' Anne begged, her blue eyes wide. 'Please teach me.'

'All right,' Samantha finally conceded, settling on the floor between Anne's feet as her inner desires got the better of her.

Lying back and parting her thighs wide, the teenager closed her eyes as Samantha kissed the gentle rise of her mons. Breathing in her girl-scent, Samantha tentatively pushed her tongue out and licked the protective hood of Anne's inflating clitoris. Wondering whether the young girl masturbated, she tasted the pinken flesh of her sex crack, repeatedly sweeping her tongue around her stiffening pleasure button. Breathing heavily, Anne parted her thighs further, her slender fingers peeling her love lips open, exposing the intricate folds nestling within her sex valley to Samantha's inquisitive tongue.

Moving back, Samantha gazed at the girl's gaping sex hole, the intact membrane of her hymen. Should she tear

open Anne's curtain of innocence? She thought about this, licking the pink funnel of creamy-wet flesh surrounding the teenager's vaginal entrance. Pushing her tongue into the girl's sex hole, licking the creamy walls of her tight pussy, Samantha sucked out her lubricious juices of desire. Mouthing and sucking on the girl's inner lips, repeatedly driving her tongue into her wet hole, Samantha felt her own juices of lesbian lust seeping between her engorged vaginal labia and soaking into the tight material of her panties.

'That's nice,' Anne breathed, her naked body beginning to tremble. 'I like the feel of your tongue inside me.'

'You taste heavenly,' Samantha gasped, lapping up the girl's sex juices. 'Would you like to feel my fingers inside you?'

'Yes, yes, I would,' Anne groaned, her naked body squirming as her pleasure built.

Slipping a finger into the tight sheath of the little virgin's vagina, Samantha massaged her inner flesh. She was so tight, Samantha mused, the exquisite sheath of her sex-wet cunt lovingly hugging Samantha's massaging finger. Sucking on Anne's erect clitoris, her tongue snaking over the sensitive tip, Samantha drove a second finger deep into the young girl's vaginal duct. Watching her stomach rising and falling, Samantha knew that she was about to come as she pistoned her virginal sex sheath. Gasping, her naked body shaking uncontrollably, Anne arched her back and let out a rush of breath.

'Coming,' she cried, clutching Samantha's head and grinding her rubicund cunt-flesh hard against the older girl's mouth. Her orgasming juices spewing from her pistoned vagina, running in rivers of milk over Samantha's hand, she moaned as if in agony while her

orgasm peaked. Samantha was amazed by the girl's copious flow of sex juices. Streaming from her bloated sex sheath, her cunt-milk splattered the pale flesh of her inner thighs as her vaginal muscles spasmed. Slipping her fingers out of the wailing girl's pussy, Samantha drove her tongue into her drenched sex duct and licked the creamy walls of her contracting cunt.

Breathing heavily, Anne shuddered as Samantha's finger slipped between the firm cheeks of her rounded bottom and drove deep into her tight rectal sheath. Sucking hard, Samantha drew out the young girl's orgasmic milk, repeatedly swallowing the cream as she finger-fucked Anne's tight bottom. Anne cried out again, her young body squirming as her pleasure rocked her very soul. This was probably the most intense orgasm the girl had ever experienced, Samantha mused, driving a second finger into her tightening anal canal. Shaking violently, her whimpers of sexual pleasure resounding around the room, Anne lifted her legs and pressed her knees against the firm mounds of her young breasts to allow Samantha deeper penetration of her rectal duct. Losing control to her base desires, Samantha forced a third finger into Anne's spasming anal canal, stretching her tight brown hole open to the extreme as she finger-fucked her hot arse.

'No,' Anne breathed as Samantha tried to push her fourth finger past the taut tissue of her rectal ring. Ignoring the girl, Samantha managed to impale her on all four fingers as she sucked her pulsating clitoris into her wet mouth. 'God, my bum,' Anne gasped, her anal sphincter muscles gripping Samantha's thrusting fingers like a velvet-jawed vice. This was lesbian sex at its crudest, Samantha mused, deciding to tongue-fuck the

girl's rectum once she'd come down from her shuddering climax. Debased in the extreme, crude, vulgar . . .

Wondering what sort of person she'd become as she slipped her slimed fingers out of the girl's rectal sheath, Samantha knew that she couldn't help herself as she forced her young victim to roll over. Yanking the rounded cheeks of Anne's buttocks wide apart as she knelt on the floor and rested her head on the sofa cushion, Samantha gazed longingly at the tight brown entrance to her anal sheath. Gripping the girl's buttocks, her fingernails biting into the firm flesh of her young bottom, she repeatedly swept her tongue up Anne's anal valley. Tasting the brown tissue of the girl's rectal inlet, she pushed the tip of her tongue into her tight hole and savoured the bitter-sweet dankness of her tight arse.

'No,' Anne breathed again, obviously thinking the crude act was wrong. 'Sam, please . . . You shouldn't be . . .' Letting out a rush of breath as Samantha drove four fingers deep into the wet sheath of her tight cunt, Anne clung to the sofa cushion, whimpering in the new-found pleasure she was deriving from her abused rectum. Her tongue darting in and out of the girl's anus, Samantha locked her full lips to the sensitive brown tissue surrounding Anne's most private hole and sucked hard.

'Sam,' Anne murmured. 'Sam, this is . . . this is obscene. You can't be enjoying it.' Still sucking hard, Samantha ignored Anne's remark. This *was* obscene, she knew as the crude act sent quivers through her contracting womb. Tasting the girl's rectal tube, breathing in the intoxicating perfume of her gaping anal gully, she continued to massage her inner vaginal flesh. Lost in her sexual delirium, Samantha fervently mouthed and sucked Anne's anal hole, delighting in the bitter-sweet taste of her inner core.

Abandoning her protests, Anne writhed and breathed heavily as her lesbian lover tongue-fucked her rectum. Her young body quivering, her juices of lust streaming down Samantha's thrusting fingers, she buried her face in the sofa cushion as her incredible pleasure rocketed. Sinking her teeth into the brown flesh of Anne's anal portal, Samantha forced half her fist into her once-virginal cunt. Yelping, Anne could do nothing to halt the crude abuse of her tight sex holes as Samantha bit harder into her brown ring.

'Sam,' the girl breathed, her young body wriggling. 'Sam, that hurts.' After biting even harder on her anus, Samantha finally parted her teeth and again sucked hard. 'You *can't* be enjoying this,' Anne repeated, gasping as Samantha's tongue drove deep into her tight anal duct. Licking the dank walls of her rectum, Samantha pressed her wet lips harder against Anne's anal ring and forced her tongue deeper into her rectal canal. Deciding to force Anne to reciprocate, to push her tongue into Samantha's bottom-hole, Samantha finally moved back and licked her rectum-slimed lips. Again pressing her mouth hard against the girl's anus, she slipped her tongue into her secret hole. She couldn't get enough she knew as she mouthed and sucked, her tongue repeatedly darting into Anne's rectal core. Massaging her inner vaginal flesh with her fingers, Samantha finally moved back and tugged her panties down.

'Lick me,' she breathed, kneeling on the floor and resting her head on the sofa cushion. Her short skirt pulled up over her back, she yanked the firm orbs of her bottom wide apart. 'Lick me there,' she again ordered the girl.

'Sam, I—'

'Just do it, Anne. You'll love it, I know.'

'It's not right to do this,' the girl protested weakly, moving behind Samantha and kissing each rounded buttock in turn.

'Right or wrong, it doesn't matter. Try it, Anne. You won't know whether or not you like it until you try.'

Feeling the girl's wet tongue tentatively licking the brown tissue surrounding her tight bottom-hole, Samantha let out a rush of breath. Wondering what Anne was thinking, whether or not she was enjoying the experience, Samantha yanked her naked buttocks further apart. Her anal hole gaping wide open, she shuddered as the teenager's tongue entered her rectal tube. Anne's wet lips pressed hard against Samantha's anal ring as she pushed her tongue deeper into her hot duct and licked the dank walls of her rectum.

'God, you taste beautiful,' Anne breathed, slipping her tongue out of Samantha's rectal hole and licking her gaping anus. 'I'd never have thought that I'd love doing this. Especially to another girl. Sam, why have you shaved?'

'I prefer to be that way. Why don't you try it?'

'Yes, yes – I might do that.'

'I want you to suck hard,' Samantha breathed, her slender fingers holding her tight bottom-hole wide open. 'Suck hard on my bumhole.'

Complying with her mistress's crude wish, the girl locked her lips to Samantha's anal portal and sucked as hard as she could. Samantha could feel the vacuum building within her rectal tube, the sensations driving her wild as she shuddered in her lesbian ecstasy. Her eyes closed, her face buried in the sofa cushion, Samantha parted her knees further and jutted her buttocks out to

allow Anne deeper penetration of her rectum. Breathing heavily as her teenage lover repeatedly drove her tongue into her gaping bottom-hole, Samantha again wondered what to do about Anne as she drifted in her sexual ecstasy.

The girl would make a perfect live-in lesbian lover, she reflected. Housekeeper, sex-slave . . . Anne was ideal. But was that what Samantha really wanted? Unsure of her sexual feelings as she thought about sucking sperm from an orgasming knob, she knew that Anne couldn't satisfy her every sexual need. Although Samantha's lesbian desires were becoming increasingly powerful, she knew that she'd also need a penis to drive deep into her cock-hungry pussy.

Letting out a sigh of pleasure as she felt the girl's finger enter her rectal duct, Samantha began quivering uncontrollably. Her inner rectal flesh massaged, the sleeping nerve endings there stirring, she shuddered as Anne's teeth sank into the rounded cheek of her firm buttocks. The girl was learning fast, she mused as a second finger forced its way deep into her arse. Or was she? Samantha's curiosity mounted as Anne's fingers slipped out of her arse, leaving her anal sphincter muscles twitching expectantly.

'What are you doing?' she asked, hearing Anne moving about behind her.

'You'll see,' Anne giggled. 'Be patient, and you'll find out.'

Waiting in expectation, Samantha jolted as she felt something hard and cold press against the delicate tissue of her anal ring. Anne had obviously found something to use as a dildo, she mused, her anus dilating as the object began to drive deep into the tight tube of her spasming

rectum. Trying to guess what the object was, Samantha let out a gasp as her anal canal stretched wide open to accommodate the phallus. Guessing that it must have been the candle from the mantelpiece, she grinned. Anne was certainly imaginative, Samantha thought as the waxen shaft glided slowly into the hot depths of her bowels.

'Is that nice?' the girl asked, twisting the candle.

'God, yes,' Samantha breathed, holding her naked buttocks wide apart. 'Are you sure you're not experienced?'

'Well, a girl at school . . .'

'I thought so,' Samantha giggled. 'OK, tell me what happened.'

'My parents were out and I was trying on some new clothes. My friend was helping me, telling me what she thought about a skirt and blouse my mum had bought me. I was wearing my panties and bra, about to try a dress on, when she suggested that I take my bra off. I didn't want to at first but she said that I'd look better in the dress without a bra. Anyway, I took it off and . . . She gave me a strange look. Her eyes were glazed. She stared at my nipples and then reached out and squeezed my breast. It went from there.'

'Tell me more,' Samantha murmured, her eyes rolling as Anne pistoned her anal canal with the candle.

'I ended up taking my panties off and lying on the bed. She sat beside me and . . . and rubbed my clitoris. She made me come.'

'Was that your first orgasm?'

'Yes, yes, it was.'

Picturing two young girls playing around on a bed, one masturbating the other to orgasm, Samantha realized that the notion was turning her on as never before.

Had they licked each other's pussies? she wondered, her juices of arousal streaming down her inner thighs as Anne arse-fucked her with the wax dildo. Had they tasted each other's sex juices? The candle finally sliding out of her rectal duct, Samantha shuddered as the girl's tongue entered her inflamed hole. The feel of Anne's saliva running down to her swollen vaginal lips sending delightful quivers through her contracting womb, she wondered what Anne was up to as the teenager leaped to her feet and left the room.

'You'll like this,' Anne chuckled, returning and settling on the floor behind Samantha. Saying nothing, Samantha waited expectantly as she felt something extremely cold pressing against her burning anal ring.

'What is it?' she finally asked, a cooling sensation permeating the sheath of her rectum.

'Wine,' Anne giggled. 'I'm filling your bottom with wine. I'll drink it out of you when you're full up.'

Unable to believe the girl's ingenuity, Samantha gasped as her bowels flooded with cold wine. She could hear the bottle emptying as her pelvis quivered and her young womb rhythmically contracted. Was this what Anne had done with her young schoolfriend? The bottle drained, Anne pressed her warm lips to Samantha's anus and sucked hard. This was incredibly arousing, Samantha thought, listening to the teenager sucking and gulping down the wine. Deciding to reciprocate once Anne had drained her bowels, she imagined drinking wine from the girl's anus.

'This is going to my head,' Anne giggled, slurping and sucking on Samantha's sensitive anus.

'I've another bottle in the fridge,' Samantha said, squeezing her muscles and squirting wine into Anne's

mouth. 'I'll drink it from your bottom when you've finished drinking from mine.'

Shuddering as her clitoris pulsated expectantly, Samantha knew that she needed the relief of orgasm. A young teenage girl drinking from her rectal tube was the most incredible experience imaginable, she mused, her inner thighs sticky with wine and girl-juice. The girl was going to end up drunk, she reflected, listening to the sucking and gulping between her firm buttocks. Not only on alcohol, but drunk with sex. Feeling incredibly wicked as her bowels drained, Samantha turned and faced Anne. Images of her young body bound with rope flooding her mind, she ordered her to wait while she went to get something.

Leaving the room, wine oozing from the inflamed eye of her bottom-hole, Samantha grabbed two leather belts from her bedroom. Returning to the lounge, she grinned as Anne gazed at the belts with a puzzled look in her eyes. Ordering her to lie on her back, Samantha knelt beside her and fixed each end of one belt to her ankles. Taking the centre of the belt and lifting her legs up, she hooked it around the back of Anne's head.

'There,' she said, gazing at the gaping valley of her young victim's vulva.

'It's uncomfortable,' Anne complained, her knees pressing hard against the small mounds of her firm breasts.

'You'll soon get used to it,' Samantha said, running her fingertip over the exposed brown tissue of her anus. 'I can get to both your holes now,' she giggled.

'Sam, the belt is hurting the back of my neck. Do I have to—'

'Yes, you do.' Samantha interrupted the girl. 'I want your holes fully exposed so that I can . . . You'll see what I'm going to do.'

Lying on her stomach, Samantha ran her tongue over the girl's anus and up along the creamy valley of her vagina to her ripening clitoris. The different taste driving her wild as her tongue repeatedly swept over her bottom-hole and her vaginal entrance, she grabbed the candle from the floor and drove it deep into Anne's young cunt. Quivering, Anne let out a gasp and Samantha stirred her vaginal cream with the candle before withdrawing the waxen phallus and pressing the dripping end hard against the teenager's anal eye. Driving the shaft deep into her bowels, Samantha forced three fingers into the tight sheath of the girl's vagina. Squirming and gasping, Anne grimaced as Samantha twisted and bent her fingers, tearing down what was left of Anne's hymen as she pistoned her hot arse with the candle.

'Like it?' Samantha asked, massaging the exposed nub of the girl's sensitive clitoris with her free hand.

'God, yes,' Anne breathed, her bound body shaking wildly.

'I'll give you a good spanking in a minute. You'll enjoy that.'

Using and abusing the girl was sending Samantha's libido sky-high, inducing her cunt-milk to flow between the hairless lips of her vagina. But she knew that she was going to have to solve the problem of Anne's future before long. Eight years ahead of her time, unable to return to her parents' home, no money or place to live . . . This was a major problem, Samantha knew. Listening to the girl's gasps of sexual pleasure, she decided to talk to her parents at some stage. If she said that Anne had lost her memory . . . The idea was bound to work, she mused. Amnesia would solve all the problems.

'I'm . . . I'm coming,' Anne whimpered, her nostrils

flaring, the smooth plateau of her stomach rising and falling jerkily. Shaking violently, she let out a scream of immense pleasure as her solid clitoris erupted in orgasm beneath Samantha's massaging fingertip. The girl convulsed fiercely and Samantha thought that she was having some kind of fit as she screamed out again. Her juices of lust gushing from the gaping entrance of her sex sheath as Samantha repeatedly rammed the candle deep into the duct of her rectum, Anne involuntarily let out a trickle of golden liquid between her splayed vaginal lips.

'*That* deserves a spanking,' Samantha said, leaving the candle embedded deep within the teenager's anal canal and grabbing the spare leather belt. Raising it, she brought it down across the girl's pouting vaginal lips with a loud crack. Screaming, Anne convulsed wildly again as the belt strapped the sensitive flesh of her outer labia. Her golden liquid now gushing from her urethral opening, the candle shooting out of the barrel of her rectum like a bullet, she begged for mercy as Samantha changed her target and brought the belt down across the rounded cheeks of Anne's naked buttocks with a deafening crack.

'Please, no,' the girl cried, the belt alternately striking her protruding inner labia and her quivering arse-globes. Her naked buttocks turning a fire-red, her vaginal cream blending with her urine and coursing down between the firm cheeks of her bottom, she screamed out again as the leather belt briefly lashed the backs of her slender thighs. Her whimpered protests only serving to drive Samantha on, the girl struggled against her bonds, desperately trying to unhook the first belt from behind her head. Her knees pressed hard against the petite mounds of her newly-developed breasts, her feet virtually either side of her head, there was no way Anne could escape the degrading bondage.

Again and again the leather belt lashed the crimsoned flesh of her pouting vulval lips, the cracking sound reverberating around the room as Samantha giggled wickedly. As if possessed, Samantha lashed the girl's naked buttocks and vulval flesh as hard as she could. Her arm beginning to ache, she continued the gruelling thrashing until she was forced to drop the belt to the floor. Anne whimpered and sobbed as Samantha gazed at her handiwork. The girl's pouting love lips glowing scarlet, her buttocks crimsoned . . .

'Where the hell could they have gone?' the younger man asked as Samantha found herself back in the barn.

'Fuck knows,' the middle-aged man replied, leaving the small room as Samantha ducked behind several bales of straw. 'That older woman . . . she must have led the girl somewhere. How the fuck they got past us, I don't know.'

'Neither do I. But I *do* know that this place will be crawling with cops before long. We'd better get out of here.'

'OK. We'd better clear up. Get rid of all evidence of the girl being here.'

Leaving the barn as the men returned to the small room, Samantha surveyed the surrounding countryside. A village lay at the other side of a field and, judging by the sound of heavy traffic, a main road wasn't too far away. Noticing a car parked by the side of the barn, she went to investigate. On the front seat, she found several letters addressed to a Mr Robertson. Grinning, she made a note of the address and slipped behind some bushes as she heard voices.

'I just don't understand it,' the older man complained.

'There was no way they could have left without us seeing them.'

'But we didn't see them, did we? We should never have—'

'What's done is done. Let's go to the Duck and have a beer. I think we both need a drink.'

Watching as the two men climbed into the car and drove off, Samantha emerged from the bushes and wandered across the field towards the village. Her intervention *had* changed history she knew as she approached a row of cottages. The girl was never found, the men never caught . . . and Anne's parents had obviously thought the worst. Eight years on and the dust had settled, they'd probably accepted the situation . . . But that still left the problem of what to do with the girl.

Deciding that there was no point in wandering around the village, Samantha decided to return to her own time. She now knew the identity of one of the men and . . .

Finding herself standing in her lounge, Samantha gazed at Anne's naked body, her scarlet vulval flesh. She'd treated the girl no better than the men would have done, she reflected. Complaining about her neck aching, Anne announced that she was going to thrash Samantha's buttocks the minute she was free.

'It's only fair,' she said, her blue eyes focusing on Samantha.

'Maybe,' Samantha replied, grinning as she was about to release her victim.

'You thrashed me with the belt, so I'll thrash you and—'

'Anne, we're going to have to think of something to do with you. You can stay here for the time being but—'

'Take this belt off me and we'll talk about it,' the girl cut in.

'You look great with your feet either side of your head,' Samantha breathed, her arousal rising as she gazed longingly at Anne's swollen cunt lips. 'In fact, you look most appealing with your little pussy gaping open. Would you like me to shave you?'

'Yes, but take the belt off first.'

Slipping into the bathroom and grabbing a razor, Samantha took the can of shaving foam from the shelf and returned to the lounge. Again asking to be released, Anne pulled against her bonds as Samantha settled on the floor and massaged the foam into the swell of the teenager's pouting vulval lips. Saying nothing as the girl continued to protest, Samantha had no intention of releasing her. Dragging the razor over the rise of Anne's mons, leaving smooth, hairless flesh in its wake, Samantha thought that this might be her last opportunity to enjoy the young girl's naked body. The girl might decide to leave, perhaps go to her parents' house, and Samantha would never see her again. Unless she enjoyed her young body now . . .

'Take this belt *off*,' Anne snapped as Samantha dragged the razor over the swell of her vulval lips. Ignoring her, Samantha worked the razor over her vulval flesh, stripping years from her as her blonde pubes fell away. The job of depilation finally complete, she grabbed a wet flannel from the bathroom and wiped away the foam and shaved-off golden curls. Admiring her handiwork, Samantha focused on the girl's erect clitoris protruding alluringly from beneath its pinken hood. She looked so young without her pubic fleece, she thought. Leaning forward, she licked the full length of

Anne's vaginal slit, lapping up the flowing sex-cream as the girl quivered and gasped in her sexual ecstasy.

A chill running up Samantha's spine, as if someone had just walked over her grave, she looked around the room. Feeling as if someone was watching her, spying on her, she sat back on her heels as she thought that she heard a distant voice calling her. It sounded like a girl crying, calling for help . . . Releasing Anne, she told the girl that she had to go out for a while.

'Where to?' Anne asked, clambering to her feet and rubbing her aching neck.

'I have to go and see someone,' Samantha replied, hearing a distant voice again.

'You suddenly have to go out?' the girl asked, frowning in puzzlement.

'I . . . I'd forgotten that I'd arranged to meet someone. It won't take long. Stay in the flat while I'm out, OK?'

'OK,' Anne replied. 'I'll dry my clothes and make something to eat.'

'Yes, yes, you do that. I'll see you later.'

Leaving the flat, Samantha knew that someone wanted her, needed her. But who? Feeling that she should head for the woods behind the village church at home, she walked briskly down the street to the railway station. The journey to her home village would only take half an hour she knew as she bought a ticket and waited on the platform for the train. Someone, or something, needed her to go to the woods. She had no idea what she was going to find there. Perhaps she was mistaken, she pondered. But the feeling grew stronger as the train pulled into the station and she knew that this was no mistake.

7

Standing beneath the trees, Samantha looked around her. Memories flooding back, she thought about Chris, the time they'd made love on the soft grass. She remembered playing in the woods after school, meeting friends there and . . . But what was she doing there now? Samantha became lost in thought, tramping along a path that took her deeper into the woods. Had she really been called by someone? Perhaps her imagination had played tricks on her.

'Hi, Sam,' a male voice called from behind.

'Oh,' she gasped, spinning round on her heels and staring at a grey-haired man.

'Don't you recognize me?' he asked. 'I recognized you the minute I saw you walking past the church.'

'No, I'm sorry,' she replied, sure that she knew him from somewhere.

'I know that it's been a long time, but . . . God, it must be ten years. You've aged well.'

'Aged?' she echoed, puzzlement reflected in her blue eyes.

'You're the same age as me,' he said, smiling at her. 'I'm fifty-five this year.'

'God,' Samantha breathed, looking down at the wrinkled skin on the backs of her hands. 'Fifty-five? I've gone forward,' she murmured, feeling her face.

'Gone forward? What do you mean?'

'Sorry, I . . . I was thinking aloud. Yes, of course I recognize you.'

There was an air of sadness about him, Samantha reflected. Almost desolation. She thought that he'd probably been deeply hurt, no doubt by a woman. She felt that he needed love, and was tempted to reach out and take him in her arms. But she had no idea who he was. Had she been called to the woods to meet him? she wondered. If so, then why? He was well dressed, she observed. His white shirt was crisp and clean, his trousers pressed. Someone must have been looking after him, although she instinctively knew that he was alone in the world.

'So, how are you?' she asked him, hoping for a clue to his identity.

'The same as I've always been since we split up. Very sad, still very much in love with you . . .'

'Split up? Oh, yes, of course.'

'Are you still with Sarah?'

'Sarah?'

'Your sister.'

'Oh. Er . . . yes, yes, I am.'

'It's funny when I think back. I was all for your sister moving in with us. It seemed like such a good idea at the time. Little did I know that you'd end up . . . Well, that's history.'

'What happened?'

'You know what happened, Sam. I discovered that you were sleeping with your sister. And had been since before we were married.'

'Married?'

'Are you all right? You don't seem to recall anything about us. Ten years isn't *that* long.'

'No, no . . . I'm fine. I've been having a few problems recently, that's all.'

'It's great to see you, Sam. I don't think a day goes by without my thinking about you. I remember when we first got together. We bumped into each other in that dreadful pub,' he laughed. 'Do you remember that awful barmaid?'

'Yes, I remember,' Sam lied, still trying to recall who he was.

'To think that we were in our early thirties back then. Why did you give up the dancing school?'

'Well, I thought . . .'

'The day I asked you to marry me, you gave it up. You never did tell me why.'

'Oh, I don't know. I suppose I wanted to move on.'

'I would have had no trouble competing with the dancing school, Sam. I know that it took up a great deal of your time but . . . You loved it. It was your life, and I would have accepted that. But I could never compete with Sarah. Anyway, you're no longer Mrs Rogers, so it doesn't matter.'

'Rogers? Oh, er . . . no, no I'm not.'

'I fell in love with you when I first set eyes on you in the office. They used to call me *John the Prat* at the newspaper, do you remember? Dave always called me *John the Prat*. Shall we sit on that log over there?'

Following him, Samantha couldn't believe that she'd ended up marrying John. Sitting beside him on the log, she thought how good-looking he was. He seemed so kind, softly spoken, gentle . . . Perhaps he wasn't such a prat after all, she reflected. Perhaps *she*'d been the prat. So the dancing-school idea had worked, she mused. She'd stayed with Anne, obviously told people that

the girl's name was Sarah and that she was her sister and
. . . Wondering why she'd been attracted to the woods,
why she'd gone forward in time, she thought that it
might be to show her the mistakes she'd made. If she
could change the way things had turned out . . . She'd
obviously fallen in love with John. She'd married him
and—

'I saw Barry the other day,' John said. 'I'd like to see
more of him but, as he's living up north, it's not easy.
He's just like his mother.'

'Is he?' she asked, wondering who Barry was.

'He's the image of you, Sam. Both our sons are the
image of you. Anyway, Barry's doing well on the newspaper and young Greg seems happy at university.'

'Greg, yes,' Samantha murmured.

'I'm hoping that they'll contact you soon. I've done my
best to explain that it wasn't your fault, that the end of
our marriage . . . They're pretty headstrong, I'm afraid.'

'John, if things had been different . . .'

'If I could turn back time . . . I'm still in love with you,
Sam. I always will be.'

'John . . . I don't think I want to know any more about
the future.'

'The future? What do you mean?'

'I meant . . . I'm sorry, but I've had a lot on my mind
recently.'

'People used to think that I'd married you for your
money. Some even said as much. Just because you owned
the mansion . . . Are you still living there?'

'Er, yes, I am,' she sighed, realizing that she must have
earned a fortune from the dancing school.

'I married you because I loved you, Sam. I would have
married you if you'd been penniless. Still, there we are.

Do you ever hear from Gerry? Since he went to Australia . . .'

'No, I don't. We lost touch long ago.'

'Oh, right. I suppose he's still with Kitty. I didn't know them well but, on the odd occasion I met them, I thought that they were made for each other. They were both potty,' he laughed. 'Well suited.'

'What are you doing here?' she asked. 'In the village, I mean.'

'I saw no reason to leave the village. When we moved here, I fell in love with the place. And when you left to live in the mansion with Sarah . . . The village is home to me, Sam. It always was and always will be.'

'I'd better be going,' Samantha sighed.

'Shall we . . . Sam, how about us meeting again?'

'John, I . . .'

'It's all right. I'm sorry, I should never have asked you. You were my first love. I was a late starter,' he said, forcing a laugh. 'But you were my first and only love. Just seeing you here . . . At least I now have a fresh picture of you in my mind. You're as beautiful as ever, Sam. As beautiful as the day I started at the paper and first laid eyes on you.'

'You could have done better, John. I was never any good for you.'

'Don't say that, Sam. Whatever your feelings were for Sarah . . . You had to go with your feelings, I understand that. I've explained that to the boys.'

'I was no good, John. Someone like you deserves far better than the likes of me.'

'You were my life, Sam. You still are. What's that song? "If I could turn back the hands of time . . ."'

'It might not come to this, John.'

'Come to what?'

'I have to go now. I'll see you . . . I'll see you again. And, this time, I'll get it right.'

Walking away, tears flooding down her cheeks, Samantha ran back along the lane to the railway station. She was going to fuck her life up, she mused as the train pulled in. Two sons? She thought about that. Two sons who were obviously not speaking to her. And for good reason. But she might have the chance to change things. Anne was going to be the problem, she thought, stepping onto the train and finding an empty seat. The dancing-school scam was going to be successful, she'd buy the mansion . . . Anne had to be out of her life before she married John.

Reaching home, she found Anne watching television in the lounge. The girl looked so young, so innocent, she thought, eyeing her naked thighs emerging alluringly from beneath her short skirt. Samantha had about ten years before John came into her life. Nothing was going to change during that time, she was sure. The dancing school, the mansion, living with Anne . . . But the day John asked her to marry him, she'd not only close the dancing school but get Anne out of her life.

'You were away a long time,' Anne said, looking up from the sofa.

'Sorry, I was held up. Anne . . . God, I don't know where to begin. When I get married—'

'You're getting married?' the teenager trilled excitedly.

'No . . . I mean, yes, eventually. Not for about ten years.'

'Sam, what are you on about? Who is this man? That's a hell of a long time to wait.'

'You won't understand this now, but . . . In ten years, you'll understand. When I tell you that I'm getting married, you must get out of my life.'

'In ten years' time?'

'Yes.'

'OK, whatever you say. Shall we go out to eat? I'm starving.'

'Anne, I want you to understand that . . . Oh, never mind. Make something to eat if you're hungry. I'm tired. I'm going to have a lie-down for a while and then we'll talk about the future.'

'OK,' the girl sighed.

In her bedroom, Samantha locked the door and lay down on top of her quilt. She wasn't tired. She wanted to return to the mansion to discover exactly what Gerry and Kitty were up to. If she was going to own the dancing school, and the mansion, she needed a clue about how she'd end up in that situation. Where would her dancing school be located? In the mansion? Closing her eyes, she concentrated on the mansion, the 'doctor's surgery'. No one would see or hear her she knew as she felt herself drifting through time. She'd hover and listen, listen and learn . . .

'What the hell are you doing here?' Kitty asked, staring hard at Samantha.

'Oh, I . . .' Samantha stammered, wondering why the woman could see her.

'Making out that you wanted me to supply you with young girls, stealing Jane's diary . . .'

'How do you know that?' Samantha asked, wondering whether she'd travelled forward in time again.

'I don't like your prying. I don't know who you are or

what you want, but . . . Carl,' she called. 'Come here.'

'Yes, ma'am,' a young man said, entering the surgery.

'This young lady requires a doctor, Carl. Put her on the couch and give her a damned good examination.'

'Certainly, ma'am.'

As the man lifted her off her feet and laid her on the examination couch, Samantha knew that she was in serious trouble. Concentrating on her lounge as the man tore her blouse from her trembling body, she tried to return to her own time to save herself. Again concentrating as her bra was ripped from the firm spheres of her young breasts and her hands were cuffed behind her head, she realized that she couldn't return. Her skirt and panties torn from her trembling body, her feet forced wide apart, her ankles cuffed, she lay naked on the couch awaiting her fate as Kitty towered over her.

'The breast rings,' Kitty ordered the young man. 'Start with the breast rings.' Samantha watched with bated breath as he took two steel rings with screw attachments from a shelf and placed them over the globes of her firm breasts. Tightening the screws, the rings closing, she watched her mammary spheres inflate. Her nipples standing painfully proud from her darkening areolae, she grimaced as the rings tightened further. The pale flesh of her breasts turning blue as Carl continued to turn the screws, she cried out and begged for mercy.

'And now the nipple clamps,' Kitty chuckled, ignoring Samantha's pleas as she gazed at her ballooning breasts. Pulling two thin chains down from the ceiling, Carl placed the metal clips attached to the ends over her erect nipples and moved to the wall. Turning a handle, he chuckled as the chains tightened, the metal clips pulling

on her brown milk-teats. The pain permeating her mammary globes, Samantha gasped as her nipples stretched into long protrusions of brown flesh. She couldn't take this she knew as the woman ordered Carl to take a vaginal speculum from the instrument trolley.

'Please, no,' she breathed as her vaginal lips were painfully yanked wide open.

'You came here to nose around,' Kitty said accusingly. 'You came here to pry. And, now that you're here, you're going to find out exactly what we do.'

'I wasn't nosing around,' Samantha whimpered. 'I came here to see—'

'Jenny is our mistress of correction,' the woman cut in. 'I'm sure that she'll be only too pleased to deal with you. Insert the speculum, Carl,' she ordered the young man as she walked to the door. 'I'll bring Jenny in.'

Samantha had already witnessed Jenny at work, and she wasn't relishing being on the receiving end of the sadistic woman's cruel attention. The breast rings and nipple clamps were nothing in comparison to what Jenny was going to do to her tethered body she knew as she felt the cold steel speculum slip deep into the wet sheath of her tightening vagina. As the man squeezed the levers together, stretching her vaginal duct wide open, she tried not to cry out. At least she knew now what the future held, she reflected. But when was the dancing school going to be hers? And when would she buy the mansion? What did the next ten years hold?

'Ah, we have a specimen,' Jenny chuckled as she walked into the room and stood by the examination couch. 'A very nice specimen, too.'

'Do your stuff,' Kitty said, standing in the doorway. 'Carl, you come with me.'

'I'll do my stuff, all right,' Jenny laughed as Carl left the room and closed the door. 'So, where shall I begin?'

'Please . . .' Samantha breathed.

'Please, what? Please torture your pretty little cunt? I don't know who you are or what you're doing here. And I don't really care. I don't know why Kitty wants me to . . . All I know is that you have a beautiful young body.'

'I came here to ask whether I could work for Kitty,' Samantha said, futilely hoping to be released.

'Work for Kitty?' the girl laughed. 'You're far too old to work for Kitty. Her girls are young, very young. But your arrival is most convenient. We have some new apparatus to try out. Kitty was saying only this morning that we need someone to test the new equipment on.'

Taking a thin rubber pipe from below the examination couch, Jenny placed the open end over the exposed protrusion of Samantha's sensitive clitoris and flicked a switch below the couch. Samantha could feel the suction building, her clitoris swelling, as a soft buzzing sound emanated from beneath her. Her clitoris becoming painfully hard as the suction increased, she let out a rush of breath. Jenny chuckled as her young victim arched her back and grimaced. The sadist had only just begun Samantha knew as her clitoris swelled to an incredible size.

'And now for the anal pump,' Jenny murmured, taking something from the trolley. The firm orbs of her buttocks yanked wide apart by the girl's slender fingers, Samantha felt something long and thin slip into her rectum. She dreaded to think what the device was, what horrendous act Jenny was going to commit on her naked body. Her nipples painfully stretched, her clitoris solid as the vacuum continued to build, she gasped as her bowels suddenly flooded with cold liquid.

'There will be around eight men,' Jenny announced, turning the handle on the wall and watching Samantha's already painfully stretched nipples pull still further away from her ballooning breasts. 'They'll all want to fuck your sweet little bottom-hole. That's why I'm washing you out. And, before the men take their pleasure, I'd like to test a new machine. Basically, it's a huge dildo on the end of a piston. The motorized machine thrusts the dildo in and out . . . Once your tight little arse is cleaned out, I'll give you a demo.'

Her eyes closed, Samantha breathed unsteadily as her clitoris began to pulsate. The vacuum rapidly rising and falling, her clitoris throbbing, she prayed that she wouldn't come as her vaginal muscles rhythmically contracted around the steel speculum. She didn't want to give Jenny the pleasure of watching her shudder in orgasm and derive sexual gratification from the vacuum hose. She knew that she had to endure the incredible blend of pain and pleasure and . . . Watching the girl drag a machine across the surgery, she gazed in awe at the huge rubber dildo fixed to the end of a metal rod.

'God, no,' she murmured.

'This is the fucking machine,' Jenny enlightened her proudly. 'It fucks young girls.'

'One day, I'll own this place,' Samantha breathed. 'And when I do, you're going to—'

'Own this place?' the girl laughed. 'Don't talk crap. Anyway, we're not here to have a chat. We're here to test out various devices on your beautiful young body. I design most of the equipment myself and a friend of mine constructs it from my plans. Once I've got the fucking machine operating, I'll show you my latest creation.'

Sliding the speculum out of Samantha's inflamed vaginal sheath, Jenny positioned the machine at the end of the couch and drove the rubber dildo deep into the abused duct of Samantha's wet pussy. Samantha grimaced, her eyes squeezed shut as she waited anxiously for the machine to start up. Again wondering why she couldn't return to her own time, she gasped as the machine whirred and the rubber dildo moved in and out of her contracting vagina. Listening to the squelching sounds of her sex juices as the dildo gathered speed and rocked her naked body, she actually found the experience rather pleasant.

Her bowels still flooding with the cooling liquid, Samantha listened to the splashing sound on the floor as she lifted her head and gazed at her painfully stretched nipples. This was abuse beyond belief, she mused as the machine speeded up, the dildo repeatedly ramming into her tightening vaginal tube. Watching Jenny hovering by the instrument trolley, she wondered what horrendous device she was going to force her to endure next. Taking something from the trolley, the blonde girl stood beside Samantha and removed the nipple clamps. Tightening the breast rings, she watched Samantha's sore nipples balloon. Giggling, she leaned over and sucked her victim's milk-teats into her wet mouth.

'I think they're ready,' Jenny said, standing upright. 'These little things slip over your nipples, like this,' she said, placing two clear plastic cups over Samantha's areolae. 'These two hoses fix onto the cups, like this, and then the suction builds.' Grimacing, Samantha lifted her head and watched her nipples inflate to an incredible size within the cups. 'Nipple vacuum pumping is a speciality of mine,' Jenny announced. 'I prefer younger

girls as their breasts are rock-hard, their nipples unripe.
It's amazing how they expand to three or four times their
normal size. And they stay that way.'

Her nipples continuing to inflate, Samantha bit her lip
as she watched the delicate brown tissue of her areolae
expanding at the tips of her already ballooning mammary
spheres. This was sexual torture, she thought fearfully,
dreading to think what the other girl was up to as she
fiddled with the instruments on the trolley. Switching
the machine off, the dildo coming to rest deep within the
inflamed duct of Samantha's vagina, Jenny fixed something to her young victim's fleshy outer lips.

'This is my pussy-lip stretcher,' she giggled, taking the
chains hanging from the ceiling and fixing the ends to what
Samantha thought were metal clamps. 'I think your arse
is clean now,' she said, slipping the long object out of
Samantha's cold rectal duct. 'Nice and clean and ready to
be pumped full of spunk.' Pushing the machine away, the
rubber dildo sliding out of Samantha's tight vagina, she
turned as Kitty entered the room. The men were ready, the
woman announced. Samantha feared the worst as Jenny
removed the vaginal lip clamps and asked for the clients to
be sent in. Removing the plastic cups from Samantha's
inflamed nipples, she left the steel rings in place and sighed.

'I'll have to try my toys out later,' she said. 'The men
will want to get at all your tight holes, so . . . Ah, here
they are.'

'There are only six,' Kitty said, leading the naked men
into the room.

'That'll do,' Jenny replied. 'I'm sure six cocks will be
more than enough for this little tart.'

'I'll leave you all to enjoy yourselves,' Kitty said,
closing the door as she left the room.

'Right,' Jenny breathed. 'She's all yours. Do whatever you wish to the little cow.'

Mumbling to each other, the naked men surrounded the examination couch as Samantha gazed in awe at the erect shafts of their huge cocks. Her naked body completely defenceless, she watched as one man stood behind the couch and lowered the padded headrest. Her head dropping back, she gazed at the view of his upside-down penis as he offered the swollen knob of his cock to her pursed lips. Taking him into her pretty mouth, she sucked on his bulbous glans as he gasped in his male pleasure. Rocking his hips, he repeatedly drove his solid glans to the back of her throat, fucking her wet mouth as another man clambered onto the couch and drove the shaft of his huge cock deep into the inflamed sheath of her tight cunt.

This was the beginning of a long session of crude sex Samantha knew as the sore nipples of her ballooning breasts were sucked into two hot mouths. The steel rings gripping the base of her breasts, her mammary spheres painfully inflated, she jolted as a finger slipped between the rounded cheeks of her pert buttocks and drove deep into the cleansed shaft of her rectum. Alleviating her fears by concentrating on the idea that one day she would own the corrupt business and the mansion, she knew that she wouldn't come to any harm. But she was desperate to know exactly *how* she'd take over the dancing school and earn enough cash to buy the mansion.

'She's got a tight little cunt,' the man driving his solid penis into her moistening vagina gasped. Samantha gobbled and sucked on the bulbous glans bloating her hot mouth as she pondered on the future. In a way, she wished that she'd not discovered her fate. It was nice to

know that she was going to be rolling in money, living in a huge mansion, but she wanted a few surprises in her life. There again, she knew that the next ten years probably held many surprises.

Her gobbling mouth flooding with sperm, she did her best to swallow the creamy fluid. The man rocking his hips, repeatedly driving his orgasming knob to the back of her throat as he mouth-fucked her, she felt the contracting sheath of her vagina filling with the product of male orgasm. Her young body jolting with the double-ended fucking, teeth sinking into the brown teats of her sore nipples, her rectal canal massaged by intruding fingers, she knew that she'd reached the pinnacle of sexual debauchery. There was nothing more debased anyone could do to her naked body, was there?

Listening to the men's gasped comments, Samantha tried again to return to her own time, to the comfort of her lounge. Hoping that she wasn't stuck in the future, she closed her eyes and concentrated hard. Nothing changed. Her mouth still flooding with sperm, her spasming vagina squelching with the crude fucking, she couldn't understand why she'd lost the ability to travel through time. Perhaps, she thought, she had to experience the debauchery. For whatever reason, she might have to endure the gruelling sexual abuse of her young body by six men. About to concentrate on her lounge again, her thoughts were derailed by another man forcing his swollen knob into her mouth alongside the first deflating glans.

Her pretty mouth bloated by the two cockheads, spunk streaming down her cheeks and matting her blonde hair, she shuddered as the spent penis slipped out of her mouth and was immediately replaced by a fresh glans.

They were both going to come at once she was sure as the knobs drove to the back of her throat, bloating her mouth to capacity. Her full lips stretched tautly around the solid shafts, the silky penile bulbs massaging her wet tongue, she breathed heavily through her nose as her feet were released and her legs lifted high into the air.

The spent cock leaving the spermed sheath of her tight cunt, Samantha moaned through her nose as two penises entered the inflamed duct of her vagina. She couldn't take four cocks fucking her wet orifices she knew as her naked body rocked back and forth. This was crudity beyond belief, she mused, almost choking as the two purple plums drove to the back of her throat. Breathing in the male scent of the pubic curls tickling her nose, she did her best to concentrate on returning to her own time.

As one penis slipped out of her vaginal duct, the bulbous glans moving down and pressing hard against the tightly closed eye of her anus, she felt that her legs would snap as her feet were pulled apart to the extreme. Her sex holes gaping, a jolt running through her young pelvis, she squeezed her eyes shut as a solid cock drove deep into the restricted tube of her hot rectum. All three holes crudely fucked, she felt as if her young body would explode when the two penises fucking her bloated mouth erupted in orgasm. Swallowing the double load of creamy sperm as the men gasped and grunted, she again felt spunk streaming down her upside-down head, flowing through her blonde hair and into her ears.

Never had her curvaceous body taken so much sperm, Samantha reflected, her vaginal sheath squelching with the first man's sperm as a fresh knob pummelled her ripe cervix. Horrified as two men held their cocks above her face and wanked out their copious flow of semen, she

thought that she was going to drown in the male sex fluid. Was this, she wondered, what was going to happen to her in the future? Or had the men simply taken advantage of her untimely visit? Was this really happening . . .?

'Come in,' an ageing man said as Samantha found herself standing on the doorstep of a house. 'I've been looking forward to this.'

'Er, yes . . . so have I,' she returned, following him into the lounge.

'I hope they're really dirty.'

'Dirty?' she echoed, frowning as she looked around the unfamiliar room.

'Your panties. I hope you've been wearing them since we last met.'

'Oh, yes, yes – of course.'

'Lift your skirt up and I'll have a sniff,' he said, kneeling in front of her.

Lifting her skirt, Samantha looked down as the grey-haired man pressed his nose to the tight material of her panties and breathed in. She had no idea who he was but she reckoned that he must be a client from sometime in the future. Did her life hold nothing but perverted sex? She mused on this possibility as he licked her panties, wetting the crotch. What had happened to make her turn to a life of prostitution? Frowning as the old man announced that it was time for her bath, she followed his instructions and sat on the sofa with her legs wide apart. She wanted to ask him a hundred questions, but knew that she had to play it by ear. Pressing his face against her moist panties, he looked up at her and grinned.

'Good girl,' he praised her. 'You haven't washed since I last saw you.'

'No, no, I haven't,' she murmured, watching his tongue licking away again at the tight crotch of her panties.

'Mmm, you taste absolutely heavenly,' he chuckled. 'Slip your panties off and I'll give you your tongue bath.'

Complying, Samantha slipped her panties down her long legs and reclined on the sofa with her thighs spread wide. The old man moved in, his wet tongue working up and down her sex valley as he cleansed her there. She was going to have to discover why she was going to lead a life of debauchery she knew as the man parted the fleshy swell of her vaginal lips and snaked his tongue around the inflating nub of her clitoris. She could hardly accept that she'd become nothing more than a common whore. No matter how much money prostitution paid, she couldn't believe that she would stoop so low.

'I need some answers,' she said.

'Oh?' he murmured, his dark eyes looking up at her pretty face.

'How did you find out about me? Where did you first make contact?'

'The dancing school,' he replied. 'But you already knew that, surely.'

'I can't explain things now. But you must tell me how you found out about the school and how you made contact with me.'

'I don't understand,' he breathed, frowning at her. 'You've been coming to see me once a week for over a year, and yet you seem to know nothing about—'

'I'm . . . I'm writing a book,' she said, smiling at him. 'No names, of course. But I'd like to hear your side of the story.'

'Well,' the man sighed, sitting back on his heels. 'I first

heard about the dancing school from Kitty, the woman who lives a few doors away. She suggested that I might help out at the school, cleaning and the like. She knew that I had plenty of money, of course. She knew that I could afford the fees. That's why she came up with her ploy to invite me to the school. Anyway, I saw the dancers and I was hooked.'

'So when did *I* come on the scene?' Samantha asked.

'I would have thought that was obvious,' he chuckled, leaning forward and running his tongue up her creamy sex slit.

'Of course, but . . . tell, me anyway.'

'You owned the school. Kitty introduced us and—'

'And when was this? The date, I mean.'

'Last December.'

'Two thousand and . . .?'

'Three. Two thousand and three.'

'That's next year. I mean . . . So, Kitty works for me?'

'Yes. Are you sure this is for a book? I mean, to write about the school and . . .'

'Don't worry, it's for my private diaries. It's a long story, but . . . Tell me, where does Gerry Andrews fit into all this?'

'Ah, the man who gave you the mansion?'

'*Gave* me?'

'I don't know what the arrangement was, but he signed the place over to you. That's what Kitty said, anyway.'

'And he stayed on?'

'No, no. He went off to Australia. There is talk that Kitty might join him at some stage. Do you mind if I get on with the job in hand?' the oldster asked her, licking his pussy-smeared lips.

'No, no. I'm sorry. You carry on and enjoy yourself.'

As the man slipped his wet tongue between the fleshy hillocks of her outer labia, Samantha pondered on his words and thought about what she'd learned from him. Why would Gerry Andrews give her the mansion? There were too many unanswered questions, she reflected. Not least, why had she been gifted with the ability to travel through time? There must have been a reason, she thought, as the old man drove his tongue deep into the drenched sheath of her hot vagina. Wondering what would happen if she tried to go one hundred years forward in time, she felt a shudder run up her spine. Realizing how dangerous her travels could be, she concentrated on the man's tongue as he licked the creamy inner walls of her vagina.

'You *are* enjoying yourself, aren't you?' she giggled, parting her firm thighs and moving her naked buttocks over the edge of the sofa cushion. 'Do I taste good?'

'God, yes,' he replied, his cunny-dripping face beaming as he looked up at her. 'As always, I'm saving the best bit till last.'

'Best bit?' she echoed, her head cocked to one side.

'Your sweet little bottom-hole,' he replied gleefully.

'Oh, right. I was forgetting how much you like my bottom.'

'My tongue sliding deep into your tight arse, tasting the slimy walls of your . . . God, I can hardly wait. Before that, though, we'll do the usual in the garden.'

'Yes, yes, of course,' Samantha said, wondering what the hell *the usual in the garden* entailed.

Realizing that she had no qualms about allowing an old man to tongue her young cunt, Samantha wondered again why she'd fallen so deep into the pit of depravity. She'd felt no embarrassment whatsoever as the man had talked about

tonguing deep inside her bottom. As the future had unfolded, she'd obviously had so many men that she thought nothing of offering them her bared sex holes for their debased pleasures. Even now, after relatively few exploits, she was beginning to look upon her young body as a potential commodity from which she could earn vast sums of money. And she had to admit that she'd derived immense pleasure from both male and female tongues.

Looking around the room as the elderly man slurped and sucked at the juice-dripping entrance to her hot vagina, Samantha thought that he must live alone. He probably relied on her weekly visits to satisfy his male lust, she mused. Thinking that it was a sad way to end up, she looked at the ceiling as she heard a dull thud. *No one's up there, surely*, she thought. Perhaps the man's wife was bedridden and—

'It's the cat,' the old man said, grinning at Samantha.

'Oh, right.'

'Well, I'm getting very thirsty now. Are you going to give me a drink in the garden?'

'Er . . . yes, of course.'

Clambering to her feet, Samantha followed him through the kitchen and out onto the patio. She had no idea what he wanted her to do as he lay on his back on the lawn. Walking towards him, puzzlement reflected in her blue eyes, she waited for him to instruct her in whatever act he wanted her to perform. *Thirsty?* she mused, suddenly wondering whether her thinking was right and he wanted her to . . .

'Stand over my face, then,' he said.

'Stand over . . . Yes, right.'

'After this, I'll tongue your sweet little bottom. The blend of—'

'I'm not sure that I can manage this,' Samantha cut in, lifting her skirt as she stood with her feet either side of his head.

'I hope you've been drinking plenty of water,' he murmured. 'You always drink plenty of water before visiting me.'

'Yes, yes, I have,' she lied, praying that she could please the sad old man as she squeezed her muscles.

Her golden liquid raining over the old man's face, Samantha looked down in disgust. He was obviously deriving immense pleasure from her crude act, she thought, as he opened his mouth and drank. *And why not?* she ruminated, realizing that she was as bad as he was. Her disgust waning, she peeled the wet lips of her pussy apart, spraying his face with her clear yellow flow as her pleasure heightened. No one knew about her lewd behaviour, she mused, her flow stemming to a trickle. Whatever she did, no one at the newspaper, her family, friends . . . She was free to do as she wished.

Lowering her skirt, her inner thighs wet, Samantha stepped aside as the man sat up and wiped his face on the back of his hand. Was he so sad? The question made her think. She'd enjoyed the lewd act as much as he had. Was there really anything wrong with two adults playing dirty games? Watching as he knelt in front of her and lifted her skirt high up over her stomach, she grinned as he administered another tongue bath, licking her inner thighs and cleansing her wet sex crack.

'I have to be going,' she murmured, his tongue entering the sex-wet sheath of her vaginal duct.

'Yes, of course,' he said, his glistening face grinning as he looked up at her. He'd obviously decided against finishing his session with a tongue-fucking of

Samantha's anus. Maybe he thought the additional excitement would bring on a heart attack, she thought. 'As always, you've made me very happy.'

'That's good. After all, that is what I'm here for.'

'I'll see you next week, as usual.'

'Yes, next week,' she replied as they walked towards the house.

As he showed her out, she walked down the path to the street and looked around her . . .

Hearing the old guy's front door close, Samantha suddenly found herself sitting in her parents' garden. Her mother was pouring tea from a pot and talking about someone called Archie, a name that meant nothing to Samantha. Looking down at her clothes, she knew that she must be nearing her thirties. Her mother looked older, too, she mused, wondering why she'd been transported to this particular place and time.

'You're going to have to make up your mind,' the woman said, passing Samantha a cup of tea. 'The way he's been carrying on, you should dump him.'

'Yes, I will,' Samantha murmured, reckoning that Archie must be a future cheating boyfriend.

'You know what your father thinks about your relationship. And to find out now that Archie has been seeing another girl all along . . .'

'I'll do something about it,' Samantha sighed, not really wanting to know about the man.

'She's a dreadful girl, Samantha. I really can't think why you—'

'Who is?' Samantha queried.

'Archie, of course.'

'Archie is a—' Samantha began. 'But I thought . . .'

'When you announced that you were having a lesbian relationship, your father . . . Well, you know all about that. You should never have finished with Zak.'

'Mother, Zak was sleeping with Angela.'

'So you've said. I really don't think he was.'

'Look, I haven't come here to talk about my relationships.'

'Oh? Then what have you come here for? To talk about that dancing school?'

'What do you mean?'

'All you ever go on about is the dancing school. Why you've never allowed us anywhere near the place, I really don't know. You seem to be doing so well, Samantha. And yet . . . What is it about the school that you want to keep secret?'

'Nothing, Mother. It's just that . . . Oh, I don't know.'

'It seems that we know nothing about your life. Apart from your lesbian relationship, of course. Still, now that Archie has shown *her* true colours . . .'

'What's the date, mother?'

'The twenty-fifth. Why do you ask?'

'What year is it?'

'What year . . .'

'It's a trick question. I'll add the date of the month and . . . Just tell me what year it is.'

'Two thousand and six.'

'Right, er . . . Oh, I forget how to do it.'

'Samantha, instead of playing silly games—'

'Have I told you about Anne?'

'That girl you share your flat with? What about her?'

'She's looking for a new job and—'

'I thought she was your live-in housekeeper?'

'Well, yes, she is.'

'She's a strange girl. In fact, most of your friends are strange. Look at Jane and Geoff. Now there really *is* something weird about that couple. Do you remember that barbecue of theirs we went to? That young girl they had acting as a waitress?'

'Oh, er . . . yes, I remember.'

'She was half naked, for goodness' sake. And God only knows how old she was. She was far too young to be—'

'Where's father?'

'You know where he is, Samantha.'

'No, I don't.'

'He left last year.'

'Left?' Samantha gasped. 'Oh, yes . . . What I meant was, *how* is he? What's he doing?'

'He's living with that girl he picked up.'

'I meant . . . Never mind.'

Watching her mother sipping her tea, Samantha thought again that she'd be better off not knowing what the future held. Her father leaving? Living with a girl he'd picked up? This was too much to take in, Samantha mused, again wondering who Archie was and where she'd meet the girl. Looking around the garden as her mother went to answer the doorbell, Samantha was desperate to know why she was learning about her future. Was there a reason for everything? She reflected on the question as her mother approached with a young man in tow.

'Young Brian's here,' her mother said, grinning at Samantha. 'I'll go and make a fresh pot of tea.'

'Hi, Sam,' the good-looking man greeted her.

'Hi,' Samantha murmured, wondering who he was as her mother went into the house.

'I'm pleased to have a minute alone with you,' he said,

glancing over his shoulder. 'I wanted to ask you about the photographs.'

'Oh?'

'There's a German magazine. They've shown great interest in buying the pics.'

'Oh, er . . . that's good news.'

'Is it? God, you've changed your tune. I thought you were dead against having your open fanny plastered across a centrefold?'

'My open . . . well, I . . .'

'I've got some new pics here,' Brian said, taking an envelope from his jacket pocket. 'Take a look.'

Opening the envelope, Samantha gasped as she stared wide-eyed at a couple of dozen photographs of her naked body. Several shots showed her gaping pussy with a huge purple knob jetting sperm between her hairless lips. These were hard-core porn, she mused, looking at another photograph of two purple knobs shooting spunk over her face. Her life really was going to become debased in the extreme, she thought, wondering again why she would leave journalism behind to sink into a pit of decadence. Sure that she couldn't change the next ten years, she thought about John, her future husband. He'd obviously have no idea that he'd be marrying someone who could only be described as a wanton slut.

'What are you doing?' she asked, gazing at Brian's erect penis sticking out of his trousers.

'You know how much you like a little suck now and then,' he chuckled. 'Go on, slip it into your mouth and suck out my spunk.'

'Not *here*, Brian,' she retorted.

'What's the matter, Sam? You usually yank my cock out at every opportunity. Look at the times you've

sucked me off virtually in public. On the train last week, behind the hedge at that party . . . and in your mother's lounge the other day while she was fiddling with the video. She could have turned round and . . . You've always said that it's the danger of getting caught that turns you on. Go on, you know that you can't resist drinking my spunk.'

Gazing at his huge glans, his sperm-slit, Samantha knew that she had to comply with his lewd request. If she'd previously been eager to suck him off at every opportunity, he'd think it odd that she was now rejecting him. He obviously wasn't just a passing boyfriend, she thought, wondering how many photographs he'd taken of her naked body. Perhaps the dancing school was also a front for a photographic studio, she mused. Unless the porn pics were a sideline to bring in some extra cash. She wondered whether her future revolved around making money. Sex, cocksucking, prostitution, porn pics . . .

Leaning forward, she sucked Brian's swollen glans deep into her wet mouth and rolled her tongue over its silky-smooth surface. She *was* a wanton slut she knew as he gasped and clutched her head. Gobbling on his bulbous glans, sinking her teeth into the solid shaft of his huge cock, Samantha knew instinctively that she was in her element. The danger of her mother returning heightening her libido, she hauled the man's heavy balls out of his trousers and kneaded his sperm eggs.

'They don't call you the cock-swallower for nothing,' he breathed, driving his purple plum to the back of her throat. 'As we were saying the other day, you've made a name for yourself. You have quite a reputation, Sam.'

'Tell me more,' she giggled, slipping his cock out of

her mouth and licking his sperm-slit. 'I like listening to you talking about my reputation.'

'When I heard that you'd sucked the spunk out of forty-two cocks in one day, I didn't believe it. Then I saw you in action at the dancing school. I thought that you were going to drown in spunk as you sucked off those men. Twenty men, all lined up with their cocks sticking out. Watching you sitting on that chair swallowing spunk from cock after cock . . .'

'You don't mind my infidelity?' she asked, licking his heaving balls.

'You know that I love it,' Brian chuckled. 'After all, I'm the one who brings you fresh cock. You'd better be quick. Your mother will be back any minute now.'

Taking his purple globe between her succulent lips, Samantha realized that her arousal was soaring as she snaked her tongue around the rim of his helmet. Listening to Brian talking of her debauched acts had turned her on, stiffened her clitoris and induced her cunt-milk to ooze between the swollen lips of her yearning pussy. Wondering for the umpteenth time why she'd turned out to be a dirty slut, she breathed heavily through her nose as Brian's spunk jetted from his throbbing knob and bathed her snaking tongue. Swallowing hard as her cheeks filled with his orgasmic cream, she was becoming used to crude sex with strangers. It was odd to think that Brian obviously knew her intimately and yet she didn't know him.

Swallowing the last of his sperm, Samantha ran her tongue around his deflating glans and cupped his drained balls in her hand. Gripping his fleshy shaft as he tried to pull away, she clutched her prize and sank her teeth into his glans. She was desperate for more she knew as she felt

her clitoris pulsating and her juices of desire streaming from her hot vaginal opening. Feeling herself drifting away, she clung to Brian's cock. But she was leaving him, travelling to another time and place. As she slipped away, she wondered: would she find herself with another man's cock in her mouth?

8

Standing in Angela's lounge, Samantha wondered why the girl couldn't see or hear her. Sometimes Samantha was visible, and other times . . . Having no control over her time travelling, she thought again that someone or something was pulling the strings. Why was she now in Angela's lounge? She pondered the question, hearing movements in the hall. Was this the past or the future?

'Hi, babe,' Zak said, entering the room and kissing Angela's cheek.

'You're late,' the girl complained.

'Sorry, but I couldn't get away from Sam.'

'Is she going to take you back or not?'

'I'm not sure,' Zak sighed, slipping his hand inside Angela's blouse.

'All that money, and we can't get our hands on it. How much did you say her father had given her?'

'One hundred thousand.'

'I'm getting pissed off with this, Zak. I thought you said that she was talking about making plans for the wedding?'

'That's right. She seemed keen enough but . . . Don't worry, babe. Everything's going to work out. Now she believes that we're finished, that it was only a stupid fling, I reckon that she'll marry me. Once she does, I'll get hold of the money and—'

'And we'll go abroad.'

'Yes, we will. Greece, Spain . . . Somewhere where the sun shines. Somewhere far away from Sam.'

Watching Zak unbuttoning Angela's blouse, Samantha reckoned that this was happening in the near future. He obviously thought that she was about to take him back and marry him. He was in for quite a surprise, Samantha reflected. Not only was there going to be no wedding, but she'd make sure that Angela dumped him. Eyeing Angela's huge nipples as Zak lifted her bra clear of her firm breasts, Samantha wondered whether to stay and witness her boyfriend's act of infidelity. There was really no point, she mused, about to attempt to return to her own time.

'Get the clamps,' Angela said as Zak tweaked the ripe protrusions of her breasts.

'I was hoping you'd say that,' Zak replied, grinning.

'You know how much I like you torturing my titties,' she chuckled as Zak took two metal clamps from the mantelpiece.

As Angela lay on the couch, Samantha watched Zak place the clamps over the erect teats of her firm breasts and tighten the screws. Zak was a bastard, she reflected. But Angela was . . . Samantha had never really known the girl. Although they'd been friends for many years, Samantha had had no idea that she was into breast torture. Noticing thin weals fanning out across the pale flesh of Angela's mammary spheres, she wondered whether the other girl had been whipped there. Her face grimacing as the clamps bit into the sensitive flesh of her ripe nipples, she gasped.

'More,' Angela breathed as Zak continued to tighten the screws. 'God, that's beautiful. Get the cane.' Grab-

bing a thin cane from the corner of the room, Zak knelt by the sofa and raised it above his head. Samantha grimaced as the thin bamboo stick swished through the air, striking Angela's breasts with a loud crack. The girl writhed on the sofa, gasping as Zak administered the gruelling tit-thrashing.

Yet more crude sex, Samantha reflected, wondering what had happened to her life. Any semblance of normality had gone, she mused. Although she enjoyed sex, lewd sex with both men and women, she realized that she wanted to be in a permanent and stable relationship. But she'd eventually marry John and . . . and she wouldn't ruin it. Ten years was a long time, she thought, as Angela's screams resounded around the room. Ten years to enjoy her young body, to experience sex with anyone and everyone. Ten years – and then settle into a good marriage.

'Do my cunt now,' Angela gasped, yanking her short skirt off. 'I want you to whip my cunt, Zak.' Frowning as the girl slipped her panties off and lay on the sofa with her thighs spread wide, Samantha watched Zak bring the cane down across the hairless lips of Angela's naked vulva. The protruding wings of her inner labia turning a fire-red as the merciless caning continued, Angela screamed out in the grip of her agony and pleasure.

Once more trying to return to her own time, Samantha closed her eyes and shut out Angela's screams. She'd seen and heard enough about the future, she thought, concentrating on her flat . . .

Opening her eyes as she felt a draught whip around her ankles, Samantha looked around what appeared to be a very old pub. Wearing Victorian clothes, she instinctively knew that she'd travelled way back in time. There

were wooden beer barrels lined up behind the bar, scrubbed tables around the large room, pewter mugs hanging from low beams on the ceiling . . .

'Don't stand about, girl,' a bearded man snapped as he walked behind the bar. 'Get the floor cleaned up and then get out to the kitchen.'

'I . . . Where am . . .' Samantha stammered.

'What's the matter with you?' the man asked, tossing a dishrag over his shoulder. 'Mother's ill in bed and we have to get this place cleaned up. We're not going to allow the house to grind to a halt just because Mother's ill, are we?'

'No, of course not,' Samantha replied.

'I know it's hard, Meg,' he said, placing his hand on her shoulder.

'Meg?' she echoed.

'Don't tell me that you've forgotten your own name,' he chuckled. 'Look, I'll clean up down here. You go up and see whether your mother wants anything.'

Walking through a doorway, Samantha climbed the creaking stairs to a small landing. Wondering why she'd travelled so far back in time, she thought that she must have returned to a previous life. But why? Looking out of a small window, she gazed at a hansom cab pulled by a horse. This was eighteen hundred and something, she mused as a horse and cart passed by. This was also very dangerous, she knew. If she couldn't return to her own time . . .

'Is that you, Meg?' a woman called.

'Yes, it is,' Meg replied, walking into a bedroom.

'Do something with my pillow, there's a dear,' the woman said, propping herself up on her elbows. 'How's your father doing without me?'

'Oh, he's . . . he's fine.'

'Ah, that's better,' the woman breathed as Samantha pulled her pillow up. 'If you could just fill my water jug, I'll be fine.'

Taking the jug, Samantha left the room and wandered into another, smaller bedroom. This was her room she knew as she looked at the dolls propped up on the windowsill. But, she wondered again, why had she gone back to a previous life? She placed the jug on a small table and sat on the bed. This had to be a dream she was sure as she looked down at her long dress. There was no such thing as a previous life, was there?

'You'd better come with me,' a young man said, standing in the doorway.

'Who are you?' Samantha asked, looking at his crisp white shirt and tie as he held his hand out.

'I've been trying to catch up with you,' he said, taking her hand as she stood up and walked towards him. 'You've been flitting here and there . . . You shouldn't be doing this.'

'I . . . I've not been able to—'

'Come with me.'

'Where to?'

'To your own time. There's about to be a huge fire. You have to save the girl who's sleeping rough. Malthadrew . . .'

Waking to find herself lying on her bed, Samantha looked around the room. Positive that she'd been dreaming, she slipped off her bed and sat at her dressing table. Brushing her long blonde hair, she was thankful to be back in her flat. She was definitely back in her own time she knew as she gazed at her reflection in the mirror. The dream had

seemed so real, she reflected, pondering on the young man's words. A girl, a fire . . . a previous life? She shook her head, grinning as a loud knock sounded on the door.

'Sam, someone's here to see you,' Anne called.

'Who?' Samantha asked, opening the door.

'Me,' Dave said, standing behind Anne in the hall. 'Your boss, remember?'

'Sorry,' Samantha sighed. 'I was going to ring you but . . . Anne, would you make some coffee?'

'OK,' the girl trilled.

'Dave, I've been working on a story,' Samantha said, leading him into the lounge.

'Sammy baby, where the hell have you been?'

'It's a long story.'

'What, the one you're working on? Or the one you're about to dream up?'

'Seriously, Dave. Things have been happening to me. I can't explain because you'd never believe me.'

'No, I wouldn't. And you won't believe this. I've been doing some snooping around that mansion. Andrews is turning the hall into a dancing school.'

'A dancing school?' Samantha echoed.

'Yes, but this is no ordinary dancing school. I'm onto something, but I don't know what.'

'How do you mean?'

'I didn't have a great deal of time but I discovered a surgery, a doctor's surgery. There's something going on at that mansion, Sammy.'

'Perhaps Gerry Andrews has come up with another moneymaking idea.'

'Oh, yes, that's for sure. But a dancing school? Presumably the surgery is for checking the dancers over or something.'

'What's odd about that?'

'I can't quite put my finger on it, but I've a feeling that the school is a front for something. Unfortunately, I didn't have a chance to look around properly because some woman asked me what I wanted. I told her that I was looking for ghosts, which seemed to satisfy her. Anyway, I want you to go there and ask about dancing lessons.'

'*Me?*' Samantha gasped, wondering whether she'd ever escape from this nightmare.

'I don't think John the Prat would be a suitable candidate for dancing lessons, do you?'

'No, I suppose not. Dave, this dancing school . . . is it really worth bothering with?'

'If Gerry Andrews is involved, yes, it is.'

'You've got something against him, haven't you?'

'No, of course I haven't. It's just that I know he's up to something. The haunted-mansion scam was one thing, but . . . OK, get this. As I was leaving, I saw a couple of young girls hanging about in a corridor.'

'Dave, if it's a dancing school, then—'

'They weren't dancers. They were pretty young and the way they looked at me . . .'

'Don't say that they were eyeing you up, for God's sake.'

'Yes, I believe they were. Anyway, this other story of yours about a sex den.'

'I was wrong about that. I was given a false lead and . . . Someone was pissing me about.'

'Shit. We could have done with something juicy like that.'

'Two coffees,' Anne said, placing a tray on the table.

'Thanks,' Samantha murmured. 'Er . . . close the door on your way out.'

'Sammy, tell me what's been going on,' Dave said as the girl left the room.

'Nothing's been going on,' she sighed. 'Apart from wasting my time on duff leads.'

'I haven't seen you for bloody ages,' he said, sipping his coffee. 'Or heard from you.'

'I'll be back in the office tomorrow, I promise you. I've wasted enough time.'

'Yes, you have. Oh, by the way. We've got a new photographer.'

'Really? What about Derek? Is he still—'

'Derek's leaving. This new bloke seems OK. His name's Brian.'

'Brian?' Samantha gasped.

'What's the matter?'

'Nothing. So, what's he like?'

'Youngish, good-looking . . . He seems very keen, which is good. He's been doing a lot of nude photography.'

'Yes, I know. I mean, I know that he'll be all right. If he's keen, then he'll be all right. Dave, do you believe in past lives?'

'I've never really thought about it. Besides, it's the present life I'm interested in. And, in particular, the newspaper. So, we need a damned good story.'

'Dave, have you heard the name Malthadrew?'

'Yes, it's a paint factory. Why do you ask?'

'Where is it?'

'The industrial estate out by Toddington's Farm. Are you onto something?'

'I . . . I don't know,' Samantha sighed, wondering whether there was a girl sleeping rough close to the factory.

'I won't bother to ask you to keep me posted because I know you won't,' he chuckled, finishing his coffee. 'Look, I'd better be going.'

'Yes, yes . . . I'll see you tomorrow.'

'You'd better.'

As Dave left, Samantha grabbed her car keys and told Anne that she had to go out. The girl was getting used to Samantha coming and going, and seemed happy enough to watch the TV news to learn more about the new era she'd been transported to. Leaving the flat, Samantha drove to the paint factory and parked in what appeared to be a disused yard. She was sure that she'd been dreaming, but the young man's words were haunting her. *There's about to be a huge fire. You have to save the girl who's sleeping rough.*

Leaving her car, she looked around the yard at the piles of rubbish and a couple of dumped cars. The factory, with smoke billowing from a tall chimney, was a hundred yards or so away. No one would be sleeping rough in the old yard she was sure as she peered into one of the scrapped cars. Had she been dreaming? The young man had mentioned the name of the factory, and yet she'd never heard of it. Perhaps she'd heard the name somewhere and it hadn't registered she concluded as she walked back to her car.

Noticing a girl hiding behind some wooden boxes, Samantha started the engine and drove back down the track. The girl was obviously frightened, she thought, parking around the corner where her car was obscured by a group of trees. Walking back along the track, Samantha ducked behind some bushes and watched the girl walking towards the factory. Following at a safe distance, she ducked behind a clump of bushes again as the girl slipped into an old shed.

Looking around her, Samantha realized that, if there was a huge fire, the girl might not be able to escape. Three sides of the shed were surrounded by a high fence, the only escape route taking her past the back of the factory. Wondering what to do, Samantha walked back to her car. She doubted that the girl would talk to her. She'd probably run off the minute she was confronted, only to return later to the shed. Calling the police would only get the girl into trouble, she mused, sitting in her car. Sure now that she hadn't been dreaming, she finally drove to the main entrance of the factory and wandered into a reception area.

'Can I help you?' a woman sitting behind a desk asked.

'Er . . . well, I'm not sure. The land behind the factory. What's it used for?'

'Nothing, really. It's become a dumping ground. Why do you ask?'

'I was out walking and I saw some kids playing around there. I thought it wasn't a safe place for them.'

'You're right there,' the woman sighed. 'It's a fire hazard. The powers that be won't listen. They've been told to clear the rubbish but . . . One of these days there'll be a fire, you mark my words. I'd better go and tell the kids to clear off.'

'I've already done that,' Samantha said. 'They've gone, but they'll probably be back.'

'Well, thanks for letting me know. I'll keep my eyes open.'

Leaving the building, Samantha now knew that she hadn't been dreaming. She also knew that her gift of time travel wasn't purely for her own sexual gratification. This was serious, she thought, returning to her car. It was one thing learning the identity of the man she'd

eventually marry, but to discover that a young girl was going to lose her life . . . The fire might not start for several days, or even weeks, she mused. If she chased the girl off, she'd only return. Again driving to the back of the building, she parked her car and walked to the shed. She had at least to talk to the girl, she knew, as she yanked the door open.

'Shit,' she breathed, realizing that the girl must have heard the car and run off. Noticing a sleeping bag on the floor, she decided to come back later. If she could catch the girl in the shed, it might be possible to persuade her to find somewhere else to sleep. And, if that didn't work, she could threaten to call the police. Returning to her car, she drove to the park near her flat to do some thinking.

Sitting on a bench in the corner of the park, the afternoon sun warming her, she pondered on her life. She'd discovered too much she knew as she thought about marrying John. And now she had the girl behind the paint factory to worry about. Wishing she'd never visited the old mansion, she wondered whether the place held the key to her ability to travel through time. It had begun when she'd been in the basement, she reflected, wondering whether there was some kind of paranormal presence in the bowels of the old building.

'Hi, Sam,' Zak said, walking towards her. 'I saw you park your car and . . . Any chance of having a chat?'

'Yes, of course,' she replied, smiling as he sat down beside her. 'I'm sorry I've not been in touch but I've been pretty busy at work.'

'That's OK. So how are you?'

'I'm fine.'

'Sam, I thought we might go away for a while. A holiday would do us both good.'

'Yes, you're right. I've been doing a lot of thinking recently. We've always been good together, Zak. When we split up . . . well, I was devastated. This holiday. Have you anywhere in mind?'

'I thought Spain might be nice. We need some time together, don't you agree?'

'We certainly do. A month in the sun, just the two of us . . .'

'A month?'

'Why not?'

'Yes, OK. Shall I book something?'

'You book a hotel, and then I'll pay my half. Don't tell me where it is. I like surprises, Zak.'

'Right, I'll book a month in a top-class hotel. Er . . . I'm pretty short of cash at the moment.'

'Use your credit card and I'll pay you . . .'

'OK. Can you get the time off work?'

'God, yes. Dave owes me several holidays. Make it a five-star hotel, Zak.'

'That'll cost a bit, but—'

'Don't forget that my father gave me plenty of money. While we're away, we'll make the wedding plans.'

'Great. So, what are you doing here?'

'Actually, I'm waiting for a woman who works for the council. She wants to spill the beans about something. You'd better make yourself scarce.'

'How about this evening? Are you doing anything?'

'No, I'm not. You go and book a holiday and I'll meet you in the wine bar. About eight?'

'OK, I'll be there. Sam, I—'

'We'll talk later, Zak. This woman will be here at any minute and I don't want to blow it. Go and book the holiday and we'll talk later.'

'OK, I'll see you in the wine bar.'

Concealing a grin as he kissed her cheek and walked away, Samantha knew that he'd go straight to the nearest travel agent and book an expensive holiday. She felt bad about conning him into spending what little money he had, but her guilt quickly faded when she thought about his despicable behaviour with her so-called best friend. She'd discovered too many things about too many people, she reflected. Not least herself. Digging out skeletons had initially been intriguing, but now . . . now she didn't want to know.

Watching a young man walking across the park towards her, she knew that she didn't want to travel through time any more. It had been interesting and extremely enlightening. But it wasn't doing her any good. Now that she knew what the future held, she was determined to live her life in the present. No more dark secrets revealed, no more surprises . . . Frowning as the young man hovered a few yards away, she wondered what he was up to.

Leaving the bench and walking alongside the wooden fence concealing the railway line, she glanced over her shoulder. He was walking slowly behind her, obviously following her. She didn't need this, she mused, quickening her pace. She'd come to the park to be alone, to think. First Zak and now . . . Turning a corner, she slipped through a gap in the fence and waited. Much to her relief, the young man walked past.

Sitting on the short grass, she looked down at the railway line in the cutting below. The steel rails catching the sunlight, the air still and warm, she felt at one with herself as she lay back on the grass and closed her eyes. Anne, it seemed, had moved into the flat for good she thought as a train rumbled through the cutting. Kitty,

Gerry Andrews . . . There were too many problems, too many people to worry about.

'Excuse me,' the young man said, towering over her.

'Oh, God,' Samantha gasped, sitting upright. 'You made me jump.'

'I'm sorry. I was—'

'Following me. Yes, I know.'

'I wanted to ask you whether you'd seen a girl waiting in the park.'

'A girl?'

'I'd arranged to meet her here and . . . I suppose she's not going to turn up,' he sighed.

'That might not be such a bad thing,' Samantha breathed, eyeing his unruly black hair cascading over his forehead.

'What do you mean?'

'She's obviously not making you happy.'

'No, she . . . The thing is, my older brother has been after her and I think they're seeing each other.'

'Nice brother.'

'He's got money, a car . . . I suppose that's what she's attracted to. I can't even drive yet. And I don't have much money since I'm still at college.'

'I'm Samantha, by the way.'

'Oh, sorry . . . I'm Chester.'

'That's an unusual name.'

'Yes,' he sighed abstractedly, pulling a blade of grass from the ground.

'How old is this girl?'

'Sixteen.'

'Forget about her, Chester. As I said, she's obviously not making you happy. What's the point in being with someone who makes you unhappy?'

'I know, but . . .'

'There are no buts. I was with a man for several years. It wasn't so much that he made me unhappy. But I've realized how much happier I am now that he's not around. There are plenty of other girls, Chester. Besides, you're young. You have your whole life ahead. You don't have to get tied up with anyone yet.'

'No, I suppose not. It's just that she . . . Jodie is special.'

'Yes, she sounds it. Special to you, your brother, and anyone else who takes her fancy.'

Pondering on happiness, Samantha knew that she was better off without Zak. Before she'd discovered his infidelity, she'd thought she'd found happiness, but all she'd found was someone to share her flat with. Anne was nothing more than a flatmate, she reflected. She was fun, extremely sexual . . . But she wasn't someone Samantha wanted to spend the rest of her life with. So many marriages were just based on habit, she thought, wondering when her father was going to run off. People thought that they were in love, married, and then discovered that they'd made a mistake.

'It's good to talk to someone,' Chester murmured, toying with the blade of grass.

'Yes, it is,' Samantha agreed. 'I don't think that people talk to each other enough. They bottle things up, get sucked into the mire of their minds.'

'Are you seeing anyone at the moment?'

'Er . . . not exactly,' Sam chuckled.

'I suppose you'll say that you're too old for me.'

'Too old for what?'

'To see me, go out with me.'

'Go out with you?' she echoed, realizing that he was

gazing at the naked flesh of her slender thighs. 'Well, I
. . . I wouldn't mind meeting you here again.'

'Really?' He beamed. 'I think I need someone older
like you. Oh, I didn't mean that you're old.'

'I know what you meant.'

Samantha was about to have sex with the young man,
she knew, as she eyed the crotch of his jeans. Unable to
help herself, to deny her rising arousal, she reclined on
the grass and allowed her short skirt to ride up her naked
thighs. No one would know what she'd done, she con-
soled herself. Hidden behind the fence beneath the
summer sun, no one would know that she'd seduced a
young teenage boy. She wondered whether this was
really what she wanted, discreetly tugging her short skirt
up as he watched a train speeding through the cutting.

Closing her eyes as she felt Chester's fingers running
up the sensitive flesh of her inner thigh, she let out a long
sigh of pleasure. This *was* what she wanted, she reflected,
as his fingertips pressed into the soft swelling of her tight
panties. Crude sex with a young teenager she'd never met
before . . . This had nothing to do with time travel, she
mused, grinning as his finger followed the divide between her inflating love lips, running up and down the
valley of her vagina. This was here and now, the present.

As Chester pulled the front of her panties down and
stroked the warm flesh of her hairless sex lips, Samantha
breathed heavily and arched her back. To allow a teenager to explore her young body, examine her vulval flesh,
was incredibly arousing she mused as he tugged her
panties down her long legs. Slipping her shoes off, he
removed her panties and parted her legs wide. He seemed
to have no qualms, no embarrassment, she thought
happily. Perhaps he was desperate for sex. As his young

girlfriend hadn't shown up, he was probably stiff, his balls full, his teenage hormones running rampant. Wondering what sort of experience he'd had, Samantha imagined taking his purple cockhead into her wet mouth and sucking out his creamy spunk. Hopefully, he didn't know a great deal about sex. She'd teach him, she decided. Teach him mouth-fucking, cunny-licking, anilingus . . .

'Don't you mind me doing this?' he asked in his obvious naivety.

'Mind?' she giggled. 'I love it.'

'Oh, right. I just thought that . . .'

'What did you just think?'

'That, usually, girls won't allow . . .'

'Chester, some sixteen-year-olds might hesitate before allowing you to have sex with them. I'm twenty-two. I've seen it all, done it all. You carry on and enjoy yourself because I'm enjoying your attention very much.'

'I think that we're made for each other, Samantha.'

'Chester, just because . . . yes, perhaps you're right.'

Made for each other? she giggled inwardly as he slipped his finger deep into the hugging sheath of her hot vaginal duct. *One glimpse of a fanny, and he thinks he's in love.* Spreading her thighs wide, Samantha peeled the fleshy lips of her vulva apart and displayed the intricate inner folds of her creamy-wet sex valley. Chester might have had sex with a sixteen-year-old, but the girl wouldn't have opened her cunt wide and revealed her inner flesh she was sure as she wondered whether he'd lick and suck her inner labia.

Driving a second finger into her tightening vaginal duct, he began to piston her young body. This was all very well, she mused, but it was his tongue she wanted to

feel inside the creamy sheath of her young cunt. His tongue, and then his solid cock. Lifting her head, she watched the inner petals of her sex slit dragging back and forth along his thrusting finger. Her flowing vaginal cream lubricating the intimate union, she brought her knees up to her firm breasts and reached behind her thighs.

'Put your tongue in my hole,' she said, yanking her sex lips wide apart as he slipped his finger out of her drenched vagina. 'Tongue-fuck my hot cunt and make me come. Have you ever tongued a girl before?'

'Er . . . no, I haven't,' he confessed sheepishly, his dark eyes transfixed on her gaping vaginal inlet.

'See my sex cream? I want you to tongue fuck me and suck out my juices. Drink from my cunt, Chester.'

Without hesitation, he lay on his stomach on the ground and drove his tongue deep into the tight sheath of her young pussy. Samantha moved her fingers down and parted the firm cheeks of her buttocks, hoping that he'd lick the sensitive brown ring of her anus as she felt his wet tongue snaking around the pink funnel of flesh surrounding her vaginal portal. Shuddering as her clitoris swelled, she straightened her legs and unbuttoned her blouse, pulling the garment open and exposing the alluring mounds of her young breasts.

The teenager's tongue sweeping over the solid nubble of her sensitive clitoris, Samantha brought her knees up against her breast again and yanked the entrance to her bottom-hole wide open. Her young body almost naked, she tossed her head from side to side as she imagined his wet tongue slipping into the hot duct of her rectum. He'd never licked a girl's cunt out, she ruminated, her juices just gushing from her spasming vaginal sheath, let alone

performed the delightfully crude act of anilingus. He had a lot to learn she knew as his tongue left her ripe clitoris and delved into the gaping hole of her wet cunt once again.

'My arse,' she breathed in her soaring lust for crude sex. 'Tongue-fuck my tight arse.' Hesitating, the boy finally ran his tongue up and down her gaping anal gully. Wondering what he was thinking, Samantha waited patiently for the feel of his wet tongue deep inside her hot rectum. Her bottom-hole presented an acquired taste, she mused, recalling her own first experience of analtonguing. Once he'd licked her anus, moistened her there, he was sure to want more and drive his tongue deep into her anal canal.

His saliva running down her anal crevice, trickling between the splayed hillocks of her vulval lips, Chester finally took the plunge and entered her tight bottom-hole. Gasping as her secret nerve endings came alive, Samantha yanked her anus open wider and exposed her inner flesh to his darting tongue. He was going to be a young man of great sexual experience before the day was out, Samantha reflected. Cunnilingus, anilingus, oral sex, vaginal, anal . . . There'd be nothing he wouldn't have tried before leaving the park.

'Shove your cock up my wet cunt,' she gasped, her vaginal muscles aching for something hard to grip. Grinning as he unbuckled his belt and tugged his jeans down, Samantha jolted as Chester suddenly drove the entire length of his hard rod deep into her sex-dripping cuntal sheath. Her head lolling from side to side as he began his fucking motions, her nostrils flaring, she dug her fingernails into the soft ground and arched her back as she let out a cry of sheer sexual bliss. Hoping that he

was virile enough to fuck all three of her sex-hungry orifices, she listened to the squelching sounds of her bubbling vaginal juices as he repeatedly rammed his swollen cockhead deep into her rhythmically contracting cunt. He'd spunk her cervix, and then spunk down her throat before completing his session of lewd sex by filling the hot depths of her bowels with his gushing orgasmic cream.

That was one advantage of young teenage lads, she reflected, her quivering body jolting with the illicit fucking. They had virility, staying power, and were extremely keen to be taught the baser side of sex. Older men were obviously into crude sex, but young teenage boys had an unrivalled eagerness to commit sexual acts, an unquenchable thirst for debauched sex. But, Samantha reflected, hadn't she been the same? Not only during her younger years – even now she was hungry to experience obscene sex.

Time travelling wasn't necessary, she thought, as her young pupil began gasping, his swinging balls battering the rounded globes of her firm buttocks as he fucked her. Why visit other times and places when there were the likes of Chester roaming the park? He'd have friends, she mused, imagining taking several lads behind the fence and sucking their swollen knobs in turn. They'd all be eager to mouth-fuck her, cunt-fuck and arse-fuck her, she knew.

'I'm . . . I'm coming,' Chester announced as if in pain. His solid cock-shaft swelling within the hugging sheath of Samantha's tight cunt, his glans ballooning, he let out a long moan of satisfaction as his fresh sperm jetted from his slit and filled her spasming vaginal cavern. Samantha could feel his male cream lubricating his thrusting piston

as he continued to fuck her with a vengeance. Collapsing over Samantha's trembling body as he made his last thrusts and drained his swinging balls, Chester sucked each ripe nipple into his wet mouth and sucked hard. Mouthing like a babe at the breast, he shuddered, ramming his solid cock deep into her quim before stilling his spent organ deep within the hugging duct of her sperm-flooded cunt.

'Kneel over my face,' Samantha ordered him. Grinning as he slid his cock out of her tight vagina, licking her succulent lips, she watched as he positioned his cunny-dripping penis above her sperm-thirsty mouth. Pulling him down, taking his creamy glans to the back of her throat, she sank her teeth into his glistening shaft and sucked out the remnants of his sperm. Breathing in the heady scent of his pubic curls, savouring the blend of her pussy juice and his spunk, she gobbled and sucked fervently on his stiffening cock.

He'd soon be fully erect she knew as his gasps filled her ears. Once he was rock-hard, she'd order him to mouth-fuck her and shoot his second load of sperm down her throat. Kneading his hanging balls, she moved her hand up and pressed her fingertip against the sensitive brown tissue of his anal iris. He jolted, gasping as she pushed her inquisitive finger past his anal sphincter muscles and massaged the inner flesh of his tight rectal tube. Sure that he'd never experienced the pleasure of an anal finger-fucking as he'd fucked a girl's mouth, Samantha wasn't surprised when his purple glans swelled and he pumped his second load of fresh spunk into her gobbling mouth.

His orgasm obviously extremely intense, Chester shuddered and writhed as his balls drained again. Driv-

ing a second finger into his rhythmically contracting rectal sheath, Samantha gobbled and mouthed on his throbbing glans, swallowing his gushing spunk as he whimpered in his uncontrolled ecstasy. Her mouth overflowing with his gushing cream, the white liquid running down her cheeks and over her neck, she thought again that young lads were not only more energetic than older men but produced more sperm. Repeatedly swallowing his orgasmic offering, she felt her anal canal spasm as she imagined the feel of his solid cock shafting her rectal tube. Her juices of lust mingling with spunk issuing from her inflamed vagina as her muscles contracted, she sucked the last of his salty liquid from his sperm-slit and licked her lips as he rolled to one side.

'Was that nice?' she asked, her fingers sliding out of his rectum.

'God, yes,' he murmured, his eyes rolling as he lay on his back with his deflated cock snaking over his hairy ball bag.

'There's one more thing before you go,' she giggled, wiping spunk from her cheeks with the back of her hand. 'I need a damned good arse-fucking.'

'What?'

'Chester, I want you to push your beautiful cock deep into my arse and fuck me.'

'Oh, er . . . yes,' he stammered, obviously surprised by her lewd request.

Positioning herself on all fours, Samantha jutted out her rounded buttocks, presenting her anal hole to his wide eyes as he knelt behind her and wanked his shaft to another erection. Samantha could feel her anal ring spasming, dilating and contracting as she worked her muscles in readiness to grip the boy's solid cock-shaft.

The taste of his sperm lingering on her full lips, his male cream oozing from her gaping vaginal entrance, this would be her third and final orifice to receive his creamy spunk.

'Yes,' she breathed as she felt the silky-smooth globe of his glans pressing against her saliva-wet anus. Pushing hard, trying to gain access to her tight inner duct, Chester gasped as his bulbous knob was sucked into her rectum. The taut tissue of her brown anus gripping his cock just beneath the rim of his swollen helmet, he grabbed her shapely hips and moved his body slowly towards hers. His veined shaft sinking into her trembling body, his purple knob journeying along the dank sheath of her anal canal, he let out a sigh of immense pleasure as he impaled her completely on his teenage penis. Withdrawing, he watched her anal tissue clinging to his slimed shaft, dragging along its veined surface until his purple globe appeared.

'God,' he breathed, ramming his knob-head back deep into the very core of her young body. Withdrawing again, slowly pulling his greasy cock out of her dank rectal tube, he once more rammed his solid glans deep into the fiery heat of her bowels. He was loving every minute of the crude act Samantha knew as he withdrew his rock-hard organ again until her delicate anal tissue hugged his knob-rim. Driving into her again, letting out a rush of breath as his balls smacked against her hairless vulval lips, he at last quickened his anal-fucking rhythm.

Her quivering body rocking back and forth, Samantha felt her pelvic cavity inflate and deflate as the lad's piston repeatedly glided along her rectal passage and withdrew. This was heaven, she reflected, her face resting on the soft grass as she projected her naked buttocks out

further. His swinging balls hammering the wet flesh of her swollen vulval lips, her juices of lust seeping from her hot love-hole and running down her inner thighs, she reached between her legs and massaged the solid nubble of her sensitive clitoris.

Her vaginal muscles contracting as her self-induced climax approached, her juices of desire streaming down her thighs in rivers of milk, she cried out as the teenager pumped her hot bowels full of sperm. Gasping, writhing as her own orgasm erupted within the pulsating protuberance of her swollen clitoris, she felt her rectal muscles tighten, gripping the lad's pistoning cock like a vice as his gushing sperm lubricated the illicit union. Listening to the squelching of her bowels as his copious flow of spunk continued to pump deep into the very core of her young body, she knew that she'd found her domain. She didn't need time travel, she thought again. The past was dead and gone, the future had yet to arrive, but the present was bringing her more than enough sexual gratification. *Cuáál seráá*, she mused. The future shouldn't be seen.

As the lad stilled his spent cock within the tight sheath of her spunk-flooded rectal tube, Samantha massaged the solid nodule of her pulsating clitoris to another mind-blowing orgasm. Her anal sphincter muscles gripping the deflating cock embedded deep within her inflamed arse, she cried out as he yanked his slimed penis from her anal canal with a loud sucking sound. To her great surprise, and immense pleasure, he locked his mouth to her anal inlet and slipped his tongue into her spasming rectum, at the same time thrusting at least three fingers into the neglected duct of her burning cunt as she continued to massage her palpitating clitoris and sustain her shuddering orgasm.

Chester's tongue massaging her inner anal flesh as he sucked out his sperm, drinking his own orgasmic fluid from the hot cavern of her bowels, he yanked her firm buttocks apart to open her anus wide. Samantha shook violently as her orgasm peaked, sending tremors of crude sex through her perspiring body as she fervently massaged her throbbing clitoris. On and on her pleasure coursed through her young body, tightening every muscle, reaching every nerve ending as the young lad finger-fucked her tight cunt and drained her rectal duct.

'God,' Samantha finally gasped, collapsing to the ground in a trembling heap as Chester's fingers left the inflamed sheath of her vagina. 'You certainly learn fast.'

'You're a good teacher,' he chuckled, grinning as he licked his cunny-dripping fingers.

'Ever been into spanking?' she asked, running her fingers over the firm globes of her naked buttocks as she rolled over onto her stomach.

'No, I've never been spanked,' he replied in his naivety.

'Me, silly,' she giggled. 'I meant, spank me.'

'Oh, I see.'

'Have you ever spanked a girl?'

'No, I haven't.'

'Well, now's your chance,' she breathed huskily, parting her legs wide and exposing the swell of her cunny lips nestling between her wet thighs. 'What are you waiting for? Go on, give my bottom a good spanking.'

Closing her eyes as Chester settled beside her, Samantha rested her head on the soft grass and tensed her naked buttocks in readiness for the spanking. His palm slapping each buttock in turn, she breathed heavily,

squirming on the ground as her libido again rocketed. The very thought of a young teenager spanking the rounded orbs of her bottom-cheeks driving her wild, she parted her thighs further, fully exposing the swollen lips of her vagina to the boy's wide eyes. He brought his hand down again and again, watching her juices of arousal spewing from her gaping vaginal entrance as he spanked her naked bottom harder and harder.

'More,' Samantha gasped. 'Do it as hard as you can.' The burning cheeks of her naked bottom reddening as he thrashed her mercilessly, she whimpered and squirmed in the grip of her decadent act of debauchery. 'Use something,' she breathed. 'Find a stick or something and thrash me.' Grabbing a branch from the ground, Chester lashed her naked buttocks, gazing in awe as the rough branch bit into her anal orbs and left broad weals in its wake. The branch swishing through the air, repeatedly landing across her tensed buttocks with loud cracks, he pinned her down with his free hand and increased his rhythm. Crying out as the blend of pain and pleasure permeated her young body, Samantha dug her fingernails into the soft grass as she felt her clitoris inflate and her vaginal juices flow from her neglected cunt.

'Fuck my arse again,' she ordered him.

'I'm not sure whether—'

'Do it, for God's sake. Fuck my arse and spunk me again.'

'All right,' he conceded, discarding the branch and settling between her legs.

Wanking his semi-erect cock, Chester grinned as his organ stiffened fully in his hand. Stabbing at her sperm-bubbling anal mouth, he pressed his swollen glans past

her defeated anal sphincter muscles and into the burning heat of her rectal duct. Samantha could feel his bulbous knob gliding deep into the very core of her young body, his solid shaft stretching her duct of illicit pleasure open to capacity as he impaled her fully on his beautiful organ. This was real sex, she reflected, her face pressing against the grass as he withdrew his erect shaft and rammed his solid glans deep into her bowels.

Rocking with the crude anal fucking, the teats of her firm breasts rubbing against the ground, Samantha's young body trembled as her clitoris stiffened fully again. Reaching beneath her trembling body, she slipped her fingers between the swollen hillocks of her dripping vaginal lips and masturbated her ripe clitoris as the young lad fucked the tight sheath of her inflamed rectum. Reaching another earth-shuddering orgasm, her juices of desire issuing from her spasming vaginal sheath, she thought that she'd pass out as the young lad gasped and flooded her rectal duct again with his creamy spunk.

'God,' Samantha breathed, her head spinning in her sexual delirium as the sound of squelching sperm filled her ears. Again and again, Chester rammed his cockhead deep into the dank heat of her fiery bowels, filling her inner cavern with his spunk as his balls drained. The eye of her anus burning, the delicate tissue inflamed, she murmured incoherent words of debased sex as the boy made his last thrusts and finally stilled his cock within her spunked arse. His purple glans absorbing the inner heat of her abused body, his balls resting against the hairless lips of her aching vagina, he lay on top of her, gasping for breath in the aftermath of his debauched act.

'No more,' he breathed, his deflating penis slipping out of her spunked arse. 'I can't do any more.'

'Neither can I,' Samantha murmured, her eyes rolling, her perspiration-matted blonde hair veiling her face as she lifted her head. 'God, I've never been fucked so much.'

'And I've never fucked so much,' he chuckled, rolling off her near-naked body and lying on his back. 'You really are amazing.'

'You're pretty amazing, too,' she giggled, lying on her back next to him. 'I'm pleased that we ran into each other.'

'When I first saw you . . . well, I must admit that I never thought I'd fuck every hole in your body. You've obviously done this sort of thing before.'

'Actually, I haven't,' she lied to please him. 'I've had sex, straight sex, but I've never done anything else. You're the first, Chester.'

'Am I really?' he asked, his face beaming as he turned and faced her.

'Oh, yes. No one's ever touched my bottom, let alone . . . well, you know.'

'I thought that you were really experienced?'

'Not at all. I'm like you, Chester, eager to learn.'

'In that case, we'll meet again and . . .'

'I was hoping you'd want to meet again. To be honest, I've never had a lover as good as you. Whatever you do, dump that girlfriend of yours. Let your brother have the two-timing bitch if he wants her. You've got me now, Chester.'

'Yes, right,' he chuckled. 'So, when shall I see you again?'

'We'll meet here tomorrow, at the same time.'

'Right, I'll be here,' he said, rising to his feet and zipping his jeans. 'See you.'

'Yes, I'll see you, Chester.'

Straightening her clothes and pulling her panties on as Chester slipped through the gap in the fence, Samantha pondered on her latest exploit. He was a nice lad, she reflected. And very good with his seemingly everlasting cock. He still had a lot to learn, but he'd already knocked spots off Zak's performance. Wondering how many more lads she could seduce by hanging around the park, she slipped through the fence and made her way home. Screwing teenagers in the park was safer than time travelling, she thought, as she neared her flat. Perhaps Anne would like to meet Chester, she mused. The reality of the situation hitting home, she knew that she was going to have to do something about the girl. But what?

9

'Where the hell have you been?' Samantha asked, opening the front door to Anne at nine o'clock the following morning. 'I was up half the night wondering where on earth—'

'I'm sorry,' the girl sighed, walking past Samantha into the hall. 'I . . . I went to my parents' house.'

'Bloody hell. What did they say?'

'They were out.'

'Thank God for that. Why did you go there, Anne? After all we've talked about . . . still, I suppose it's understandable. I'd want to see my parents if I'd been away.'

'I borrowed some money from your dressing table and bought a return train ticket.'

'So, when you discovered that they were out, why the fuck didn't you come back?'

'I lost the ticket. I had to get a lift.'

'You thumbed a lift? I told you not to leave the flat, Anne,' Samantha snapped. 'Had you done as I—'

'You're never here, Sam. You're always out and I have to sit here on my own.'

'Yes, I know. Look, I'm sorry. God, look at the state of you. Get out of those filthy clothes and into the shower.'

'I fell over crossing a field,' the girl murmured, looking

down at the mud smeared over her short skirt. 'It's a short cut to the station from my parents' house.'

'You've been out all night, you're covered in mud . . . I don't suppose you've eaten anything since yesterday?'

'No, I haven't.'

'Go and have a shower and I'll make us a cooked breakfast.'

Shaking her head as the girl mooched into the bathroom, Samantha knew that the time had come to make some concrete plans. Anne couldn't hang around the flat all day every day. There again, if she went out, someone was bound to recognize her. Her photographs had been plastered over all the newspapers, every TV station . . . Although eight years was a long time, someone was sure to remember her. Deciding to try to make the girl appear older, Samantha broke a couple of eggs in the frying pan in preparation for breakfast.

Food was running low, she thought, taking the last two rashers of bacon from the fridge. If Anne wanted to get out of the flat for a while, it might be an idea if she did some shopping. Wearing a hat and dark glasses would help to disguise her, Samantha mused, cutting up the last tomato and tossing it into the pan. The main problem was her long blonde hair, Samantha thought, wondering whether to get some black hair dye. Make-up and hair dye was the only option as far as ageing the girl was concerned, she reckoned, filling the kettle for coffee. Make-up, change her hairstyle . . . To conceal Anne's young legs, she'd have to wear trousers, not a short skirt. Perhaps even frump clothes, Samantha speculated, tossing what was left of the mushrooms into the frying pan. Pouring the coffee as she heard Anne leave the bathroom, Samantha laid the table and served the breakfast.

'Just in time,' she said, smiling as the teenage beauty wandered into the kitchen, wrapped in a towel. 'To get you out of the flat for a while, you can go shopping this morning.'

'New clothes?' she asked, her pretty face beaming.

'Food, Anne. We need food. I'll buy you some clothes today. Trousers, a baggy jumper . . .'

'What?' Anne gasped. 'There's no way I'm going to wear—'

'You'll wear what I tell you,' Samantha cut in as they sat at the table. 'I have some dresses that will fit you. You can wear a dress until I can get you some new clothes.'

'I don't like dresses.'

'I don't care what you like or don't like. Remember that you've been wearing the very same clothes you wore eight years ago, when you were kidnapped. The same clothes, the same age . . . It's only a matter of time before someone recognizes you, Anne.'

'Yes, I suppose you're right.'

'We have to make you look older. It's no good you running around in miniskirts and skimpy tops. Perhaps a baggy jumper is going too far, but do you see what I'm getting at?'

'Yes, I do,' Anne sighed, prodding the bacon with her fork.

'So, you'll be my sister and . . . I think we'll call you Sarah. Yes, I like that name.'

'I don't.'

'Tough. Like it or not, you're now Sarah. Anyway, that's what you're going to be known as in the future so—'

'In the future?'

'John said that . . . Never mind.'

'What about a job? I'll have to get a job, Sam.'

'That's not going to be so easy. You've got no National Insurance number, which will present a major problem. No one's going to employ you without . . . I'll have a word with someone at the office. He might be able to arrange something. In the meantime, you can go shopping. You can't laze around the flat all day doing nothing.'

'I've not been lazing around. I've been watching the news, trying to catch up with the latest. Things have changed in eight years, Sam.'

'Yes, I suppose they have. OK, finish your breakfast and we'll have a go at applying some make-up. We'll do something with your hair, too.'

After breakfast, Samantha led the girl into her bedroom and sat her at the dressing table. Standing behind Anne, she pulled her hair up, trying to decide which style would age her by a few years. Cut in a bob and dyed black . . . A pair of glasses might be an idea, she mused, imagining a librarian lookalike. Realizing that Anne would still be around in ten years, Samantha felt a little easier as she brushed the girl's long hair. John had said that Anne had come to live with them, so . . . Perhaps some aspects of the future were worth knowing, after all, she reflected as the phone rang.

'Sammy baby,' Dave said as Samantha sat on the bed and grabbed the phone. 'I've been up half the night thinking about—'

'Look, I'll try to get into the office this morning,' Samantha sighed. 'I'm chasing a lead at the moment and—'

'No, no, it's not about that. Who was that girl at your place? When I called round to see you . . .'

'Sarah? She's my sister.'

'I didn't know you had a sister.'

'She's staying with me for a week or so. I'm sorry, I should have introduced you.'

'It didn't register until later, but . . . I've been digging out some photographs. The kidnapping, eight years ago. You were asking about it, weren't you?'

'Yes, I was. Dave, what's this all about?'

'It's about Anne Wilkinson.'

'The kidnapped girl? What about her?'

'It's about you asking about the kidnapping, the girl in your flat, and putting two and two together.'

'You've lost me, Dave.'

'I don't think I have, Sammy. That girl is Anne Wilkinson. I've got the pics here on my desk. There's no doubt about it. That girl is—'

'Dave, my sister is . . .'

'I'll be there in ten minutes with the pics. Put the kettle on for coffee.'

Hanging up, Samantha knew that she was going to have to tell Dave the truth. He wasn't stupid, and there'd be no denying who Anne was once the photographs were spread out on the table. The truth? He'd never believe that Samantha was able to travel through time, let alone save Anne from the kidnappers and bring her into the future. Ordering the girl to find a dress in the wardrobe, she decided not to say anything about Dave's suspicions.

'My boss is coming round,' she said. 'Stay in here while I talk to him, OK?'

'OK,' Anne trilled, looking through the wardrobe. 'Oh, I like this skirt.'

'Anne, I said find a *dress*. I don't want you wearing miniskirts.'

'All right.'

'I'll try not to be too long with Dave. Switch the TV on and watch the news. The remote is by the bed.'

Leaving the room, Samantha closed the door and went into the kitchen. Although she knew that Anne would still be with her in ten years, she didn't know what those years held. Anything could happen, she mused, refilling the kettle and taking two cups from the cupboard. The girl might even be reunited with her parents. One thing was certain. If word about Samantha's time travelling got out, no one would believe it. But Anne's identity might be questioned, she reflected. Perhaps another trip into the future would reveal . . . But no. She'd decided not to dabble with time travel. Pouring the coffee as the doorbell rang, she took a deep breath. This wasn't going to be easy she knew as she walked through the hall.

'Come in,' she invited Dave as she opened the front door.

'We need to talk, Sammy baby,' he chuckled. 'My little girlie is keeping secrets from me, isn't she?'

'No, I'm not,' Samantha sighed, closing the door and leading him into the kitchen. 'There's your coffee,' she said, sitting at the table.

'Right, where shall we begin?' he asked, sitting opposite her. 'Let's start with you telling me all about Anne Wilkinson.'

'Dave, I . . . You're not going to believe this.'

'Try me.'

'OK, here goes. I've been travelling through time.'

'Er . . . right.'

'I went back eight years and found Anne Wilkinson in a barn. She'd been kidnapped and . . .'

'And you brought her back here, to our time?'

'Yes, that's right.'

'Sammy . . . I really don't think . . .'

'I knew that you wouldn't believe me. How the hell do you think Anne got here? She's the same age as she was when she was kidnapped, Dave.'

'I must admit that she hasn't aged,' he sighed, taking an envelope from his jacket pocket. 'These were taken just before she was kidnapped. Where is she now? Let's take a look at her and . . .'

'Dave, I don't think she's accepted what's happened yet. She's leaped forward eight years and . . .'

'Sammy baby, go and get her. She should be in on this, don't you agree?'

'Yes, but . . . You're not going to plaster this all over the front page, are you?'

'Girl travels back in time and saves kidnap victim? No, I don't think so. I want to sell newspapers, not get myself laughed at.'

'All right, I'll get Anne,' Samantha finally conceded.

Opening the bedroom door, Samantha explained the situation to Anne. The girl raised her gaze to the ceiling. She obviously wasn't keen to talk about her experiences, and Samantha couldn't blame her for that. It must have been difficult enough coping with the kidnapping, let alone suddenly finding herself whisked eight years into the future. Finally following Samantha into the kitchen, she leaned against the worktop as Dave's eyes darted between her and the photographs.

'So, you're Anne Wilkinson?' he asked her.

'Yes,' she replied.

'And Sammy brought you here, eight years in the future?'

'It looks that way.'

'Doesn't that worry you?'

'Worry me?' she breathed. 'What is there to worry about? I was locked in a barn by two men. *That* worried me.'

'Yes, yes, of course. The thing is—'

'Dave,' Samantha cut in. 'You're either going to have to accept that Anne has come here, to our time, eight years ahead of *her* time, or . . .'

'Or what? Come to the conclusion that you're both mad? I can see that this is Anne Wilkinson simply by looking at the photographs. OK, she appears to be the same age. I can't explain that, and I'm not going to accept your explanation unquestioningly. OK, so Anne is here and she appears to be about eight years younger than she is – I mean, than I would have expected.'

'Take a look at these,' Samantha said, taking Anne's miniskirt and blouse out of the washing machine. 'These are the clothes she was wearing in the barn. Look at the photographs, Dave. They are the same clothes.'

'Yes, they appear to be,' he murmured. 'Have you contacted her parents?'

'Anne did ring but . . . They thought that she was some kind of crank, Dave. Anne went missing eight years ago. She was never seen again. To face her parents eight years later and . . . She's the same age that she was when she was kidnapped. She has the same clothes she was wearing. How the hell would we explain that? You don't believe it, so why should her parents?'

'I can prove who I am,' Anne said, pouring herself a cup of coffee.

'You don't have to,' Dave said. 'I've known Sammy long enough to trust her. And there's no denying that you're the girl in the photographs. Why you've not aged is another matter. And one that I don't think I'll ever understand. The point is, what happens now?'

'That's a good question,' Anne sighed. 'As Sam said, I have no National Insurance number or—'

'I can fix that,' Dave interrupted the girl. 'What about your parents? They should be told but . . .'

'Dave, how about Anne working on the paper? I know she's too young, but we're going to do her hair and make-up. By the time we're done, she'll pass for—'

'I could use someone around the office. OK, she can work on the paper and I'll sort out some ID for her. You'll have to think of a new name.'

'We already have. Anne is my younger sister. Her name's Sarah.'

'Sarah it is. I'll sort out some ID and . . . You might have aged a little, Anne,' he said, looking at the photographs again. 'Some people don't age. It might be that you've kept your young looks and—'

'Lift your dress up,' Samantha ordered the girl.

'There,' Anne said, pulling her dress up to her neck. 'Is that the body of a—'

'Jesus,' Dave gasped, his wide eyes focusing on the hairless lips of Anne's vulva. 'Er . . . yes, well . . .'

'You can see that she's the same age,' Samantha said as the girl lowered her dress.

'This is either time travel or medical history. OK, I have to get back to the office. When you've completed your ageing effect on young Anne, bring her into the office.'

'OK, Dave,' Samantha said, seeing him to the front door. 'Thanks.'

'Take care, baby. By the way, why were you asking about the paint factory?'

'Shit, I'd forgotten about that.'

'About what?'

'Nothing. Er . . . I'll see you soon.'

'OK. And keep me posted.'

'As always, Dave. As always.'

Returning to the kitchen, Samantha knew that she was going to have to do something about the girl who was sleeping rough behind the paint factory. All she could do was go there again and try to speak to her, she decided. There'd been so many things going on that she'd forgotten about it. What with Zak and . . . Wondering whether he'd booked the holiday, she suggested that she should have a go at cutting Anne's hair and applying some make-up to add a few years to her tender age. Following Samantha into the bedroom, Anne slipped her dress off and placed a towel around her shoulders as Samantha grabbed a pair of scissors and announced that she wasn't too bad at hairdressing.

'A bob,' Samantha said, standing behind the girl and brushing her hair. 'And then I'll get some black dye.'

'Black?' Anne echoed despondently. 'I prefer auburn.'

'Black, auburn . . . It doesn't matter what colour, as long as it's not blonde.'

'Dave seems nice,' the girl said. 'He didn't believe the time travelling, but he seems like a nice man.'

'He *is* nice,' Samantha replied. 'A bit of a rogue at times, but nice.'

The towel slipped off the girl's shoulders and Samantha eyed the ripe teats of her young breasts in the mirror. Her stomach somersaulting, she did her best not to think about lesbian sex as she brushed the teenager's long blonde hair. Turning her thoughts to Dave, she knew that he wouldn't say anything to anyone about Anne. He certainly wouldn't mention time travelling. Perhaps she should never have mentioned it, she re-

flected. There again, what other explanation could she have given for Anne's presence? Realizing that the young girl was going to be around for the next ten years, she knew that it was futile trying to deny her feelings for her as she focused on the elongated teats of her young breasts again.

'You're beautiful,' Samantha murmured, running her fingertip up and down her spine.

'Shall we forget about my hair?' Anne asked, turning her head and grinning at Samantha.

'Well, we really should . . . I suppose we can do it later,' she finally conceded. 'It seems strange having you live with me. Apart from the fact that you've lost eight years . . .'

'I try not to think about it,' Anne sighed. 'I'll never see my parents again, will I?'

'There might be a way,' Samantha said, taking the girl's hand and leading her to the bed. 'If you write to them, say that you've been abroad . . .'

'It's no good,' Anne sighed despondently. 'No matter how old I say I am, they'll ask too many questions. How did I end up abroad? What happened to me? Where have I been living? Why haven't I contacted them before?'

'Yes, I see what you mean,' Samantha said as Anne lay on the bed and spread her limbs.

'Still, there's no point in going on about it.'

'So, what am I going to do with you?' Samantha asked, eyeing the girl's swollen vaginal lips rising alluringly either side of her young sex crack.

'Do whatever you want to do with me,' Anne replied impishly, her blue eyes sparkling as she licked her succulent lips.

Grinning, Samantha sat on the edge of the bed and ran

'Fuck the sun,' Anne snapped. 'I'm not going to the park to get laid by some dirty old sod.'

'I'll be there to vet the . . . I'll be with you to vet any potential customers. Come on, slip into a dress and we'll go and take a look at the park.'

Complaining as she clambered off the bed, Anne chose a dress from the wardrobe and pulled it over her head. She couldn't have been totally against the idea, Samantha thought as Anne slipped her shoes on and walked into the hall. Had she really not wanted to go to the park, she'd have stayed on the bed rather than get dressed. Following her out of the flat, Samantha walked by her side as they made their way down the street.

'It's this way,' Samantha said, turning a corner. 'Are you all right?'

'I suppose so,' Anne sighed. 'It's just that I thought I'd be working on the newspaper with you. Not getting laid by dirty old men.'

'Anne, stop going on about old men. I'm talking about young lads, not ageing men.'

'I'll still be a prostitute.'

'Whatever you want to call it, we need some money. I want you to do some shopping later. Where's the money for that going to come from?'

'My fanny, I suppose,' Anne quipped.

'Let's sit on that bench over there,' Samantha said, heading across the park towards the fence.

'Now what?' Anne asked grumpily as they reached the bench and sat down. 'Wait for some old pervert to come along and—'

'Shut up, Anne,' Samantha snapped. 'Good grief, there's nothing wrong with having a teenage lad fuck you. It's either that, or you leave the flat and—'

'OK, OK,' the girl sighed. 'I suppose I don't mind teenage boys.'

'Good. Of course . . . I mean, if someone a little older comes along with cash . . .'

'Yes, all right.'

Concealing a smile, Samantha looked around the park. Someone was bound to come along before long, she thought, hoping to build up a few regular customers. It wasn't so much the money, she reflected. Although the cash would come in useful, she was looking forward to watching a huge cock drive into young Anne's little pussy. She wondered if she was a voyeur as she watched a middle-aged man walking across the grass. The thought of a huge penis slipping between the girl's hairless pussy lips making her panties wet, she nudged Anne as the man approached.

'He'll do,' she whispered.

'He's an old man,' Anne complained. 'Besides, he might not have any money on him.'

'Don't be so negative,' Samantha reproached the young girl. 'He's bound to have something in his wallet. Pull your dress up and show your thighs.'

'What are you going to say to him?' she asked, pulling her dress up. '*Hello, do you want to fuck my friend?*'

'Shush,' Samantha murmured as the man stood by the bench and smiled.

'Excuse me,' he said. 'Do you know where the railway station is? I was told to cut through the park, but . . .'

'Yes, you can get to it that way,' Samantha replied, eyeing the crotch of his trousers. 'Follow the fence and you'll come to a road. Cross the bridge and the station is on the left.'

'Thanks,' he said, eyeing Anne's naked thighs.

'Where are you off to?' Samantha asked as Anne parted her legs a little. 'Anywhere interesting?'

'Oh, er . . . no, not really,' he replied abstractedly, his dark-eyed stare fixed on Anne's naked thighs as she opened her legs further.

'If you're not in a hurry, stay with us for a while.'

'Yes, yes, I will. I'm only going to visit a friend, so there's no rush.'

Unable to take his eyes off Anne's inner thighs, the man crouched in front of her, obviously hoping for a glimpse of her tight panties. Wondering what he'd think when he discovered that the young girl was naked beneath her dress, Samantha introduced herself and said that Anne was her sister. His name was Don, he told her. He was in his mid-forties and not bad-looking. He probably had a wife, Samantha mused, wondering how big his cock was. Did his wife suck out his spunk?

'Do you like Anne's legs?' Samantha asked unashamedly.

'Er . . . well . . .' he stammered, rising to his feet.

'She should be at school today, shouldn't you, Anne?'

'Yes, I should. But I thought I'd come to the park instead.'

'Anne wants to learn about sex,' Samantha said, wondering how to broach the subject of offering Don the girl's young body in return for cash. 'She's a virgin and she wants to experience sex.'

'Aren't you a little young?' he breathed, frowning darkly.

'All my friends have had sex,' Anne sighed. 'I must be the only virgin in my class.'

'You're obviously not into young girls,' Samantha said.

'Well, it's not that I'm . . . I just thought she seemed rather young.'

'She might be young, but she's got what it takes,' Samantha giggled. 'Show him your pussy, Anne.'

Lifting her dress high up over her stomach, Anne parted her legs wide and displayed the hairless lips of her naked vulva to the shocked man. Grinning, Samantha watched the bulge in his crotch growing as his cock stiffened. He must have thought them a couple of tarts, she mused. With her pussy shaved, Anne looked far younger than her already tender age. Perhaps she appeared rather *too* young, Samantha thought. There again, how could he resist such a little beauty?

'We're hoping to find a young lad to initiate her in the fine art of sex,' Samantha said as Anne massaged the fleshy lips of her vagina.

'Nice,' Don murmured. 'Very nice. Er . . . a young lad? The trouble with young lads is that they don't have any experience. Anne would be better off with someone who knows what they're doing.'

'Yes, you're probably right. Would *you* like to teach her?'

'What? Er . . .'

'How much money do you have?'

'Well, I . . .'

'She wants to follow in my footsteps, you see. I earn money from sex, and Anne wants to do the same.'

'Yes, yes – of course I would. God, she's absolutely beautiful.'

'One hundred pounds,' Samantha said firmly.

'One hundred . . . I only have about fifty.'

'That'll do,' she said as he took his wallet out of his jacket pocket. 'Right, come this way,' she ordered him.

Grabbing the money, Samantha led Anne and her stunned client through the gap in the fence. This was easy, she mused, instructing Anne to slip out of her dress as the man watched with bated breath. Anne had a beautiful young body, Samantha observed again as the girl stood naked on the soft grass. Her boyish figure gave her an air of innocence, her hairless vulva adding to the fantasy of her being a young virgin girl. Her barely formed breasts topped with ripe nipples, her long blonde hair cascading over her shoulders, she licked her lips provocatively as the man scrutinized her naked body.

'What do you think?' Samantha asked the man.

'I think she's lovely,' he replied, his trousers almost bursting open with his obvious arousal.

'Why don't you start by licking her pussy?' she suggested, her own juices of desire seeping between her pouting outer lips.

'Er . . . yes, yes – I will.'

Kneeling in front of Anne, Don wasted no time in running his wet tongue up and down the tightly closed crack of her naked vulva. Samantha could hear his heavy breathing, the slurping of his tongue as he tasted the fresh juices of the young girl's vaginal slit. Gripping her slender hips as she spread her feet wide, he pushed his face hard against the softness of her naked vulva and slipped his tongue into the virginal – he thought – hole of her young pussy. Anne trembled, her naked body swaying as he worked between her legs, his tongue teasing the inner flesh of her tightening sex sheath.

Kneeling behind Anne, Samantha parted the rounded cheeks of her firm buttocks and tasted the brown tissue of her anus. Shuddering as the two tongues licked and slurped, Anne gasped as Samantha pushed her tongue

deep into her anal hole and caressed her rectal flesh. Samantha was unable to help herself, succumbing to her base lesbian yearnings as she parted the girl's buttocks wide, her thumbs opening her rectal inlet. The man must have thought it odd that she should lick her sister's bottom-hole, Samantha reflected. Whatever he thought, she knew that the 'incestuous' act of lesbianism would send his arousal soaring.

Hoping that she wouldn't suddenly be transported to another time and place, Samantha pressed her wet lips against Anne's anal ring and sucked hard. Savouring the bitter-sweet taste of the girl's rectal tube, she sank her fingernails into the firm flesh of Anne's naked buttocks and parted the rounded cheeks of her young bottom further. She could hear the man's tongue slurping as Anne whimpered in the beginnings of her climax. Her bottom-hole tightening, she cried out as her solid clitoris finally exploded in orgasm beneath the man's sweeping tongue.

'Yes,' she gasped, clinging to Don's head as her naked body shook violently. Two mouths sucking, two tongues teasing out her pleasure, her cuntal milk gushed from the gaping entrance of her vagina and streamed down the pale flesh of her inner thighs. The man's cock would be solid by now Samantha knew as she slipped her tongue out of Anne's hot bottom-hole and pushed her finger deep into her rectal tube. Pistoning her young flatmate's tight arse, Samantha reached between Anne's legs and grabbed the bulging crotch of the man's trousers. His cock was indeed rock-hard, and she knew that he'd be desperate to force his penis deep into the young girl's tight cunt and pump out his spunk. But he was going to have to wait for the illicit pleasure, she decided.

Slipping her finger out of Anne's rectal canal, Samantha ran her tongue up and down the younger girl's anal gully, delighting in the bitter-sweet taste of her rectal opening. Breathing in the teenager's anal musk, she felt herself beginning to slip away through time. Clinging to Anne's naked buttocks, she knew she didn't want this. If she was going to travel to another time and place, then she wanted to be in control, decide when and where she was going. Besides, she couldn't simply dematerialize, leaving Anne alone with . . .

'I want to get out of here before too long,' Gerry Andrews said as Samantha found herself outside the correction-room door. 'The place costs too much to run. Even with the dancing school bringing good money . . .'

'You're no businessman, that's the trouble,' Kitty broke in. 'You allow the punters to owe you money and you end up losing out.'

'I was trying to boost the numbers, Kitty. Not everyone can afford our fees. I thought that—'

'You thought that, by not charging some people, you'd eventually get more clients and make more money? It doesn't work like that, Gerry. If a man can't afford our fees, then he should pick up a tart from a street corner. We're not running some seedy backstreet brothel.'

'I know that. I just thought—'

'Leave the thinking to me, Gerry. As far as running the mansion is concerned, you're right. It costs far too much to keep this place. You should have sold it, as I suggested.'

'No one would buy this place. It's falling down, for God's sake.'

'If it's a liability, then get rid of it and we'll move the school . . . Ever thought of living abroad?'

'Abroad? Yes, I have, as it happens.'

'How about moving the school to another country?'

'How would that help, Kitty?'

'Find somewhere cheap to buy. A secluded villa in Spain or Greece.'

'That's hardly cheap.'

'If we start putting money away, it won't take too long to build up enough cash to set up abroad.'

'No, I suppose not,' Andrews murmured. 'Our expenses would be a fraction of what we have to pay out for the upkeep of this place. OK, let's start making some plans. The first thing to decide is what to do with the mansion.'

'Give it away.'

'*What?*' he gasped. 'Just *give* it to someone?'

'I'll cost less in the long run. Think about it. You put it up for sale and it could take months or even years before you find a buyer.'

'I'll sell it off cheap.'

'You'll never sell it, Gerry. If it's cheap, no one will want it because they'll think there's some major problem with the place. And, if someone was interested, they'd have surveyors crawling all over the place and—'

'I see your point, Kitty. But to simply give it away . . .'

'You work out what it costs per month to run the place, and then assume that it could take twelve months or more to sell it. Add to that the fact that the building is falling down around your ears . . .'

'Yes, you're right. I won't give it away, though. I'll get fifty grand or so for it.'

'Try, if you wish. But remember this – the longer you

keep this place, the more money we're going to have to part with. We have a new girl arriving soon. I'll go and wait in the hall.'

Slipping along the corridor into the surgery, Samantha began to wonder whether she'd want to own a mansion that was falling down and cost a fortune to run. At least she now knew why she was going to be given the place, she reflected. She'd make a go of it she knew as she looked around the surgery. It wouldn't be too difficult to bring in more than enough cash to run the place and make a tidy profit.

Again wondering why she'd been transported through time, she closed her eyes and concentrated on Anne. She had to get back to the park she knew as she pictured the man licking the full length of the young girl's hairless sex slit. To flit from one place to another like this had no apparent purpose. She wasn't learning anything in particular, she mused. Nothing of any importance, anyway . . .

Slipping through time, Samantha frowned as she realized that she was in an old church. This wasn't the church she'd attended when she was young she was sure as she looked around her. As her eyes adjusted to the dimly lit church, she noticed several naked men standing in front of the altar. This involved crude sex she knew as she turned and looked at the closed doors. She wondered why she had been brought here as she sat on a pew at the back of the church where the shadows concealed her.

A realization hitting her, she thought back to her early teens. She'd been heavily into fantasizing during her masturbation sessions. Vicars, schoolteachers, groups of men . . . Her fantasies had often worried her and, at

times, she'd thought that she wasn't normal. Her fantasies had usually involved several men. As she'd rubbed her clitoris to orgasm, she'd imagine several men pleasuring her naked body. She'd probably had fantasies about vicars because of her sexual experiences after Sunday school each week. Thinking about her schoolteacher during masturbation was understandable.

Wondering whether her trips to different times and places had something to do with her fantasies, Samantha realized that someone or something paranormal might *not* be pulling the strings. There might *not* be an unseen being at the bottom of this, she reflected, as she recalled one particular fantasy she'd had. She was held prisoner in a small room – several men had captured her and stripped her, laughing at her tearful pleas and her pathetic attempts to struggle free of their brutal grasp. She hadn't been able to escape as they'd run their hands over her naked body and pressed the stiff shafts of their huge penises against her. She wondered if that was why she'd travelled to the barn. Thinking about the dancing school, she recalled the times during her early teens when she'd thought about becoming a ballerina. It had been the thought of wearing a tight leotard and doing the splits in front of an audience that had excited her.

Confused, she bit her lip as she realized that the power pulling the strings, the force that had transported her to different times and places where she experienced crude sex, might be her own subconscious mind. If that was the case, then these were her fantasies coming true, she reflected fearfully. There was no way she could control her subconscious she was sure as the naked men turned and walked up the aisle towards her.

Gazing at the men's huge penises snaking over their

heavy balls as they approached, she realized that sucking Brian off in her parents' garden had been another fantasy that she'd enjoyed in her early teens. A man's cock in her mouth, the danger of her mother catching her committing the debased act . . . The more she thought about it, the more she realized that her subconscious thoughts were emerging from the shadowy depths of her mind into the light of day.

'Satan has brought her unto us,' one man said, taking Samantha's arm and pulling her off the pew and into the aisle. 'Satan has risen from the dark and brought unto us a virgin.' Saying nothing as the man led her towards the altar, Samantha knew that this was another of her teenage fantasies coming true. She'd found a book at a friend's house and had avidly read a story about a young girl taken to a church by several men. The girl had been stripped and laid on the altar as a sacrifice to Satan. The men had fucked her, each one taking his turn to drive his solid cock deep into the hitherto virginal sheath of her tight cunt. The story had excited Samantha and driven her to masturbate vigorously several times every day until the fantasy eventually faded from her young mind.

'Satan has sent his daughter,' the man said, his deep voice echoing around the old church. 'Strip her and lay her on the altar.' Remaining still as several men tore her clothes away from her young body, exposing the small mounds of her barely developed breasts, she realized that she'd travelled back in time to her early teens. She wasn't sure how old she was, but her breast buds were small, the lips of her pouting vulva devoid of hair. This had been a major fantasy, she reflected. And one that had not only sent her arousal soaring, but had terrified her.

As the men laid her young body on the altar, she knew

that she could do nothing to prevent the imminent horrendous sexual abuse. Recalling the book she'd read, she remembered the scene where Satan had materialized and pushed his massive penis deep into the young girl's virginal cunt and fucked her. Was that what was going to happen? Her sexual experiences had been real enough during her various time travels. Thinking again that none of this made sense, she puzzled over Anne, knowing that her subconscious didn't have the power to take the girl eight years forward in time.

Her legs pulled wide apart, her feet hanging down either side of the altar, Samantha knew that the hairless valley of her vagina was gaping wide open as the men gazed longingly at her naked body. A cushion was placed beneath her head and she realized that they wanted her to be able to see her yawning vaginal crack, witness the crude shafting of her young pussy as she gazed between the small mounds of her breasts and focused on the gentle rise of her naked mons. Wondering why they wanted her to view the crude fucking of her young cunt, she watched a man part the fleshy lips of her vulva with his long fingers. The intricate folds of her vaginal valley bared in front of her audience, her ripening clitoris emerging from beneath its pink hood, she let out a rush of breath as two fingers drove deep into the tight sheath of her pussy.

Watching her lower stomach rise as the man's fingers bent and twisted inside the creamy sheath of her young cunt, Samantha knew that she was in for several hours of barbaric sex. But she'd endure whatever they did to her young and completely defenceless body. The future lay ahead and would unfold as it should. The dancing school, the mansion, marriage . . . She'd survive her horrendous time in the church, she knew.

'Satan, we offer this virgin girl unto you in the name and the power of darkness,' the man standing behind Samantha's head chanted. 'Through us, oh master, we offer you defilement of her virgin body. Through our flesh, we invite you to desecrate the sanctity of the virgin state. By employing our bodies, we beckon you to defile the sacredness of this girl's virginity.'

Her eyes wide, Samantha watched as one man climbed onto the altar and knelt between her splayed thighs. The solid shaft of his huge penis hovering above the hairless flesh of her vulva, his purple plum swollen in readiness to tear down the curtain of her innocence, he ran the glans of his penis up and down the moist gully of her quim. There were seven men, she counted, realizing that each in turn would drive his solid cock into her pink pussy and fuck her. Seven men, seven cocks . . .

'Through the flesh of my penis, oh master,' the man cried, looking up to the roof of the church, 'I offer you the power to defile the virgin girl.' His bulbous glans forcing its way past Samantha's inner lips and driving deep into the restricted sheath of her vagina, he impaled her fully on his staff of lust. Shuddering as she gazed at the hairless lips of her vagina stretched tautly around the broad base of the man's penis, Samantha felt that her pelvic cavity was bloated to capacity by the huge cock-shaft.

Gazing in awe as the outer lips of her vulva rolled back and forth along the man's veined shaft as he began his fucking motions, she watched her lower abdomen rise and fall with the vaginal pistoning. She could feel the sensitive nub of her clitoris inflating, swelling as her debased arousal rocketed. The thought of her naked body lying on an altar, with the first of seven men fucking

the tight duct of her young vagina, was driving her into a sexual frenzy. Her juices of desire squelching with the illicit fucking, streaming from her bloated vaginal canal and flowing down between the firm cheeks of her buttocks, she knew that she'd once more found her domain.

Was this a dream? Was she still with Anne behind the fence, watching the middle-aged man mouthing and slurping between the fleshy lips of the young girl's cunt? Her confusion mingling with her amazing arousal, her eyes rolling, Samantha felt herself drifting as if on a cloud of sheer ecstasy as the teats of her young breasts were pinched and squeezed. She knew that she was going to experience a massive orgasm as the man fucking her tight cunt began gasping in his Satanic fucking.

'In the name of darkness,' the man gasped, repeatedly ramming his bulbous cockhead deep into Samantha's spasming cunt. 'In the name of darkness, I . . . I strip the girl of her virginity and . . . and fill her with the seed of Satan.' Samantha could feel his spunk jetting from his throbbing knob, bathing the soft firmness of her ripe cervix as his swinging balls battered the tensed cheeks of her naked bottom. Again and again, he thrust his orgasming knob deep into her trembling body, his sperm lubricating the inflamed sheath of her vagina as he fucked her with a vengeance.

The other men stood watching the lewd act of defilement, awaiting their turn to flood her orifices with their sperm. Samantha cried out as her orgasm erupted within the cock-massaged protrusion of her pulsating clitoris. Her young body shaking violently, she arched her back delighting in the pain and pleasure emanating from her firm breasts as two men sank their teeth into the dark

discs of her areolae and sucked hard on the brown protrusions of her sensitive nipples. Her whole body alive with sex, her head lolling from side to side, her screams of ecstasy echoed around the church as her orgasm peaked.

The first man finally withdrawing his deflating cock, Samantha whimpered in the aftermath of her enforced orgasm as she waited for the next cock to drive deep into her sperm-flooded cunt and fuck her to another mind-blowing orgasm. As two men lifted her feet high into the air, pressing her knees hard against the mounds of her small breasts, she knew that the brown ring of her anus was fully exposed between the taut globes of her naked bottom. Were they going to fuck her there? She trembled in anticipation as spunk oozed from her inflamed cuntal opening and streamed over the delicate tissue of her bottom-hole.

'Satan, we offer you the girl's body in the name of debased sex.' Someone's voice resounded around the church as another man climbed onto the altar. His bulbous knob pressing against the sperm-covered entrance to Samantha's rectum, he grabbed her hips and drove his solid cock-shaft deep into her bowels with such force that her naked body slid along the altar. Her delicate brown ring stretched painfully around the massive root of his huge cock, her bowels inflated by his swollen knob, she felt as if she was going to split open. The anal fucking commencing, the man's solid cock repeatedly withdrawing and driving deep into the very core of her teenage body, Samantha grimaced as she writhed and squirmed on the altar.

Her legs lifted higher, her feet wide apart above her head, she could feel the sperm squeezing out of her

vaginal shaft as her rectal tube repeatedly inflated and deflated with the illicit fucking. The spunk dribbling down between the tensed cheeks of her naked buttocks, lubricating the thrusting male organ, she thought that her naked body would split in two as her legs were pulled further apart. Again and again, the man forcefully propelled the veined shaft of his solid cock deep into the core of her bowels, gasping in his forbidden act as his swinging balls pummelled the smooth orbs of her young arse.

Another man climbing onto the altar and pressing his swollen glans hard against her pursed lips, Samantha opened her mouth wide and sucked on his salty knob. She had no choice she knew as she ran her pink tongue over the silky-smooth surface of his purple crown. But, she wondered, did she *want* a choice? Taking the naked man's cockhead to the back of her throat and sinking her teeth gently into the solid rod of his penis, she knew that this was crude sex, illicit sex, sex so debased . . . This was Samantha . . .

'No,' she breathed, looking around her as she lay on her bed in her parents' house with a young lad licking between the swollen lips of her pink pussy. This had been another fantasy she'd enjoyed while masturbating in her early teens. A boy licking her vaginal crack, pushing his tongue deep into the virgin duct of her sex-drenched cunt as she'd massaged her clitoris to orgasm. 'I don't want this,' Samantha murmured, desperate to return to the church, to the crude abuse of her naked body.

10

'That was great,' Anne giggled, her naked body lying on the soft grass next to Samantha.

'What happened?' Samantha asked, wondering why she'd returned to the railway cutting. 'Didn't you wonder where I'd got to?'

'What?' the girl murmured, frowning at Samantha. 'When?'

'I left you here with the man.'

'Left me?' Anne chuckled. 'I know that Don fucked you to a massive orgasm, but I didn't realize he'd blow your mind away in the process.'

'I . . . I've been here all the time?'

'Of course you have. Are you all right, Sam? Where do you think you've been?'

'I . . . You're right. I must have had such a massive orgasm that my mind blew away. But I'm OK now.'

'You had me worried for a minute. I thought you were going to say that you'd been off on one of your time travelling escapades.'

'No, no, of course not.'

Looking down at her naked body, Samantha couldn't understand how she'd been in two places at the same time. But it *hadn't* been the same time, she reflected. Different times, different places . . . Perhaps it wasn't so difficult to understand, she thought. She was at the office

during the day and in her bed at night. Different times, she mused. In the church, and by the railway cutting . . . Although she was confused, she was beginning to see that it was perfectly feasible to be at different places, as long as there was a time difference.

'I've got his wallet,' Anne giggled.

'You stole it?' Samantha asked.

'Why not? He was only going to pay fifty.'

'Yes, and I agreed to that.'

'Now we have two hundred.'

'Two hundred? Anne, you can't steal money . . .'

'I had his wallet out of his pocket before he had time—'

'That's it,' Samantha broke in . . . 'Before time.'

'What?'

'Time travel. If I travelled back in time by a split second, you wouldn't be able to see me.'

'I'm not with you, Sam.'

'Exactly. You wouldn't be with me because I'd be a split second before your time. I'd always be just behind you, never catching up with you so you wouldn't see me. But I'd see you because you'd just been in my time. I'd be watching your every move, but a split second behind you. Imagine that you're filling the kettle at one minute past twelve. My time is exactly twelve, one minute before you. When my time reaches one minute past, I can see you filling the kettle. Of course, you're then at two minutes past and might be taking the milk out of the fridge . . .'

'Yes, yes, I see what you're getting at. But what about it?'

'That explains why I've been back in time and I've seen people but they've not seen me.'

'Oh, right,' Anne sighed, frowning at Samantha.

'How that fits in with living out fantasies, I don't know. Do you ever fantasize?'

'Of course. Doesn't everyone?'

'Yes, I suppose they do,' Samantha murmured pensively. 'My mother always says be careful what it is you want because you might get it.'

'Now you *have* lost me.'

'Fantasies are a sort of wanting, aren't they? They're wishful thinking, imagining scenarios that you'd like to happen, scenes that you'd like to be part of.'

'And?'

'I have no idea,' Samantha sighed, grabbing her clothes and dressing. 'I know what I'm talking about, but I don't know what it means.'

'Perhaps *you*'re a fantasy,' Anne giggled. 'Perhaps you don't exist. You're just a fantasy in my mind.'

'You could be right there.'

'I was joking, Sam,' the girl laughed, pulling her dress over her head. 'Of course you're not a fantasy. You're real.'

'Am I? I'm beginning to wonder. Take this split-second business a step further. There might be other people here, by the railway cutting, but they're a split second before our time so we can't see or hear them.'

'But they can see and hear us?'

'Yes. No, I mean . . . Now I'm confusing myself. I'm going to give this some serious thought,' Samantha said eagerly as she finished dressing. 'I've hit upon something, I'm sure of it.'

'There's no one here a split second ahead of us.'

'What?'

'We'd see them, wouldn't we? If they were just ahead of us in time, we'd see them.'

'Oh, er . . . yes, yes, we would.'

'What are you doing here?' a young man asked as he slipped through the gap in the fence. 'This is railway property. Besides, it's dangerous. You could fall down the embankment and—'

'Don't be so pompous,' Samantha cut in. 'We're not children, for goodness' sake.'

'No, but this *is* railway property.'

'Then why doesn't the railway have the fence repaired? If kids got in . . .'

'What are you doing here?'

'Relaxing beneath the sun,' Samantha sighed. 'At least, we were.'

'And train-spotting,' Anne giggled.

'Yes, well . . . you'd better leave. And be sure you don't trespass again.'

'You don't have a wife or a girlfriend, do you?' Samantha asked him.

'Er . . . no, no, I don't.'

'I thought as much. With your attitude, I'm not surprised.'

'Now you listen to me, young lady.'

'Young lady? You're no older than me,' Samantha laughed.

'And she's no lady,' Anne chuckled.

'Thanks,' Samantha murmured.

'Shall we wank him off?'

'Anne, for God's sake.'

'Would you like me to suck your cock?' the girl asked him impishly.

'Suck . . . Good grief . . .' he stammered.

'Go on, get your cock out and I'll suck it and you can come in my mouth.'

Shaking her head as Anne knelt in front of the young man and tugged his zip down, Samantha couldn't help but laugh. His face was a picture, she thought, as the girl hauled his flaccid cock out of his trousers and sucked his purple knob into her wet mouth. Gazing down in disbelief as she gobbled on his cockhead, his face flushing, he began gasping as his involuntary arousal stiffened the shaft of his penis. As Anne slipped her hand behind the man and eased his wallet out of his back pocket, Samantha knew that she was going to have to do something to correct her young friend's thieving ways. It was one thing taking money in return for sex but just stealing it like that was despicable. Watching as Anne tossed the wallet into the long grass behind the young man, Samantha moved to the fence and picked it up.

He only had a twenty-pound note, she discovered, looking through his wallet. He was probably saving it for a drink in the pub that evening or . . . Taking the money, she slipped the wallet back into his pocket. This was cash in exchange for a mouth-fucking, she decided, slipping the rolled-up note into the deep gully of her mammary cleavage. Besides, having his money taken would serve him right for being a pompous git.

'God,' he gasped, his legs swaying as he clutched Anne's head and flooded her gobbling mouth with his creamy sperm. Samantha could hear the girl gulping down his orgasmic fluid as the man's low moans of pleasure filled the summer air. A train rumbling through the cutting below, drowning out the sounds of Anne's spunk-drinking, Samantha realized that the girl was fun to be with. She was young, too young perhaps for this sort of thing. But she was good company and enjoyed a laugh.

'God,' the man breathed again, slipping his spent cock out of Anne's sperm-flooded mouth and zipping his trousers. 'I . . . I'd better be going.'

'Now you've come, you can go,' Anne giggled, licking her spunk-glossed lips.

'Er . . . yes, right. And don't trespass on railway property again,' he growled as he slipped through the fence.

'Where's the wallet?' Anne asked, searching through the long grass.

'I put it back in his pocket,' Samantha said. 'Stealing is a terrible thing, Anne.'

'You put it *back*?' the girl asked, frowning furiously.

'I emptied it first,' Samantha giggled, pulling the twenty-pound note from her deep cleavage. 'You mustn't steal, Anne. It's not right to—'

'*You* stole,' the girl returned. 'You've taken twenty—'

'No, I didn't. I took the money by way of payment for him fucking your pretty little mouth. Anyway, he was an arse and he deserves to have his money taken.'

'Let's find some more men,' Anne breathed excitedly, licking her salty lips again. 'I'm quite enjoying this.'

'We'll come back later. We should go home and do something with your hair. We'll get some hair dye on the way.'

Leaving the park with Anne in tow, Samantha thought again about time travelling. She was going to have to use her gift to her advantage, she decided. Flitting from one debased sexual experience to another was all very well, but she knew that she should use her gift for something other than fun. She also needed more control over where she travelled to, she reflected. Wondering what to do about her job as Anne went into a chemist and chose

some auburn hair dye, she turned her thoughts to journalism. Was that what she really wanted? There was more than enough money to be made from prostitution, but . . . The terrible word jolting her mind, she tried to convince herself that all she was doing was having some fun and making money in the process.

As Anne went into the bathroom to dye her hair, Samantha filled the kettle. At least the girl would be able to go out shopping without having to worry about people recognizing her. Things were going to work out well Samantha knew as she poured herself a cup of coffee. Now that Dave was in on the secret, he'd be able to help with some ID and . . . Anne really should work on the paper, Samantha reflected guiltily. She was far too young to be selling her body for sex. Answering the phone, Samantha frowned as a man asked for Anne Wilkinson.

'Who?' Samantha breathed shakily.

'Anne Wilkinson,' he repeated.

'I'm sorry but you have the wrong number.'

'I don't think so,' he chuckled. 'I know she's there so you might as well let me talk to her.'

'I'm sorry, but I don't know anyone by that name,' Samantha returned, feeling that he was going to threaten her. 'You have the wrong number.'

'I'm not going to waste time,' he snapped. 'Anne Wilkinson is there with you. Where she's been for the last eight years, I don't know. But I'm going to find out. And when I contact her parents . . .'

'If you're talking about that girl who was kidnapped—'

'You know damned well I am.'

'What is it you want?'

'Money,' he murmured. 'I reckon that you were in on the kidnapping.'

'That's ridiculous,' Samantha retorted. 'I was only a kid at the time.'

'You've been to the park with the girl. I saw you walking through the park with Anne Wilkinson so don't deny it. I'll meet you there in one hour. Both of you.'

As he hung up, Samantha felt her stomach churning. She'd learned nothing about this during her time travels, she reflected. Apart from discovering that she was going to own the mansion and marry John, she'd learned nothing of any real value. *Was* she going to marry John? She began to wonder. She'd never fantasized about the man, but . . . Sipping her coffee, she sat at the table and tried to formulate a plan.

'Shit,' she breathed, wondering who had recognized the girl. They must have followed Anne and Samantha back to the flat and then somehow discovered the phone number. If this man *did* contact Anne's parents . . . It didn't bear thinking about Samantha knew as she wondered what the hell to do. Once Anne had auburn hair, the chances of anyone realizing who she was were minimal. Even her parents probably wouldn't recognize her. Besides, they'd be expecting a girl eight years older.

This was going to work out, Samantha thought as she finished her coffee. If the man did start blabbing, then Anne would simply say that it was a case of mistaken identity. Her name was Sarah. She was Samantha's sister and she . . . This might not be so easy after all, Samantha thought. There was no way to prove that the girl was her sister. Deciding to meet the man in the park, Samantha knew that her only option was to use her gift of time travel to find out more about him. If she could go to the park a split second before he arrived . . .

'Well?' Anne trilled as she breezed into the kitchen.

'God, that's amazing,' Samantha gasped. 'You look nothing like . . . Once we've cut your hair, no one will ever recognize you. And I love the make-up. The transformation really is amazing.'

'I'll go shopping now.'

'No, no . . .'

'Why not? I thought you wanted me to—'

'Anne, I've just had a phone call from a man who says that he recognized you. He saw us walking through the park.'

'Who is he?'

'I don't know. But he wants money to keep quiet.'

'Blackmail?' the girl gasped. 'What has he threatened to do?'

'Go to your parents. He wants to meet us in the park in one hour.'

'What shall we do? How much does he want?'

'I don't know what to do yet, and he hasn't said how much he wants to keep quiet. Whatever happens, we're not giving him a penny.'

'But if he goes to my parents and—'

'Don't worry, I'll think of something.'

'Do you want another coffee?' Anne asked, switching the kettle on.

'I could do with some vodka,' Samantha laughed. 'No, no, I'm fine.'

As the girl made herself a cup of tea, Samantha rested her chin on her clasped hands. Trying to think back to the park, she didn't recall seeing anyone. Apart from the middle-aged man . . . That was it, she thought. And the young man who'd complained about trespassing. Thinking back, Samantha realized that she'd used Anne's name. He'd obviously put two and two together and

followed them back to the flat. There again, perhaps it was the middle-aged man, she reflected.

'I'm going to the park,' she announced, standing up and moving to the door.

'What about me?' Anne asked. 'I thought I was going with you.'

'That's what he wants, but I think it's best if I go alone. Beside, you look different now. We don't want to give away your new look.'

'Be careful, Sam,' the girl murmured, frowning.

'I will. You stay here, all right? Don't go wandering off anywhere.'

'I'll stay here, I promise. And don't worry, I won't answer the phone or the door.'

'Good girl. OK, I'll see you later.'

Leaving the flat, Samantha kept her eyes peeled as she walked down the road. This was all she needed, she thought as she neared the park. There were enough problems without some bastard trying to make some easy money out of her predicament. Sure that she'd not been followed, she crossed the park to the bench and sat down. She was fifteen minutes early, but had wanted to get there first to have time alone to think.

The plight of the girl sleeping rough behind the paint factory playing on her mind, she knew that it was pointless driving out there again. The girl would hear her and do a runner. Besides, even if she did get to talk to her, she'd never believe that the factory was going to burn down. Perhaps there wasn't going to be a fire, Samantha mused. She'd never fantasized about fires, so . . . Not knowing what to think, she wondered whether Zak had booked the holiday. Hoping that he'd blown several thousand pounds on his credit card, she

couldn't wait to see his face when she announced that she'd changed her mind. Zak would go mad, but there'd be nothing he could do about it.

Grinning, Samantha imagined Zak trying to get his money back, or suggesting that Angela help him with the debt. They could both go off and enjoy the holiday, she mused. There again, they'd have to get the tickets changed. They'd have to change Samantha's name to Angela, and that might not be possible. And Zak would still be unable to pay off his credit card. Her thoughts turning to Kitty, she recalled Julie, the young girl lying on the bed in the woman's house. Wondering what had happened to the girl, she thought that she was probably still working at the so-called dancing school. And what was Jane up to? she mused. She must have realized that her diary had gone and—

Noticing a man walking towards her, she didn't recognize him. He was in his fifties, smartly dressed in a light suit and shirt and tie. His greying hair swept back from his suntanned face, he wasn't bad-looking for his age. But Samantha had to drag her thoughts away from prostitution and concentrate on the blackmailer. The pompous young man who'd complained about trespassing was the culprit, she was sure. He'd heard Samantha use Anne's name, he'd had more than a good look at the girl . . .

'Mind if I join you?' the grey-haired man asked, sitting beside Samantha.

'No, not at all,' she replied. This wasn't the blackmailer, was it? 'It's a nice day for a walk in the park.'

'Yes, yes, it is. I thought I'd get out of the house for a while and enjoy the sunshine. My wife's got a couple of friends round. I thought I'd be better off out of her way. I know it's a terrible line but, do you come here often?'

'No, I don't,' Samantha replied abstractedly, scanning the park for her blackmailer.

'Do you live far away?'

'Er . . . just up the road.'

'I'm sorry if I'm intruding. Perhaps I'd better leave you in peace.'

'No, not at all. I've got a lot on my mind, that's all.'

'A problem shared.'

'I . . . I don't want to talk about it. I'm Sam, by the way.'

'Rob,' he said, shaking her hand. 'Is it money? The problem, I mean.'

'Er . . . no, no. It's not money.'

'A relationship problem?' he persisted. 'I must admit that my wife and I don't get on at all well. We should never have married, I suppose. But we did, and now we're stuck with each other.'

'You could always get divorced,' Samantha suggested.

'It's too late for that,' he chuckled. 'We've been together too long to part company now. I must say it's quite refreshing, talking to a beautiful young girl like you. My wife and her old cronies . . . Ah, well. Not to worry. I take it that you're not married?'

'What makes you think that?'

'I don't know. You don't seem to be the type to marry young.'

'You're right, Rob. I'm not married.'

'I don't suppose you'd consider . . . No, of course you wouldn't.'

'Consider what?' Samantha asked, having a pretty good idea of what he was about to say.

'I just thought that we might meet again. Just for a chat, of course.'

'Are you really that unhappy in your marriage?'

'Yes, I suppose I am.'

'That's terrible,' Samantha sighed. 'You should get out of the marriage if it's no good. I wouldn't stay in a relationship . . .'

'I'm too old to start again, Sam.'

'Never,' she chuckled. 'You're good-looking. You'd have no trouble finding someone.'

'Would you like to go out for a meal one evening?'

'Er . . . well . . .'

'I can see that you don't want to. I'm sorry, I shouldn't have asked you.'

'No, no, it's not that I don't want to. The truth is, I'm supposed to be meeting someone here. Not a boyfriend. Far from it, in fact. It's someone who's demanding money from me.'

'So, you *do* have money worries?'

'No, no . . . He's trying to blackmail me. He knows something about me and . . . Oh, I don't know. It's a long story.'

'So, where is he?'

'He said he'd be here . . . Perhaps he's seen me with you and gone away.'

'Oh. You should have said. Look, I'll go if—'

'No, I want you to stay. I should never have agreed to meet this man. Even if I did give him money, he'd only come back for more.'

'This thing he's got on you . . . Would it really matter if he told people about it?'

'Actually, it's not to do with me. It's a friend of mine. This man knows that my friend is . . . It's all rather complicated.'

'Tell me about it.'

'My friend is in hiding. No, that doesn't sound right. She's starting a new life. She's going under a different name and trying to begin a new life. This man, whoever he is, knows about her old life and is threatening to tell her parents about her.'

'Oh, I see,' Rob murmured, rubbing his chin. 'Well, I don't know what to suggest. Your friend could move away from the area.'

'Yes, we'd thought of that. She's living with me at the moment but . . . Anyway, we'll work something out.'

'I like you, Sam,' he said, placing his hand on her knee. 'I'd like to get to know you.'

'Yes, well . . .'

'I have money.'

'Money?'

'I mean . . . This will sound terrible, but . . . I'd like to see you again and, if it takes money, then so be it.'

'What are you getting at? You mean that you'd pay me to go out with you?'

'It sounds awful, doesn't it?'

'I don't know. But it does show how unhappy you are in your marriage.'

'Marriage?' he chuckled. 'It's a farce. I haven't had sex for . . . You don't want to know about that.'

'If it's sex you want . . .'

'Yes?'

'You're going to think *me* awful now,' Samantha sighed.

'Go on.'

'I *am* rather short of money. I suppose I could . . .'

'I'm very desperate, Sam. God, that sounds terrible. You're so young, attractive . . .'

'Come with me,' she said, leaving the bench. 'I'm pretty desperate too, so . . . Come with me.'

Leading the man through the gap in the fence, Samantha knew that she shouldn't be doing this. But she felt sorry for him. Stuck in an unhappy marriage, no sex life . . . She also needed something to take her mind off her own problems. Sitting on the short grass, she lay back beneath the summer sun and spread her legs. He sat beside her, obviously wondering what to do as he gazed at the firm flesh of her inner thighs. Pulling her skirt up, exposing the tight material of her panties to his wide eyes, she smiled.

'Well?' she said huskily. 'I'm all yours.'

'Sam, I . . . I don't know what to say,' Rob breathed, running his fingertip up her inner thigh to the triangular patch of her moist panties.

'You don't have to say anything, Rob. You're unhappy, lonely . . . I need something to relax me, take my mind off my worries . . .'

'What about money?' he asked, pressing his fingertip into the soft swelling of her panties. 'How much do you want?'

'Let's not talk about money. Let's not talk about anything.'

'It's been years since I last—'

'Then you'd better make up for it.'

Closing her eyes and spreading her legs further as he stroked the wetting crotch of her panties, Samantha couldn't help but think about the blackmailer. There was nothing the man could do, she mused, her young body trembling as Rob slipped his finger between the top of her thigh and her panties. If he told Anne's parents that he'd seen their daughter, they'd never believe him.

And, as Rob had suggested, Anne could always move to another area. If Samantha was asked about the girl, she'd deny all knowledge of her. After all, no one could prove that Anne Wilkinson had been living in her flat.

'You're beautiful,' Rob murmured, his finger moving beneath the tight material of her panties, massaging the fleshy lips of her vulva.

'Mmm, that's nice,' Samantha breathed, all thoughts of the blackmailer fading as her clitoris swelled and her juices of desire seeped between her swollen love lips. 'You certainly know what to do.'

'It's been a long time, but I'll never forget. Have you . . . have you shaved?'

'Yes, I have. I was wondering when you'd realize.'

'I've always been . . . I used to fantasize about girls shaving. There's something about it that really turns me on.'

'I prefer it that way,' Samantha giggled. 'Why don't you pull my panties down and take a look?'

Bringing her legs together briefly as he tugged her panties down and slipped them off her feet, Samantha then parted her thighs wide again, exposing the yawning valley of her expectant pussy to Rob's wide eyes. Stroking the hairless cushions of her outer lips, he settled between her legs and kissed the smooth flesh of her naked mons. She could feel his hot breath, his wet tongue, as he licked each outer lip in turn. Her girl-juices flowing freely from her gaping vaginal entrance, trickling down between the firm cheeks of her buttocks, she dug her fingernails into the soft grass as his inquisitive tongue swept over the sensitive tip of her erect clitoris. The exquisite sensations rippling throughout her trembling body driving her wild, she unbuttoned

her blouse and exposed the firm mounds of her rounded breasts.

As she'd hoped, Rob reached up and squeezed her ripe nipples as he continued his clitoral licking. Moving down the sex-drenched valley of her vulva, he drove his tongue deep into the tight sheath of her vagina, licking the creamy walls of her pleasure duct as she gasped and squirmed on the soft grass. His tongue slurping inside her vulval tube, lapping up her lubricious juices of lust, he moved up to her neglected clitoris and sucked the solid protrusion into his hot mouth.

'Yes,' Samantha breathed as he thrust two fingers deep into her spasming vagina. Nearing her orgasm, she rocked back and forth with the finger-fucking, her whimpers of arousal drifting through the summer air as a train rumbled through the cutting below. Older men certainly knew how to please a young girl, she reflected as he massaged the inner flesh of her tight cunt. Her bubbling sex juices streaming over his hand as he repeatedly drove his fingers deep into her sex hole, she shook uncontrollably, arching her back as her clitoris swelled to an incredible size beneath his snaking tongue.

'Coming,' she cried, her face grimacing, her nostrils flaring, as her orgasm erupted within the pulsating nubble of her solid clitoris. Shock waves of ecstasy rolling through her quivering body, her juices of lust squelching within her finger-fucked vagina, she again cried out as her orgasm peaked and rocked her very soul. Rob's penis would be solid she knew as she imagined his cock-shaft driving deep into her spunk-thirsty cunt. Imagining licking his purple knob, sucking the spunk out of his knob-slit as he mouth-fucked her, she felt wicked as she lay beneath the sun with her body laid open

to a total stranger. Never had she known an orgasm of such intensity and duration, she reflected, as her clitoris transmitted tremors of sex throughout her young body. Of all those who had licked her clitoris, fucked her tight cunt . . . Rob understood what it was a girl needed.

'Fuck me,' Samantha gasped, riding the crest of her shuddering climax. 'I want your cock . . . Fuck me really hard.' Wasting no time, Rob pulled his cunny-dripping fingers out of her vaginal duct and yanked his jacket and trousers off. Massaging her clitoris with her fingertips, sustaining her orgasm, Samantha was amazed by the sheer size of the man's cock as he slipped his swollen glans between the engorged petals of her inner lips and thrust his veined shaft deep into her shaking body. His bulbous knob pressing against the creamy ring of her cervix, his heaving balls squeezed against the rounded cheeks of her naked bottom, he withdrew his cock and again rammed his weapon of lust deep into her writhing body.

'God, you're big,' Samantha breathed, lifting her head and gazing at the sheer girth of his pussy-slimed cock as he partially withdrew. His purple glans still encompassed by her crimsoned inner lips, he drove into her again, forcing her young body across the grass as he fully impaled her on his beautiful penis. Gliding across the grass with each thrust of his mighty joybone, Samantha reached another mind-blowing orgasm as she dug her fingernails into the ground. Her head bobbing with each inthrust of his massive prick, her young breasts bouncing, she'd never been fucked like this, she reflected. Never had she experienced such a huge cock, never had she been fucked so hard.

'Here it comes,' Rob gasped, his ramrod swelling

within the hugging sheath of her drenched cunt. Samantha could feel his sperm gushing into her, bathing her cervix, lubricating the forceful fucking of her young cunt. Grunting with each thrust, he pumped her full of spunk, his balls draining as he took his pleasure from her young body. He'd never forget this Samantha knew as she felt his swinging balls repeatedly smacking the taut globes of her naked bottom. She'd never forget it, either, she thought as her climax peaked and shook her to the very core.

Finally collapsing over her quivering body, Rob stilled his spent cock deep within the sperm-flooded duct of Samantha's inflamed cunt. Breathing heavily, he kissed her full mouth, their tongues meeting as they writhed in the aftermath of their illicit fucking. Samantha could taste her cunt milk on his tongue as he kissed her. She could feel his penis deflating, his sperm oozing. Satisfied as never before as he finally slipped his limp cock out of her vagina and rolled onto the grass beside her, Samantha shuddered as her young womb contracted and her vagina drained.

'You really are amazing,' Rob breathed, his cock snaking over the hairy sac of his balls as he lay on his back, gasping for breath.

'Do you believe in past lives?' Samantha asked, recalling herself as Meg in the old pub.

'Past lives? I've not really thought about it. Although I suppose it's possible. Why do you ask?'

'I had an experience,' Samantha began, feeling that she could talk to Rob. 'It wasn't a dream. I don't really know what it was, to be honest. I went back in time and found myself working in my parents' pub. Back in the nineteenth century.'

'You must have been dreaming,' he chuckled.

'No, no, I wasn't. They called me Meg and . . . It was so real, Rob. I've had a few experiences like that.'

'You might check the records,' he suggested. 'Check the pub, the names of the people and whether they had a daughter called Meg.'

'The daft thing is that I don't even know the name of the pub, let alone the surname of . . . Hang on. I recall seeing a sign above the bar. Welcome to the . . . God, what was it? Yes, that's it. Welcome to the Gypsy's Tavern.'

'That's a start. There are records you can look through. Mind you, if you don't know the name of the people, or the time they were there . . . What other experiences have you had?'

'Several. Usually concerning going back in time. What would you do if you could go back in time?'

'I wouldn't have got married. Apart from that, I don't think I'd change much. I've been quite happy with my life. I'd like to have had children. Perhaps that's what's wrong with my marriage. If we'd had kids . . . Still, you can't change the past, can you?'

'Can't you? I'm not so sure about that. It would be interesting to travel forward in time to see how your life turned out.'

'No, I wouldn't like that at all. I might discover something that . . . I just wouldn't want to know, Sam.'

'Neither would I. Anyway, let's not talk about that. Would you like me to clean you up?' she asked, gazing at his sperm-glistening cock.

'Clean me up? What do you mean?'

'I'll show you,' she giggled, positioning herself between his legs.

Licking Rob's sex-wet cock, Samantha ran her tongue
over the hairy sac of his scrotum. Breathing in his male
scent as he moaned deeply in his rising arousal, she
hoped that he'd be able to come again as she rolled his
fleshy foreskin back and sucked his purple knob into her
hot mouth. Tasting the heady blend of his sperm and her
own girl-juice, her clitoris stiffening between the inflamed lips of her pussy, she wondered why the blackmailer hadn't turned up. She might have been able to pay
him off by having sex with him, she mused. There again,
he'd be back for more and more.

'You're good at that,' Rob gasped, his cock stiffening
fully as Samantha mouthed and gobbled on his ripe
plum. Happy to think that she was pleasing him, she
decided to meet him again in the park. The young lad had
been fun, but she wouldn't bother to see him again. Rob
was different, she reflected. She could talk to him, as well
as fuck him. He was good company, a good fuck, and she
wondered why he didn't get on with his wife. Perhaps the
woman was boring in bed, she thought as she repeatedly
took his swollen knob to the back of her throat and
bobbed her head up and down. Rob's wife might not
have been into oral sex, spunk-swallowing and tongue-
fucking. Marriage didn't suit everyone she knew as she
turned her thoughts to her father.

To run off with some young girl and leave her mother
was despicable, Samantha reflected. He'd obviously gone
off with the girl for sex. To leave his wife and home . . .
But what did the future hold for Samantha? Wasn't she
destined to leave her husband for Anne? But she was
determined to change the future. John was going to be a
good husband, and she'd prove to be a good wife. She
had ten years to play around, she thought happily,

wanking the solid shaft of Rob's cock as she ran her tongue around the helmet of his purple knob. Ten years to fuck and lick and suck and—

'God, I'm coming again,' Rob gasped, his penis twitching, his glans swelling. Fervently sucking his throbbing knob and wanking his cock, Samantha moaned through her nose as her mouth suddenly filled with his salty sperm. Moving her head up and down, mouth-fucking his solid penis, she repeatedly swallowed hard as his sperm-flow continued. Rob shook uncontrollably, his head tossing from side to side as she kneaded his heavy balls and wanked his fleshy shaft. His spunk gushing into her thirsty mouth, overflowing and running down his shaft to her hand, he propped himself up on his elbows and watched Samantha's crude act.

Wanking him faster, she slipped his glans out of her mouth and allowed his spunk to splatter her flushed face. He'd enjoy watching his spunk giving her a facial she knew as she engulfed his purple globe within her hot mouth again and drank from his fountainhead. Briefly slipping his knob out of her mouth once more, his sperm still jetting over her cheeks, her forehead, she swiftly took his orgasming plum to the back of her throat one last time and swallowed the remnants of his sperm. The white liquid streaming down her cheeks, running over her eyes, she sucked out the last of his creamy semen as he rested his head on the grass and shuddered in the waning of his orgasm.

'You taste good,' she murmured huskily, slipping his cock out of her mouth and lapping up the sperm from his rolling balls.

'You've obviously done this before,' he chuckled.

'Only once or twice. I've never known a man with such a big cock. It's massive.'

'So I've been told,' he said proudly. 'Mind you, that was years ago. Decades ago, in fact. I wish we'd met decades ago.'

'I wasn't alive decades—'

'You know what I mean,' he sighed, grabbing his trousers as Samantha sat upright.

'Yes, yes, I do. Well, I don't know what happened to the man I was supposed to be meeting. Perhaps the bastard—'

'Sam, I have something to tell you.'

'Oh?'

'Our bumping into each other wasn't coincidence. I've seen you around town before. I've also seen you in the park a couple of times.'

'Did you phone me?' Samantha asked, wondering whether he was the blackmailer.

'Phone you? No, I don't know your number. I don't even know where you live. I happened to see you in the park with another girl and thought I'd come back. I've been back several times, hanging around, hoping that I'd see you.'

'You didn't know I'd be here, then?'

'How could I have known? It was on the off-chance that we met. I happened to see you on the bench and . . . well, you know the rest.'

'I see,' Samantha murmured, wondering whether he'd spied through the gap in the fence and seen her antics with Anne and other men. 'Where was I when you saw me with my friend?'

'In the park, as I said.'

'Yes, but . . . where, exactly?'

'Walking towards the road.'

'Did you follow me home?'

'Sam, I've already said that I don't know where you live. No matter what you might think, I'm not into stalking. Besides, what good would it have done me to follow you home?'

'You've seen me around before. You obviously realized that you fancied me and . . . You might have thought about calling at my flat.'

'Hardly. For all I knew, you might have been married or something. Imagine me knocking on your door and being confronted by your husband. Or you might have been living with your parents. God, imagine your father opening the door and finding me on the step. I'll bet he's younger than I am. I'm telling you the truth, Sam. Everything I've said is true. Yes, I am married. My wife doesn't like me. When we met, I suppose we thought that we were in love. We were still in our teens – what did we know? Now I realize that we weren't even friends, let alone lovers.'

'How long have you been married?'

'Thirty-five years. Like I said, I've seen you around town and . . . to be honest, I fancied you something terrible. Obviously, I still do. More so than ever now that we've . . . well, you know.'

'How old are you?'

'Fifty-two.'

'You'll be pleased to hear that my father is older than you. And he's going to run off with some young girl or other.'

'I'm sorry to hear that.'

'That's in the future . . . I mean, he's not going off just yet.'

'Sam, I . . . I'd better be going. I want to stay but . . . This isn't a good idea. No matter how old your father is, *I'm* still old enough to be your parent.'

'So?'

'So . . . we're years apart, Sam. Generations apart.'

'Only one generation. Look, you don't have to worry about your age. It's how well we get on together that matters. We certainly get on all right sexually,' she giggled.

'Yes, yes, we do. So, you want to see me again?'

'Of course I do, Rob. I don't just go around fucking men without having any feelings for them,' she lied, crossing her fingers behind her back. 'I have real feelings for you, Rob. It's early days yet and I'm not sure what those feelings are, but . . .'

'OK, we'll meet here again,' he said, his girl-wet face beaming.

'Yes, yes, we will. Perhaps tomorrow morning, if you can get out of the house?'

'That's easy,' he laughed, standing and buckling his belt. 'She *wants* me out of the house. The more often, the better.'

'OK, we'll say about ten o'clock.'

'Right, I'll be here. Shall I walk with you?'

'No, no. I'm going to sit here for a while and watch the trains.'

'You need to think about this man who's threatening you?'

'I suppose so.'

'I'll leave you with your thoughts, Sam. You'd, er . . . you'd better get dressed,' he chuckled as he moved to the gap in the fence. 'I'll see you tomorrow.'

'Take care, Rob. And, thanks.'

'Thank *you*. Until tomorrow.'

When he'd gone, Samantha dressed and brushed her long blonde hair back with her fingers. She liked Rob. No matter how old he was, she liked him. More than liked him, she realized, lying on the grass and closing her eyes. Listening to another train trundling through the cutting, the sun warming her, she wished that she'd never seen the future. Knowing what was to come wouldn't do her any good, she decided. The dancing school, the mansion, John . . .

Wondering what the future held as far as Rob was concerned, she grinned. She really didn't want to know, she mused. It was best to live for the moment. Enjoy what she had while she had it. If it fell apart within a month or two, there'd be nothing lost. *Love?* She pondered on the word. Was she in love? She'd thought that she'd been in love with Zak but . . . There again, perhaps she hadn't really thought that. Perhaps she'd known that she wasn't in love with him. She wondered – had she ever been in love? No, she hadn't, she decided.

Anne would be wondering where she was, she thought, checking her watch. But the girl would just have to wonder for a while longer. Samantha needed to relax, to spend some time alone with her thoughts and unwind. Quite a lot had happened since she first went to the mansion, she reflected. More than enough to fill a lifetime. Sex with men and women, whipping, caning, anal-fucking, mouth-spunking, clit-licking . . . Would Rob still want her if he discovered the sordid truth? Would anyone want her if they knew about . . . Anne would, she mused, drifting in and out of sleep.

Plans had to be made she knew as she listened to the birds singing. The girl behind the paint factory . . .

Samantha would never forgive herself if the girl died. She'd try to talk to her. Frightening her off by threatening her with the police might work, she mused. Perhaps she'd already found somewhere else to sleep. If the woman on the reception desk had gone to chase the kids away from behind the building, she might have bumped into the girl and . . . Sleep engulfing her as the sun warmed her young body, Samantha dreamed her dreams of sex and orgasms. And fires.

11

'Morning, Dave,' Samantha trilled as she breezed into his office.

'Er . . . who are you? Oh, yes. You used to work here,' he quipped.

'Shut up, Dave. OK, here's the story,' she said, passing him several sheets of A4 paper.

'What story? What's this? *Bosses were warned of fire.* What bosses, where?'

'Read it and you'll find out.'

'The paint factory? But there hasn't been a fire.'

'No, but there will be. I contacted the local fire station. The fire inspector has told the company to clear the dumping ground behind the factory. And the receptionist said that—'

'Sammy baby, there hasn't been a fire. How can I run a story—'

'Run the story *after* the fire, silly.'

'But . . .'

'There was a girl sleeping rough behind the factory. I rang the police and they're going to deal with her.'

'What?'

'All will be revealed before long.'

'You're not saying that you're going to start the fire, are you? I know we need to sell papers but—'

'Of course I'm not. Right, I have work to do. See you.'

'Wait . . . Sammy, where are you going?'

'To buy a can of petrol and some matches. I'll keep you posted.'

Leaving the office, Samantha wondered whether Anne had woken up as she drove to her flat. The girl had gone to bed by the time Samantha had got back from the park, presumably because she was exhausted after her sex sessions. Wondering about the blackmailer as she let herself into the flat and made a cup of coffee, Samantha again reckoned that he must have seen her in the park with Rob and had decided not to approach her. Perhaps he'd ring again, she thought, deciding not to arrange to meet him again. If he went to Anne's parents with his insane allegations about their daughter, they'd send him packing. Turning as the phone rang, Samantha gazed at the instrument, sure that it was the blackmailer calling with more threats.

'Hello,' she murmured, her trembling hand pressing the receiver to her ear.

'Hi, Sam,' Jane trilled. 'How are you?'

'Oh . . . er, I'm fine.'

'I thought I'd give you a ring to find out how you're getting on with your story.'

'Story?'

'Your investigation into this den of iniquity involving a schoolteacher or whatever it was.'

'Oh, that. I'm getting there, but progress is slow. How's Geoff?'

'He's all right. So, have you discovered any more?'

'I have one or two leads to follow up. It's all rather hush-hush at the moment.'

'Oh, do tell me. I'm intrigued.'

'I'd rather not say anything just yet, Jane.'

'I had a diary stolen from my place.'

'Really? What, you've had burglars?'

'And a phone call was made from here.'

'What do you mean?'

'I was just wondering whether *you*'d been here, Sam.'

'Yes, I came to see you. You must remember—'

'I mean, when I was out.'

'No, I've not called when you've been out. Hang on. Are you suggesting that *I* broke in?'

'No, no. It's just that . . . A blonde woman fitting your description arranged to meet a friend of mine. They met in a wine bar and—'

'I'm sorry, Jane. You've completely lost me. What have your friend and a wine bar got to do with the burglary?'

'That's what I want to know. Do you have a mobile phone?'

'Yes, of course.'

'Is the number—'

'Hang on, Jane. My phone was stolen a week ago. I've just got a new phone and a new number.'

'Oh, I see. It's just that my friend was given the mobile number by someone pretending to be me. They were using my home phone.'

'This is becoming incredibly complicated, Jane,' Samantha sighed. 'My mobile was stolen from my car so I would imagine that it was a local thief. There again, it's quite a coincidence that my stolen phone and your friend . . . Anyway, who would want to steal your diary?'

'I really don't know. The thing is . . . Geoff and I do have a little sideline we run from home.'

'A sideline?'

'As you're looking into this den-of-iniquity thing . . . Why don't you come round and we'll have a chat?'

'All right,' Samantha said, thinking that this could be a trap. 'About fifteen minutes?'

'Yes, yes, that's fine.'

'OK, see you soon.'

Hanging up, Samantha bit her lip. What with the dancing school and the problems with Anne's untimely arrival, she'd pushed Jane's illicit exploits to the back of her mind. Grabbing her keys, she left the flat and walked down the street. On reflection, she became uncertain whether this was a trap. How could it be? Jane would hardly imprison her in the torture chamber and . . . Or would she? The best thing to do would be to deny all knowledge of Jane's friend. The friend was obviously Kitty, she mused. But if Kitty was there waiting for her . . . That was a bridge she might have to cross.

Deciding to cut through the park, she looked about her as she headed for the bench. It was another hot summer day, and she recalled lying on the soft grass by the railway cutting with Rob pleasuring the most private part of her young body with his wet tongue. Half hoping to bump into him again, she knew that speaking to Jane was more important than having sex in the park. Maybe she'd come back via the park, she thought, following the fence to the railway bridge.

'Oh, hi,' Jane said, smiling as she opened the front door. 'Come in. I've put the kettle on.'

'Thanks,' Samantha said, following the woman into the kitchen. 'I was thinking about the break-in. There's been a spate of burglaries in the area. Your diary, my mobile phone . . . I suppose it's a sign of the times.'

'I don't think my break-in was an opportunist thief,' Jane said mysteriously. 'I reckon that someone was actually looking for my diary.'

'Why on earth would anyone do that? I mean, dental appointments, hairdresser . . . No one would be interested, Jane.'

'There was far more in my diary than dental appointments, Sam.'

'Oh? You've not been having an affair? Perhaps Geoff got a private detective onto you and—'

'That's ridiculous,' Jane laughed. 'No, no, you don't understand. Kitty, this friend of mine . . . I'm going to be honest with you, Sam. But first, you must tell me all you know about this den-of-iniquity business.'

'What is your interest in that?' Samantha asked. 'You seem to be—'

'I know who's involved,' Jane cut in. 'I . . . if I'm not careful, I could be implicated.'

'*What?*'

'Just tell me what you've discovered. More to the point, tell me who else knows about this.'

'It's nothing more than a couple of a vague leads, Jane. Yes, there is a house in this area that is being used by a married couple to abuse young girls. Yes, there is a schoolteacher involved . . . How on earth could *you* be implicated?'

'Kitty is the schoolteacher and this is the house,' Jane confessed. 'Geoff and I are the married couple.'

'God,' Samantha gasped, her eyes wide as she feigned shock. 'So, you mean to say that . . .'

'It's all perfectly legal. Or it was. For the time being, due to this coming to light, we've dismantled the sex den.'

'You had a sex den?'

'It was only for fun, for goodness' sake. Geoff and I like others to join in with our sex games. That's all it was. The girls were all eighteen or older and . . .'

'I see,' Samantha breathed, wondering why the woman had owned up.

'Once the newspaper . . . once you realize that there is no story, we'll probably carry on having our fun. This business about girls being abused is nonsense. We play adult games with consenting adults, Sam. The reason we dismantled the sex den was because some people might have got the wrong idea. Start talking about abusing girls and . . . well, you can understand why we've temporarily stopped our games.'

'Yes, yes, I can. Do you know anything about a dancing school?'

'A dancing school? No, I don't. What are you getting at?'

'Oh, nothing. So there is no story after all?'

'No, there isn't, Sam,' Jane sighed, obviously relieved. 'There never was a story. Not unless you think that playing adult games in the privacy of your own home should make newspaper headlines.'

'No, of course not.'

'So that's it. I've come clean. If you'll excuse the pun.'

'The young girl I spoke to . . .' Samantha murmured. 'She told me that she'd been tied up and sexually abused.'

'Well, I know nothing about that. Unfortunately, word does get around sometimes. She might have heard about our sex den and . . . I really don't know, Sam. Perhaps she overheard an adult talking about it. Some of our friends do have daughters. Needless to say, they're kept well away from here.'

'Yes, of course. Well, I suppose that just about wraps it up.'

'Yes, I think it does. There's your coffee.'

'Thanks. I know that you'll get your sex den going again.'

'I hope so. There again . . .'

'You will, believe me.'

'You seem very sure.'

'I am. Anyway, I'm going to have to find another juicy story.'

'So you're definitely dropping this one?'

'Yes, of course. Now that you've told me that it's just fun between consenting adults, there's no point in going on with it.'

'You'll have to come round one evening and . . . if you're into that sort of thing, of course.'

'That might prove interesting,' Samantha giggled, sipping her coffee. 'On the other hand, I'm not sure that I'd want to . . .'

'You won't know until you've tried it, Sam.'

'No, I suppose not. Well, I have work to do,' Samantha said, finishing her coffee. 'I'd better be going.'

'OK. It's been nice talking to you, Sam. We must meet up more often.'

'Yes, we must.'

'And I'm pleased to hear that you're no longer looking into sex dens and things.'

'To be honest, I really didn't think that I was going to get anywhere with it. OK, I'll be in touch.'

As Jane saw her to the door, Samantha wondered whether the woman really knew the true ages of the girls. Perhaps she'd said that they were eighteen or so to lessen Samantha's interest. Whatever Jane thought didn't matter. She was having some fun with Geoff, harmless fun. The same applied to the dancing school, Samantha reflected. The punters were enjoying them-

selves, the girls were getting paid for having obscene sex, so what the hell?

'Where have you been?' Anne asked as Samantha wandered into the kitchen.

'Working,' Samantha snapped. 'You're not my keeper, for fuck's sake. I *do* have to go to work sometimes, Anne.'

'What, fucking in the park?'

'No, no,' Samantha laughed, feeling a little less uptight. 'I've been working for the paper. I was up early this morning, typing up a story.'

'Oh, right. Some man phoned.'

'Why did you answer the phone? I told you not to . . .'

'It kept ringing. On and on and on . . .'

'Who was it?'

'The man who reckons that I'm Anne Wilkinson.'

'Oh, God. What did he say?'

'He wants me to meet him in the park.'

'I reckon that this man is going to become a nuisance. He already *is* a nuisance. What else did he say?'

'He said that he saw you yesterday with another man. I didn't know you'd taken someone to the park.'

'I didn't. I bumped into an old man and we got chatting, that was all. I did think that our blackmailer would back off when he realized that I was with someone else.'

'He said that I was to go there alone and meet him by the bench.'

'When?'

'Now. He said that he'd be waiting and I was to get there as soon as I could.'

'That's odd,' Samantha breathed, checking her watch

as she recalled that she'd arranged to meet Rob in the park at ten o'clock.

'What's odd?'

'When did he ring?'

'About ten minutes ago. Why, Sam? What is it?'

'I'm not sure. Perhaps it's just my suspicious mind doing overtime. All right, this is what we'll do. I'll go there and pretend that I'm Anne Wilkinson. I'm about the right age, aren't I?'

'Well, yes, but—'

'I'm the age you would have been by now and I'm blonde. I'll ask him why he's interested in me. I won't deny who I am. If I say that I've been abroad and I've come back to see my family . . .'

'I can feel confusion grabbing me, Sam.'

'So can I,' Samantha laughed. 'Look, if he thinks that I'm Anne Wilkinson, so what?'

'But he's seen me, hasn't he? He thinks that I'm Anne. Sod it, I *am* Anne Wilkinson.'

'All I can do is play it by ear. I'll try to confuse him.'

'You've confused *me* all right Look, I've got an idea. Say that you've come back to see your friends, not your family. If you tell him that you argued with your parents years ago and—'

'So, if he contacts them, they'll deny all knowledge . . . Yes, that sounds good. OK, I'll get going.'

'Good luck, Sam.'

'Thanks. I'll see you later. I hope. And don't answer the bloody phone.'

'OK, I promise.'

Walking back to the park, Samantha realized that she was going to have to shut this man up once and for all. Phoning a second time and talking to Anne . . . She

wasn't going to stand for it, she decided. He could do what the hell he liked. Contact the girl's parents, go to the police . . . The man would look a fool if he told people that Samantha was Anne Wilkinson. If she was questioned, she would just laugh and prove her identity.

Lurking behind a clump of bushes, she thought it odd that Rob was due to arrive at the same time as the blackmailer. Wondering why Anne had been ordered to go alone to the park, she kept her eye on the bench from her hiding place. There was no way the blackmailer would believe that Samantha was Anne, she was sure. Shaking her head and sighing, she felt despondent as she watched a distant figure growing larger. It was a middle-aged man, she observed, as he approached the bench. Was this her man?

Gazing at Rob as he sat on the bench, Samantha tried not to put two and two together. Rob and the blackmailer weren't one and the same, were they? If it had been Rob who'd phoned and spoken to Anne, he might have had it in mind to threaten her. Anne hadn't met him, so she'd be none the wiser. Perhaps he wanted to screw the girl, Samantha thought. If he said that he knew her true identity and he'd keep quiet in return for sex . . . but then, Rob would hardly order Anne to meet him by the bench at the same time he'd arranged to meet Samantha.

After fifteen minutes, Samantha realized that the blackmailer wasn't going to turn up. Unless he, too, was lurking somewhere. Perhaps he'd seen Rob, thought that Anne wasn't going to turn up and . . . This was a bloody mess, Samantha reflected, wondering what the hell she was doing hiding in the bushes like a thief in the night. Watching as Rob finally wandered across the park and disappeared from view, she emerged from the bushes

and sat on the bench. If her man was still there, he'd show himself now, she was sure. Slipping her hand between her thighs as she watched from the bushes, she pressed her fingertips into the warm swelling of her tight panties. Feeling incredibly aroused, she slipped a finger beneath her panties and caressed her protruding inner lips. She desperately needed to come she knew as her clitoris swelled, her juices of desire oozing from her tight sex hole. Unable to help herself, she lay on the ground and slipped her panties down her long legs.

'God, I'm wet,' she murmured, slipping a finger into the hot, creamy sheath of her drenched vagina. Looking up at the trees wavering high above her, the sun sparkling through the foliage, she massaged her inner flesh and breathed heavily in her self-loving. Time travel, blackmail . . . She had to move on, get away from her problems, she knew, as she slipped her wet finger out of her vagina and massaged the solid nub of her ripe clitoris. Apart from the paint factory story, she'd done nothing for the newspaper.

Feeling that her life was going nowhere, Samantha tried not to think about the vicar as images of his office loomed in her mind. Concentrating on the newspaper as she massaged her solid clitoris, she thought about the new photographer. She'd not met Brian yet, she mused. But, before long, she would not only meet him but would allow him to take photographs of her naked body, the gaping valley of her young pussy. The vicar had taken photographs of her legs, her tight panties . . .

'Lift your dress up and bend over my desk,' the vicar said sternly.

'But . . . Please, I . . .' Samantha stammered, looking down at her Sunday dress.

'Do as I tell you, Samantha,' he snapped. 'Unless you want me to tell your parents that I caught you stealing money from the collection tray.'

'I wasn't stealing it,' she whimpered, her tear-filled eyes looking up at him. 'You told me to take the money out of the tray and put it in the—'

'You *were* stealing it, Samantha. Where have you put the five-pound note that was in the tray?'

'There wasn't a—'

'Stealing, lying . . . Lift your dress up and bend over my desk.'

Samantha remembered this well. The vicar had tricked her, had told her to empty the tray and place the money on his desk and had then accused her of stealing. Her parents knew that she wasn't a thief, but an accusation of stealing coming from the respected vicar . . . He was a clever man, she reflected, as he again ordered her to lift her dress up over her back and bend over his desk. Clever – and extremely evil.

'I'm going to spank you,' he announced as she leaned over the desk. She had no idea how old she was as his fingers ran over the tight material of her pink panties clinging to the rounded cheeks of her young bottom. She remembered the episode, the accusation, but she couldn't recall how old she'd been at the time. This had happened after the priest had begun his photo sessions, she was sure. He'd already promised her that she'd be a model one day and his photographs were the start of a successful career.

'Where is the five-pound note?' he asked again, slapping the firm flesh of her tensed buttocks.

'I haven't taken any money,' she whimpered, her hands clinging to the far edge of the desk as she rested her face on the polished wood.

'Are there any pockets in your dress?'

'No. I haven't got any pockets – or a bag or anything.'

'Then you must have hidden the money in your clothing,' he murmured, yanking the back of her panties down.

'I haven't hidden—'

'What's this?' he asked, holding up a five-pound note. 'What was this doing in your panties, Samantha?'

'I . . . I didn't put it there. I promise, I . . .'

'That's evidence enough for me. And, no doubt, for your parents.'

Yanking her panties down to her ankles, the vicar ordered Samantha to step out of the garment and then spread her feet wide. Complying, she couldn't understand how the money had come to be hidden in her panties. She hadn't recalled seeing a note in the tray. There were coins, but no notes. Naive, innocent, trusting . . . Had she known then what she knew now . . . But now she did know, of course. Trembling as the vicar's fingertip ran up and down the tightly closed crevice of her buttocks, she was dreading what he had in mind as she listened to his heavy breathing.

'I'm going to spank you, Samantha,' the cleric said, clutching the warm globes of her naked buttocks in his hand. 'I don't want to have to do this but . . . It's either a spanking, or I go to your parents. What's it to be?'

'I . . . I didn't steal the money,' she sobbed.

'I found it in your panties, girl. What else do you hide in your panties?'

'Nothing.'

'I don't believe you. You put your hand down the front of your panties, don't you?'

'No, honestly . . .'

'I've seen you, Samantha. I've seen you during Sunday school. You sit at the back and slip your hand down the front of your panties.'

'No, I never do that.'

'Why do you insist on lying, girl? What would your mother say if she discovered that you not only steal money from the collection tray but that you put your hand down the front of your panties? Spread your feet further, as wide as you can. I'm sure you'd rather have a spanking than have to face your parents.'

The palm of the priest's hand slapping the taut flesh of her rounded bottom, Samantha's young body jolted as she clung to the desk. Her buttocks stinging as he repeatedly brought his hand down across her naked bottom, she felt her fresh vaginal milk oozing between the firm lips of her young pussy. The spanking wasn't severe, but it was still hard enough to redden her buttocks, the stinging sensations numbing her tensed flesh as she gripped the far side of the desk. Again and again, the vicar brought his hand down, swiping each globe in turn as her whimpers resounded around the small office.

Although she was enjoying the experience, Samantha wondered again why she'd been taken back in time. Was this, she asked herself, purely as a result of her subconscious thoughts? Her vaginal juices trickled down her inner thighs as her arousal heightened. She'd often fantasized about spanking, she reflected. During her masturbation sessions, she'd frequently imagined a man spanking her naked bottom, reddening her bare flesh. Her schoolteacher, her father, even the man in the local shop . . .

Wondering what the vicar was up to as he halted the punishment, Samantha smiled as she felt his fingers

sliding down the gully of her bottom, venturing dangerously close to the fleshy lips of her vulva nestling between her naked thighs.

'I think that's enough,' the cleric said shakily, his
fingertip pressing into the moist divide of her outer
labia. 'No, don't get up,' he said as Samantha lifted
her head off the desk. 'I haven't finished with you yet.'

'But you said . . .'

'Don't worry, I'm not going to spank you again. Move
forward across the desk, Samantha. Lift your feet off the
floor and move forward so that your head is over the far
side of the desk.'

Following his command, Samantha slid forward until
her head was hanging over the edge of the desk. Her legs
wide apart, her bared vulval lips fully exposed beneath
the tight brown ring of her bottom-hole, she heard the
vicar pull a chair up and sit between her splayed thighs.
He'd have a perfect view of the most intimate part of her
young body she knew as he moved her legs even further
apart. His fingertip running up each milk-wet inner
thigh in turn, tantalizing her sensitive flesh, he leaned
forward and planted a kiss on the firm mounds of her
rounded buttocks.

'You're a lovely girl, Samantha,' he breathed, his lips
brushing against the tensed flesh of her naked buttocks,
his breath warming her there. Now, are you going to
admit that you put your hand down the front of your
panties?' he asked.

'Yes,' she breathed, knowing what he wanted to hear.

'I thought as much. Tell me, do you rub yourself
between your legs?'

'Yes, yes, I do,' she murmured, her juices flowing
from her tightly closed sex hole.

'Do you look at yourself there? I mean, when you're in the bath, do you look inside your crack?'

'I have done,' she confessed. 'I have looked inside my crack.'

'*I*'m going to look inside your crack, Samantha,' he breathed, parting the fleshy cushions of her vaginal lips.

Quivering as she felt the priest's fingertip circling the pink funnel of flesh surrounding her virginal pussy hole, Samantha could feel her lubricious sex-milk lubricating his illicit massaging. This was the only aspect of time travelling that she enjoyed, she reflected. Returning to the nineteenth-century pub had been of no value, and certainly hadn't been fun. Flitting forward in time to the dancing school had been interesting. But her visits to the church, to the vicar's office – those were what had really excited her. She'd do this again, she decided. Whatever happened with Anne, whatever the next ten years held . . . She'd slip back in time to the vicar's office and enjoy his illicit attention.

'Have you ever pushed your finger in there?' the man of God asked, the tip of his finger slipping between the petals of her inner lips.

'Yes, yes, I have,' Samantha gasped, trying to conceal her arousal as her young body trembled.

'You like me doing this to you, don't you?'

'I . . . I don't know,' she replied, raising her buttocks and swivelling her hips in the hope that he'd massage the solid bud of her ripening clitoris.

'I'll slip my finger inside you,' he said. 'Just relax and I'll make you feel good.'

His finger gliding deep into the tight duct of her vagina, the cleric massaged her inner flesh as Samantha did her best not to writhe on the desk. He was gazing at

the naked hillocks of her outer lips stretched tautly around his intruding finger she knew as he bent and twisted that finger, sending quivers through her young pelvis. Kissing her rounded buttocks again, his lips moving to her anal gully, he pushed his tongue out. Trembling uncontrollably, Samantha breathed deeply as she felt the wet tip of his tongue slip between the rise of her crimsoned buttocks, seeking out the tight brown hole of her anus.

His tongue teasing the delicate flesh of her bottom-hole, the vicar parted her naked buttocks with his free hand as he continued to massage the inner flesh of her vaginal sheath. The sensations were heavenly, Samantha mused as she relaxed completely. Hoping that he'd push his tongue deep into her rectum, she couldn't stop herself from gasping and writhing as he tasted her anal ring. His tongue repeatedly sweeping over her brown hole, he parted her firm buttocks further. The secret portal to her anal canal opening wide, he drove his wet tongue into her dank tube and licked the inner walls of her sheath of illicit pleasure.

Drowning in the exquisite sensations of forbidden pleasure as the vicar tongued her rectal sheath and fingered the tight duct of her virgin cunt, Samantha grimaced as he forced her firm buttocks further apart and fully opened her brown hole to his darting tongue. She'd enjoyed the spanking, she reflected, as he licked inside her rectal tube, savouring the bitter-sweet taste of her young bottom. And she was enjoying his most intimate attention to her anal canal. She'd definitely visit the cleric again, she decided, as he slipped a second finger deep into the rhythmically contracting sheath of her virgin cunt.

'Do you like me licking your bottom?' he asked her, his fingers gliding in and out of her sex-drenched vagina.

'Yes, I think so,' she murmured, her eyes rolling as her clitoris swelled.

'When you rub yourself, rub between your lips, do you . . . do you reach the point where you shudder?'

'Yes, every time I rub myself there,' she replied.

'Where do you rub, exactly?'

'There's a hard spot just at the top of my crack. That's where I rub.'

'And you'd like me to rub your hard spot?'

'I . . . I think so.'

His fingers sliding out of Samantha's juice-flooded vaginal canal, the priest moved up the valley of her vulva and massaged the sensitive tip of her exposed clitoris. Her creamy juices lubricating the illicit masturbation, he rubbed her pleasure spot faster as she whimpered and squirmed in the grip of her soaring arousal. He wouldn't stop here she knew as his tongue entered the dank sheath of her rectum again. He'd push his huge cock into her tight pink pussy and fuck her, she was sure.

His tongue snaking deep inside her rectum, his fingertip massaging the painfully hard protuberance of her ripe clitoris, the vicar locked his lips to the brown tissue of her anus and sucked hard. Lost in her sexual delirium, Samantha felt her young womb contracting, her clitoris pulsating in the onset of her forbidden coming as the man of God licked her rectal duct and increased the pace of his clitoris-masturbating rhythm. This was sheer sexual bliss she mused as the buds of her small breasts pressed hard against the desk. The vicar might have been evil, but he certainly knew how to pleasure a girl.

Bending her knees, her calves pressing against the

backs of her thighs, Samantha reached behind her back and grabbed her ankles. Pulling her feet up to meet the back of her head, her spine curving as the sexual centre of her young body gaped wide open, she knew that the vicar's arousal would rocket. Managing to pull her feet either side of her head, she shuddered as her clitoris swelled and erupted in orgasm when the man slipped his wet tongue out of her tight bottom-hole and drove a finger deep into her rectal sheath.

Crying out as her climax rocked her young body, Samantha listened to the squelching of her vaginal juices as the man drove at least two fingers into the tight sheath of her virgin cunt. Her orgasm peaking, her young body shaking violently, she parted her thighs as far as she could to allow her abuser deeper access to her sex holes. Sucking hard on her rectal inlet again, his tongue darting in and out of her arse, he continued his clitoris massaging and vaginal fingering. Again and again, shock waves of pure sexual bliss rolled through her shaking body, tightening her muscles, gripping her very soul, and she screamed with pleasure.

His fingers finally leaving the spasming tube of Samantha's vagina, his tongue sliding out of her rectal duct, the cleric lifted his cassock and pressed the solid bulb of his purple glans between the inflamed lips of her vulva. This was what he'd been longing for Samantha knew as her clitoris was forced out from beneath its pinken bonnet when his penile shaft glided along the tight sheath of her cunt. Her inner lips dragged along his veined shaft, his bulbous knob pressing hard against the creamy ring of her cervix, he completely impaled her on his huge cock.

'No,' she cried. 'You . . . you shouldn't be doing this.' Ignoring her protest, his arousal taking control, he forced

his finger deep into her anal canal and massaged the restricted duct. Samantha could hardly believe the incredible sensations coursing through her young body as he withdrew his solid cock and again drove his purple crown deep into the wet heat of her once-virgin cunt. He was going to spunk her young pussy, she knew, as his swinging balls battered the naked flesh of her mons and he crudely finger-fucked her tight arse.

His finger leaving her rectum, his cock sliding out of her inflamed cunt, the vicar pressed the bulbous globe of his glans hard against Samantha's saliva-wet anal ring. Again ignoring her perfunctory cries of protest, he drove his knob deep into the tight shaft of her rectum until his knob absorbed the fiery heat of her bowels and his heaving balls pressed hard against her sex-dripping vaginal lips. Feeling as if her pelvic cavity had bloated to capacity, she shuddered as he grabbed her feet and parted her legs wide. Clinging to the edge of the desk, she felt his massive tool withdrawing, her anal ring dragging along his veined shaft until the delicate brown tissue hugged the rim of his helmet.

'Please,' Samantha gasped as the man of God's penile length drove forcefully back into her inflamed anal canal, the dilated sphincter of her anus gripping the root of his monster cock as he again impaled her completely. Withdrawing once more, his slimed cock gliding slowly out of her fiery rectum, he held her feet high in the air and rammed his glans deep into her bowels. Increasing his anal fucking rhythm, he repeatedly drove his bulbous cockhead deep into the very core of her young body as she clung to the desk to steady herself.

'Tight-arsed little slut,' the vicar breathed, his hips swinging back and forth as he anal-fucked Samantha's

young body. Obviously losing control, he gasped his crude expletives as he held her feet high in the air and repeatedly propelled his knob-plum deep into the burning core of her bowels. His full balls bouncing, his slimed shaft gliding in and out of her inflamed rectum, he was about to reach the climax of his illicit act, Samantha knew, as she clung to the desk in sheer desperation.

'Yes,' cried the cleric, his throbbing knob pumping out his creamy spunk, the liquid of male orgasm lubricating his pistoning of her anal duct. Samantha could feel his sperm filling her, bubbling deep within her bowels as again and again he rammed his pulsating cockhead deep into her young body. Her vaginal muscles spasming, her hot cunt-milk spewing from her gaping sex hole, she thought that she was going to slip into unconsciousness as her clitoris exploded in orgasm. Her long blonde hair veiling her flushed face, her eyes rolling, she screamed out in ecstasy as she rode the crest of her mind-blowing orgasm.

'God, you're a tight-arsed slut,' the vicar cried, the last of his sperm jetting from his knob-slit and flooding Samantha's bowels. Making his final thrusts, he reached beneath her shaking body and massaged her pulsating clitoris, sustaining her incredible orgasm as he stilled his deflating cock deep within her contracting rectal sheath. Finally drifting down from her sexual heaven, her young body convulsing wildly, Samantha lay sprawled across the desk, gasping for breath as sperm oozed from the burning portal of her anus.

'Are you all right?' the vicar asked, his fingers leaving the sex-drenched sheath of her cunt as he withdrew his cock slowly from her sperm-brimming rectum.

'Yes, yes . . .' she managed to gasp, her legs twitching as he lowered her feet.

'That was amazing,' he breathed, sitting on the chair.
'You really are quite a little—'

'You . . . you shouldn't have done that,' Samantha
whimpered, her dress up over her back, the sperm-
dribbling mouth of her anus blatantly exposed to the
vicar's sparkling eyes. 'You shouldn't have—'

'Now, you listen to me, young lady,' he interrupted
her sternly. 'You'll say nothing about this, do you understand?'

'But I—'

'You'll say *nothing*, Samantha. If you do, then you'll
find yourself in serious trouble, not only for stealing
money but for allowing another girl to touch your crack.'

'But I . . .' Samantha whined as she managed to
clamber off the desk and stand on her sagging legs.

'I saw you, Samantha. You were with another girl in
the churchyard with your dress up and your panties
down. She was fingering your crack, Samantha.'

'But . . .'

'There are no buts, girl. Now, are you feeling all
right?'

'Yes, yes, I think so,' she replied, grabbing her panties
from the floor and tugging them up her legs.

'Good. Would you like another girl to finger your
crack?'

'No, I wouldn't.'

'Have you never allowed a girl to touch you there?
Perhaps you've touched another girl's crack?'

'Only a couple of times,' she confessed, again knowing
exactly what he wanted to hear.

'Tell me about it. What happened?'

'We . . . we were playing in my bedroom after school
and . . . I rubbed her crack, her hard spot.'

'And?'

'I was telling her how I rubbed myself and she wanted me to teach her. She pulled her knickers down and lay on the bed. I sat beside her and rubbed her spot until she shook and shuddered.'

'What was her name . . . Oh, I think someone's just come into the church,' the vicar said, straightening his cassock. 'You may go home now. And remember what I said.'

'I'll remember,' she sighed, walking across the office and opening the door.

'I want you to come back this evening. Tell your mother that you're going to help me with some tidying-up.'

Leaving the office, Samantha smiled as she passed a woman in the aisle and finally made her escape through the main doors. Out in the sunshine, she slipped around the back of the church and sat on a bench. Her bottom-hole burning, sperm oozing from her rectum and seeping into the tight material of her panties, she grinned as she recalled her debased act. The innocent young girl and the dirty old man, she mused. Little did the dirty old man know that the girl had the mind of a twenty-two-year-old.

As she was about to close her eyes and return to her own time, Samantha noticed a middle-aged man wandering through the churchyard. As he approached, she eyed the crotch of his tight jeans. He was in his late forties, not bad-looking, with dark, swept-back hair. But it was his bulging crotch that she was interested in. Catching his eye, she smiled and licked her lips provocatively. He'd enjoy slipping his hand up her dress and toying with the lips of her hairless pussy, she knew as he

stopped by the bench. Feeling wicked, her clitoris swelling expectantly, she lay back on the bench and parted
her thighs.

'Do you like young teenage girls?' she asked him
unashamedly.

'Like them?' he said, frowning as she pulled her dress
up, revealing her naked thighs.

'Their little pink pussies,' she said softly, knowing that
she could return to her own time whenever she wished.

'Well, yes,' the man replied, obviously shocked.

'Do you want to see *my* pussy?'

'OK,' he said, looking around the churchyard. 'Are
you here on your own?'

'Yes, I've been to Sunday school.'

'You really want to show me your . . . your pussy?' he
asked incredulously.

'If you want to see it,' she giggled impishly.

'Yes, yes, I do. Let's go into those bushes.'

Following him, Samantha felt her stomach somersault
as they slipped into the clump of bushes. Time travel
wasn't so bad after all, she thought, standing in the small
clearing in the middle of the bushes. Lifting her dress up
over her stomach, she pulled the front of her pink panties
down and exposed the pouting lips of her hairless vulva
to the astonished man. He stared in disbelief at her young
sex crack, obviously wondering why she was doing this as
he knelt on the ground and scrutinized the most private
part of her body.

'Do you like my crack?' Samantha asked, her cunny-
wet panties around her knees.

'Yes, yes – I do,' he replied, daring to stroke her outer
labia.

'No one's ever seen my crack before,' she lied, know-

ing that his cock would be solid within his tight jeans. 'Are you married?'

'Er . . . yes, I am,' he murmured, moving forward and kissing the naked mound of her mons.

'So, you know about sex, then?'

'Oh, yes. I know everything about sex. Would you like me to finger you?'

'I don't know what that is,' she lied. 'I've never had a boyfriend so you'll have to teach me.'

Allowing her panties to fall around her ankles, Samantha stepped out of the garment and lay on the ground with her legs wide apart. This was fun, she mused, as the man settled between her naked thighs and ran his tongue up and down the pinken slit of her pussy. She'd eventually return to her own time and would never meet him again. No embarrassment, no explanations . . . Just cold sex for the sake of sex. Naughty young girl, middle-aged man with a rampant hard-on . . . This was the sort of fun Samantha was going to enjoy with her gift of time travelling.

'No one's licked you before?' he asked, slipping his finger deep into the creamy duct of her vagina.

'No one's seen my pussy,' she replied. 'Teach me about sex. I want to know everything.'

'You're amazing,' he breathed, his finger massaging the drenched walls of her vaginal canal. 'What made you ask me . . . I mean, why did you offer to show me your pussy?'

'My friend was telling me that her next-door neighbour played with her pussy. He's taught her how to fuck and everything. I want to learn how to fuck. When I saw you, I thought that you might be able to teach me.'

'I can teach you, all right,' the man chuckled, standing

and tugging his jeans off. 'Have you ever seen a cock?'

'No, never.'

'There it is,' he said, proudly displaying the solid shaft of his penis. 'Sit up and suck it,' he ordered her, rolling his foreskin back.

Sitting up, Samantha knelt in front of him, took his purple plum into her wet mouth and rolled her tongue around the rim. Gasping as he looked down at her succulent lips encompassing the purple globe of his cock, he clutched her head and rocked his hips. His swollen glans gliding back and forth over her wet tongue, her lips rolling along his veined shaft, he ordered her to fondle his swinging balls. Complying, Samantha kneaded his ball sac, feeling his sperm eggs through the fleshy bag as he mouth-fucked her.

'That's good,' he breathed. 'I'm going to come in your mouth, fill your mouth with my milk. Make sure that you swallow it.' Holding the fleshy shaft of the man's cock, Samantha ran her hand up and down his solid rod, wanking him as she sucked and gobbled on his bulbous glans. This had never happened, she reflected. This was a fantasy, something she'd often thought about while masturbating on her bed when she was young. What other fantasies could she live out? She mused on the subject, breathing in the heady scent of the man's pubic curls.

'Don't stop,' he gasped as she suckled fervently on his knob. 'God, I'm going to come.' His sperm jetting from his knob-slit, gushing into her hot mouth and bathing her snaking tongue, he gripped her head and increased his mouth-fucking rhythm. Swallowing hard, Samantha hoped that he'd restiffen quickly after the illicit act and fuck the tight sheath of her pussy. His sperm overflowing

from her mouth and running down her chin, she'd never known a man pump out so much spunk. His seemingly never-ending flow of semen filling her cheeks, dripping from her chin and splattering the front of her dress, she swallowed repeatedly until she'd drained his huge balls and he swayed on his sagging legs.

'Was that all right?' she asked, sperm dribbling down her chin as she looked up at him.

'God, yes,' the man breathed, dropping to his knees as she lay on her back with her thighs wide.

'Are you going to fuck me now?'

'Yes, yes. In a minute. I'll have to wait until it's stiff again.'

'Will this make you stiff?' Samantha asked, tugging her dress over her head and exposing the unripe buds of her small breasts. 'They're not very big yet, I'm afraid.'

'God, they're beautiful,' he breathed, leaning over her naked body and sucking her milk teat into his wet mouth.

His cock fully erect, Samantha lay with her limbs spread, the crack of her vagina bared in readiness to take his huge organ. Her nipple leaving his mouth, she grinned as he positioned himself between her slender thighs and pressed the bulb of his cock into the divide of her fleshy cunny lips. His glans entering her, gliding past the inner lips of her pussy and driving along the tight passage of her young cunt, her breathed heavily as he rested his weight on his hands and looked down at the petite mounds of her breasts.

'Oh, I'm going to tear apart,' she whimpered as his knob pressed hard against her cervix.

'No, you won't,' he reassured her. 'Does it feel nice?'

'Yes, yes, it does,' she replied, licking her sperm-glossed lips.

'I'm going to fuck you now,' he said, partially withdrawing the huge shaft of his cock and ramming into her again. 'I'm going to fuck your pretty little cunt and spunk up you.'

Gasping, Samantha closed her eyes as she listened to the arousing sound of her slurping vaginal juices. The man's thrusting cock rocking her naked body, he sank his teeth into the disc of her areola and sucked hard on the teat of her small breast. Her clitoris swelling, the sensitive tip massaged by his pistoning cock, she knew that she was going to come. Trying to hold back, she knew that his pleasure would be heightened if her wet cunt spasmed in orgasm in time with his own coming.

'Fuck me harder,' she breathed as her clitoris pulsated, the birth of her orgasm stirring within her rhythmically contracting womb. 'Fuck me and spunk me.' Letting out a long low moan of pleasure, he rammed his swollen knob repeatedly into the tightening sheath of her cunt, his swinging balls battering the rounded cheeks of her buttocks as he fucked her. Gasping, his sperm flooding her convulsing vagina, Samantha shook violently as she reached her massive orgasm and her vaginal muscles gripped his thrusting cock.

'Oh, oh,' she whimpered, her virgin gasps adding to his pleasure as her climax rolled through her naked body. Her clitoris pulsating against his cunny-wet shaft as he fucked her tight cunt, she reached beneath her legs and kneaded his swinging balls. She could feel his spunk oozing from her stretched vaginal canal, running down to her anus and mingling with the vicar's spunk as she shuddered in the grip of her multiple orgasm. Listening to the man's gasped expletives as his balls drained, she imagined him returning to his wife and spilling out his lies.

Marriage, Samantha pondered as he slowed his adulterous fucking. Were *any* men faithful? Given the opportunity, any man would fuck a young girl she knew as he finally withdrew his deflating cock and rolled off her naked body. No man could refuse the offer of Samantha's young body. A passing stranger, a vicar . . . There wasn't a man in the world who'd walk away, declining the offer of her pretty pink cunt.

Her vaginal crack streaming with sperm, Samantha looked up at the blue sky as she recovered from her illicit coming. She could feel the man's sperm bubbling within the tight sheath of her vagina, her clitoris retreating beneath its pinken hood, as she lay on her back and breathed heavily in the aftermath of her crude fucking. This was real sex, she reflected again, as she ran her fingertips around the sensitive teats of her breasts. She'd return to the church again she knew as her nipples stiffened and her clitoris began to swell. She'd return and fuck the vicar, fuck the married man in the churchyard, suck cocks and swallow spunk. She'd return whenever she felt the need for crude sex. But right now she had to go back to her flat, to her own time.

12

'Hi,' Zak said as Samantha opened the front door. 'I've booked the holiday.'

'Holiday?' Samantha echoed, frowning at him. 'What holiday?'

'Greece. A five-star hotel for a month. You'll love it, Sam.'

'Oh, *that* holiday. Sorry, but I've changed my mind.'

'What? You can't—'

'I'm sorry, Zak. I suppose I should have called you or something. I really don't want to spend one day with you, let alone a month.'

'Sam, this has cost me thousands. You can't just back out like that. You said that you'd pay . . . I thought we were getting back together?'

'I don't think so, Zak. Seeing as all you want is my father's money so that you can run off with that slag, I decided—'

'Sam, I don't know what you're talking about. The thing with Angela is over, has been for ages. In fact, there never really was anything between us.'

'Zak, I know what the plan is. Angela rang me and told me about it. You want to marry me, get your hands on the money my father gave me, and then run off to Spain or Greece with Angela.'

'She . . . she told you that?' he asked her, his dark eyes frowning. 'I can't believe that she . . .'

'That was the plan, Zak. Angela told me everything. She said that I'd be better off without you. She reckons that she's going to dump you.'

'Dump me? I don't understand any of this, Sam. Angela and I have nothing to do with each other. I thought that you and I were going to get back together. In fact, you said that we'd start planning the wedding.'

'That was until Angela told me what your intentions were.'

'This is crazy,' he moaned. 'My bloody credit card is fucked now that I've booked the holiday. Fucking thousands . . .'

'It's a shame that Angela is going to dump you. You could have taken *her* on holiday.'

'The tickets have our names – yours and mine – on them. I can't change the fucking things. Shit, now I'm really fucked.'

'Was there anything else? I have things to do, so . . .'

'Thanks, Sam. Thanks a fucking lot.'

'Thank you for fucking Angela behind my back. Thanks for fucking her cunt, her arse, her mouth and—'

'Sam, Sam . . . This is all rubbish. I've never . . .'

'Goodbye, Zak.'

Closing the door, Samantha grinned as she went into the lounge and joined Anne on the sofa. Zak would probably row with Angela, she reflected, eyeing Anne's naked thighs as the girl lounged on the sofa in her bra and panties. Zak must have thought that there'd be no way Samantha could have known about the plan unless Angela had told her. They'd argue and, with any luck, split up. Zak would have credit card problems and no fanny to fuck, she mused happily. No money, no pussy . . .

'Who was that?' Anne finally asked as the news pro-gramme she'd been watching came to an end.

'An ex-boyfriend,' Samantha replied, again eyeing the girl's thighs, the triangular patch of her panties straining to contain her full sex lips. 'He wants us to get back together but I don't need him any more.'

'Do you need *me*?' Anne asked, parting her thighs wide, revealing the narrow strip of her panties that barely concealed her outer labia.

'You know I do,' Samantha giggled. 'What would I do without you?'

'Fuck men, I suppose.'

'Yes, but what would I do when I need pussy milk?'

'Do you need pussy milk now?' Anne laughed. 'I'm feeling pretty wet.'

'In that case, you'd better slip your panties off.'

As the girl yanked her panties off and reclined on the sofa, Samantha knelt on the floor between her feet and gazed longingly at the hairless lips of her naked vulva, the gaping valley of her creamy-wet sex crack. Opening Anne's slit wide with her fingers, Samantha exposed the intricate folds of her vagina, the pinken funnel of flesh surrounding the entrance to her young pussy. Leaning forward, sweeping her tongue over the girl's intimate flesh, Samantha breathed in the aphrodisiacal scent of the teenager's genitalia.

'You taste nice,' she murmured, her wet tongue snak-ing around the solid nub of Anne's sex-sensitive clitoris.

'I haven't had a shower yet,' Anne said. 'Shall I go and—'

'You're not going anywhere,' Samantha giggled. 'Kneel on the floor and rest your head on the sofa. I think I'd better tongue-bath your bottom for you.'

'Are you sure you want to . . .?'

'I'm sure, all right,' Samantha breathed, licking her cunny-wet lips provocatively. 'You should know me by now. I can't get enough of your sweet little bottom-hole.'

As Anne knelt on the floor and projected the rounded cheeks of her buttocks, Samantha knelt behind her and gazed longingly at the swell of the younger girl's smooth vaginal lips bulging between the tops of her parted thighs. Peeling the firm cheeks of her bottom apart, Samantha moved forward and pushed her tongue into Anne's gaping anal gully. Running her wet tongue over her anal tissue, Samantha breathed in the heady perfume of the girl's valley of illicit pleasure as she savoured the bitter-sweet taste of her secret hole.

'Do I taste nice?' Anne asked, her breathing becoming fast and shallow as her lesbian arousal heightened.

'Heavenly,' Samantha replied, parting her firm buttocks further, opening the inlet to her rectal tube. 'You taste absolutely heavenly.'

'I suppose I'll never need to take a shower if you're going to tongue-wash me every day.'

'Now that's a thought,' Samantha giggled. 'Yes, that's what I'll do. I'll wash you with my tongue. I'll lick you clean. Your pussy, your bottom, under your arms . . . I'll tongue-wash your beautiful young body every day.'

Pushing her tongue into the girl's yawning anal portal, Samantha licked the dank walls of her rectal canal. Savouring the taste of her secret duct, she pressed her wet lips against the delicate tissue of her anus and sucked hard. She was addicted to anilingus she knew as she felt dizzy in her arousal. The perfume of the girl's anal gully, the taste of her bottom-hole . . . Deciding to refresh the taste, she moved to the mantelpiece and grabbed the

candle that Anne had used as an anal dildo on Samantha's bottom. Running her fingertips along the waxen shaft as she settled behind the girl, she licked the rounded end, lubricating the dildo in readiness for the penetration of the teenager's rectum.

'You'll like this,' she breathed, easing the end of the candle into the girl's contracting anal inlet. 'This is the candle you pushed up my bum. Now it's *your* turn for a dildo bum-fucking.' Giggling, Samantha watched the waxen phallus sink inch by inch into the girl's anal hole. Gasping, Anne trembled uncontrollably as the tapered shaft progressively opened her tight anus, stretching the delicate tissue surrounding her private portal as Samantha continued to push the phallus deep into the hot core of her young body.

Twisting the candle, she withdrew the phallus until the rounded end emerged and again eased it deep into Anne's anal canal. Anal-fucking the girl slowly, gently, she grinned as she noticed a trickle of cunt-milk glistening on the pale flesh of Anne's inner thigh. The girl was loving the anal abuse she knew as she continued her pulling and pushing. The anal-slimed wax shaft repeatedly emerging and sinking deep into the girl's bowels, Samantha slipped her free hand between Anne's thighs and located the solid bulb of her clitoris with her fingertip.

'That's nice,' Anne breathed as Samantha continued the crude anal pistoning and massaged the sensitive tip of her erect clitoris. The girl's vaginal juices filling the palm of her hand, Samantha massaged Anne's clitoris faster, taking her ever nearer to her sexual heaven as she arse-fucked her tight rectum with the candle. The girl's naked body shaking uncontrollably, her cunt-milk flowing

freely from her gaping vaginal entrance, she began whimpering as her clitoris swelled to an incredible size. Moving forward, Samantha licked her bottom-hole as the sensitive tissue of her anus rolled back and forth along the waxen dildo. Tasting her there, her saliva lubricating the candle, she massaged Anne's clitoris fervently as the girl screamed out in the grip of her lesbian-induced orgasm.

'Yes,' she cried. 'Fuck my arse harder and faster.' Increasing her anal thrusting rhythm, Samantha licked the girl's stretched anal tissue and massaged her pulsating clitoris more rapidly still as her hand filled with the teenager's lubricious orgasmic juices. Anne lifted her head off the sofa, her eyes rolling as her orgasm peaked and shook her young body to the core. Again and again, waves of orgasmic bliss crashed throughout her trembling body as her lesbian lover dildo-fucked her spasming rectum and sustained her cuntal pleasure with her vibrating fingertips.

The candle shooting out of Anne's anal canal like a bullet as Samantha momentarily released the shaft, the girl's bottom-hole lay bared, gaping wide open as if inviting a wet tongue. Wasting no time, Samantha locked her lips to Anne's anal ring and drove her tongue deep into the dank heat of her rectum. Breathing in the refreshed scent of her anal gully, her taste buds alive, her mouth watering, she tongue-fucked the girl with a vengeance. Her hand overflowing with the girl's vaginal fluid, she massaged the lubricious cream into the swollen pads of the teenager's outer lips as she continued her lesbian masturbating and arse-tonguing.

'No more,' Anne finally cried, her naked body shaking violently as she rested her head on the sofa, panting for

breath. Slowing her clitoral massaging to a gentle
rhythm, bringing out the last ripples of sex from the
girl's deflating clitoris, Samantha pushed her tongue
deep into her anal canal, savouring the taste of her inner
core. Sliding her tongue out of Anne's hot duct, she
licked the full length of her rectal-scented gully, holding
her firm buttocks wide apart to allow better access to her
secret flesh. Anne's naked body calming as she recovered
from her massive orgasm, her breathing slow and deep,
she closed her eyes and wallowed in the illicit pleasure
that her lover's tongue was bringing her.

'I love your bottom-hole,' Samantha murmured, rubbing her mouth over Anne's anus.

'I'd never have guessed,' Anne giggled, lifting her
head off the sofa. 'You can tongue-bath me every day
from now on.'

'Mmm, I'd love that,' Samantha murmured, rubbing
her face against the inner flesh of the younger girl's anal
crevice. 'God, you taste heavenly. I love breathing in the
perfume of your sweet bottom. It's like a drug, I just
can't get enough.'

'Well, that's going to have to be enough for now. I
must get dressed and—'

'Oh no, you don't,' Samantha cut in, sitting back on
her heels. 'You'll walk around the flat naked.'

'What, all the time?'

'Yes, why not?'

'So you can lick my bottom-hole whenever you feel
like it?'

'Of course. No dress, no panties . . . Completely naked
at all times.'

'Even now?' Anne laughed as the front doorbell
rang.

'Even now,' Samantha said, leaping to her feet. 'Hide your panties and bra and I'll see who it is.'

'I'll go to the bedroom and—'

'Oh no, you won't. You'll stay here, naked.'

'But . . . Sam, you don't even know who it is.'

'I'm about to find out. Wait there.'

Walking through the hall, the scent of Anne's anal ring filling her nostrils as she licked her full lips, Samantha imagined taking Dave into the lounge and watching his expression as he gazed at Anne's naked body. She was surprised that Anne hadn't dashed into the bedroom when the doorbell had rung. Perhaps she relished the idea of showing off her beautiful young body. Opening the door, Samantha frowned as she stared at Rob. He must have followed her home from the park and . . .

'What are *you* doing here?' she asked him.

'I've been to the park a couple of times but you weren't there. We were supposed to meet at ten . . .'

'Something came up,' Samantha said, wondering whether to invite him in. 'So, you *did* follow me home.'

'Yes, I did. I'm sorry, Sam. I know it was wrong but . . . well, here I am.'

'You'd better come in,' she said, opening the door further. 'Er . . . my sister is in the lounge,' she murmured. 'Come through and I'll introduce you.'

'Oh, right. Thanks. I really do apologize for following you, Sam.'

'That's OK,' she said, walking into the lounge and grinning at Anne. 'Sarah, this is Rob. Rob is a friend of mine.'

'Pleased to meet you,' Anne said, smiling as the man focused on the barely developed mounds of her breasts

before lowering his eyes to the hairless flesh of her vulva. 'Sorry, I was about to get dressed.'

'Oh, er . . .' Rob stammered, his wide-eyed stare fixed on her naked pussy crack. 'Sorry, I . . .'

'Sarah doesn't mind people seeing her naked,' Samantha said, wondering what Rob thought of her boyish figure. 'Sorry I couldn't meet you in the park, Rob. Things got pretty hectic and I just couldn't make it.'

'That's all right,' he replied, unable to take his gaze off the young girl's naked body.

'Did you wait long?'

'Er . . . about half an hour or so.'

'Sit down, Rob,' Samantha invited him, pointing to the sofa. 'Would you like a tea or coffee?'

'No, no, I'm fine, thanks,' he replied, sitting on the sofa.

Gazing in amazement as Anne turned her back to him and bent over, Rob focused on the hairless vaginal lips nestling beneath her bottom-hole. Anne was fiddling with the video recorder, her feet wide apart as she took a tape out of the machine. Samantha knew that she was deliberately displaying the swollen lips of her young pussy as she pushed the tape back into the machine. She had the right idea, Samantha mused. She was a girl after her own heart, there was no doubt about that.

Sitting next to Rob as Anne finally left the video recorder and plonked herself down in the armchair, Samantha concealed a grin as the girl lay back and parted her thighs. Rob must have thought it odd that she should blatantly display her young body, Samantha thought. His disbelieving stare glued to her partially open sex crack, the bulge in his trousers was all too obvious. He'd have given anything to mouth-fuck the young girl,

Samantha was sure, as Anne nonchalantly parted her thighs a little further.

'We'll have to go out for a drink one evening,' Rob said, finally managing to drag his stare away from Anne's vulval crack.

'Yes, I'd like that,' Samantha replied.

'I didn't realize that you lived with your sister. It must be nice to have some company.'

'Yes, it is. Sarah came to live with me when our parents moved abroad. What with Sarah's school and everything, they thought it best.'

'School, yes,' Rob murmured.

'We get on pretty well, don't we, Sarah?' Samantha asked the girl, sure that Rob was dying to ask how old she was.

'Yes, we do,' Anne replied. 'You're not as strict as Mum.'

'I can be, my girl,' Samantha giggled. 'Especially if you don't do your homework.'

'She's got a thing about homework,' Anne sighed, smiling at Rob.

'And so she should have,' he said, his eyes again locked to the pouting lips of Anne's vulva. 'It's important to do well at school.'

'I suppose I'd better get dressed,' Anne said, leaving the armchair and deliberately standing close to Rob as she asked Samantha about her school uniform.

'It'll be ready by the morning,' Samantha said. 'Don't worry about it.'

Gazing at the girl's rounded buttocks as she left the room, Rob was obviously amazed by the way she had no qualms about displaying her young body. Samantha noticed again the bulge in his trousers, and wondered whether

to haul his cock out and give him a quick wank. But it was Anne he'd want to get his hands on, she was sure. Slipping his huge cock into the sheath of her little pink pussy, sucking on the unripe teats of her petite breasts . . . There was no doubt that he'd love to fuck her senseless.

'I saw you with a young girl in the park the other day,' Rob said. 'Only she was blonde.'

'Ah, that was a friend of mine,' Samantha replied, wondering when he'd seen her with Anne.

'It looked like Sarah, but . . . Has Sarah changed her hair colour?'

'No, no, she hasn't. The blonde girl was a friend. It wasn't Sarah.'

'Oh, right. Would her name be Anne?'

'Anne?' Samantha echoed, reckoning that Rob must have spied through the gap in the fence and seen her with Anne – and heard her mention her name to the young man. 'I don't know anyone called Anne.'

'That's odd.'

'Why, Rob? What is it?'

'It's just that . . . I'm sure that it's the same girl.'

'Sarah hasn't dyed her hair, Rob,' Samantha stated firmly, her suspicion rising as she recalled the blackmailer wanting to meet Anne at the same time that Samantha was supposed to have met Rob. 'Sarah lives with me, Rob. My sister is auburn-haired, always has been.'

'Oh, well. Not to worry,' he sighed. 'I'd better be going. Thanks for inviting me in. And I really am sorry that I followed you to your flat.'

'And phoned me? Are you sorry about that?'

'Phoned . . .? OK, I'll put my hand up.'

'So it *was* you, Rob? Why try to blackmail me, for God's sake?'

'I saw you and Anne – Sarah – behind the fence with some man and . . . I thought that perhaps I'd get the opportunity to—'

'Screw her?'

'Well, yes.'

'Christ, you didn't have to use blackmail.'

'Sam, I . . . I don't know what to say. She *is* Anne Wilkinson, isn't she?'

'Yes, I am,' Anne said, appearing in the doorway in all her naked glory.

'I thought so. How come you look—'

'So young?' Samantha asked. 'It's a long story, Rob. And one that you'd never believe. So much for all this crap about wanting to be with me, wanting to go out with me. You just wanted to get your cock up Anne's cunt.'

'I . . . I meant what I said, Sam. Yes, I would like to . . .'

'We're wasting time,' Samantha breathed. 'Fifty pounds, and she'll do anything.'

'Sam,' Anne gasped. 'You're making me out to be—'

'Not in front of a client, please, Anne. I can be strict, remember? Start by sucking Rob's cock. He likes that.'

Settling on the floor between Rob's feet, Anne unzipped his trousers and hauled out his erect penis. Rob lifted his buttocks clear of the sofa as she released his belt and tugged his trousers down. Tossing the trousers and his shoes to one side, she spread his thighs and licked the fleshy sac of his scrotum. He gazed at her angelic face, her succulent lips, her pink tongue, as she licked the base of his twitching cock. Running her tongue up and down the veined shaft of his huge organ, Anne held his foreskin between her finger and thumb and fully retracted the fleshy hood. Sitting beside Rob, Samantha watched the

young girl as she tasted the rim of Rob's glans, her eyes sparkling as she finally swallowed his purple knob. Her taut lips encompassing the veined shaft of his cock, she kneaded his rolling balls, adding to his obviously amazing pleasure as he gasped and trembled.

'She's good at cocksucking,' Samantha said, gazing at the expression of sheer ecstasy on Rob's face.

'God, yes,' he breathed. 'She's . . . she's amazing.'

'She always swallows,' Samantha giggled. 'She can't get enough spunk.'

'She's so young,' he murmured. 'Anne Wilkinson was—'

'She's not Anne Wilkinson,' Samantha laughed as Anne bobbed her head up and down, repeatedly taking the man's bulbous knob to the back of her throat. 'I must admit that she looks very much like the girl from what I remember of the photographs in the paper at the time. But she's not her.'

'God, that's nice,' Rob gasped, watching Anne's full lips hugging the rim of his helmet as she expertly tongued his knob-slit.

Was this how things were meant to turn out? Samantha pondered the matter, listening to the slurping sounds of crude sex. A young girl living in her flat, sucking off a client, offering crude sex in return for money . . . Samantha wondered if the dancing school was her destiny. If she moved to Australia, far away from the school, would she find herself returning to England and owning the mansion? Could the future be changed? She contemplated these questions, gazing at Anne's pink tongue running around the purple rim of Rob's glans. Her marriage to John, two sons . . . Doubting that she could change her fate, she slipped her panties down her

long legs and grabbed Rob's hand. Placing his fingers on the fleshy swell of her naked vulval lips, she ordered him to bring her off.

'You two really are amazing,' he breathed, massaging the solid nub of Samantha's clitoris as Anne gobbled and sucked on his ballooning glans.

'We get better,' Samantha giggled. 'You can fuck Anne's tight little bottom-hole later, and mine.'

'I think I'm going to become a regular visitor,' he chuckled, slipping his finger deep into Samantha's sex-drenched pussy sheath. 'God, I'm . . . I'm coming.'

His face grimacing as Anne held his throbbing knob between her full lips and tongued its silky-smooth plum, he pumped out his creamy spunk and gave a long moan of pleasure. Samantha watched his orgasmic cream running down his twitching shaft as the girl's mouth overflowed. Doing her best to swallow his gushing spunk, she wanked his huge shaft, his balls bouncing as he parted his thighs wider and finger-fucked Samantha's rhythmically contracting cunt.

The sound of Anne's slurping mouth as she gobbled and drank the man's spunk, the squelching of her own vaginal juices as Rob pistoned her tight cunt . . . Samantha relaxed and wallowed in her sea of debauchery, drowning in her lust as the sounds of debased sex resounded around the lounge. It was a good idea to have Anne wander naked around the flat, she decided. Callers would part with their money in exchange for the chance to fuck the girl's naked body. They'd see the wares on display. Anne's tightly closed vaginal slit, the hairless lips of her young pussy, the underdeveloped mounds of her petite breasts . . . And they'd be unable to refuse the delights she had to offer.

Pulling Rob's fingers out of her contracting vagina, Samantha stood on the sofa with her feet either side of his hips, her gaping valley of desire only inches from his face as Anne continued to drink from his orgasming knob. Wasting no time, the man grabbed her hips and pulled her forward, her hairless pussy lips pressing hard against his mouth as he drove his tongue deep into her pleasure sheath.

'Lick my dirty cunt out,' she breathed, her crude words heightening not only Rob's arousal but hers. She could feel her juices of lust mingling with his saliva, streaming from her tongued cunt and running in rivers down the pale flesh of her inner thighs. Anne's tongue probing between the firm cheeks of her naked buttocks, she knew that the girl had drained his balls and sucked his cock dry before the temptation to tongue-fuck her lesbian lover's bottom-hole had got the better of her.

Two tongues, darting in and out of her sex holes, her cunt-milk gushing from her vaginal entrance, Samantha cried out as Rod moved up her drenched vulval crack and sucked the solid bud of her clitoris into his wet mouth. Her orgasm finally erupting within her pulsating joy buzzer, she clung to Rob's head to steady her shaking body as Anne's tongue delved even deeper into the dank heat of her rectum. Never had she known such pleasure, never had she realized the amazing delights her young body held. Her time with Zak had been . . .

Trying not to think of Zak, she shuddered as her orgasm finally began to recede. Unable to stand on her sagging legs as the wet tongues slurped around her love holes and repeatedly entered her sex ducts, she almost fell off the sofa and lay on the floor on her back. Shuddering, her long blonde hair wet with the

perspiration of sex, she watched as Anne grabbed Rob's solid cock and began sucking on his bulbous knob again. The man was incredible, Samantha mused. Despite his age, he had the staying power of a teenage lad.

'Wait,' Samantha breathed, dragging her trembling body off the floor and sitting on the sofa. 'Stand up and turn round,' she ordered Anne. 'That's it. Now, bend over and I'll guide Rob's cock deep into your sweet little bottom.' As the girl took her position, Samantha eyed the tight hole of her anus. Anne needed a little lubrication, she decided, ordering Rob to lick her there. Immediately complying, the man leaned forward and parted the girl's pert buttocks, his wet tongue snaking around Anne's anal inlet as Samantha grabbed the massive shaft of his cock and rolled his foreskin back and forth over his purple globe.

When the girl was ready, saliva running over the brown tissue surrounding her gaping bottom-hole, Samantha pushed Rob back and instructed Anne to lower her naked body and part her buttocks with her fingers. Pressing the man's purple plum hard against her brown ring, Samantha thought that his cock was too big to penetrate the girl there. His glans swelling as he watched Samantha trying to force his cock up Anne's tight arse, he gasped.

'It'll never go in,' he breathed, his huge balls rolling. 'She's far too young and tight to . . .'

'You were saying?' Samantha giggled as his purple glans was suddenly sucked into the fiery heat of the girl's rectum.

'God, that . . . that's incredible,' he murmured, his body trembling uncontrollably.

'More,' Anne cried as Rob's solid shaft glided along her duct of forbidden pleasure. 'I want all of it.'

Bouncing up and down on the man's solid cock, Anne gasped and shuddered in the crude arse-fucking as Samantha moved to the floor and thrust two fingers deep into the constricted cavern of the teenager's neglected cunt. Finger-fucking the young girl, her hand bathed with her juices of lust, Samantha knew that they were going to rake in a lot of money. Rob was bound to have male friends who'd enjoy using and abusing a young teenage girl. They'd hand over cash in return for sex once they laid eyes on Anne's naked body. They'd pay up front to fuck the tight sheath of her arse, mouth-fuck her, spunk her young body . . .

Suddenly finding herself sitting on a log by a bubbling stream, Samantha looked around her. The sunlight filtering through the trees high above her, she had no idea where she was, let alone why she'd been taken there. The undergrowth was profuse, the huge leaves of the plants growing alongside the stream reminding her of the jungle. Was that where she was? She felt confused, the hot and humid air stifling her.

'You again?' she breathed as the young man she'd met in the nineteenth-century pub approached her.

'Samantha,' he said softly, smiling at her. 'You can change certain aspects of the future. Minor incidents. But you cannot change your destiny.'

'Who are you?' she asked, gazing up at his angelic face. 'Where am I?'

'You're in the garden.'

'What garden? Who are you?'

'I'm a friend,' he replied, his dark eyes sparkling. 'When you return, I want you to take care of Anne. Look after her, love her.'

'Yes, yes, I will. Tell me who you are.'

'I told you, Samantha. I'm your friend. My name is Charles. I keep watch over you, guide you. You saved the girl from the fire. She fled and has now found another place to sleep. Go back now, Samantha. You have your life ahead of you. Enjoy it.'

As he slipped into the undergrowth, Samantha frowned. Why had she been chosen to get the girl away from the factory and save her life? Why had she been chosen to care for Anne? *You can change certain aspects of the future. But you cannot change your destiny.* Pondering on his words, she felt herself slipping through time again. Where was she supposed to go now? she wondered, looking about her as she materialized in the dancing school . . .

'There you are,' Kitty said, smiling as she approached. 'I've heard from Gerry. He's settled in Australia and found a nice house. I'm joining him in a couple of days.'

'Oh, right,' Samantha replied.

'I wish you luck with the mansion and the school. I know you'll do well.'

'Yes, I hope so. Er . . . Kitty, what . . .'

'Don't worry about anything. You've done very well so far and I don't see why you shouldn't continue to do so. How's Mike?'

'Mike? Er . . .'

'It must be nice, having a brother to help.'

'A brother?' Samantha gasped. 'But I . . .'

Standing in her lounge, Samantha gazed at Anne. Rob must have gone, she thought, watching the girl panting for breath as she lay back on the sofa. Wondering who

Mike was, she sat next to Anne and wiped the creamy sperm from her chin. Anne smiled, parting her slender thighs and displaying the spunk-dripping valley of her young pussy. She needed a tongue-wash, Samantha decided, slipping off the sofa and settling between her feet.

'I'll clean you,' she breathed, lapping up Rob's sperm from the younger girl's valley of desire.

'Mmm, that's nice,' Anne breathed. 'I'll tell you what I'd like.'

'My tongue lapping up Rob's spunk from your sweet bottom-hole?'

'No . . . yes, that, too. I'd like to make some plans for the future. I don't think I want to work for the newspaper. I think, in the future—'

'Don't talk about the future,' Samantha interrupted. Licking her cunny-wet lips, she smiled. 'The future's not ours to see.'